I went into a bar.

"Gimme a drink," I said to the bartender.

"Brother, don't take that drink," said a voice at my elbow. I turned and there was a skinny little guy in his fifties. Thin, yellow hair and a smile on his face. "Brother, don't take that drink," he said.

I shook him off.

"Where'd you come from?" I said. "You weren't there when I sat down here one second ago." He just grinned at me.

"Gimme a drink," I said to the bartender.

"Not for you," said the bartender. "You had enough before you came in here." A fat bartender polishing shot glasses with his little finger inside a dishtowel. "Get your friend to take you home."

"He's no friend of mine," I said.

"Brother," said the little man, "come with me."

"I want a drink," I said. An idea struck me. I turned to the little man. "Let's you and I go someplace else and have a drink," I said.

We went out of the bar together, and suddenly we were somewhere else.

GORDON R. DICKSON

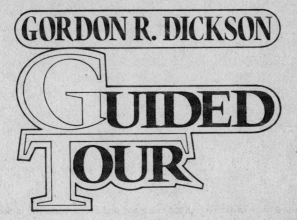

GUIDED TOUR

A TOM DOHERTY ASSOCIATES BOOK

GUIDED TOUR

Copyright © 1988 by Gordon R. Dickson

First printing: February 1988

A TOR Book

Published by Tom Doherty Associates, Inc.
49 West 24 Street
New York, N.Y. 10010

ISBN: 0-812-53589-8
CAN. ED.: 0-812-53590-1

Printed in the United States of America

0   9   8   7   6   5   4   3   2   1

Acknowledgments

Contents

Guided Tour

Please keep close—
We enter by this new pale arch of hours
Into the greystone corridor of years,
Which at this end is still under construction.
Please note the stained glass windows which depict
A number of historic episodes.
A legal green here—further back they're purple—
Before that, bright iron, bronze, and last—grey flint,
From which the hall derives its general tone.
One legend goes that at the furthest part,
Where it begins, there're only two small stones
Placed one on top the other for a start
By some half-animal—but others think
The whole was laid out from the very first
By some big architect whose spirit still
Directs construction. Well, you take your pick.
. . . And now, I thought I heard somebody ask
About our future thoughts for building on.
Well, there's now building quite a fine addition
Of plastic, steel and glass, all air-conditioned,
Also there's planned a nucleonic part
Built up from force-fields. But beyond *its* end
We butt, unfortunately, on a space—
A pit, or void, through which the right of way
May be disputed, and is still in doubt. . . .

The Monkey Wrench

Cary Harmon was not an ungifted young man. He had the intelligence to carve himself a position as a Lowland society lawyer, which on Venus is not easy to do. And he had the discernment to consolidate that position by marrying into the family of one of the leading drug-exporters. But, nevertheless, from the scientific viewpoint, he was a layman; and laymen, in their ignorance, should never be allowed to play with delicate technical equipment; for the result will be trouble, as surely as it is the first time a baby gets its hands on a match.

His wife was a high-spirited woman; and would have been hard to handle at times if it had not been for the fact that she was foolish enough to love him. Since he did not love her at all, it was consequently both simple and practical to terminate all quarrels by dropping out of sight for several days until her obvious fear of losing him for good brought her to a proper humility. He took good care, each time he disappeared, to pick some new and secure hiding place where past experience or her several years' knowledge of his habits would be no help in locating him. Actually, he enjoyed thinking up new and undiscoverable bolt-holes, and made a hobby out of discovering them.

Consequently, he was in high spirits the grey winter afternoon he descended unannounced on the weather station of Burke McIntyre, high in the Lonesome Mountains, a jagged, kindless chain on the deserted shorelands of

3

Venus' Northern Sea. He had beaten a blizzard to the dome with minutes to spare; and now, with his small two-place flier safely stowed away, and a meal of his host's best supplies under his belt, he sat revelling in the comfort of his position and listening to the hundred-and-fifty-per-hour, subzero winds lashing impotently at the arching roof overhead.

"Ten minutes more," he said to Burke, "and I'd have had a tough time making it."

"Tough!" snorted Burke. He was a big, heavy-featured blond man with a kindly contempt for all of humanity aside from the favored class of meteorologists. "You Low-landers are too used to that present day Garden of Eden you have down below. Ten minutes more and you'd have been spread over one of the peaks around here to wait for the spring searching party to gather your bones."

Cary laughed in cheerful disbelief.

"Try it, if you don't believe me," said Burke. "No skin off my nose if you don't have the sense to listen to reason. Take your bug up right now if you want."

"Not me." Cary's brilliant white teeth flashed in his swarthy face. "I know when I'm comfortable. And that's no way to treat your guest, tossing him out into the storm when he's just arrived."

"Some guest," rumbled Burke. "I shake hands with you after the graduation exercises, don't hear a word from you for six years and then suddenly you're knocking at my door here in the hinterland."

"I came on impulse," said Cary. "It's the prime rule of my life. Always act on impulse, Burke. It puts the sparkle in existence."

"And leads you to an early grave," Burke supplemented.

"If you have the wrong impulses," said Cary. "But then if you get sudden urges to jump off cliffs or play Russian Roulette then you're too stupid to live, anyway."

"Cary," said Burke heavily, "you're a shallow thinker."

"And you're a stodgy one," grinned Cary. "Suppose

you quit insulting me and tell me something about yourself. What's this hermit's existence of yours like? What do you do?"

"What do I do?" repeated Burke. "I work."

"But just how?" Cary said, settling himself cosily back into his chair. "Do you send up balloons? Catch snow in a pail to find how much fell? Take sights on the stars? Or what?"

Burke shook his head at him and smiled tolerantly.

"Now what do you want to know for?" he asked. "It'll just go in one ear and out the other."

"Oh, some of it might stick," said Cary. "Go ahead, anyhow."

"Well, if you insist on my talking to entertain you," he answered, "I don't do anything so picturesque. I just sit at a desk and prepare weather data for transmission to the Weather Center down at Capital City."

"Aha!" Cary said, waggling a lazy forefinger at him in reproof. "I've got you now. You've been lying down on the job. You've the only one here; so if you don't take observations, who does?"

"You idiot!" said Burke. "The machine does, of course. These stations have a Brain to do that."

"That's worse," Cary answered. "You've been sitting here warm and comfortable while some poor little Brain scurries around outside in the snow and does all your work for you."

"Oh, shut up!" Burke said. "As a matter of fact you're closer to the truth than you think; and it wouldn't do you any harm to learn a few things about the mechanical miracles that let you lead a happy ignorant life. Some wonderful things have been done lately in the way of equipping these stations."

Cary smiled mockingly.

"I mean it," Burke went on, his face lighting up. "The Brain we've got here now is the last word in that type of installation. As a matter of fact, it was just put in recently—up until a few months back we had to work with a job that was just a collector and computer. That is, it

5

collected the weather data around this station and presented it to you. Then you had to take it and prepare it for the calculator, which would chew on it for a while and then pass you back results which you again had to prepare for transmission downstairs to the Center."

"Fatiguing, I'm sure," murmured Cary, reaching for the drink placed handily on the end table beside his chair. Burke ignored him, caught up in his own appreciation of the mechanical development about which he was talking.

"It kept you busy, for the data came in steadily; and you were always behind since a batch would be accumulating while you were working up the previous batch. A station like this is the center-point for observational mechs posted at points over more than five hundred square miles of territory; and, being human, all you had time to do was skim the cream off the reports and submit a sketchy picture to the calculator. And then there was a certain responsibility involved in taking care of the station and yourself.

"But now"—Burke leaned forward determinedly and stabbed a thick index finger at his visitor—"we've got a new installation that takes the data directly from the observational mechs—all of it—resolves it into the proper form for the calculator to handle it, and carries it right on through to the end results. All I still have to do is prepare the complete picture from the results and shoot it downstairs.

"In addition, it runs the heating and lighting plants, automatically checks on the maintenance of the station. It makes repairs and corrections on verbal command and has a whole separate section for the consideration of theoretical problems."

"Sort of a little tin god," said Cary, nastily. He was used to attention and subconsciously annoyed by the fact that Burke seemed to be waxing more rhapsodic over his machine than the brilliant and entertaining guest who, as far as the meteorologist could know, had dropped in under the kind impulse to relieve a hermit's boring existence.

Unperturbed, Burke looked at him and chuckled.

"No," he replied. "A *big* tin god, Cary."

The lawyer stiffened slightly in his chair. Like most people who are fond of poking malicious fun at others, he gave evidence of a very thin skin when the tables were turned.

"Sees all, knows all, tells all, I suppose," he said sarcastically. "Never makes a mistake. Infallible."

"You might say that," answered Burke, still with a grin on his face. He was enjoying the unusual pleasure of having the other on the defensive. But Cary, adept at verbal battles, twisted like an eel.

"Too bad, Burke," he said. "But those qualities alone don't quite suffice for elevating your gadget to god-hood. One all-important attribute is lacking—invulnerability. Gods never break down."

"Neither does this."

"Come now, Burke," chided Cary, "you mustn't let your enthusiasm lead you into falsehood. No machine is perfect: A crossed couple of wires, a burned out tube and where is your darling? Plunk! Out of action."

Burke shook his head.

"There aren't any wires," he said. "It uses beamed connections. And as for burned out tubes, they don't even halt consideration of a problem. The problem is just shifted over to a bank that isn't in use at the time; and automatic repairs are made by the machine itself. You see, Cary, in this model, no bank does one specific job, alone. Any one of them—and there's twenty, half again as many as this station would ever need—can do any job from running the heating plant to operating the calculator. If something comes up that's too big for one bank to handle, it just hooks in one or more of the idle banks—and so on until it's capable of dealing with the situation."

"Ah," said Cary, "but what if something *did* come up that required all the banks and more too? Wouldn't it overload them and burn itself out?"

"You're determined to find fault with it, aren't you, Cary," answered Burke. "The answer is no. It wouldn't. Theoretically it's possible for the machine to bump into a problem that would require all or more than all of its banks to handle. For example, if this station suddenly popped into the air and started to fly away for no discernible reason, the bank that first felt the situation would keep reaching out for help until all the banks were engaged in considering it, until it crowded out all the other functions the machine performs. But, even then, it wouldn't overload and burn out. The banks would just go on considering the problem until they had evolved a theory that explained why we were flying through the air and what to do about returning us to our proper place and functions.''

Cary straightened up and snapped his fingers.

"Then it's simple," he said. "I'll just go in and tell your machine—on the verbal hookup—that we're flying through the air."

Burke gave a sudden roar of laughter.

"Cary, you dope!" he said. "Don't you think the men who designed the machine took the possibility of verbal error into account? You say that the station is flying through the air. The machine immediately checks by making its own observations; and politely replies, 'Sorry, your statement is incorrect' and forgets the whole thing.''

Cary's eyes narrowed and two spots of faint color flushed the tight skin over his cheekbones; but he held his smile.

"There's the theoretical section," he murmured.

"There is," said Burke, greatly enjoying himself, "and you could use it by going in and saying 'consider the false statement or data—this station is flying through the air' and the machine would go right to work on it."

He paused, and Cary looked at him expectantly.

"But—" continued the meteorologist, triumphantly, "it would consider the statement with only those banks not then in use; and it would give up the banks whenever a section using real data required them.''

He finished, looking at Cary with quizzical good humor. But Cary said nothing; only looked back at him as a weasel might look back at a dog that has cornered it against the wall of a chicken run.

"Give up, Cary," he said at last. "It's no use.

Neither God nor Man nor Cary Harmon can interrupt my Brain in the rightful performance of its duty."

And Cary's eyes glittered, dark and withdrawn beneath their narrowed lids. For a long second, he just sat and looked, and then he spoke.

"I could do it," he said, softly.

"Do what?" asked Burke.

"I could gimmick your machine," said Cary.

"Oh, forget it!" boomed Burke. "Don't take things so seriously, Cary. What if you can't think of a monkey wrench to throw into the machinery? Nobody else could, either."

"I said I could do it," repeated Cary.

"Once and for all," answered Burke, "it's impossible. Now stop trying to pick flaws in something guaranteed flawless and let's talk about something else."

"I will bet you," said Cary, speaking with a slow, steady intensity, "five thousand credits that if you leave me alone with your machine for one minute I can put it completely out of order."

"Forget it, will you?" exploded Burke. "I don't want to take your money, even if five thousand *is* the equivalent of a year's salary for me. The trouble with you is, Cary, you never could stand to lose at anything. Now forget it!"

"Put up or shut up," said Cary.

Burke took a deep breath.

"Now look," he said, the beginnings of anger rumbling in his deep voice. "Maybe I did wrong to needle you about the machine. But you've got to get over the idea that I can be bullied into admitting that you're right. You've got no conception of the technology that's behind the machine, and no idea of how certain I am that you, at least, can't do anything to interfere with its operation. You think that there's a slight element of doubt in my mind and that you can bluff me out of proposing an astronomical bet. Then, if I won't bet, you'll tell yourself you've won. Now listen, I'm not just ninety-nine point nine, nine, nine, nine, per cent sure of myself. I'm one hundred per cent sure of myself and the reason I won't bet you is because that would be robbery; and besides, once you'd lost, you'd hate me for winning the rest of your life.''

"The bet still stands," said Cary.

"All right!" roared Burke, jumping to his feet. "If you want to force the issue, suit yourself. It's a bet."

Cary grinned and got up, following him out of the pleasant, spacious sitting room, where warm lamps dispelled the grey gloom of the snow-laden sky beyond the windows, and into a short, metal-walled corridor where the ceiling tubes blazed in efficient nakedness. They followed this for a short distance to a room where the wall facing the corridor and the door set in it were all of glass.

Here Burke halted.

"There's the machine," he said, pointing through the transparency of the wall and turning to Cary behind him. "If you want to communicate with it verbally, you speak into that grille there. The calculator is to your right; and that inner door leads down to the room housing the lighting and heating plants. But if you're thinking of physical sabotage, you might as well give up. The lighting and heating systems don't even have emergency controls. They're run by a little atomic pile that only the machine can be trusted to handle—that is, except for an automatic setup that damps the pile in case lightning strikes the machine or some such thing. And you couldn't get through the shielding in a week. As for breaking through to the machine up here, that panel in which the grille is set is made of two-inch-thick steel sheets with their edges flowed together under pressure."

"I assure you," said Cary. "I don't intend to damage a thing."

Burke looked at him sharply, but there was no hint of sarcasm in the smile that twisted the other's thin lips.

"All right," he said, stepping back from the door. "Go ahead. Can I wait here, or do you have to have me out of sight?"

"Oh, by all means, watch," said Cary. "We machine-gimmickers have nothing to hide." He turned mockingly to Burke, and lifted his arms. "See? Nothing up my right sleeve. Nothing up my left."

"Go on," interrupted Burke roughly. "Get it over with. I want to get back to my drink."

"At once," said Cary, and went in through the door, closing it behind him.

Through the transparent wall, Burke watched him approach the panel in line with the speaker grille and stop some two feet in front of it. Having arrived at this spot, he became utterly motionless, his back to Burke, his shoulders hanging relaxed and his hands motionless at his sides. For the good part of a minute, Burke strained his eyes to discover what action was going on under the guise of Cary's apparent immobility. Then an understanding struck him and he laughed.

"Why," he said to himself, "he's bluffing right up to the last minute, hoping I'll get worried and rush in there and stop him."

Relaxed, he lit a cigarette and looked at his watch. Some forty-five seconds to go. In less than a minute, Cary would be coming out, forced at last to admit defeat— that is, unless he had evolved some fantastic argument to prove that defeat was really victory. Burke frowned. It was almost pathological, the way Cary had always refused to admit the superiority of anyone or anything else; and unless some way was found to soothe him he would be a very unpleasant companion for the remaining days that the storm held him marooned with Burke. It would be literally murder to force him to take off in the tornado velocity winds and a temperature that must be in the minus sixties by this time. At the same time, it went against the meteorologist's grain to crawl for the sake of congeniality—

The vibration of the generator, half-felt through the floor and the soles of his shoes, and customarily familiar as the motion of his own lungs, ceased abruptly. The fluttering streamers fixed to the ventilator grille above his head ceased their colorful dance and dropped limply down as the rush of air that had carried them, ceased. The lights dimmed and went out, leaving only the grey and ghostly light from the thick windows at each end of the corridor to illuminate the passage and the room. The cigarette dropped unheeded from Burke's fingers and in two swift strides he was at the door and through it.

"What have you done?" he snapped at Cary.

The other looked mockingly at him, then walked across to the nearer wall of the room and leaned his shoulder blades negligently against it.

"That's for you to find out," he said, his satisfaction clearly evident.

"Don't be insane—" began the meteorologist. Then, checking himself like a man who has no time to lose, he whirled on the panel and gave his attention to the instruments on its surface.

The pile was damped. The ventilating system was shut off and the electrical system was dead. Only the power in the storage cells of the machine itself was available for the operating light still glowed redly on the panel. The great outside doors, wide enough to permit the ingress and exit of a two-man flier, were closed, and would remain that way, for they required power to open or close them. Visio, radio, and teletype were alike, silent and lifeless through lack of power.

But the machine still operated.

Burke stepped to the grille and pressed the red alarm button below it, twice.

"Attention," he said. "The pile is damped and all fixtures besides yourselves lack power. Why is this?"

There was no response, though the red light continued to glow industriously on the panel.

"Obstinate little rascal, isn't it?" said Cary from the wall.

Burke ignored him, punching the button again, sharply.

"Reply!" he ordered. "Reply at once! What is the difficulty? Why is the pile not operating?"

There was no answer.

He turned to the calculator and played his fingers expertly over the buttons. Fed from the stored power within the machine, the punched tape rose in a fragile white arc and disappeared through a slot in the panel. He finished his punching and waited.

There was no answer.

For a long moment he stood there, staring at the calculator as if unable to believe that, even in this last hope, the machine had failed him. Then he turned slowly and faced Cary.

"What have you done?" he repeated dully.

"Do you admit you were wrong?" Cary demanded.

"Yes," said Burke.

"And do I win the bet?" persisted Cary gleefully.

"Yes."

"Then I'll tell you," the lawyer said. He put a cigarette between his lips and puffed it alight; then blew out a long streamer of smoke which billowed out and hung cloudily in the still air of the room, which, lacking heat from the blowers, was cooling rapidly. "This fine little gadget of yours may be all very well at meteorology, but it's not very good at logic. Shocking situation, when you consider the close relationship between mathematics and logic."

"What did you do?" reiterated Burke hoarsely.

"I'll get to it," said Cary. "As I say, it's a shocking situation. Here is this infallible machine of yours, worth, I suppose, several million credits, beating its brains out over a paradox."

"A paradox!" the words from Burke were almost a sob.

"A paradox," sang Cary, "a most ingenious paradox." He switched back to his speaking voice. "Which, in case you don't know, is from Gilbert and Sullivan's 'Pirates of Penzance.' It occurred to me while you were bragging earlier that while your little friend here couldn't be damaged, it might be immobilized by giving it a problem too big for its mechanical brain cells to handle. And I remembered a little thing from one of my pre-law logic courses—an interesting little affair called Epimenides Paradox. I don't remember just how it was originally phrased—those logic courses were dull, sleepy sort of businesses, anyway—but for example, if I say to you 'all lawyers are liars' how can you tell whether the statement is true or false, since I am a lawyer and, if it is true, must be lying when I say that all lawyers are liars? But, on the other hand, if I am lying, then all lawyers are not liars, and the statement is false, i.e., a lying statement. If the statement is false, it is true, and if true, false, and so on, so where are you?''

Cary broke off suddenly into a peal of laughter.

"You should see your own face, Burke," he shouted. "I never saw anything so bewildered in my life—anyway, I just changed this around and fed it to the machine. While you waited politely outside, I went up to the machine and said to it, 'You must reject the statement I am now making to you, because all the statements are incorrect.' ''

He paused and looked at the meteorologist.

"Do you see, Burke? It took that statement of mine in and considered it for rejecting. But it could not reject it without admitting that it was correct, and how could it be correct when it stated that all statements I made were incorrect. You see . . . yes, you do see, I can see it in your face. Oh, if you could only look at yourself now. The pride of the meteorology service, undone by a paradox.''

And Cary went off into another fit of laughter that lasted for a long minute. Every time he would start to recover, a look at Burke's wooden face, set in lines of utter dismay, would set him off again. The meteorologist neither moved, nor spoke, but stared at his guest as if he were a ghost.

Finally, weak from merriment, Cary started to sober up. Chuckling feebly, he leaned against the wall, took a deep breath and straightened up. A shiver ran through him, and he turned up the collar of his tunic.

"Well," he said. "Now that you know what the trick was, Burke, suppose you get your pet back to its proper duties again. It's getting too cold for comfort and that daylight coming through the windows isn't the most cheerful thing in the world, either.''

But Burke made no move toward the panel. His eyes were fixed and they bored into Cary as unmovingly as before. Cary snickered a little at him.

"Come on, Burke," he said. "Man the pumps. You can recover from your shock sometime afterward. If it's the bet that bothers you, forget it. I'm too well off myself to need to snatch your pennies. And if it's the failure of Baby here, don't feel too bad. It did better than I expected. I thought it would just blow a fuse and quit working altogether, but I see it's still busy and devoting every single bank to obtaining a solution. I should imagine''—Cary yawned—"that it's working toward evolving a theory of types. *That* would give it the solution. Probably could get it, too, in a year or so.''

Still Burke did not move. Cary looked at him oddly.

"What's wrong?" he asked irritatedly.

Burke's mouth worked, a tiny speck of spittle flew from one corner of it.

"You—" he said. The word came tearing from his throat like the hoarse grunt of a dying man.

"What—"

"You fool!" groaned out Burke, finding his voice. "You stupid idiot! You insane moron!"

"Me? Me?" cried Cary. His voice was high in protest, almost like a womanish scream. "I was right!"

"Yes, you were right," said Burke. "You were too right. How am I supposed to get the machine's mind off this problem and on to running the pile for heat and light, when all its circuits are taken up in considering your paradox? What can *I* do, when the Brain is deaf, and dumb and blind?"

The two men looked at each other across the silent room. The warm breath of their exhalations made frosty plumes in the still air; and the distant howling of the storm deadened by the thick walls of the station, seemed to grow louder in the silence, bearing a note of savage triumph.

The temperature inside the station was dropping very fast—

The Star-Fool

No one knows who first pinned that unkind name upon the wandering scholars of the galaxy but it is not hard to guess from what class of men he came. Undoubtedly he was some one of the pioneering element, miner, merchant, middleman, or any of the other various groups that tore into the endless planetary frontier during the twenty-eighth century. To these men, exploitation, pure and simple, was the only worthwhile occupation. They looked with contemptuous scorn on the geologists, archeologists, paleontologists, all those whose aim was the acquisition of pure knowledge.

Consequently, there was a certain amount of ironic humor in a situation that arose on Krynor IV near the close of the twenty-eighth century. It began when an epidemic of nerve-disease broke out among the pioneering element there. It grew when the officials of the Federation Government tried to get in touch with their medical station on Tarn II, where the remedy for that particularly virulent plague was cultured in a serum made from native blood. They were answered by the ravings of a madman. And it reached its peak of humorous irony when those same officials discovered that the only human within reasonable distance of the station was a star-fool, an insignificant little geologist by the name of Peter Whaley . . .

*   *   *

It is not true that every man must have some kind of companion if he is going to wander the depths of space. There are some few self-sufficient individuals who find the company of their work quite sufficient, and, in fact, prefer it to the society of their own kind. Peter Whaley was one of these. A young man with an addiction to sloppy, comfortable clothes and a distaste for combing his hair, he had not the slightest objection to company—when he was not busy. When he was busy, the existence of the rest of the human race was superfluous.

At the present moment, on the airless moon of Tarn II, he was busy.

"George," he said, gazing into the large scanner set into one wall of his control-room, "bring me a specimen from that large black boulder to your right."

Fifty miles away, a small robot chirped an acknowledgement of the order, rolled, hopped and jumped to the boulder in question, and excised a small chunk of it. Having done so, it tucked the specimen into a place in its body and chirped again to signify that the specimen was secured.

"Very good, George," said Peter Whaley, approvingly. "Now bring all the specimens you've got back to the ship."

The little robot chirped and began to roll. Peter turned away from the screen. No need to watch further. George was the last word in specimen-collectors, and could be relied on to return safely over any kind of terrain.

He was laying out his apparatus for chemical analysis, when the deep-space communicator buzzed. With a puzzled frown, he laid down the test-tube he was holding and walked over to the communicator screen, switched it on.

There was a second of blurring motion as the tubes warmed; then the features of Rad Dowell, Commissioner, Thirty-Ninth Galactic Sector, spring into sharp relief on the screen. To Peter, who had seen them twice before during news space-casts, they were only vaguely familiar, as the face of someone known a long time ago.

"Whaley, geologist, speaking," said Peter, automatically. There was a long pause as his voice and image crossed lightyears of distance, to Thirty-Ninth Headquarters on Tynan V. Then the image in the ships' screen spoke again.

"Rad Dowell, Sector Commissioner, calling," said the grey-haired man in the dark blue uniform of a Federation official. "Are you at present on the moon of Tarn II?"

"I am," answered Peter. "There is a black basalt here which, in my opinion, is decidedly unusual for a moon of this type. Not only its prevalence, but its peculiar structure reflect a kind of igneous action in the local strata—" He broke off noticing a look of exasperation on the Commissioner's lined face. "I beg your pardon," he said. "What did you call me about?"

The commissioner sighed. The words star-fool were so obviously passing through his mind that they might as well have been printed on the screen. This, then, was the only man available to handle a crisis that meant life or death to literally millions.

"Whaley," said the Commissioner, heavily, "do you know what nerve disease is?"

"No, I don't," answered Peter, truthfully.

"It's a virus infection that strikes humans whose natural resistance has been lowered by exposure to cosmic radiation," explained the older man. "If we catch it in time, we can cure it—with the proper serum. The only difficulty is that it has a three-month incubation period and can only be detected during the last two or three weeks of that period. Since it is highly infectious, that means that by the time an epidemic breaks into the open, it has usually spread over half a dozen or more planets and thousands of people are already infected. That means that when an epidemic does break out, we have to rush serum immediately to all possible danger points and start general inoculations. Whaley, we have an epidemic on our hands right now—

19

and that planet below you is the galaxy's only source of serum!''

And, swiftly, the Commissioner outlined the situation to Peter Whaley.

"You are not government personnel," he wound up. "You have absolutely no training in handling alien races and the situation down there is probably dangerous as hell. I can't order you to go, and I don't know what you can do if you do go. All I can do is ask—will you?"

It was quite a question.

Peter Whaley, geologist, looked at his chemical apparatus spread out on the workbench, and thought of the little robot skittering back over the moon's airless surface even now. That was his work, not this. What could he do, if he went, seeing that he was without training and without experience? Barring a minor miracle he would probably do no more than make a ridiculous mess of things and die a stupid death. And the Lord only knew what he would find down there.

But, when he opened his mouth to refuse, a sudden irrational pride mixed with anger came swelling up in his throat like a bubble to choke off his words. Wasn't he, after all, as good as the next man, as good as these hard-headed empire builders? Abruptly a tingling urge for adventure ran hotly through his veins, and he threw logic and common sense together to the winds.

"Of course, Commissioner," he said. "I'll leave right away."

Surprise and hope mixed themselves for a moment in the expression on Rad Dowell's face.

"Good man!" he answered. "There's a ship on the way from here to pick up the serum. See if you can have a load ready for them when they get there. Every day's delay means several thousand lives. And—good luck."

"Thanks," said Peter, feeling suddenly embarrassed, and cut the connection.

For a moment he stood, bemused, until an insistent chirping brought him from his trance and set him to opening the airlock. The little robot had hit a stretch of smooth rock and made good time on the way back. Peter closed the outer lock, opened the inner, and the squat mechanical rolled in, blinking its red toplight furiously in warning that it was still too cold from exposure to airless space to be safely touched.

"It's all right, George," said Peter, wryly. "We won't be getting to work on those samples for quite some time. Just dump them into the storage bin and get ready for takeoff."

George turned and wheeled off in the direction of the storage bin, and Peter settled himself at the controls. Actually, although it was not really necessary with the almost automatic ship he drove, Peter was a better than average pilot and he procrastinated a little, checking various dials and indicators until there was no longer any real excuse for delaying the takeoff. When there was no more reason for delay, he sighed once, cleared his tubes with a short blast, and took off.

From above, the station looked like a small colony of ant-hills. Only the metallic sheen of the domed huts and the signal tower denied the impression. There was no answer to Peter's beamed announcement of landing; and neither human nor alien stirred in the clearing. He cut his power and dropped to the baked clay of the landing spot.

Still, nothing moved. Peter sat at the silent controls and wondered. The first emergency call from Sector Headquarters, they said, had been answered by a blank screen from which came senseless ravings in a voice which could no longer be identified as one of the station members. Since then, the station had not answered at all. The question was: was the madman still alive and waiting for Peter, someplace out there?

Peter rubbed his nose, thoughtfully. Inside him, a cold little voice was regretting his hasty acceptance of the Commissioner's request. What are you doing here? the voice was asking. This is not your line of business. Leave adventure for the men who are trained for it. At the same time, however, an innate stubbornness rose up to combat

his uneasiness. Peter had the dogged persistence character-
istic of his kind, and he had never yet abandoned, unfin-
ished, a job to which he had committed himself. Madman
or not, it was necessary that Peter investigate the station.
Consequently, there was no point in delaying further.

He rose from the controls and put on an air-helmet.
Then, from a dusty and almost forgotten locker, he dug
out an explosive pellet handgun and clipped it to his belt.
This done, he activated the airlocks, keyed them for re-
entrance, and went out into the clearing.

Outside the ship, he headed for the nearest cone,
which was the communications-shack. His visual image,
checked by the automatic scanner and passed as human,
opened the door before him, and he stepped inside.

Within, the body of a man lay sprawled before the
deep-space communicator. His skull had been crushed from
behind, and the evidence of the blood dried brown on the
floor and the partial decay of his body bore witness that he
had been dead for some time.

Peter looked around without touching anything; then
went back outside and continued his search through the
other buildings. It was as he had suspected. No living
human remained in the station. Only five silent bodies.
And of these, four had been murdered and one was a
suicide.

He returned to the communications-shack and called
Sector Headquarters.

"Well?" asked Rad Dowell, as soon as his face
appeared on the screen.

"How many men," asked Peter, "were here at the
station?"

"Five," answered the Commissioner. "One psychol-
ogist, three medical technicians, and the station chief, a
sort of medical administrator and contact man with the
natives."

"They're all dead," said Peter, and went on to recite
what he had seen. "Evidently one of the technicians went
insane and was confined to the infirmary. Somehow he
killed his attendant, broke out and killed the rest of the

men, and then hung himself. There's evidence of a struggle in the infirmary, but all the others were killed evidently without warning."

The lines on the Commissioner's face deepened.

"And the serum?" he asked. "It should be in the storehouse next to the culture lab?"

"I checked," answered Peter. "The storehouse is empty."

Incredulity replaced the worry etched on the Commissioner's features. "Empty?" he said. "You mean that the drums in the storehouse are empty?"

"I mean there are no drums," Peter informed him.

"But where could they have gone to?" said the Commissioner, bewilderedly. "There must be drums . . . And some of them must contain serum! Find out where they've gone to, Whaley. Ask the natives. There's a translator in the main office that'll make you intelligible to them."

Peter set his jaw.

"There are no natives," he said.

In the screen the Commissioner seemed to sag within his uniform.

"There's hundreds sick here," he said, in a hollow voice, "and nobody knows how many more infected that don't know it yet. On the frontier planets where it started, twenty per cent of the population are dying. And all those people have their hopes pinned on a ship which is on its way to you to pick up the serum that should be stored there. And now you tell me that there isn't any." There was something almost pathetic in the tone of his concluding words.

Peter looked steadily at him.

"What do you want me to do?" he asked.

"I don't know," said Rad Dowell. "Find the drums. They must be somewhere. There must be some serum in them. If you can't do that—" his voice trailed off on a note of hopelessness—"wait until the ship comes, I suppose. Perhaps—"

But what the rest of his sentence was, Peter never heard. For at that moment, there was the crash of a heavy body striking the wall of the communications-shack, and the set went dead. The abrupt violence shocked him into a momentary paralysis. For a second he stood there, staring stupidly at the screen as if he expected it to light up again of its own accord. Then, when the patent absurdity of this had penetrated his mind, he reacted swiftly with an action that was as foolish as it was brave. Unclipping the hand-gun from his belt, he walked to the door with it held in his right hand, and stepped out into the open.

"Halt!"

For a second, the scene had all the appearance of a tableau. There was Peter, brought to an abrupt halt by what he saw, the pellet gun upraised in one hand, and there was the cause of the disturbance, a group of Tarnian natives, frozen, holding the treetrunk they had been using as a battering ram on the tower of the communications-shack.

"Halt," he said again, foolishly, for of course it meant nothing to the Tarnians.

After that things began to happen quickly.

The natives, losing their nerve at the actual appearance of the human they had been threatening, dropped the treetrunk and went bounding in great kangeroo-like hops for the forest at the edge of the clearing. Peter yelled—a quite meaningless and thoroughly instinctive battle-sound—and fired the gun at random. The pellets streamed from its muzzle at ten-thousand feet per second, missed the natives by a wide margin, and blew some fifty square meters of the forest beyond to smoking fragments. The natives, convinced that their doom was inescapably upon them, skidded to a halt and stood, their large, fish-like eyes rolling in terror, antennae quivering, too frightened to either advance into the devastated area or return toward Peter.

"Halt!" yelled Peter, a wild exhilaration filling him at finding himself in command of the situation. "Don't move. I'll be right back."

He might as well have spoken in Sanskrit for all the natives understood but the command was unnecessary.

Nothing short of an earthquake could have moved the Tarnian raiding party at that moment.

Peter ducked hurriedly into the main office building, picked up the translator—a dark colored box with two adjustable helmets attached—and ducked out again. He walked up to the raiding party and dropped the "alien" helmet on the antennaed head of the first squat green creature he came to. Then he put the "human" helmet on his own head and switched on the power.

"Who's in charge here?" Peter demanded.

"Not this one, Lord, not this one," chattered the earphones terrifiedly in his ear. "This one loves the lords. This one was made to come here by that one chief—" and a trembling green paw indicated a scowling Tarnian who was glaring at Peter's informant with murder in his eyes.

"Ha!" said Peter. He lifted the "alien" helmet from the head of the one he had been talking to, walked over, and dumped it on the native indicated.

"Are you the chief?"

"This one chief," was the sullen acknowledgement.

"Why did you break the communications tower?" Peter asked.

"Don't want tower," growled the native.

"Why not?"

"This one tower not tree. Break down. This one lord not Tarn-man. Go away."

"Just as I thought," said Peter grimly. "So you were trying to scare me off. Well, I don't scare. What made you decide that you didn't want humans here?"

"Lords take Tarn-blood. Those ones Lords say these ones Tarn-men give blood and those ones Lords protect Tarn-men from devils. Those ones Lords lie."

"Oh?" said Peter. "And what made you think they lied?"

"Those ones lords dead long time now. No devils."

Peter grimaced a trifle wryly.

The native's logic was simple but definite enough. He thought fast.

"Did it ever occur to you," he said, "that something might still be protecting you from devils?"

"Yes."

The answer stopped Peter. He blinked.

"Oh?" he said. "Who, then?"

"The old gods," was the complacent and surprising answer. "The spirit who lives in the village idols protects those ones villages."

Peter shook his head inside the helmet. This kind of crisis in native-human relations called for a trained administrator. Best to let it ride until the ship got here. But there was one thing he could do.

"In that one building," he said, slipping into the Tarnian phraseology, and indicating the storehouse, "were a lot of large metal drums. Where are they?"

"These ones take," answered the native.

"Bring them back!" snapped Peter.

"Gods say no," returned the other stubbornly. "Those ones drums have Tarn-blood in them."

"But it isn't Tarn-blood any longer, you fool," said Peter desperately. "It's serum."

"Tarn-blood," repeated the native doggedly. "Sacred."

Peter stared at him. The frustrations, he thought, must be making him ill. A strange sort of dizziness made his head swim. Abruptly, he lost all control of his temper—

"Bring them back, damn you!" he screamed, lashing out with his fist at the small native. "Bring them back!"

The native ducked, and the helmet flopped from his head. Finding himself free, he began to run. The others bolted after him, and in a second the clearing was empty, except for Peter.

Dizzily, he turned and headed back toward his ship. Have to report this, he thought, and, with the communications-shack out of order, the only transmitter was aboard his vessel. His emotions seemed oddly difficult to control. Once he turned about in a sudden fit of rage and, screaming curses, sent a stream of pellets to explode into the forest where the Tarnians had disappeared. Then he made his way into the ship and switched on his set, calling Sector Headquarters.

· The face of Rad Dowell took form on the screen.

"Hello, Whaley," the Commissioner said. "Any luck?"

"Why should I have luck?" asked Peter, sourly. "The natives are trying to break away from human control. They've reverted to worship of their village idols. They've stolen the serum from the storehouse and won't bring it back."

Rad Dowell shook his head despairingly.

"It looks hopeless," he said.

"Of course it's hopeless," snapped Peter. "You knew that when you sent me here."

The Commissioner's eyes narrowed suddenly; he looked suspiciously at Peter.

"Tell me, Whaley," he asked, "you had inoculations yourself before you left for the Tarn moon, didn't you?"

"What inoculations?" demanded Peter.

"Why—Tarn itself is the home of the nerve disease!" said the Commissioner. "I thought you knew that. That's why the native blood can be used as a culture for the preventive serum. Only on Tarn it's that much worse, because while the disease runs for the regular two weeks through alternate periods of excitement and lassitude before it kills the patient, there's no incubation period required if you catch it directly from a native carrier. But you must have been inoculated before they gave your ship clearance papers for Tarn from your last stop."

Peter looked at him dully.

"I didn't have clearance papers for Tarn," he replied. "Just for the moon of Tarn." He paused. Somewhere within him, a thick black vein of anger pulsed and throbbed feverishly; the screen in front of him seemed to shake in time with its beating. Then, abruptly, it rose like a fiery tide inside him and rage spewed words from his mouth.

"You knew it!" he screamed, as the walls of the ship spun crazily about him. "You sent me to my death. To my death! *To my death!*" And, whipping the handgun from his belt, he sent it crashing, butt first, directly into the screen.

There was an instantaneous flash of intense, blue-violet light, and the set went dead.

"If you want my opinion, Cushey—" began third-mate Ron Parker.

"Which I don't," interrupted the little doctor, bristling.

"As I say," continued the young officer, imperturbably, "if you want my opinion, he's already dead; and we two are going to look like damn fools, leaping off the ship the minute she lands and rushing up to a corpse with revivicator and half the medical equipment the City of Parth carries on board."

He looked moodily out the airlock scanner, watching the medical station of Tarn II float up to them as the big government-ship eased in for a landing.

"And what if he isn't, hey?" barked Major Cushey. "What if there's a flicker of life left in him and we can bring him back enough to tell us something of what's been going on around here . . . what if he finally found out where the drums are kept, hey? Isn't a thousand to one chance worth a little physical effort, even to you, if it means halting an epidemic? Lazy young lout!"

"Not lazy. Just no point in expecting—" Ron began. A slight jar announced that they had grounded. "Oh, well, here we go, ready or not—" and the two men flipped their air-helmets down over their heads and clipped them tight.

Before them, the outer lock swung open. They leaped out and hit the ground running, Major Cushey bouncing ahead like a particularly energetic, if overfed rabbit, and Ron loping clumsily along behind, the long, awkward bulk of the revivicator clutched lovingly to his chest.

"Try the office building first," Cushey's voice shrilled in the young officer's earphones. Ron cursed and followed the shorter man to the building with the Federation flag flying above it. They reached it. The scanner, noting their speed, checked them hastily, and the door swung open. They plunged inside . . .

. . . And skidded to a shocked and startled halt. For rising from a chair to greet them, unsteady, pale, but undeniably alive, was the man they had come to save.

"You'll excuse me for not going outside to meet the ship," he said. "I heard you landing, but I'm a little too weak to walk that far yet."

They stared at him.

"But you're not sick!" said Cushey peevishly, as if it were rather unkind of Peter to be alive at all.

"Not any more," answered Peter, sinking back in his chair.

"How did this happen, this—this cure," barked the little doctor.

"In the most ordinary way," said Peter, "I took some of the serum."

"But you told the Commissioner the natives had taken all the serum there was."

"They had," said Peter. He closed his eyes and chuckled. "I—er—persuaded them to bring it back. The storehouse is full of drums of it right now—a full load for you to take back."

The two officers looked at each other.

"Pardon me," said Cushey, and stepped forward to curl two fingers over Peter's pulse.

Peter chuckled again. "No, I'm quite well," he said. "Look in the storehouse if you don't believe me."

"But how could you do it?" cried Ron . . . *a star-fool, like you!* his words implied.

"Simple," answered Peter. "They thought that their village idols were ample protection against devils—that they didn't need human protection. So I supplied them with a devil that their idols were no protection against. They came crying to me for help. I tottered out into the clearing, challenged It, and when It showed up, blew It to bits." He paused, "After that, they fell over themselves to be good to me. Brought the serum back, and offered to bleed all over the place for me—'course I couldn't take them up on that, not knowing how to make the serum. But when you're ready for them, I can whistle them up in a jiffy.''

"But I still don't understand," protested the bewildered Ron. "What was the devil? Where would you get a devil?"

"The devil?" echoed Peter. "Oh, that was George, my specimen collector. Poor George. I hated to blow him to pieces, but it was him or me.''

"Specimen collector?" repeated the medical major in an odd tone of voice, applying his stethoscope to Peter's chest. "But I know what they are. They're just small robots that chip off pieces of rock and bring them to you for examination. Ruggedly built, of course; but I don't see what devil-like aspects one of those could have. Your George was utterly harmless.''

Peter laughed out loud. And this time he opened his eyes and looked them both full in the face.

"Not," he said, cheerfully, "when he went around on my orders collecting specimens from all of the village idols, he wasn't.''

Hilifter

It was locked—from the outside.

Not only that, but the mechanical latch handle that would override the button lock on the tiny tourist cabin aboard the *Star of the North* was hidden by the very bed on which Cully When sat cross-legged, like some sinewy mountain man out of Cully's own pioneering ancestry. Cully grinned at the image in the mirror which went with the washstand now hidden by the bed beneath him. He would not have risked such an expression as that grin if there had been anyone around to see him. The grin, he knew, gave too much of him away to viewers. It was the hard, unconquerable humor of a man dealing for high stakes.

Here, in the privacy of this locked cabin, it was also a tribute to the skill of the steward who had imprisoned him. A dour and cautious individual with a long Scottish face, and no doubt the greater part of his back wages reinvested in the very spaceship line he worked for. Or had Cully done something to give himself away? No. Cully shook his head. If that had been the case, the steward would have done more than just lock the cabin. It occurred to Cully that his face, at last, might be becoming known.

"I'm sorry, sir," the steward had said, as he opened the cabin's sliding door and saw the unmade bed. "Off-watch steward's missed making it up." He clucked reprovingly. "I'll fix it for you, sir."

"No hurry," said Cully. "I just want to hang my clothes; and I can do that later."

"Oh, no, sir." The lean, dour face of the other—as primitive in a different way as Cully's own—looked shocked. "Regulations. Passenger's gear to be stowed and bunk made up before overdrive."

"Well, I can't just stand here in the corridor," said Cully. "I want to get rid of the stuff and get a drink." And indeed the corridor was so narrow, they were like two vehicles on a mountain road. One would have to back up to some wider spot to let the other past.

"Have the sheets in a moment, sir," said the steward. "Just a moment, sir. If you wouldn't mind sitting up on the bed, sir?"

"All right," said Cully. "But hurry. I want to step up for a drink in the lounge."

He hopped up on to the bed, which filled the little cabin in its down position; and drew his legs up tailor-fashion to clear them out of the corridor.

"Excuse me, sir," said the steward, closed the door, and went off. As soon as he heard the button lock latch, Cully had realized what the man was up to. But an unsuspecting man would have waited at least several minutes before hammering on the locked door and calling for someone to let him out. Cully had been forced to sit digesting the matter in silence.

At the thought of it now, however, he grinned again. That steward was a regular prize package. Cully must remember to think up something appropriate for him, afterward. At the moment, there were more pressing things to think of.

Cully looked in the mirror again and was relieved at the sight of himself without the betraying grin. The face that looked back at him at the moment was lean and angular. A little peroxide solution on his thick, straight brows, had taken the sharp appearance off his high cheekbones and given his pale blue eyes a faintly innocent expression. When he really wanted to fail to impress sharply discerning eyes, he also made it a point to chew gum.

The present situation, he considered now, did not call for that extra touch. If the steward was already even vaguely suspicious of him, he could not wait around for an ideal opportunity. He would have to get busy now, while they were still working the spaceship out of the solar system to a safe distance where the overdrive could be engaged without risking a mass-proximity explosion.

And this, since he was imprisoned so neatly in his own shoebox of a cabin, promised to be a problem right from the start.

He looked around the cabin. Unlike the salon cabins on the level overhead, where it was possible to pull down the bed and still have a tiny space to stand upright in—either beside the bed, in the case of single-bed cabins, or between them, in the case of doubles—in the tourist cabins once the bed was down, the room was completely divided into two spaces—the space above the bed and the space below. In the space above, with him, were the light and temperature and ventilation controls, controls to provide him with soft music or the latest adventure tape, food and drink dispensers and a host of other minor comforts.

There were also a phone and a signal button, both connected with the steward's office. Thoughtfully he tried both. There was, of course, no answer.

At that moment a red light flashed on the wall opposite him; and a voice came out of the grille that usually provided the soft music.

"We are about to maneuver. This is the Captain's Section, speaking. We are about to maneuver. Will all lounge passengers return to their cabins? Will all passengers remain in their cabins, and fasten seat belts. We are about to maneuver. This is the Captain's Section—"

Cully stopped listening. The steward would have known this announcement was coming. It meant that everybody but crew members would be in their cabins and crew members would be up top in control level at maneuver posts. And that meant nobody was likely to happen along to let Cully out. If Cully could get out of this cabin, however, those abandoned corridors could be a break for him.

However, as he looked about him now, Cully was rapidly revising downward his first cheerful assumption that he—who had gotten out of so many much more intentional prisons—would find this a relatively easy task. On the same principle that a pit with unclimbable walls and too deep to jump up from and catch an edge is one of the most perfect traps designable—the tourist room held Cully. He was on top of the bed; and he needed to be below it to operate the latch handle.

First question: How impenetrable was the bed itself? Cully dug down through the covers, pried up the mattress, peered through the springs, and saw a blank panel of metal. Well, he had not really expected much in that direction. He put the mattress and covers back and examined what he had to work with above-bed.

There were all the control switches and buttons on the wall, but nothing among them promised him any aid. The walls were the same metal paneling as the base of the bed. Cully began to turn out his pockets in the hope of finding something in them that would inspire him. And he did indeed turn out a number of interesting items, including a folded piece of notepaper which he looked at rather soberly before laying it aside, unfolded, with a boy scout type of knife that just happened to have a set of lock picks among its other tools. The note would only take up valuable time at the moment, and—the lock being out of reach in the door—the lock picks were no good either.

There was nothing in what he produced to inspire him, however. Whistling a little mournfully, he began to make the next best use of his pile of property. He unscrewed the nib and cap of his long, gold fountain pen, took out the ink cartridge and laid the tube remaining aside. He removed his belt, and the buckle from the belt. The buckle, it appeared, clipped on to the fountain pen tube in somewhat the manner of a pistol grip. He reached in his mouth, removed a bridge covering from the second premolar to the second molar, and combined this with a small metal throwaway dispenser of the sort designed to contain antacid tablets. The two together had a remarkable resemblance to the magazine and miniaturized trigger assembly of a small handgun; and when he attached them to the buckle-fountain-pen-tube combination the resemblance became so marked as to be practically inarguable.

Cully made a few adjustments in this and looked around himself again. For the second time, his eye came to rest on the folded note, and, frowning at himself in the mirror, he did pick it up and unfold it. Inside it read: "O wae the pow'r the Giftie gie us" Love, Lucy. Well, thought Cully, that was about what you could expect from a starry-eyed girl with Scottish ancestors, and romantic notions about present-day conditions on Alderbaran IV and the other new worlds.

". . . But if you have all that land on Asterope IV, why aren't you back there developing it?" she had asked him.

"The New Worlds are stifling to death," he had answered. But he saw then she did not believe him. To her, the New Worlds were still the romantic Frontier, as the Old Worlds Confederation newspapers capitalized it. She thought he had given up from lack of vision.

"You should try again . . ." she murmured. He gave up trying to make her understand. And then, when the cruise was over and their shipboard acquaintance—that was all it was, really—ended on the Miami dock, he had felt her slip something in his pocket so lightly only someone as self-trained as he would have noticed it. Later he had found it to be this note—which he had kept now for too long.

He started to throw it away, changed his mind for the sixtieth time and put it back in his pocket. He turned back to the problem of getting out of the cabin. He looked it over, pulled a sheet from the bed and used its length to measure a few distances.

The bunk was pivoted near the point where the head of it entered the recess in the wall that concealed it in Up position. Up, the bunk was designed to fit with its foot next to the ceiling. Consequently, coming up, the foot would describe an arc—

About a second and a half later he had discovered that the arc of the foot, ascending, would leave just enough space in the opposite top angle between wall and ceiling so that if he could just manage to hang there, while releasing the safety latch at the foot of the bed, he might be able to get the bed up past him into the wall recess.

It was something which required the muscle and skill normally called for by so-called "chimney ascents" in mountain climbing—where the climber wedges himself between two opposing walls of rock. A rather wide chimney—since the room was a little more than four feet in width. But Cully had had some little experience in that line.

He tried it. A few seconds later, pressed against walls and ceiling, he reached down, managed to get the bed released, and had the satisfaction of seeing it fold up by him. Half a breath later he was free, out in the corridor of the Tourist Section.

The corridor was deserted and silent. All doors were closed. Cully closed his own thoughtfully behind him and went along the corridor to the more open space in the center of the ship. He looked up a steel ladder to the entrance of the Salon Section, where there would be another ladder to the Crew Section, and from there eventually to his objective—the Control level and the Captain's Section. Had the way up those ladders been open, it would have been simple. But level with the top of the ladder he saw the way to the Salon section was closed off by a metal cover capable of withstanding fifteen pounds per square inch of pressure.

It had been closed, of course, as the other covers would have been, at the beginning of the maneuver period.

Cully considered it thoughtfully, his fingers caressing the pistol grip of the little handgun he had just put together. He would have preferred, naturally, that the covers be open and the way available to him without the need for fuss or muss. But the steward had effectively ruled out that possibility by reacting as and when he had. Cully turned away from the staircase, and frowned, picturing the layout of the ship, as he had committed it to memory five days ago.

There was an emergency hatch leading through the ceiling of the end tourist cabin to the end salon cabin overhead, at both extremes of the corridor. He turned and went down to the end cabin nearest him, and laid his finger quietly on the outside latch-handle.

There was no sound from inside. He drew his put-together handgun from his belt; and, holding it in his left hand, calmly and without hesitation, opened the door and stepped inside.

He stopped abruptly. The bed in here was, of course, up in the wall, or he could never have entered. But the cabin's single occupant was asleep on the right-hand seat of the two seats that an upraised bed left exposed. The occupant was a small girl of about eight years old.

The slim golden barrel of the handgun had swung immediately to aim at the child's temple. For an automatic second, it hung poised there, Cully's finger half-pressing the trigger. But the little girl never stirred. In the silence, Cully heard the surge of his own blood in his ears and the faint crackle of the note in his shirt pocket. He lowered the gun and fumbled in the waistband of his pants, coming up with a child-sized anesthetic pellet. He slipped this into his gun above the regular load, aimed the gun, and fired. The child made a little uneasy movement all at once; and then lay still. Cully bent over her for a second, and heard the soft sound of her breathing. He straightened up. The pellet worked not through the blood stream, but immediately through a reaction of the nerves. In fifteen minutes the effect would be worn off, and the girl's sleep would be natural slumber again.

He turned away, stepped up on the opposite seat and laid his free hand on the latch handle of the emergency hatch overhead. A murmur of voices from above made him hesitate. He unscrewed the barrel of the handgun and put it in his ear with the other hollow end resting against the ceiling which was also the floor overhead. The voices came, faint and distorted, but understandable to his listening.

"... Hilifter," a female voice was saying.

"Oh, Patty!" another female voice answered. "He was just trying to scare you. You believe everything."

"How about that ship that got hilifted just six months ago? That ship going to one of the Pleiades, just like this one? The *Queen of Argyle—*"

"*Princess of Argyle.*"

"Well, you know what I mean. Ships do get hilifted. Just as long as there're governments on the pioneer worlds that'll license them and no questions asked. And it could just as well happen to this ship. But you don't worry about it a bit."

"No, I don't."

"When hilifters take over a ship, they kill off everyone who can testify against them. None of the passengers or ship's officers from the *Princess of Argyle* was ever heard of again."

"Says who?"

"Oh, everybody knows that!"

Cully took the barrel from his ear and screwed it back onto his weapon. He glanced at the anesthetized child and thought of trying the other cabin with an emergency hatch. But the maneuver period would not last more than twenty minutes at the most and five of that must be gone already. He put the handgun between his teeth, jerked the latch to the overhead hatch, and pulled it down and open.

He put both hands on the edge of the hatch opening; and with one spring went upward into the salon cabin overhead.

He erupted into the open space between a pair of facing seats, each of which held a girl in her twenties. The one on his left was a rather plump, short, blond girl who was sitting curled up on her particular seat with a towel across her knees, an open bottle of pink nail polish on the towel, and the brush-cap to the bottle poised in her hand.

The other was a tall, dark-haired, very pretty lass with a lap-desk pulled down from the wall and a handscriber on the desk where she was apparently writing a letter. For a moment both stared at him, and his gun; and then the blonde gave a muffled shriek, pulled the towel over her head and lay still, while the brunette, staring at Cully, went slowly pale.

"Jim!" she said.

"Sorry," said Cully. "The real name's Cully When. Sorry about this, too, Lucy." He held the gun casually, but it was pointed in her general direction. "I didn't have any choice."

A little of the color came back. Her eyes were as still as fragments of green bottle glass.

"No choice about what?" she said.

"To come through this way," said Cully. "Believe me, if I'd known you were here, I'd have picked any other way. But there wasn't any other way; and I didn't know."

"I see," she said, and looked at the gun in his hand. "Do you have to point that at me?"

"I'm afraid," said Cully, gently, "I do."

She did not smile.

"I'd still like to know what you're doing here," she said.

"I'm just passing through," said Cully. He gestured with the gun to the emergency hatch to the Crew Section, overhead. "As I say, I'm sorry it has to be through your cabin. But I didn't even know you were serious about emigrating."

"People usually judge other people by themselves," she said expressionlessly. "As it happened, I believed you." She looked at the gun again. "How many of you are there on board?"

"I'm afraid I can't tell you that," said Cully.

"No. You couldn't, could you?" Her eyes held steady on him. "You know, there's an old poem about a man like you. He rides by a farm maiden and she falls in love with him, just like that. But he makes her guess what he is; and she guesses . . . oh, all sorts of honorable things, like soldier, or forester. But he tells her in the end he's just an outlaw, slinking through the wood.''

Cully winced.

"Lucy—" he said. "Lucy—"

"Oh, that's all right," she said. "I should have known when you didn't call me or get in touch with me, after the boat docked." She glanced over at her friend, motionless under the towel. "You have the gun. What do you want us to do?"

"Just sit still," he said. "I'll go on up through here and be out of your way in a second. I'm afraid—" he reached over to the phone on the wall and pulled its cord loose. "You can buzz for the steward, still, after I'm gone," he said. "But he won't answer just a buzzer until after the maneuver period's over. And the stairway hatches are locked. Just sit tight and you'll be all right."

He tossed the phone aside and tucked the gun in the waistband.

"Excuse me," he said, stepping up on the seat beside her. She moved stiffly away from him. He unlatched the hatch overhead, pulled it down; and went up through it. When he glanced back down through it, he saw her face stiffly upturned to him.

He turned away and found himself in an equipment room. It was what he had expected from the ship's plans he had memorized before coming aboard. He went quickly out of the room and scouted the Section.

As he had expected, there was no one at all upon this level. Weight and space on interstellar liners being at the premium that they were, even a steward like the one who had locked him in his cabin did double duty. In overdrive, no one but the navigating officer had to do much of anything. But in ordinary operation, there were posts for all ships personnel, and all ships personnel were at them up in the Captain's Section at Control.

The stair hatch to this top and final section of the ship, he found to be closed as the rest. This, of course, was routine. He had not expected this to be unlocked, though a few years back ships like this might have been that careless. There were emergency hatches from this level as well, of course, up to the final section. But it was no part of Cully's plan to come up in the middle of a Control room or a Captain's Section filled with young, active, and almost certainly armed officers. The inside route was closed.

The outside route remained a possibility. Cully went down to the opposite end of the corridor and found the entry port closed, but sealed only by a standard lock. In an adjoining room there were outside suits. Cully spent a few minutes with his picks, breaking the lock of the seal; and then went in to put on the suit that came closest to fitting his six-foot-two frame.

A minute later he stepped out onto the outside skin of the ship.

As he watched the outer door of the entry port closing ponderously in the silence of airless space behind him, he felt the usual inner coldness that came over him at times like this. He had a mild but very definite phobia about open space with its myriads of unchanging stars. He knew what caused it—several psychiatrists had told him it was nothing to worry about, but he could not quite accept their unconcern. He knew he was a very lonely individual, underneath it all; and subconsciously he guessed he equated space with the final extinction in which he expected one day to disappear and be forgotten forever. He could not really believe it was possible for someone like him to make a dent in such a universe.

It was symptomatic, he thought now, plodding along with the magnetic bootsoles of his suit clinging to the metal hull, that he had never had any success with women—like Lucy. A sort of bad luck seemed to put him always in the wrong position with anyone he stood a chance of loving. Inwardly, he was just as starry-eyed as Lucy, he admitted to himself, alone with the vastness of space and the stars, but he'd never had much success bringing it out into the open. Where she went all right, he seemed to go all wrong. Well, he thought, that was life. She went her way and he would go his. And it was probably a good thing.

He looked ahead up the side of the ship, and saw the slight bulge of the observation window of the navigator's section. It was just a few more steps now.

Modern ships were sound insulated, thankfully, or the crew inside would have heard his dragging footsteps on the hull. He reached the window and peered in. The room he looked into was empty.

Beside the window was a small, emergency port for cleaning and repairs of the window. Clumsily, and with a good deal of effort, he got the lock-bolt holding it down unscrewed, and let himself in. The space between outer and inner ports here was just enough to contain a spacesuited man. He crouched in darkness after the outer port had closed behind him.

Incoming air screamed up to audibility. He cautiously cracked the interior door and looked into a room still empty of any crew members. He slipped inside and snapped the lock on the door before getting out of his suit.

As soon as he was out, he drew the handgun from his belt and cautiously opened the door he had previously locked. He looked out on a short corridor leading one way to the Control Room, and the other, if his memory of the memorized ship plans had not failed him, to the central room above the stairway hatch from below. Opening off this small circular space surrounding the hatch, would be another entrance directly to the Control Room, a door to the Captain's Quarters, and one to the Communications Room.

The corridor was deserted. He heard voices coming down it from the Control Room; and he slipped out the door that led instead to the space surrounding the stairway hatch. And checked abruptly.

The hatch was open. And it had not been open when he had checked it from the level below, ten minutes before.

For the first time he cocked an ear specifically to the kinds of voices coming from the Control Room. The acoustics of this part of the ship mangled all sense out of the words being said. But now that he listened, he had no trouble recognizing, among others, the voice of Lucy.

It occurred to him then with a kind of wonder at himself, that it would have been no feat for an active girl like herself to have followed him up through the open emergency hatch, and later mount the crew level stairs to the closed hatch there and pound on it until someone opened up.

He threw aside further caution and sprinted across to the doorway of the Captain's Quarters. The door was unlocked. He ducked inside and looked around him. It was empty. It occurred to him that Lucy and the rest of the ship's complement would probably still be expecting him to be below in the Crew's section. He closed the door and looked about him, at the room he was in.

The room was more lounge than anything else, being the place where the captain of a spaceship did his entertaining. But there was a large and businesslike desk in one corner of the room, and in the wall opposite, was a locked, glassed-in case holding an assortment of rifles and handguns.

He was across the room in a moment and in a few, savage, seconds, had the lock to the case picked open. He reached in and took down a short-barreled, flaring-muzzled riot gun. He checked the chamber. It was filled with a full thousand-clip of the deadly steel darts. Holding this in one hand and his handgun in the other, he went back out the door and toward the other entrance to the control room—the entrance from the central room around the stairway hatch.

". . . He wouldn't tell me if there were any others," Lucy was saying to a man in a captain's shoulder tabs, while eight other men, including the dour-faced steward who had locked Cully in his cabin, stood at their posts, but listening.

"There aren't any," said Cully, harshly. They all turned to him. He laid the handgun aside on a control table by the entrance to free his other hand, and lifted the heavy riot gun in both hands, covering them. "There's only me."

"What do you want?" said the man with the captain's tabs. His face was set, and a little pale. Cully ignored the question. He came into the room, circling to his right, so as to have a wall at his back.

"You're one man short," said Cully as he moved. "Where is he?"

"Off-shift steward's sleeping," said the steward who had locked Cully in his room.

"Move back," said Cully, picking up crew members from their stations at control boards around the room, and herding them before him back around the room's circular limit to the very entrance by which he had come in. "I don't believe you."

"Then I might as well tell you," said the captain, backing up now along with Lucy and the rest. "He's in Communications. We keep a steady contact with Solar Police right up until we go into overdrive. There are two of their ships pacing alongside us right now, lights off, a hundred miles each side of us."

"Tell me another," said Cully. "I don't believe that either." He was watching everybody in the room, but what he was most aware of were the eyes of Lucy, wide upon him. He spoke to her, harshly. "Why did you get into this?"

She was pale to the lips; and her eyes had a stunned look.

"I looked down and saw what you'd done to that child in the cabin below—" her voice broke off into a whisper. "Oh, Cully—"

He laughed mournfully.

"Stop there," he ordered. He had driven them back into a corner near the entrance he had come in. "I've got to have all of you together. Now, one of you is going to tell me where that other man is—and I'm going to pick you off, one at a time until somebody does."

"You're a fool," said the captain. A little of his color had come back. "You're all alone. You don't have a chance of controlling this ship by yourself. You know what happens to Hilifters, don't you? It's not just a prison sentence. Give up now and we'll all put in a word for you. You might get off without mandatory execution."

"No thanks," said Cully. He gestured with the end of the riot gun. "We're going into overdrive. Start setting up the course as I give it to you."

"No," said the captain, looking hard at him.

"You're a brave man," said Cully. "But I'd like to point out something. I'm going to shoot you if you won't co-operate; and then I'm going to work down the line of your officers. Sooner or later somebody's going to preserve his life by doing what I tell him. So getting yourself killed isn't going to save the ship at all. It just means somebody with less courage than you lives. And you die."

There was a sharp, bitter intake of breath from the direction of Lucy. Cully kept his eyes on the captain.

"How about it?" Cully asked.

"No brush-pants of a colonial," said the captain, slowly and deliberately, "is going to stand in my Control Room and tell me where to take my ship."

"Did the captain and officers of the *Princess of Argyle* ever come back?" said Cully, somewhat cryptically.

"It's nothing to me whether they came or stayed."

"I take it all back," said Cully. "You're too valuable to lose." The riot gun shifted to come to bear on the First Officer, a tall, thin, younger man whose hair was already receding at the temples. "But you aren't, friend. I'm not even going to tell you what I'm going to do. I'm just going to start counting; and when I decide to stop you've had it. One . . . two . . ."

"Don't! Don't shoot!" The First Officer jumped across the few steps that separated him from the Main Computer Panel. "What's your course? What do you want me to set up—"

The captain began to curse the First Officer. He spoke slowly and distinctly and in a manner that completely ignored the presence of Lucy in the Control Room. He went right on as Cully gave the First Officer the course and the First Officer set it up. He stopped only, as— abruptly—the lights went out, and the ship overdrove.

When the lights came on again—it was a matter of only a fraction of a second of real time—the captain was at last silent. He seemed to have sagged in the brief interval of darkness and his face looked older.

And then, slamming through the tense silence of the room came the sound of the Contact Alarm Bell.

"Turn it on," said Cully. The First Officer stepped over and pushed a button below the room's communication screen. It cleared suddenly to show a man in a white jacket.

"We're alongside, Cully," he said. "We'll take over now. How're you fixed for casualties?"

"At the moment—" began Cully. But he got no further than that. Behind him, three hard, spaced words in a man's voice cut him off.

"Drop it, Hilifter!"

Cully did not move. He cocked his eyebrows a little sadly and grinned his untamable grin for the first time at the ship's officers, and Lucy and the figure in the screen. Then the grin went away.

"Friend," he said to the man hidden behind him. "Your business is running a spaceship. Mine is taking them away from people who run them. Right now you're figuring how you make me give up or shoot me down and this ship dodges back into overdrive, and you become a hero for saving it. But it isn't going to work that way."

He waited for a moment to hear if the off-watch steward behind him—or whoever the officer was—would answer. But there was only silence.

"You're behind me," said Cully. "But I can turn pretty fast. You may get me coming around, but unless you've got something like a small cannon, you're not going to stop me getting you at this short range, whether you've got me or not. Now, if you think I'm just talking, you better think again. For me, this is one of the risks of the trade."

46

He turned. As he did so he went for the floor; and heard the first shot go by his ear. As he hit the floor another shot hit the deck beside him and ricocheted into his side. But by that time he had the heavy riot gun aimed and he pressed the firing button. The stream of darts knocked the man backward, out of the entrance to the control room to lie, a still and huddled shape, in the corridor outside.

Cully got to his feet, feeling the single dart in his side. The room was beginning to waver around him, but he felt that he could hold on for the necessary couple of minutes before the people from the ship moving in alongside could breach the lock and come aboard. His jacket was loose and would hide the bleeding underneath. None of those facing him could know he had been hit.

"All right, folks," he said, managing a grin. "It's all over but the shouting—" And then Lucy broke suddenly from the group and went running across the room toward the entrance through which Cully had come a moment or so earlier.

"Lucy—" he barked at her. And then he saw her stop and turn by the control table near the entrance, snatching up the little handgun he had left there. "Lucy, do you want to get shot?"

But she was bringing up the little handgun, held in the grip of both her hands and aiming it squarely at him. The tears were running down her face.

"It's better for you, Cully—" she was sobbing. "Better . . ."

He swung the riot gun to bear on her, but he saw she did not even see it.

"Lucy, I'll have to kill you!" he cried. But she no more heard him, apparently, than she saw the muzzle-on view of the riot gun in his hands. The wavering golden barrel in her grasp wobbled to bear on him.

"Oh, Cully!" she wept. "Cully—" And pulled the trigger.

"Oh, *hell!*" said Cully in despair. And let her shoot him down.

* * *

When he came back, things were very fuzzy there at first. He heard the voice of the man in the white jacket, arguing with the voice of Lucy.

"Hallucination—" muttered Cully. The voices broke off.

"Oh, he said something!" cried the voice of Lucy.

"Cully?" said the man's voice. Cully felt a two-finger grip on his wrist in the area where his pulse should be—if, that was, he had a pulse. "How're you feeling?"

"Ship's doctor?" muttered Cully, with great effort. "You got the *Star of the North?*"

"That's right. All under control. How do you feel?"

"Feel fine," mumbled Cully. The doctor laughed.

"Sure you do," said the doctor. "Nothing like being shot a couple of times and having a pellet and a dart removed to put a man in good shape."

"Not Lucy's fault—" muttered Cully. "Not understand." He made another great effort in the interests of explanation. "Stars'n eyes."

"Oh, what does he mean?" wept Lucy.

"He means," said the voice of the doctor harshly, "that you're just the sort of fine young idealist who makes the best sort of sucker for the sort of propaganda the Old World's Confederation dishes out."

"Oh, you'd say that!" flared Lucy's voice. "Of course, you'd say that!"

"Young lady," said the doctor, "how rich do you think our friend Cully, here, is?"

Cully heard her blow her nose, weakly.

"He's got millions, I suppose," she said, bitterly. "Hasn't he hilifted dozens of ships?"

"He's hilifted eight," said the doctor, dryly, "which, incidentally, puts him three ships ahead of any other contender for the title of hilifting champion around the populated stars. The mortality rate among single workers—and you can't get any more than a single 'lifter aboard Confederation ships nowadays—hits ninety per cent with the third ship captured. But I doubt Cully's been able to save many millions on a salary of six hundred a month, and a bonus of one tenth of one per cent of salvage value, at Colonial World rates.''

There was a moment of profound silence.

"What do you mean?'' said Lucy, in a voice that wavered a little.

"I'm trying,'' said the doctor, "for the sake of my patient—and perhaps for your own—to push aside what Cully calls those stars in your eyes and let a crack of surface daylight through.''

"But why would he work for a salary—like that?'' Disbelief was strong in her voice.

"Possibly,'' said the doctor, "just possibly because the picture of a bloodstained hilifter with a knife between his teeth, carousing in Colonial bars, shooting down Confederation officers for the fun of it, and dragging women passengers off by the hair, has very little to do with the real facts of a man like Cully.''

"Smart girl,'' managed Cully. "S'little mixed up, s'all—'' He managed to get his vision cleared a bit. The other two were standing facing each other, right beside his bed. The doctor had a slight flush above his cheekbones and looked angry. Lucy, Cully noted anxiously, was looking decidedly pale. "Mixed up—'' Cully said again.

"Mixed up isn't the word for it,'' said the doctor angrily, without looking down at him. "She and all ninety-nine out of a hundred people on the Old Worlds.'' He went on to Lucy. "You met Cully Earthside. Evidently you liked him there. He didn't strike you as the scum of the stars, then.

"But all you have to do is hear him tagged with the name 'hilifter' and immediately your attitude changes.''

Lucy swallowed.

"No,'' she said, in a small voice, "it didn't . . . change.''

"Then who do you think's wrong—you or Cully?'' The doctor snorted. "If I have to give you reasons, what's the use? If you can't see things straight for yourself, who

can help you? That's what's wrong with all the people back
on the Old Worlds.''

"I believe Cully," she said. "I just don't know why I
should.''

"Who has lots of raw materials—the raw materials to
support trade—but hasn't any trade?" asked the doctor.

She frowned at him.

"Why . . . the New Worlds haven't any trade on
their own," she said. "But they're too undeveloped yet,
too young—''

"Young? There's three to five generations on most of
them!''

"I mean they haven't got the industry, the commercial organization—" she faltered before the slightly satiri-
cal expression on the doctor's face. "All right, then, you
tell me! If they've got everything they need for trade, why
don't they? The Old Worlds did; why don't you?''

"In what?''

She stared at him.

"But the Confederation of the Old Worlds already
has the ships for interworld trade. And they're glad to ship
Colonial products. In fact they do," she said.

"So a load of miniaturized surgical power instruments made on Asterope in the Pleiades, has to be shipped
to Earth and then shipped clear back out to its destination
on Electra, also in the Pleiades. Only by the time they get
there they've doubled or tripled in price, and the difference
is in the pockets of Earth shippers.''

She was silent.

"It seems to me," said the doctor, "that girl who
was with you mentioned something about your coming
from Boston, back in the United States on Earth. Didn't
they have a tea party there once? Followed by a revolu-
tion? And didn't it all have something to do with the fact
that England at that time would not allow its colonies to
own and operate their own ships for trade—so that it all
had to be funneled through England in English ships to the
advantage of English merchants?''

"But why can't you build your own ships?" she said. Cully felt it was time he got in on the conversation. He cleared his throat, weakly.

"Hey—" he managed to say. They both looked at him; but he himself was looking only at Lucy.

"You see," he said, rolling over and struggling up on one elbow, "the thing is—"

"Lie down," said the doctor.

"Go jump out the air lock," said Cully. "The thing is, honey, you can't build spaceships without a lot of expensive equipment and tools, and trained personnel. You need a spaceship-building industry. And you have to get the equipment, tools, and people from somewhere else to start with. You can't get 'em unless you can trade for 'em. And you can't trade freely without ships of your own, which the Confederation, by forcing us to ship through them, makes it impossible for us to have.

"So you see how it works out," said Cully. "It works out you've got to have shipping before you can build shipping. And if people on the outside refuse to let you have it by proper means, simply because they've got a good thing going and don't want to give it up—then some of us just have to break loose and go after it any way we can."

"Oh, Cully!"

Suddenly she was on her knees by the bed and her arms were around him.

"Of course the Confederation news services have been trying to keep up the illusion we're sort of half jungle-jims, half wild-west characters," said the doctor. "Once a person takes a good look at the situation on the New Worlds, though, with his eyes open—" He stopped. They were not listening.

"I might mention," he went on, a little more loudly, "while Cully here may not be exactly rich, he does have a rather impressive medal due him, and a commission as Brevet-Admiral in the upcoming New Worlds Space Force. The New Worlds Congress voted him both at their meeting just last week on Asterope, as soon as they'd finished drafting their Statement of Independence—''

But they were still not listening. It occurred to the doctor then that he had better uses for his time—here on this vessel where he had been Ship's Doctor ever since she first lifted into space—than to stand around talking to deaf ears.

He went out, closing the door of the sick bay on the former *Princess of Argyle* quietly behind him.

Counter-Irritant

Premier Joseph MacIntosh leaned back in his swivel-chair, put the tips of his fingers together in front of his nose, and gazed over them with grave disapproval at the stocky young man on the other side of his official desk.

"Now, let's not be hasty," said MacIntosh.

The young man exploded.

"Hasty!" he bellowed. "After fifty years of wishy-washy shilly-shallying milk-and-water appeasement I ask for a little action, and you tell me not to be hasty!" He choked with anger.

"Hasty!" he repeated furiously, pounding the fragile, mirror-like surface of the Premier's desk.

"Yes, Mr. Van Brock," said the Premier firmly, "hasty. It's not a light matter to plunge the Solar System and its colonies into a probably-disastrous war. My policy, and the policy of this government will be, as always, to keep the peace."

"Government policy!" snorted Van Brock. "Poly-Sci partyline policy, you mean."

The Premier looked at him steadily. "Mr. Van Brock," he said. "You're a young representative to the lower house of the United Worlds Government, and a new representative. For that reason you're allowed occasional breaches of decorum that would not be pardoned in an older office-holder. But it might be a good idea to remember that is all you are; and that I am the executive head of this Government. The decision in these cases is mine.''

Van Brock leaned forward, gripping the edge of the Premier's desk with both hands. All the tremendous vitality of his personality was concentrated in this one unconscious gesture.

"But don't you understand, sir!" he cried. "Vega's the one big rival we have! She's as strong as we are, and growing stronger." He swung away from the desk and strode over to the three-dimensional star map on the wall.

"Look," he said, extending a finger. "Here's Vega, 26.5 light years away—three months by overdrive. Here's Arcturus, five months away. And here's Altair, only two months away. Where do most of those complaints on your desk come from? Altair. The Vegans are stepping on the toes of our colonists on every inhabitable system we've discovered so far. But if they can get the upper hand on Altair, they'll be practically squatting on our doorstep.''

"Don't you think, Mr. Van Brock," said the Premier with just a touch of sarcasm, "that Altairian barbarians would have some objection to Vegan domination?''

"What could they do?" retorted Van Brock. "Even with our help, the barbarian races on Altair are behind the Arcturians. And the Arcturians are just on the threshold of civilization. Both of them are too unhuman to help or hinder. But the Vegans are our natural enemies. They're humanoid; they're intelligent and civilized. We quit too soon in the last war with them; we should have gone on and crushed them entirely.''

MacIntosh looked at him. "You weren't alive fifty years ago," he said. "That war was a stalemate. It would have ended by exhausting Earth and Vega races together.''

"That's an opinion only.''

"It was my opinion," said the Premier, "at the time we signed the peace, and now. You're a chauvinist through ignorance Mr. Van Brock; and I don't intend to see Humanity stretched on the rack of another war simply to educate you.''

Van Brock's mouth twisted bitterly. "Don't you see," he said, "that this ostrich-like policy of deliberately ignoring friction between our colonials and Vegan traders, and exploiters on the barbarian worlds, is leading inevitably to this very war you're so frightened of?"

"I do not."

Van Brock sighed heavily. "You force me to take the whole matter to the public," he said.

MacIntosh stood up behind his desk. He stood very straight, in spite of his hundred and fifteen years, and his eyes met Van Brock's on the level at last. "I was put in office, with the rest of the Political Science Party half a century ago, to keep the peace," he said. "And as long as I'm Premier it will be kept. If you want action on Vega, you'll have to get me out."

"All right, then," said Van Brock. "I will."

The Premier smiled a bleak smile.

"And when you've tried that and failed . . ."

"I won't," said Van Brock.

". . . Come back, and have another talk with me."

Van Brock looked at him in some surprise; then shrugged his shoulders, turning away toward the door. "Why not?" he said. "But, as I say, I won't fail." And with that he left the office.

On the steps of Government Head House a thin, wiry-haired little man waited. As Van Brock came out this individual fell into step beside him.

"Well?" the individual asked.

"No luck, Harry," Van Brock answered glumly. "He's honest enough, and human enough, but he's getting old and short-sighted. When he refused to do anything, I threatened to take the whole matter to the public. He challenged me. Said I'd have to get him out of office if I wanted action."

Harry whistled. "That's a stopper," he said.

"Why?" asked Van Brock. "I think I can do it."

"What!" Harry grabbed Van Brock by the arm, swing-

55

ing him around so that the two men stood halted, facing each other. "Why, you don't have a chance! The Political Science Party has polled a clear majority on every major issue for fifty years, and they'll back MacIntosh to the limit. It's political suicide for a freshman representative like yourself."

Van Brock looked at him a trifle oddly. "I'm not doing this for myself," he said harshly. "It seems to me that the lives of a few billion people are more important than my political career."

"If you could do anything for them," said Harry. "*If* these conclusions you've drawn about Vega are true. *If. If.* Come down to earth, Van. I've been a representative's press-agent around Government Center here for nearly three quarters of a century, and I know what I'm talking about. All you'll get out of this will be six month's hard work tying a noose around your own neck."

"And yours, too—is that it?" asked Van Brock bitterly. He gave a short, unhappy laugh. "I don't blame you, Harry. I must be pretty short on persuasion if I can't convince even my own press-agent that there's real danger. Well, I can't get started on this for a couple of weeks at least. I'll help you find another job in that time."

He turned on his heel and walked away.

"Damn fool," said Harry, looking after him.

Van Brock continued to stride off. Suddenly the little man broke into a trot in pursuit.

"Hey, Van," he called. "Slow up. Wait for me."

Two weeks later, the first of Van Brock's broadcasts was aired. There was no advance publicity, but rumor had already spread its reports; a good percentage of those owning reception-boxes on the Three Worlds of Earth, Venus, and Mars, and the colonies listened.

In a billion boxes, then, light swirled, eddied, and coalesced into the thick-shouldered, tri-dimensional image of Van Brock. And his voice came, deep and vibrant, challengingly, to all of them.

"Citizens of the Three Worlds," he said, "men and women of the human race, *we have been betrayed*!"

And, in the office of Premier MacIntosh, a small handful of men listened: middle-aged men; the old guard of the Political Science Party; those who had been present at its victory.

"Young hothead!" grumbled Al Peters, of Extra-Terrestrial Trade Office.

"But dangerous," said another, turning to the Premier. "Don't you think so, Mac?"

Premier MacIntosh, sitting on a couch facing the three-dimensional image in the office reception box and sipping a before-dinner cocktail, looked up at his questioner.

"There's always danger in politics, Joe," he answered. "And Humanity knows we ought to be used to it by now. But I think, in this case, the odds are on our side."

Joe Hennesy, Premier's Aide-de-Camp shrugged, and turned back to the box, from which Van Brock's image was now pouring words in a fiery stream.

"We have been asleep! We have let ourselves be cozened by old men into paying too high a price for peace. We have slumbered in a false security while men in our far-flung colonies in other systems, and on the barbarian worlds, spoke softly and turned the other cheek to Vegan aliens. Men and women alike, of our kind, have bowed down to alien authority; men and women, such as you and I, who call ourselves free and equal to any intelligence in this wide universe.

"And shall I tell you why they have bowed down? Not, fellow humans, because it is their nature to do so. Not because they are naturally servile. Not because they fear the Vegan alien. No, there is another, more shameful reason.

"*It is the law!*

"Yes, it is the law. Our own human law, set up by a bunch of old men whose only policy is—so they say—to keep the peace. But whose peace is this they are keeping?

57

Not the peace of our colonists, who suffer almost constant friction with the Vegans. Not the peace of your children, who—if this goes on—will have to fight Vegan warriors. None of these.

"Men and women of Humanity, I say to you, tonight, from this broadcasting booth in Government Center, that it is *their* peace, and *their* peace alone, that these old men, these political veterans of the Political Science Party, are concerned with. It is the political peace of fifty years following the termination of our last war with Vega that concerns them.

"It is that peace I have broken for you, tonight."

"Whew!" said Joe Hennesy, turning from the reception box. "He's hitting us where it hurts, all right. We can't deny our own watchword. 'To keep the Peace' was the slogan that put us up into office in the first place." He turned for encouragement to the Premier sitting on the couch, who smiled back at him with quiet confidence.

"Take it easy, Joe," said MacIntosh. "We knew somebody like this was bound to come along, sooner or later. He'll whip up a storm all right. But the real test will come when he takes the matter to the Assembly; then we can begin to fight back."

And he smiled again. But he smiled less easily the next day, when liberal newspapers began to clamor for his head.

Van Brock's series of broadcasts went on. He reviewed history for the audience that listened to him. He showed that the forces of Humanity had been holding their own at the time the last peace treaty with Vega was signed. He accused the Political Science Party of taking advantage of a war-weary people to gain office. He charged them with attempting to make cowards out of the human race at the present time, in an effort to hold that office. And he reported incident after incident of Vegan-Human friction in the colonies of the barbarian worlds in the Altairian and Centaurian systems.

"You have heard the facts," he repeated constantly to his listeners. "What do you say to them?"

And, in an ever-increasing volume, in newspapers, in messages to their representatives, they responded that he was right, that the Poly-Scis were wrong, that something must be done.

After some three months of this, a tired MacIntosh said, "Well, Joe, how are things lining up in the Assembly?"

Joe Hennesy winced. "Oh, we've still got our majority in both the upper and lower houses. But I'm afraid it's going to evaporate, the minute Van Brock calls for a vote of confidence in you from the representatives. Once public attention is focused on the houses, it's every man for himself: a lot of our luke-warm members are going to desert to save their own hides."

MacIntosh looked out a window and drummed with his fingers on the top of the desk in front of him. "I didn't expect such a reaction." he murmured, half to himself. "I really didn't."

"It's this younger generation that Van Brock belongs to," said Hennesy. "They're too young to remember the last war, and this talk about old men in office has got them excited."

"And the trouble is," said MacIntosh grimly, "he's right; we *are* old men. But we've got a tiger by the tail and can't let go."

For a minute there was silence in the office. Then Hennesy spoke up again. "Well, chief," he said, finally. "Shall we play it dirty?"

MacIntosh sighed. "I guess we'll have to, Joe," he said. "Fair means or foul, we've got to win; get in touch with Lyt Marja."

Five months to the day from his challenge to MacIntosh, Van Brock received a call from the Vegan Embassy at Government Center.

"Who's this?" he asked sharply.

The light in his communication-box swirled, and the scrawny figure of a Vegan, looking (as all Vegans do) like a half-starved caricature of a human, answered him in a deep bass voice.

"I am Lyt Marja, Mr. Van Brock."

"Well?"

"I think you might find it to your advantage to talk to me."

"Go ahead," said Van Brock.

"No," the Vegan demurred, "not over the public communications system; you must come and see me at the Embassy."

"Nothing doing," said Van Brock. "You boys would like an opportunity to put me out of the way. If you can't talk over the box, you come here."

"Be reasonable, Mr. Van Brock," answered Lyt Marja. "With public excitement at the pitch it is at now, it is somewhat unsafe for a Vegan to venture out. We have been stoned here at the Embassy, and our windows broken. Moreover, for me to visit you would be to announce the matter of our meeting publicly; the result could only be an accusation that our government was meddling in the internal politics of humanity. No, you must come to me—as secretly as possible."

"No thanks," said Van Brock; and broke the connection.

But, after he had ended the conversation, he sat for a while, thinking it over. He did not consider himself to be in ignorance of the motive behind the call. Either it was a bid for the cessation of hostilities being made by the administration, through the safest possible intermediary; or it was an attempt to bribe him off on the part of either the Poly-Sci Party, or the Vegans themselves. As for the personal danger involved in such a visit, both he and the Vegan knew that this was no more than an excuse. Van Brock was far too much in the public eye right now for violence to be a safe measure against him.

He hesitated a minute, biting his lip, wishing that Harry was there to talk the matter over with. Then, making up his mind, he flipped on his communications box and called Lyt Marja back.

"Tonight at ten hundred hours," he said. The Vegan nodded; and Van Brock broke the contact.

It was dark that night when Van Brock slipped up to the Vegan embassy in a car, rented under an assumed name, and rang the bell at the service entrance.

The door opened before him automatically. He entered and it closed behind him. Down a long dark hallway, he could see a door standing ajar and bright light flooding through the opening. He went down the hall.

The door proved to be the entrance to a room comfortably furnished in the human fashion. Cigarettes, and the materials for a drink awaited him. He ignored both and sat down in an armchair to wait.

It was quiet in the room. So quiet, in fact, that he was able to hear the almost noiseless sound of the door closing behind him. His tight nerves jerked him to his feet as the faint click of its latch sounded in his ears. In three swift strides he crossed the room and threw his weight against it.

It was securely locked.

Harry Taylor, returning to the office that was their mutual headquarters, wanted Van Brock. He wanted Van Brock badly, the World Center grapevine had just informed him that a considerable segment of the younger Poly-Sci party group were ready to revolt and come over on Van Brock's side, if that gentleman would spearhead a movement for a general reelection. The little press-agent therefore came bursting into the office with his news on his lips and was quite dumbfounded when he found no one to tell it to.

He glanced hurriedly at Van Brock's check-clock, which showed that the representative had passed out of its reception-area at roughly nine hundred and twenty hours. It was now almost twelve hundred hours. That meant that, according to the rigidly-artificial time of Government Center, which divided the normal twenty-four hours into two thousand units of the same designation, Van Brock had been gone a good quarter of the evening and that it was well past midnight. Harry cursed. Why hadn't Van Brock left a message in plain sight on the automatic secretary? Then the obvious answer that Van might not have wanted his destination broadcast occured to Taylor; he looked anxiously around the room for some less-obvious clue to the representative's whereabouts.

There was little to look at. Government Center offices were fully automatic from dictagraph to disposal chute, and everything was in plain view. Helplessly he checked the blank tapes and blank document sheets in the dicta-graph. They were completely unrewarding. He checked through the filed correspondence that had come in since nine hundred hours; and here also he drew a blank. Fi-nally, his gaze fastened on the relief-image of Government Center on the office wall. If Van Brock was anywhere in the Center, his location would be represented on that map. And if he had meant Harry to know that location, Van Brock would have found some way of marking it un-obtrusively.

Taylor stepped up and began to study the image minutely.

Daylight was beginning to show at the office win-dows when Taylor found what he wanted: The image of the Vegan Diplomatic House slightly distorted. Eagerly, his fingers probed the imaged building, seeming to disap-pear as they plunged into the little grey representation. They closed over something hard, and, as he withdrew it, the image snapped back into proper shape again, its re-flecting surface being then clear.

The hard object was a tightly-folded pellet of docu-ment sheet. He unfolded it and read:

Harry: I'm to meet Lyt Marja for a talk at the Vegan Embassy at ten hundred hours tonight. Don't know about what. If I'm not back in two hundred hours, call out the Marines.

Harry left the office at a dead run.

He broke more than one traffic regulation on the way to the embassy; and he wasted little time once he got there.

Finding the main entrance locked, he tried the service entrance, as Van Brock had done, and was alarmed, rather than reassured, when it opened at his touch. He had taken the pellet-gun from his car holster, and he held it cautiously in front of him as he slipped down the dark corridor.

But there was no opposition waiting, and the door at the far end opened at a touch to reveal an exceedingly angry but unharmed Van Brock sitting in an arm chair. He sprang to his feet as Harry entered.

Harry grunted, midway between overwhelming relief and exasperation.

"What—" he began, but Van Brock cut him short.

"I don't know," he answered. "But let's get out of here fast." And he led the way at a run for Harry's car.

Once they were well away from the embassy, Harry shoved the pellet-gun back into its slot in the dashboard.

"What happened?" he demanded.

Van Brock shook his head and frowned.

"Nothing," he said. "Just exactly nothing. I can't understand it. Lyt Marja may have gotten cold feet at the last minute about telling me whatever it was he wanted to tell me. But then, why keep me locked up? And if I was to be locked up, why let me go when you came?"

"I don't get it either," said Harry. "Did you ever meet this Vegan before?"

"No," said Van Brock. "By the way, what do you know about him, Harry?"

Harry shrugged. "Nothing much. He's one of the older Vegan diplomats. If I remember rightly, he was even part of the peace-signing treaty group that came over here fifty years ago when we ended the war, and opened diplomatic relations with his kind again. For all we know, he may have a lifetime position as ambassador to Government Center. I don't know much about the internal workings of Vegan politics."

"None of us do, blast it," said Van Brock gloomily. "That's another fault we can lay at Poly-Sci's doorstep. Oh, well. Whatever was planned for tonight evidently fell through. So I guess we can forget about it."

*   *   *

The next morning he woke to find Harry standing over his bed with a face expressive of the worst possible news.

"What's up?" asked Van Brock groggily.

"Everything," said Harry quietly. "Read that." He tossed a newsheet on to Van Brock's bed.

Sleepily, the big man sat up and focused his eyes on the headlines. " 'Van Brock In Secret Communication With Vegan Embassy'," he read out loud. "What . . . ?"

"No point in reading any farther," said Harry. "They've got the whole story of how you went secretly to the Vegan Embassy last night, and the amount of time you spent there. It's just newspaper-talk so far, but I got a call warning me that if you pressed the matter any further there'd be pictures produced and a charge of treason pressed against you."

Van Brock sat stunned. Harry's voice continued, hollow and distant in his ears. "Even if you want to fight the charge, you've already lost the big battle. People are frightened now, and I doubt if you could raise half a dozen votes in the Representatives House to back you after this. There's no alternative to defeat, only degrees of it. Either you give up now, and are simply through with politics; or you keep on going and have a virtually certain conviction of treason pressed against you. And that would mean the death-penalty."

"There's too many people backing me," said Van Brock, dazedly. "Nearly all of humanity is on my side in this question. The government wouldn't dare convict me, let alone execute me."

"Nobody is behind you," said Harry. "The people who listened to you, and agreed with you yesterday, distrust you today. They're afraid of you. They, themselves, would force your conviction and execution if it came to a treason-trial."

There was a long period of silence in the room: and then Harry spoke again. "The Premier wants to see you.

He called and left a message you were to come to him immediately. It's an order.''

In a dream of unreality, Van Brock got up and slipped into his clothes. Harry, watching him, said nothing. Then the representative headed for the door. He was reaching for the latch, when a thought struck him with all the cruelty of an open-handed slap in the face. He turned to look at Harry, who avoided his gaze.

"Harry!" said Van Brock. "*You* don't think I've been hooked up with the Vegans, do you?"

The accusation hung heavy in the room.

"I don't know," said Harry slowly, looking out a window. "I'm inclined to believe you myself; but all I know about what went on last night in the Embassy is what you told me. Then I remember the last war and—I don't know."

Van Brock took a deep breath and went out of the room.

In the Premier's office, MacIntosh awaited him. So did a thin Vegan, whom Van Brock recognized.

"Ah, Van Brock," said MacIntosh. "You've met Lyt Marja."

"Only over a reception-box," answered the young man grimly. "Thanks for the frame, Vegan."

Lyt Marja inclined his head. MacIntosh's lips thinned disapprovingly. "Relax, Van Brock," he said. "What we did was necessary."

"Necessary to what?"

"Necessary to keeping the peace," returned MacIntosh.

Van Brock laughed bitterly. "Did you just get me here to gloat?" he asked. "Because, if so, I'm leaving, protocol or no protocol."

"Not at all," snapped MacIntosh. "You're attributing to us the same sort of childish reactions you're feeling yourself. I asked you here to find out whether you'd like to fill the office of Premier. *My* office, Van Brock."

The words were like a blow to the representative's

solar-plexus. The breath went out of him with a whoosh and he sat down abruptly in a chair. Then he began to laugh a trifle crazily. "What next?" he asked weakly. "Premier?"

"Not right away, of course," said MacIntosh. "But in five or ten years—after this furor has died down and been forgotten. The Poly-Sci party heads have gotten together and decided that you seem to have the kind of qualities we need in the man holding this office. With the party solidly behind you, we can eventually shove you in. We're going to need a new man soon, you know." He smiled a trifle wryly. "You were right, unfortunately when you called us old men."

Van Brock had recovered from his momentary urge to hysteria. He looked straight at the Premier. "This is the most ridiculous thing I ever heard" he said coldly. "Don't you realize that the minute I was in, I'd turn your precious keep the peace policy upside down?"

"No you wouldn't," said MacIntosh.

"Why wouldn't I?" demanded Van Brock.

"Because," said MacIntosh with the suspicion of a smile at the corners of his lips, "in the next five years we should be able to teach you a little common sense."

"Common sense?" Van Brock reared up out of his chair. "What is this you're playing? Some kind of farce?"

"Nonsense," said MacIntosh swiftly. "The Poly-Sci Party has the best reason in the world for acting as it does, although only a handful of we old men at the top know what that reason is. Will you sit still and listen to it?"

"All right," said Van Brock flatly, reseating himself, "go ahead. It must be some whale of a good reason."

"It is," answered MacIntosh. "You came to me six months ago with evidence that the Vegans were moving in and competing with our colonies in the Altairian and Arcturian systems. That evidence was correct. I knew it was correct *because it is what the Poly-Sci Party has been working toward for fifty years*. Listen to a little history, Van Brock."

"The last war with Vega was a stalemate, no matter what our earth histories tell you in your schoolbooks. When the Poly-Sci Party came to power, the war had been going on for forty years, draining the lifeblood of both races. And there was no hope of a solution. Vegans were an expanding, pioneering people; so were humans. The two civilizations were at roughly the same stage of development. Individuals of both races were similar, physically, mentally, and psychologically. We had too many points in common, people said; we were natural enemies.

"What only a few political science theorists recognized was that we were also natural allies.

"But these few intelligences were voices crying in the wilderness. Vegans were killing humans: humans were killing Vegans. It is a hopeless task to preach friendship with a murderer. So, instead, we formed a political party and threw our full weight into obtaining a peace that was little more than a truce, both sides tacitly admitting it was only a breathing-spell to give them time to build up their strength.

"But, having gained a peace, we were determined to keep it."

"And," interjected Van Brock, "merely put off the reckoning until a more bloody day."

"No!" said MacIntosh. "Our job was to put off the reckoning until Vega should come to realize that their eventual well-being rested in a friendly alliance with humans. We set out to bring them to this realization—first by keeping the two races apart, in which we were aided by a few Vegans like Lyt Marja here, who is, himself, the equivalent of a Poly-Sci man on the Vegan worlds; and by supplying a counter-irritant."

"Counter-Irritant?" asked Van Brock.

MacIntosh smiled. "The human race, in spite of a thousand years of contact with alien races, is still unsophisticated in its emotional reaction to aliens. We tend to relate them to our own solar standards; we find it hard to take an alien at face value. Instead, we are likely to assume that because he looks like a teddy bear he must act like a teddy bear—or that because he lives like a mole, he thinks like a mole. In the case of a humanoid, we cannot relate him to an animal; therefore we tend to regard him as an inferior type of human, since a belief in our own superiority is firmly fixed in our minds.

"And the Vegan attitude is the same. Minor differences bulk large in our respective eyes, because we have not yet learned to take each other at face value. Only when races with greater differences begin to claim equality, will these minor differences lose their importance. To bring the Vegans, and even our own people to this realization, the Poly-Sci party has been working to keep the two people apart until pressure from the non-humanoid races on Arcturus and Altair can bring them together. And because the Poly-Sci party is infinitely more strong here on the human worlds than it is on the Vegan, we are the ones who are encouraging trespass by the Vegans on our colonial holdings.

"That's the story Van Brock. What do you think of it?"

There was a moment's silence.

"Why don't you tell this to the people?" asked Van Brock.

"With emotional reactions," answered the Premier, "it's not a matter of telling. Intelligences must be shown."

"Then why are you trying to tell me?"

"Because," said MacIntosh; and again there was the suspicion of a smile at the corners of his mouth. "I think you're just inquisitive enough to go out to Arcturus or Altair and check for yourself on whether there's more common ground between Vegans and humans than there is between either and the barbarian races."

There was a long moment of silence in the Premier's office. Then . . . "I might do just that," said Van Brock, musingly. "I might indeed. But—" he raised his voice, looking up at both MacIntosh and Lyt Marja—"I warn you. No matter what happens to me as a result, if this story doesn't hold water, I'll spread it all over the galaxy among humans and Vegans.''

"Agreed," said MacIntosh.

"Well?" demanded the young man.

Premier Rupert Van Brock leaned back in his swivel chair, put the tips of his fingers together in front of his nose, and gazed over them with grave disapproval.

"Now, let's not be hasty," said Premier Van Brock . . .

Last Voyage

"What's up?" asked Barney Dohouse, the engineer, coming through the hatch and swinging up the three metal steps of the ladder to the control room. Both Jed Alant (the captain), and the young mate Tommy Ris were standing in front of the vision screen.

"We're being followed, Barney," said Jed, without turning around. "Come here and take a look."

The heavy old engineer swung himself forward to stand between the stocky, grizzled captain and the slim young mate. The screen was set on a hundred and eighty degrees rear—which meant it was viewing the segment of space directly behind them. Barney squinted at it. An untrained eye would have seen nothing among the multitude of star points that filled it like an infinite number of gleaming drops from the spatter-brush of an artist; but the engineer, watching closely, made out in the lower left corner of the screen a tiny dark shape that occulted point after glowing point in its progress toward the center of the screen.

The point seemed to crawl with snail-like slowness, but Barney frowned. "Coming up fast, isn't he? Who do you suppose he is?"

"There's no scheduled craft on that course," said Tommy Ris, his blue eyes serious under the carefully combed forelock of his brown hair.

"Uh," grunted Barney. "Think it's Pellies?"

"I'm afraid so." Jed sighed. "And us with passengers."

The three men fell silent, gazing at the screen. It was a reflection on their years of experience in the void that they thought of the passengers rather than themselves. Your true spaceman is a fatalist out of necessity, and as a natural result of having his nose constantly rubbed in the fact that—cosmically speaking—he is not the least bit important. With passengers, as they all three knew, the case was different. Passengers, by and large, are planet-dwellers, comfortably self-convinced of the necessity for their own survival and liable to kick and fuss when the man with the scythe comes along.

The *Tecoatepetl—Teakettle* to her friends and crew— had no business carrying passengers in the first place. She had been constructed originally to carry vital drugs and physiological necessities to the pioneer worlds, as soon as they were opened for self-supporting colonists. When the first belt of extra-solar worlds had been supplied, she was already a little outdated. Her atomic power plant and her separate drive section—like one end of a huge dumbell—balanced the control and payload section at the other end of a connecting section like a long tube. Powerful, but not too pretty, she was useful, but not so efficient, by the time sixty years had passed and the hair of her captain and engineer had greyed. As a result she had been downgraded to the carrying of occasional passenger loads—according to the standards of interstellar transportation, where human life is usually slightly less important than cargoes of key materials for worlds who lack them.

Old spaceships never die until something kills them, the demand for anything that will travel between the stars fantastically outweighing the available carrying space. An operating spaceship is worth its weight in—spaceships. To human as well as alien; which was why the non-human ship from the Pleiades was swiftly over-hauling them. Neither humans nor cargo could hold any possible interest for the insectivorous humanoids; but the ship itself was a prize.

"We're five hours from Arcturus Base," said Tommy, "and headed for it at this velocity he can't turn us. Wonder how he figures on getting us past our warships there without being shot up."

"Ask him," said Barney, showing his teeth in a grin.

"You mean—talk to him?" Tommy looked at the captain for permission.

"Why not?" said Jed. "No, wait; I'll do it. Key me in, Tommy."

The younger man seated himself at the transmission board and set himself to locating the distantly-approaching ship with a directional beam. Fifteen minutes later, a green light began to glow and wink like a cat's eye in front of him; and he grunted with satisfaction.

"All yours," he said to Jed. The captain moved over to stand in front of the screen as Tommy turned a dial and the stars faded to give an oddly off-key picture of a red-lighted control room. A tall, supple-looking member of the race inhabiting the Pleiades stars, his short trunk-snout looking like a comic nose stuck in the middle of his elongated face, looked back at him.

"You speak human?" asked Jed.

"I speak it," answered the other. The voice strongly resembled a human's except for a curious ringing quality, like a gong being struck in echo to the vowels. "You don't speak mine?"

"I haven't got the range," replied Jed. They stood looking at each other with curiosity, but without emotion, like professional antagonists.

"So," said the Pellie. "It takes a trained voice, you." He was referring to the tonal changes in the language of his race, which covers several octaves, even for the expression of simple ideas. "Why you have called?"

"We were wondering," said Jed, "how you thought you could take our ship and carry it through the warfleet we're due to pass in five hours."

73

"You stay in ship, you," answered the other, "when we pass by fleet we let you leave ship by small boat."

"I bet," said Jed.

The Pleiadan did not shrug, but the tone of his voice conveyed the sense of it. "Your choice, you."

"I'll make you a deal," said Jed. "Let us out into the lifeboats now. None of us can turn at this velocity, so we'll all ride together up as far as the base. Once our small boats are safe under the guns of the fleet, you can chase the ship here and take it over without any trouble."

"Only-one person you leave on ship blows it up," said the Pleiadan. "No. You stay. Say nothing to fleetships. We stay close in for one pip on screen Arcturus. After we pass, we let you go. You trust us."

"Well," said Jed. "You can't blame a man for trying." He waved to the Pellie, who repeated the gesture and cut the connection. "That's that," Jed went on, turning back to the other two humans, as Tommy thoughtfully returned the star-picture to the screen. The occulting shape that was the ship they had just been talking to was looming quite large now, indicating its closeness.

"D'you think there's any chance of him doing what he says?" Barney asked the Captain.

"No reason to, and plenty of reason not to," replied Jed. "That way he keeps the two lifeboats with the ship—they're valuable in their own right." This was true, as all three men knew. A lifeboat was nothing less than a spaceship in miniature—as long as you kept it away from large planetary bodies, whose gravity were too much for the simple, one-way-thrust engines.

"I suppose the passengers will have to be told," broke in Tommy. "They'll be seeing it on the lounge screen sooner or later. What do you say, Jed?"

"Let's not borrow trouble until we have to," frowned the captain. They were all thinking the same thing, imagining the passenger's reactions to an announcement of the true facts of the situation. Hysteria is a nasty thing for a man to witness just before his own death.

"I wish there was something the fleet could do," said Tommy a trifle wistfully. He knew the hopelessness of the situation as well as the two older men; but the youngness of him protested at such an early end to his life.

"If we blew ourselves up, they'd get *him*, eh, Jed?" said Barney.

"No doubt of it," said the captain. "But I can't with these passengers. If it was us . . ."

There was the sudden suck of air, and the muted slam of the opening and closing of the bulkhead door between the control section and the passengers lounge above. Leni Hargen, the chief steward swung, down the ladder, agile in spite of his ninety years, his small, wiry figure topped by a face like an ancient monkey's. He joined the circle.

"Got company have we, Jed?" he asked, his sharp voice echoing off the metal, equipment-jammed walls.

"A Pellie," Jed nodded. "The pay-load excited?"

"So-so," replied Leni. "It hasn't struck home yet. First thing they think of when they see another ship is that it's human, of course. 'Damned clever, these aliens, but you don't mean to say they can really do what we do' —that sort of attitude. No, they think it's human. And they want to know who their traveling companions are; sent me up to ask."

"I'll go talk to them," said Jed.

"Why talk?" said Leni. Living closest of them all to the passengers, he had the most contempt for them. "Won't do no good. Wait till the long-nose gets close, then touch off the fuel, and let everybody die happy."

Barney swore. "He's right, Jed. We don't have a prayer, none of us. And I want to go when the old girl goes."

He was talking about the *Teakettle*, and the captain winced. With the exception of Tommy and the assistant steward, the ship had been their life for over half a century. It was unthinkable to imagine an existence without her. The thought of Tommy made him glance at the young mate. "What d'you say, son?"

"I . . ." Tommy hesitated. Life was desperately important to him and at the same time he was afraid of sounding like a coward. "I'd like to wait," he said at last, shamefacedly.

"I'm glad to hear it," replied Jed, decisively. "Because that's what we're going to do. I know what you think of your charges, Leni; but so far as I'm concerned, human life rates over any ship—including this one. And as long as there's one wild chance to take, I've got to take it."

"What chance?" said Leni. "They promise to turn us loose?"

Jed nodded. "They did. And I'm going to have to go on the assumption that they will."

"They will like . . ."

"Steward!" said Jed; and Leni shut his mouth. "I'll go out and talk to the passengers. The rest of you wait here."

He turned and went up the ladder toward the lounge door in the face of their silence.

The hydraulically-operated door whooshed away from its air seal as he turned the handle, and sucked back into position after he had stepped through. He stood on the upper level of the lounge, looking down its length at the gay swirl of colorfully dressed passengers. For a moment he stood unnoticed, seeing the lounge as it had been in the days when it was the main hold and he was younger. Then "Oh, there's the captain!" cried someone; and they flocked around him, chattering questions. He held up his hand for silence.

"I have a very serious announcement to make," he said. "The ship you see pulling up on us is not human but Pleiadan. They are not particularly interested in humans, but they want this ship. So after we pass Arcturus Station, we may have to take to the lifeboats and abandon the ship to them—unless some other means of dealing with the situation occurs."

He stopped and waited, bracing himself for what

he knew would follow:—first the stunned silence; then the buzz of horrified talk amongst themselves; and finally the returning to him of their attention and their questions.

"Are you sure, Captain?"

"Look for yourself," Jed waved a hand at the screen at the far end of the lounge on which the ship was now quite noticeable. "And I've talked to their captain."

"What did he say?" they cried, a dozen voices at once.

"He gave me the terms I just passed on to you," said Jed.

A silence fell on them. Looking down into their faces, Jed read their expressions clearly. This threat was too fantastic; there must be someone who had blundered. The spaceship company? The captain?

They looked back up at him, and questions came fast.

"Why don't we speed up and run away from them?"

Patiently Jed explained that maximum acceleration for humans was no more than the maximum acceleration for Pellies; and that the "speed" of a ship depended on the length of time it had been undergoing acceleration.

"Can't we dodge them?"

A little cruelly, Jed described what even a fraction of a degree of sudden alteration of course would do to the people within the ship at this present velocity.

"The warships!" someone was clamoring, an eldery, professional looking man. "You can call them, Captain!"

"If they came to meet us," said Jed, "we'd pass at such relatively high velocities that they could do us no good. We can only continue on our present course, decelerating as we normally would, and hope to get safely away from the ship after we pass Arcturus station."

The mood of the crowd in the lounge began to change. Stark fear began to creep in, and an ugly note ran through it.

"It's up to you," said one woman, her face whitened

and sharply harsh with unaccustomed desperation. "You do something!"

"Rest assured," Jed answered her, speaking to them all. "Whatever I and the crew can do, will be done. Meanwhile . . ." he caught the eye of Eli Pellew, the young assistant steward, standing at the back of the room. "The bar will be closed; and I'll expect all of you to remain as quiet as possible. Pellew, come up forward when you've closed the bar. That's all ladies and gentlemen."

He turned and went back through the door, the babble of voices behind him shut off suddenly by its closing. He re-descended the ladder to find the mate, engineer and steward in deep discussion, which broke off as he came in.

"What's this?" he said cheerfully. "Mutiny?"

"Council of war," said Barney. "It's your decision, but we thought . . ."

"Go ahead," said Jed. Sixty years of experience had taught him when to stand on his rights as captain, and when to fit in as one of the group.

"We've been talking a few things over," said Barney, "proceeding on the assumption—which most of us figure is a downright fact—that the Pellie hasn't any intention of letting us go, anyway."

"Go on."

"Well," said Barney. Almost exactly Jed's age and almost his equal in rank, the engineer slipped easily into the position of spokesman for the rest of the crew. "Following that line of thought, the conclusion is we've got nothing to lose. So to start out with, why not notify the Arcturus Base ships, anyway?"

"Because he just *might* keep that promise," said Jed. Behind them, the lounge door swished and banged. Pellew came down the steps, his collar and stewards jacket somewhat messed up.

"They're steaming up in there," he announced.

"Better go back and dog that door shut then," said Jed.

"I already did," replied Eli, his round young face

under its blond hair rosy with excitement. "I locked the connecting door to the galley, too. They're shut in."

"Good job," approved Jed. "Hope it doesn't lead to panic, though. I may have to talk to them again. You were saying, Barney . . ."

"The point is," said the engineer, taking up his argument again, "we're like a walnut in its shell with the difference that they want the shell, not the meat inside it. The way to take a ship like this is with a boarding party cutting its way through the main lock. Bloody, but the least damaging to the ship, itself. They won't want to fire on us; and if they try to put a boarding party aboard between here and Arcturus Base, we'll certainly message ahead and the warships'll have no reason for not opening fire on them. *But* if we simply message ahead and stay put, they'll just have to ride along and hope to use us for hostages when we reach the Base area."

"Sensible," said Jed, "provided they really don't mean to let us get away afterward."

"You know they don't, Jed," protested the engineer. "When did they ever let crew or passengers get away? It's not in their psychology—*I* think."

"They like to tidy up afterward, that's true," said Jed. He thought for a minute. "All right; we'll call. *Then* what do you suggest?"

There was a moment's uncomfortable silence.

"At least we know *he* won't get away then," said old Leni. "The warships'll follow and take care of him."

Jed smiled a little sadly. "I thought as much." He glanced at Tommy. "Well, make a message off. How long should it take to reach the Base?"

"About ten minutes."

"All right," Jed nodded. "Let me know if you rouse any reaction from our friend behind us." He looked at the stewards. "You two keep an eye on the passengers; Barney, come along with me."

They had been shipmates and friends for a long time. Barney turned and followed without a word as the captain

79

took the three steps of the down ladder to the bulkhead door leading under the passenger quarters; and led the way through.

They stepped into a narrow passageway that was all metal, except for the rubbery plastic matting underfoot; the door sucked to behind them. Like all sections of the ship sealed by the heavy doors, it was soundproof to all other sections. But the light overhead was merely an occasional glimmer from spaced tubes; and the passageway itself was so narrow that there was barely room for two men to stand breast-to-breast and talk.

Jed, therefore, did not talk here. Instead he led the way back down the ship, ducking at the middle where the lifeboat blisters—one on each side of the ship—bulged down into the passage; and up three more steps at the far end. Here another door waited to be passed; when they had gone through it, they found themselves in the central tube that connected the payload section of the ship with the drive section where the atomics were located.

This passage was wider, being the full size of the tube, and its circular shape apparent to the eye. Two and a half meters in diameter was the tube, but its walls were relatively thin and uninsulated—except for a radiation protective coating between the two skins of metal that made the tube. In spite of the ships heating system, the ''cold of space'' seemed to seep through. Jed led the way to the midpoint of the tube where two small vision screens were set, one on each side of the tube. These relayed the picture—seen by antennae arms that extended like two huge knitting needles jutting out on each side of the ship beyond the screens—and looked back to scan each its own side of the space-going vessel. The trouble-shooting screens. Jed gestured at them, to the identical dumbbell shape imaged on each.

''What do you see, Barney?''

The engineer looked at the screens and back at his captain, puzzled. ''The ship,'' he said at last. ''Why, what do you see?''

"A fifty-fifty chance."

At that moment, there was a sudden shock that shook the vessel from end to end and sent the two men staggering. Recovering first, the captain took two quick steps back to the screen. On the rear left could now be seen, beyond the bulge of the drive section, the distant forward half of the Pleiadan ship. On the drive section itself was a black hole with outcurling ragged metal edges—the mark of a hit by an explosive shell in space.

"So they don't want to fire on us," said Jed, turning to Barney grimly.

The engineer looked shaken. "The message to Arcturus Base must have made him mad." Suddenly he turned and began plunging back down the tunnel. "I've got to find out what damage they did!" he shouted back.

Jed nodded; turning on his heel, he hurried back toward the control room. He came up the ladder to find the young first mate and Leni facing each other. Tommy was white, but the eyes of the wizened little steward glowed black with rage.

"Ram them!" shouted the small man, spinning on Jed as he came up the three steps of the ladder in one jump.

"Leni," said Jed, coldly. "You're under arrest; get to your quarters and stay there."

The steward hesitated, his old face twisted and violent. Suddenly, the expression of his features twisted and broke, leaving him looking simply ancient and pathetic. He choked on a sob and turned away, stumbling blindly toward the door on the level of the cabin floor, between the two stairways, that led to the captains and crew quarters under the upper level of the passenger lounge.

"Go with him," Jed instructed Eli Pellew, who was still at his station by the intercom screen, watching proceedings among the passengers. "Wait a second," he added, as the young second steward turned to go. "How've they been in there?"

"Noisy, but quiet now," answered the boy. "That

81

shot we took seems to have quieted them. They're praying, some of them."

Jed nodded, and Eli dived through the door leading back to crew's quarters. The captain turned back to Tommy. "Have you touched anything since we were fired on?"

"No sir," said Tommy. "I had my hands full, keeping Leni off the controls. But we're tumbling end-over-end."

"Good. We won't touch anything. Make him wonder whether he did us any vital damage, or not. Any answer from Arcturus?"

"Just before you came back," answered the mate. "They acknowledged and said they were standing by to receive or follow us."

"Also good. I've got a gamble in mind; but it's among the three of us—you, Barney, and me; and he's back looking at the drive section. There's nothing more to be done here. I don't want to answer the Pellie if he calls us, anyway; keep him guessing. Come on with me back and we'll talk with Barney."

A curious look in the younger man's eyes warned Jed he was talking with an unusual excitement. Mentally reproving himself, he turned on his heel and led the way back down below the passenger section and through the full length of the tube back to the drive section. They stepped through a further door into one vast chamber honeycombed with equipment and to be traversed only by a network of ladders and catwalks.

"Barney!" Jed yelled.

"Yo!" came a distant answer and shortly the engineer came into view whisking his heavy old bulk up and down ladders with the agility of long practice. He came forward at a level about two meters over their head and dropped hand over hand down a ladder to stand at last in front of them.

"How was it?" asked the captain.

"Not bad, thank the Lord," said Barney, wiping his face. There was a black smudge of resealing material on his forehead. "It was back of the fuel bins and the whole section sealed off automatically."

"Barney . . ." said Jed.

"Yes?" The engineer had found a cleaner-cloth in his pocket and was scrubbing at the black gunk below his receded hairline.

"You remember we were looking at the ship and I said I thought I saw a fifty-fifty chance?"

"That's right." The hand holding the cloth dropped suddenly to Barney's side and he looked at his captain with alert interest.

"Well, tell me something," said Jed. "We haven't used power since before the Pellie showed up. That means the tubes have all been closed, haven't they?"

"Of course," said the engineer, indignantly. "They're always closed immediately after firing; you know that."

"And with the tubes closed, our back end looks just like our front, doesn't it?"

"Why, sure," said Barney, "but I still don't see what good that does us."

"When we're all in one piece, it doesn't," replied Jed. "But suppose, just as we hit the Arcturus Base area, we break in the middle of the connecting tube and our two halves go in opposite directions? What's the Pellie to do then? He can run down one section only at the cost of getting separated from the other; and by that time the warships'll be up. So if we cut the ship in half, it gives us an even chance of being the section he doesn't chase."

His words left the two other men in a stunned silence for several seconds. Tommy was the first to recover. His eyes lit up at the possibility and he wheeled on the engineer. "That's terrific—isn't it Barney? We can fool him! Isn't that a fine idea?"

To the younger man's surprise, the engineer did not take fire from his enthusiasm. In fact, he pursed his heavy lips, doubtfully. "I don't know," he said slowly. "We'd have to think it over."

Jed was watching his old friend and shipmate with hard, bright eyes. "All right, cut it out, Barney."

The engineer raised innocent, wondering eyes to the captain. "Cut it out?" he echoed. "I don't know what you mean, Jed."

"You know damn well what I mean," said Jed. "I already had to put Leni under arrest in his quarters, with Eli as guard over him, because of the same attitude you're taking. She's a fine old ship, Barney and I love her, too—more than anything else I can think of. But get this straight. The passenger's lives come first and ours too. Then the *Teakettle. Is that clear?*"

The last three words came out like the crack of a whip. Barney dropped his head, and Tommy was astonished to see the glint of tears in the old man's eyes. "I don't know what I'll do without her," he mumbled.

"Nor I," answered Jed, more gently now. "But what must be, must, Barney. We can't become selfish because our remaining years are short. Now . . . how are we going to cut the tube?"

"Explosive?" suggested Tommy. "Have we got any?"

"Not a gram," said Jed, grimly.

Barney spoke up. "There's cutting torches back in the drive section."

Jed bit his lower lip. "I don't like that notion too well," he said, slowly. "It means we'd have to work in suits, because we'd loose air from the tube with the first hole made. And then, they'd see us busy at it and have time to think of some counter-move."

"The metal's thin," said Tommy. "If we pried off the inside plates with a crowbar, and chiseled out the insulation, a metal saw should do the work."

"Fine," said Barney. "Only we don't have a metal saw."

"I thought every drive section had metal saws among its tools," Tommy said.

"Do you think I carry a machine ship? Torches were all I ever needed."

The old man was still upset. Jed, who had been thinking, spoke up. "We've got signal flares, haven't we, Tom?"

"Yes sir," answered Tommy. The emergency equipment was his responsibility.

"Isn't the powder in them hot enough to melt through the outer skin of the tube here?"

"By God, yes," said Tommy. "It's got a thermite base; this stuff'd boil like water."

"Then that's it," said Jed. "Go bring us as much as you've got." Tommy started off at a run down the tube.

Jed turned to the engineer, who was leaning, his face sagging, against the curve of the wall. "Don't take it so hard, you old idiot!" he said, in a fierce, soft voice. "Chances are the Pellie'll give up when he sees us split. Then it's just a matter of running the two halves down and sticking them together again."

Barney pushed himself away from the wall and shook his head. "We'll kill her; you know we will. We'll kill her." And he turned and moved heavily off in the direction of the drive section, passing through the door and leaving Jed alone.

The young mate seemed to take a long time returning and Jed had the chance to feel his age and the loneliness that was to come; before the payload-section door opened and Tommy backed through, pushing his way with his shoulders, his arms loaded down with the long metal tubes of the flares.

"Stack them here," said Jed, taking charge. "Now, how are we going to stick the powder to the wall?"

". . . Thought of everything," grunted Tommy. He settled his armload on the floor, and, reaching around behind him, unhooked two short crowbars from his belt. His bulging pockets produced several bottles of the pitch-like emergency sealer. "We pry off the inner skin, gouge out insulation to the outer skin, and seal the powder in with gunk."

"Good boy," approved Jed.

They set to work, captain and mate together. In the narrow space of the tube, back-to-back, they grunted and pried until a half-meter width of the inner metal panelling had been removed. Then the sharp points of the crowbars came into action; they chipped and pounded at the heavy, brittle insulation until metal showed through beyond. A fine, searing dust rose from the fragmented insulation and hung in the passage. They coughed and choked but worked on.

"All done," said Tommy, finally. "Except for the control cables." He was referring to the thick metal conduits running between the control room and the drive section.

"Leave them—they'll burn, too," wheezed Jed. "Now help me with the powder."

Step by step they drew their circle around the tube; white, innocent-looking powder, held in by sticky blackness. Finally, they were done.

"Fuse?" said Jed.

"Here." Tommy pulled a coil of shining, slim wire from within his tunic. It was regulation electrical contact cable, spliced and fitted with an explosive cap. Jed took the end and wedged it into the gunk, pushing it through to the powder beneath. Then they moved back, paying it out as they went, along the tube, through the door, up the under passage and into the control room.

The two men collapsed on to seats before the equipment boards.

"Whew!" said Tommy, after a few moments. "That was a job!"

Jed nodded. He was feeling his age, and there was a sharp pain in his chest. After he had rested a few more minutes, he got up and began checking their position.

They were close to Arcturus Base Area, that imaginary globe of space which enclosed the waiting warfleet, whose duty is to guard the Arcturian planets. Jed set his viewer up to maximum range and probed the empty distances ahead. There was nothing on it, but the armed ships which might rescue them could not be too far away.

"I'll give them another fifteen minutes; then we'll split," said Jed, glancing at the younger man. Suddenly he was aware of the emptiness of the control room. "By heaven, Barney's still back in the drive section. Get him up front here!"

Tommy dived for the down stairs; and vanished through the door. Jed grimaced and glanced at the clock. He reached out to call ahead to the armed vessels, then remembered the shot that had been fired at them on the previous occasion and took his hand away. He checked the scanner.

There were a couple of pips tiny in the distance, too far to show on the screen.

The waiting seemed interminable. Finally Tommy reappeared, almost literally herding the old engineer before him.

"We aren't going to waste any more time," said Jed. "Take seats and strap yourself in." He leaned over and keyed in the intercom to the passenger lounge.

"Attention," he said. The view on the screen faded from the stars to the lounge's interior. Weary, hopeless and frightened people looked up at him without much reaction. "Will you please take seats and fasten yourself in them. We are about to attempt evasive action."

"What for?" said a tall man, standing greyfaced toward the back of the room. "You said before it was no use."

"We're almost up to the Arcturus Base Fleet," answered Jed. "It may do some good now. Will you strap yourself in, please?"

"Why should we strap ourselves in?" cried a little man who had been sitting with his head in his hands. He now raised it, his deep eyes wild. "Why did you lock the doors? What . . ."

"Strap yourselves in! That's an order!" thundered Jed suddenly, tried beyond all patience.

Stunned by the volume of the intercom amplifier, the passengers fell into their seats without further protest, stumbling over each other in their haste. Safety belts snapped; and when Jed could tell by looking at the screen that all were secured, he switched back to an outside view.

Ahead, the warships of the Base were being rapidly overhauled in spite of the fact that they were building up velocity in the same direction as the *Teakettle* and the Pleiadan at maximum bearable acceleration. The alien ship itself was hanging in close and directly behind the *Teakettle*, so that they too would show as long as possible as a single pip on the warship's screens. Now was the time to do whatever could be done.

Jed turned and threw a quick glance about the control room. Leni and young Eli Pellew had come out of the crew quarters and were strapped in side by side, in the observer seats. Tommy must have warned them. The young mate himself was strapped into the acceleration chair before the auxiliary screen; and on Jed's other side to his right, Barney sat belted to the chair before the direct drive controls. This was his proper post; and although there was nothing now for him to do there, Jed thought he understood the impulse that had pushed the old man to his accustomed place. Jed reached for the contact switch and lifted it. The cable trailed away from him on the floor, silver to the bottom of the door and disappeared beneath it.

Jed glanced once more about the control room. Tommy's face, to his left, was tense on the screen, watching the growing shapes of the warships, pale—but not so pale as the face of Eli Pellew behind him, who seemed drugged with shock. Beside Eli's young face, Leni's eyes glared up at him, black and bitter. On his right, Barney sat slumped before his board, his fingers resting laxly upon the controls, his face unreadable.

He seemed chained and bound to inertness by the depression within him. But as Jed turned his way and closed his fingers about the switch, from the corner of his eyes, he seemed to see the fingers of the old man flicker, once.

And almost in the same heartbeat, closed his own fingers, closing the switch.

The ship bucked once like an insane thing as the super-heated air in the tube exploded outward through the vaporized metal of the outer skin. The stars spun like a pinwheel on the screen; and into view swam the full length of the Pleiadan and the tumbling other half of the *Teakettle*. Fingers working on the direction finders, flickering but working on the self-contained emergency power stored in the control room itself, Jed kept the two images on the screen together.

As the warships swelled on the screen, the nose of the Pellie ship swung first in this direction, then in that, sniffing after the two fragments of what had been the *Teakettle*, like a hunting terrier after two scuttling mice. The warships were growing fast, and for the alien, death was certain. It fired once at the drive section; then, ominously, its nose swung toward the payload half. Nose-on on the screen it stood before them.

"Sweetheart . . ." whispered Barney. And at that moment, from the tattered half-tube attached to the fleeing drive section shot a sudden, long spurt of yellow flame, hurtling it further and faster . . .

. . . And the alien swung to follow it. For the first time, from its tubes came a flare of power—not a change of direction, but an additional thrust forward that, though diverging, brought it up level and close to the burning tube and ball.

And its guns began to pound the fleeing drive section.

Behind Jed, Leni sobbed once. And Jed, looking over at Barney, saw the heavy old man press back in his seat, eyes wide, but with an incomprehensible wildness on his face.

The warships were closing up now. Ranging shells from their heavy guns began to search out the alien. But before they could strike home Barney shouted like a berserker, his old voice cracking. The drive section opened up like a flower into a brilliant pure white blossom of flame whose lightest touch was extinction. And the alien ship flared like a burnt moth.

In the silence of the control room they sat and watched it burn. And when the fire had died; and the warships were far behind, but coming up fast now, Jed turned to the engineer, "Thanks, Barney," he said.

"Thank her," said Barney emptily. "All I did was to pull the damping rods."

They looked at each other across the little distance and the useless controls between; two old men understanding each other.

Jed turned away and flicked on the intercom. "Attention all passengers," he said. "You may unstrap now."

An Ounce of Emotion

I

"Well? Are the ships joined—or not?" demanded Arthur Mial.

"Look for yourself!" said Tyrone Ross.

Mial turned and went on out of the room. All right, thought Ty savagely, call it a personality conflict. Putting a tag on it is one thing, doing something about it another. And I have to do something—it could just be the fuse to this nitro-jelly situation he, I, and Annie are all sitting on. There must be some way I can break down this feeling between us.

Ty glanced for a moment across the spaceliner stateroom at the statistical analysis instrument, called Annie, now sitting silent and unimpressive as a black steamer trunk against a far wall.

It was Annie who held the hope of peace for thousands of cubic light years of interstellar space in every direction. Annie—with the help of Ty. And the dubious help of Mial. The instrument, thought Ty grimly, deserved better than the two particular human companions the Laburti had permitted, to bring her to them.

He turned back to the vision screen he had been watching earlier.

On it, pictured from the viewpoint of one of the tractor mechs now maneuvering the ship, this leviathan of a Laburti spaceliner he was on was being laid alongside and only fifty yards from an equally huge Chedal vessel. Even Ty's untrained eye could see the hair-trigger risks in bringing those hundreds of thousands of tons of mass so close together. But with the two Great Races, so-called, poised on the verge of conflict, the Chedal Observer of the Annie Demonstration five days from now could not be simply ferried from his ship to this like any ordinary passenger.

The two ships must be faced, main airlock to main airlock, and a passageway fitted between the locks. So that the Chedal and his staff could stroll aboard with all due protocol. Better damage either or both of the giant craft than chance any suspicion of a slight by one of the Great Races to a representative of the other.

For the Laburti and the Chedal were at a sparking point. A sparking point of war that—but of course neither race of aliens was concerned about that—could see small Earth drafted into the armed camp of its huge Laburti neighbor; and destroyed by the Chedal horde, if the interstellar conflict swept past Alpha Centauri.

It was merely, if murderously, ironic in this situation that Ty and Mial who came bearing the slim hope of peace that was Annie, should be themselves at a sparking point. A sparking point willed by neither—but to which they had both been born.

Ty's thoughts came back from the vision screen to their original preoccupation.

It happened sometimes, he thought. It just—happened. Sometimes, for no discernable reason, suddenly and without warning, two men meeting for the first time felt the ancient furies buried deep in their forebrains leap abruptly and readily to life. It was rapport between individuals turned inside out—anti-rapport. Under it, the animal instinct in each man instantly snarled and bristled, recognizing a mortal enemy—an enemy not in act or attitude, but simply in *being*.

So it had happened with Ty—and Mial. Back on Earth, thought Ty now, while there was still a chance to do something about the situation, they had each been too civilized to speak up about it. Now it was too late. The mistake was made.

And mistake it had been. For, practical engineer and reasonable man that Ty was, reasonable man and practical politician that Mial was, to the rest of mankind— to each other they were tigers. And common sense dictated that you did not pen two tigers alone together for two weeks; for a delicate mission on which the future existence of the human race might depend. Already, after nine days out—

"We'll have to go meet the Chedal." It was Mial, reentering the room. Ty turned reflexively to face him.

The other man was scarcely a dozen years older than Ty; and in many ways they were nearly alike. There could not be half an inch or five pounds of weight difference between them, thought Ty. Like Ty, Mial was square-shouldered and leanly built. But his hair was dark where Ty's was blond; and that dark hair had started to recede. The face below it was handsome, rather than big-boned and open like Ty's. Mial, at thirty-six, was something of a wonder boy in politics back on Earth. Barely old enough for the senatorial seat he held, he had the respect of almost everyone. But he had been legal counsel for some unsavory groups in the beginning of his career. He would know how, thought Ty watching him now, to fight dirty if he had to. And the two of them were off with none but aliens to witness.

"I know," said Ty now, harshly. He turned to follow Mial as the other man started out of the room. "What about Annie?"

Mial looked back over his shoulder.

"She's safe enough. What good's a machine to them if no one but a human can run her?" Mial's voice was almost taunting. "You can't go up with the big boys, Ross, and act scared."

Ty's face flushed with internal heat—but it was true, what Mial had said. A midget trying to make peace with giants did well not to act doubtful or afraid. Mial had courage to see it. Ty felt an unwilling touch of admiration for the man. I could almost like him for that, he thought—if I didn't hate his guts.

By the time they got to the air-lock, the slim, dog-faced, and darkly-robed Laburti were in their receiving line, and the first of the squat, yellow-furred Chedal forms were coming through. First came the guards; then the Observer himself, distinguishable to a human eye only by the sky-blue harness he wore. The tall, thin form of the robed Laburti Captain glided forward to welcome him aboard first; and then the Observer moved down the line, to confront Mial.

A high-pitched chattering came from the Chedal's lipless slit of a mouth, almost instantly overridden by the artificial, translated human speech from the black translator collar around the alien's thick, yellow-furred neck. Shortly, Mial was replying in kind, his own black translator collar turning his human words into Chedal chitterings. Ty stood listening, half-selfconscious, half-bored.

"—and my Demonstration Operator." Ty woke suddenly to the fact that Mial was introducing him to the Chedal.

"Honored," said Ty, and heard his collar translating.

"May I invite you both to my suite now, immediately, for the purpose of improving our acquaintance . . ." The invitation extended itself, became flowery, and ended with a flourish.

"It's an honor to accept . . ." Mial was answering. Ty braced himself for at least another hour of this before they could get back to their own suite.

Then his breath caught in his throat.

". . . for myself, that is," Mial was completing his answer. "Unfortunately, I earlier ordered my Operator to return immediately to his device, once these greetings were over. And I make it a practice never to change an order. I'm sure you understand.''

"Of course. Some other time I will host your Operator. Shall we two go?" The Chedal turned and led off. Mial was turning with him, when Ty stepped in front of him.

"Hold on—" Ty remembered to turn off his translator collar. "What's this about your *ordering* me—"

Mial flicked off his own translator collar.

"You heard me," he said. He stepped around Ty and walked off. Ty stood, staring after him. Then, conscious of the gazing Laburti all about him, he turned and headed back toward their own suite.

Once back there, and with the door to the ship's corridor safely closed behind him, he swore and turned to checking out Annie, to make sure there had been no investigation or tampering with her innards while he was absent. Taking off the side panel of her case, he pinched his finger between the panel and the case and swore again. Then he sat down suddenly, ignoring Annie and began to think.

II

With the jab of pain from the pinched finger, an incredible suspicion had sprung, full-armed into his brain. For the first time he found himself wondering if Mial's lie to the Chedal about an 'order' to Ty had been part of some plan by the other man against Ty. A plan that required Mial's talking with the Chedal Observer alone, before Ty did.

It was, Ty had to admit, the kind of suspicion that only someone who felt as he did about Mial could have dreamed up. And yet . . .

The orders putting the Annie Demonstration Mission— which meant Annie and Ty—under the authority of Mial had been merely a polite fiction. A matter of matching the high rank and authority of the Laburti and Chedal officials who would be watching the Demonstration as Observers.

Ty had been clearly given to understand that by his own Department chief, back on Earth.

In other words, Mial had just now stopped playing according to the unwritten rules of the Mission. That might bode ill for Ty. And, thought Ty now, suddenly, it might bode even worse for the success of the Mission. But it was unthinkable that Mial would go so far as to risk that.

For, it was one thing to stand here with Annie and know she represented something possessed by neither the Laburti nor the Chedal technologies. It was all right to remind oneself that human science was growing like the human population; and that population was multiplying at close to three per cent per year—as opposed to a fraction of a per cent for the older Chedal and Laburti populations.

But there were present actualities that still had to be faced—like the size of this ship, and that of the Chedal ship now parting from it. Also, like the twenty-odd teeming worlds apiece, the thousands of years each of post-atomic civilization, the armed might either sprawling alien empire could boast.

Mial could not—would not—be playing some personal game in the face of all this. Ty shook his head angrily at the thought. No man could be such a fool, no matter what basic emotional factor was driving him.

When Mial returned to their stateroom suite a couple of hours later, Ty made an effort to speak pleasantly to him.

"Well?" said Ty, "how'd it go? And when am I to meet him?"

Mial looked at him coldly.

"You'll be told," he said, and went on into his bedroom.

But, in the four days left of the trip to the Laburti World, where the Demonstration was to be given before a joint audience of Laburti and Chedal Observers, it became increasingly apparent Ty was not to meet the Chedal. Meanwhile, Mial was increasingly in conference with the alien representative.

Ty gritted his teeth. At least, at their destination the Mission would be moving directly to the Human Consulate. And the Consul in charge was not a human, but a Laburti citizen who had contracted for the job of representing the Earth race. Mial could hardly hold secret conferences with the Chedal under a Laburti nose.

Ty was still reminding himself of this as the spaceliner finally settled toward their destination—a fantastic metropolis, with eight and ten thousand foot tall buildings rising out of what Ty had been informed was a quarter-mile depth of open ocean. Ty had just finished getting Annie rigged for handling when Mial came into the room.

"Ready?" demanded Mial.

"Ready," said Ty.

"You go ahead with Annie and the baggage—" The sudden, soft hooting of the landing horn interrupted Mial, and there was a faint tremor all through the huge ship as it came to rest in its landing cradle of magnetic forces; the main door to the suite from the corridor swung open. A freight-handling mech slid into the room and approached Annie.

"I'll meet you outside in the taxi area," concluded Mial.

Ty felt abrupt and unreasonable suspicion.

"Why?" he asked sharply.

Mial had already turned toward the open door through which the mech had just entered. He paused and turned back to face Ty; a smile, razor blade thin and cruel altered his handsome face.

"Because that's what I'm going to do," he said softly, and turned again toward the door.

Ty stared after him for a moment, jarred and irresolute at the sudden, fresh outbreak of hostilities, and Mial went out through the door.

"Wait a minute!" snapped Ty, heading after him. But the other man was already gone, and the mech, carrying Annie and following close behind him, had blocked Ty's path. Cold with anger, Ty swung back to check their personal baggage, including their food supplies, as another mech entered to carry these to the outside of the ship.

When he finally got outside to the disembarkation area, and got the baggage, as well as Annie, loaded on to one of the flying cargo platforms that did taxi service among the Laburti, he looked around for Mial. He discovered the other man a short distance away in the disembarkation area, talking again with a blue-harnessed, yellow-furred form.

Grimly, Ty turned on his translator collar and gave the cargo platform the address of the human Consulate. Then, he lifted a section of the transparent cover of the platform and stepped aboard, to sit down on the luggage and wait for Mial. After a while, he saw Mial break off his conversation and approach the cargo platform. The statesman spoke briefly to the cargo platform, something Ty could not hear from under the transparent cover, then came aboard and sat down next to Ty.

The platform lifted into the air and headed in between the blue and gray metal of the towers with their gossamer connecting bridges.

"I already told it where to take us," said Ty.

Mial turned to look at him briefly and almost contemptuously, then turned away again without answering.

The platform slid amongst the looming towers and finally flew them in through a wide window-opening, into a room set up with human-style furniture. They got off, and Ty looked around as the platform began to unload the baggage. There was no sign of the Laburti individual who filled the role of human Consul. Sudden suspicion blossomed again in Ty.

"Wait a minute—" He wheeled about—but the platform, already unloaded, was lifting out through the window opening again. Ty turned on Mial. "This isn't the Consulate!"

"That's right," Mial almost drawled the words. "It's a hotel—the way they have them here. The Chedal Observer recommended it to me."

"Recommended—?" Ty stared. "We're supposed to go to the Consulate. You can't—"

"Can't I?" Mial's eyes were beginning to blaze. The throttled fury in him was yammering to be released, evidently, as much as its counterpart in Ty. "I don't trust that Consulate, with its Laburti playing human Consul. Here, if the Chedal wants to drop by—"

"He's not supposed to drop by!" Ty snarled. "We're here to demonstrate Annie, not gabble with the Observers. What'll the Laburti think if they find you and the Chedal glued together half of the time?" He got himself under control and said in a lower voice. "We're going back to the Consulate, now—"

"Are we?" Mial almost hissed. "Are you forgetting that the orders show *me* in charge of this Demonstration—and that the aliens'll believe those orders? Besides, you don't know your way around here. And, after talking to the Chedal—I do!"

He turned abruptly and strode over to an apparently blank wall. He rapped on it, and flicked on his translator collar and spoke to the wall.

"Open up!" The wall slid open to reveal what was evidently an elevator tube. He stepped into it and turned to smile mockingly at Ty, drifting down out of sight. The wall closed behind him.

"Open up!" raged Ty, striding to the wall and rapping on it. He flicked on his translator collar. "Open up. Do you hear me? Open up!"

But the wall did not open. Ty, his knuckles getting sore, at last gave up and turned back to Annie.

III

Whatever else might be going on, his responsibility to her and the Demonstration tomorrow, remained unchanged. He got her handling rigging off, and ran a sample problem through her. When he was done, he checked the resultant figures against the answers to the problem already established by multiple statistics back on Earth. He was within a fraction of a per cent all the way down the line.

Ty glowed, in spite of himself. Operating Annie successfully was not so much a skill, as an art. In any problem, there were from fourteen to twenty factors whose values had to be adjusted according to the instincts and creativity of the Operator. It was this fact that was the human ace in the hole in this situation. Aliens could not run Annie—they had tried on Annie's prototypes and failed. Only a few specially trained and talented humans could run her successfully . . . and of these, Ty Ross was the master Operator. That was why he was here.

Now, tomorrow he would have to prove his right to that title. Under his hands Annie could show that a hundred and twenty-five Earth years after the Laburti and Chedal went to war, the winner would have a Gross Racial Product only eight per cent increased over today—so severe would the conflict have been. But in a hundred and twenty-five years of peaceful co-existence and cooperation, both races would have doubled their G.R.P.s in spite of having made only fractional increases in population. And machines like Annie, with operators like Ty, stood ready to monitor and guide the G.R.P. increases. No sane race could go to war in the face of that.

Meanwhile, Mial had not returned. Outside the weather shield of the wide window, the local sun, a G5 star, was taking its large, orange-yellow shape below the watery horizon. Ty made himself something to eat, read a while, and then took himself to bed in one of the adjoining bedrooms. But disquieting memories kept him from sleeping.

He remembered now that there had been an argument back on Earth, about the proper way to make use of Annie. He had known of this for a long time, Mial's recent actions came forcing it back into the forefront of his sleepless mind.

The political people back home had wanted Annie to be used as a tool, and a bargaining point, rather than a solution to the Laburti-Chedal confrontation, in herself. It was true, Ty reminded himself in the darkness, Mial had not been one of those so arguing. But he was of the same breed and occupation as they, reminded the little red devils of suspicion, coming out to dance on Ty's brain. With a sullen effort Ty shoved them out of his mind and forced himself to think of something else—anything else.

And, after a while, he slept.

He woke suddenly, feeling himself being shaken back to consciousness. The lights were on in the room and Mial was shaking him.

"What?" Ty sat up, knocking the other man's hand aside.

"The Chedal Observer's here with me," said Mial. "He wants a preview demonstration of the analyzer."

"A preview!" Ty burst up out of bed to stand facing the other man. "Why should he get to see Annie before the official Demonstration?"

"Because I said he could." Underneath, Mial's eyes were stained by dark half-circles of fatigue.

"Well, I say he can wait until tomorrow like the Laburti!" snapped Ty. He added, "—And don't try to pull your paper rank on me. If I don't run Annie for him, who's to do it? You?"

Mial's weary face paled with anger.

"The Chedal asked for the preview," he said, in a tight, low voice. "I didn't think I had the right to refuse him, important as this Mission is. Do you want to take the responsibility of doing it? Annie'll come up with the same answers now as seven hours from now."

"Almost the same—" muttered Ty. "They're never exact, I told you that." He swayed on his feet, caught between sleep and resentment.

"As you say," said Mial, "I can't make you do it."

Ty hesitated a second more. But his brain seemed numb.

"All right," he snapped. "I'll have to get dressed. Five minutes!"

Mial turned and went out. When Ty followed, some five minutes later, he found both the other man and the alien in the sitting room. The Chedal came toward Ty, and for a moment they were closer than they had been even in the spaceliner airlock. For the first time, Ty smelled a faint, sickening odor from the alien, a scent like overripe bananas.

The Chedal handed him a roll of paper-like material. Gibberish raved from his lipless mouth and was translated by the translator collar.

"Here is the data you will need."

"Thank you," said Ty, with bare civility. He took the roll over to Annie and examined it. It contained all the necessary statistics on both the Laburti and Chedal races, from the Gross Racial Products down to statistical particulars. He went to work, feeding the data into Annie.

Time flowed by, catching him up in the rhythm of his work as it went.

His job with Annie required just this sort of concentration and involvement, and for a little while he forgot the two watching him. He looked up at last to see the window aperture flushed with yellow-pink dawn, and guessed that perhaps an hour had gone by.

He tore loose the tape he had been handling, and walked with it to the Chedal.

"Here," he said, putting the tape into the blunt, three-fingered hands, and pointing to the first figures. "There's your G.R.P. half a standard year after agreement to co-exist with Laburti.—Up three thousands of one per cent already. And here it is at the end of a full year—"

"And the Laburti?" demanded the translated chittering of the alien.

"Down here. You see . . ." Ty talked on. The Chedal watched, his perfectly round, black eyes emotionless as the button-eyes of a child's toy. When Ty was finished, the alien, still holding the tape, swung on Mial, turning his back to Ty.

"We will check this, of course," the Chedal said to Mial. "But your price is high." He turned and went out.

Ty stood staring after him.

"What price?" he asked, huskily. His throat was suddenly dry. He swung on Mial. "What price is it that's too high?"

"The price of cooperation with the Laburti!" snarled Mial. "They and the Chedal hate each other—or haven't you noticed?" He turned and stalked off into the opposite bedroom, slamming the door behind him.

Ty stood staring at the closed surface. He made a step toward it, Mial had evidently been up all night. This, combined with the emotional situation between them, would make it pointless for Ty to try to question him.

Besides, thought Ty, hollowly and coldly, there was no need. He turned back across the room to the pile of their supplies and got out the coffeemaker. It was a little self-contained unit that could brew up a fresh cup in something like thirty seconds; for those thirty seconds, Ty kept his mind averted from the problem. Then, with the cup of hot, black coffee in his hands, he sat down to decide what to do.

Mial's answer to his question about the Chedal's mention of price had been thoughtless and transparent— the answer of a man scourged by dislike and mind-numbed by fatigue. Clearly, it could not be anything so simple as the general price of cooperation with a disliked other race, to which the Chedal Observer had been referring. No—it had to have been a specific price. And a specific price that was part of specific, personal negotiations held in secret between the alien and Mial.

Such personal negotiations were no part of the Demonstration plans as Ty knew them. Therefore Mial was not following those plans. Clearly he was following some other course of action.

And this, to Ty, could only be the course laid down by those political minds back on Earth who had wanted to use Annie as a pawn to their maneuvering, instead of presenting the statistical analysis instrument plainly and honestly by itself to the Laburti and the Chedal Observers.

If this was the case, the whole hope of the Demonstration hung in the balance. Mial, sparked by instinctive hatred for Ty, was opposing himself not merely to Ty but to everything Ty stood for—including the straight-forward presentation of Annie's capabilities. Instead, he must be dickering with the Chedal for some agreement that would league humanity with the Chedal and against the Laburti—a wild, unrealistic action when the solar system lay wholly within the powerful Laburti stellar sphere of influence.

A moment's annoyance on the part of the Laburti— a moment's belief that the humans had been trying to trick them and play games with their Chedal enemy— and the Laburti forces could turn Earth to a drifting cinder of a world with as little effort as a giant stepping on an ant.

If this was what Mial was doing—and by now Ty was convinced of it—the other man must be stopped, at any cost.

But how?

Ty shivered suddenly and uncontrollably. The room seemed abruptly as icy as a polar tundra.

There was only one way to stop Mial, who could not be reasoned with—by Ty, at least—either on the emotional or the intellectual level; and who held the paper proofs of authority over Ty and Annie. Mial would have to be physically removed from the Demonstration. If necessary— rather than risk the life of Earth and the whole human race—he would have to be killed.

And it would have to look like an accident. Anything else would cause the aliens to halt the Demonstration.

The shiver went away without warning—leaving only a momentary flicker of doubt in Ty, a second's wonder if perhaps his own emotional reaction to Mial was not hurry-ing him to take a step that might not be justified. Then, that flicker went out. With the Demonstration only hours away, Ty could not stop to examine his motives. He had to act and hope he was right.

He looked across the room at Annie. The statistical analysis instrument housed her own electrical power source and it was powerful enough to give a lethal jolt to a human heart. Her instruments and controls were insulated from the metal case, but the case itself . . .

Ty put down his coffee cup and walked over to the instrument. He got busy. It was not difficult. Half an hour later, as the sun of this world was rising out of the sea, he finished, and went back to his room for a few hours' sleep. He fell instantly into slumber and slept heavily.

IV

He jerked awake. The loon-like hooting in his ears; and standing over his bed was the darkly robed figure of a Laburti.

Ty scrambled to his feet, reaching for a bathrobe.

"What . . . ?" he blurted.

Hairless, gray-skinned and dog-faced, narrow-shouldered in the heavy, dark robes he wore, the Laburti looked back at him expressionlessly.

"Where is Demonstration Chief Arthur Mial?" The words came seemingly without emotion from the translator collar, over the sudden deep, harsh-voiced yammering from the face above it.

"I—in the bedroom."

"He is not there."

"But . . ." Ty, belting the bathrobe, strode around the alien, out of his bedroom, across the intervening room and looked into the room into which Mial had disappeared only a few hours before. The bed there was rumpled, but empty. Ty turned back into the center room where Annie stood. Behind her black metal case, the alien sun was approaching the zenith position of noon.

"You will come with me," said the Laburti.

Ty turned to protest. But two more Laburti had come into the suite, carrying the silver-tipped devices which Ty had been briefed back on Earth, were weapons. Following them came mechs which gathered up the baggage and Annie. Ty cut off the protest before it could reach his lips. There was no point in arguing. But where was Mial?

They crossed a distance of the alien city by flying

105

platform and came at last into another tower, and a large suite of rooms. The Laburti who had woken Ty led him into an interior room where yet another Laburti stood, robed and impassive.

"These," said the Laburti who had brought Ty there, "are the quarters belonging to me. I am the Consul for your human race on this world. This—" the alien nodded at the other robed figure, "is the Observer of our Laburti race, who was to view your device today."

The word *was*, with all the implications of its past tense, sent a chill creeping through Ty.

"Where is Demonstration Chief Arthur Mial?" demanded the Laburti Observer.

"I don't know!"

The two Laburti stood still. The silence went on in the room, and on until it began to seem to roar in Ty's ears. He swayed a little on his feet, longing to sit down, but knowing enough of protocol not to do so while the Laburti Observer was still standing. Then, finally, the Observer spoke again.

"You have been demonstrating your instrument to the Chedal," he said, "previous to the scheduled Demonstration and without consulting us."

Ty opened his mouth, then closed it again. There was nothing he could say.

The Observer turned and spoke to the Consul with his translator switched off. The Consul produced a roll of paper-like material almost identical with that the Chedal had handed Ty earlier, and passed it into Ty's hands.

"Now," said the Laburti Observer, tonelessly, "you will give a previous Demonstration to me . . ."

The Demonstration was just ending, when a distant hooting called the Laburti Consul out of the room. He returned a minute later—and with him was Mial.

"A Demonstration?" asked Mial, speaking first and looking at the Laburti Observer.

"You were not to be found," replied the alien. "And

I am informed of a Demonstration you gave the Chedal Observer some hours past.''

"Yes,'' said Mial. His eyes were still dark from lack of sleep, but his gaze seemed sharp enough. That gaze slid over to fasten on Ty, now. "Perhaps we'd better discuss that, before the official Demonstration. There's less than an hour left.''

"You intend still to hold the original Demonstration?''

"Yes,'' said Mial. "Perhaps we'd better discuss that, too—alone.''

"Perhaps we had better,'' said the Laburti. He nodded to the Consul who started out of the room. Ty stood still.

"Get going,'' said Mial icily to him, without bothering to turn off his translator collar. "And have the machine ready to go.''

Ty turned off his own translator collar, but stood where he was. "What're you up to?'' he demanded. "This isn't the way we were supposed to do things. You're running some scheme of your own. Admit it!''

Mial turned his collar off.

"All right,'' he said, coldly and calmly. "I've had to. There were factors you don't know anything about.''

"Such as?''

"There's no time to explain now.''

"I won't go until I know what kind of a deal you've been cooking up with the Chedal Observer!''

"You fool!'' hissed Mial. "Can't you see this alien's listening and watching every change your face makes? I can't tell you now, and I won't tell you. But I'll tell you this—you're going to get your chance to demonstrate Annie just the way you expected to, to Chedal and Laburti together, if you go along with me. But fight me—and that chance is lost. Now, *will you go*?''

Ty hesitated a moment longer, then he turned and followed the Laburti Consul out. The alien led him to the room where Annie and their baggage had been placed, and shut him in there.

Once alone, he began to pace the floor, fury and worry boiling together inside him. Mial's last words just now had been an open ultimatum. *You're too late to stop me now*, had been the unspoken message behind those words. *Go along with me now, or else lose everything*.

Mial had been clever, He had managed to keep Ty completely in the dark. Puzzle as he would now, Ty could not figure out what it was, specifically, that Mial had set out secretly to do to the Annie Mission.

Or how much of that Mial might already have accomplished. How could Ty fight, completely ignorant of what was going on?

No, Mial was right. Ty could not refuse, blind, to do what he had been sent out to do. That way there would be no hope at all. By going along with Mial he kept alive the faint hope that things might yet, somehow, turn out as planned back on Earth. Even if—Ty paused in his pacing to smile grimly—Mial's plan included some arrangement not to Ty's personal benefit. For the sake of the original purpose of the Mission, Ty had to go through with the Demonstration, even now, just as if he was Mial's willing accomplice.

But—Ty began to pace again. There was something else to think about. It was possible to attack the problem from the other end. The accomplishment of the Mission was more important than the survival of Ty. Well, then, it was also more important than the survival of Mial— And if Mial should die, whatever commitments he had secretly made to the Chedal against the Laburti, or vice-versa, would die with him.

What would be left would be only what had been intended in the first place. The overwhelming common-sense practicality of peace in preference to war, demonstrated to both the Laburti and the Chedal.

Ty, pausing once more in his pacing to make a final decision, found his decision already made. Annie was already prepared as a lethal weapon. All he needed was to put her to use to stop Mial.

Twenty minutes later, the Laburti Consul for the human race came to collect both Ty and Annie, and bring them back to the room from which Ty had been removed, at Mial's suggestion earlier. Now, Ty saw the room held not only Mial and the Laburti Observer, but one other Laburti in addition. While across the room's width from these, were the Chedal Observer in blue harness with two other Chedals. They were all, with the exception of Mial, aliens, and their expressions were almost unreadable therefore. But, as Ty stepped into the room, he felt the animosity, like a living force, between the two groups of aliens in spite of the full room's width of distance between them.

It was in the rigidity with which both Chedal and Laburti figures stood. It was in the unwinking gaze they kept on each other. For the first time, Ty realized the need behind the emphasis on protocol and careful procedure between these two races. Here was merely a situation to which protocol was new, with a weaker race standing between representatives of the two Great Ones. But these robed, or yellow-furred, diplomats seemed ready to fly physically at each other's throats.

IV

"Get it working—" it was the voice of Mial with his translator turned off, and it betrayed a sense of the same tension in the air that Ty had recognized between the two alien groups. Ty reached for his own collar and then remembered that it was still turned off from before.

"I'll need your help," he said tonelessly. "Annie's been jarred a bit, bringing her here."

"All right," said Mial. He came quickly across the room to join Ty, now standing beside the statistical analysis instrument.

"Stand here, behind Annie," said Ty, "so you don't block my view of the front instrument panel. Reach over the case to the data sorting key here, and hold it down for me."

"This key—all right." From behind Annie, Mial's

long right arm reached easily over the top of the case, but—as Ty had planned—not without requiring the other man to lean forward and brace himself with a hand upon the top of the metal case of the instrument. A touch now by Ty on the tape control key would send upwards of thirteen thousand volts suddenly through Mial's body.

He ducked his head down and hastily began to key in data from the statistic roll lying waiting for him on a nearby table.

The work kept his face hidden, but could not halt the trembling beginning to grow inside him. His reaction against the other man was no less, but now—faced with the moment of pressing the tape control key—he found all his history and environmental training against what he was about to do. *Murder*—screamed his conscious mind—*it'll be murder!*

His throat ached and was dry as some seared and cindered landscape of Earth might one day be after the lashing of a Chedal space-based weapon. His chest muscles had tensed and it seemed hard to get his breath. With an internal gasp of panic, he realized that the longer he hesitated, the harder it would be. His finger touched and trembled against the smooth, cold surface of the tape control key, even as the fingers of his other hand continued to key in data.

"How much longer?" hissed Mial in his ear.

Ty refused to look up. He kept his face hidden. One look at that face would be enough to warn Mial.

What if you're wrong?—screamed his mind. It was a thought he could not afford to have, not with the future of the Earth and all its people riding on this moment. He swallowed, closed his eyes, and jammed sideways on the tape key with his finger. He felt it move under his touch.

He opened his eyes. There had been no sound.

He lifted his gaze and saw Mial's face only inches away staring down at him.

"What's the matter?" whispered Mial, tearingly.

Nothing had happened. Somehow Mial was still alive. Ty swallowed and got his inner trembling under control.

"Nothing . . ." he said.

"What is the cause of this conversation?" broke in the deep, yammering, translated voice of one of the Laburti. "Is there a difficulty with the device?"

"Is there?" hissed Mial.

"No . . ." Ty pulled himself together. "It'll handle it now. You can go back to them."

"All right," said Mial, abruptly straightening up and letting go of the case.

He turned and went back to join the Laburti Observer.

Ty turned back to his work and went on to produce his tape of statistical forecasts for both races. Standing in the center of the room to explain it, while the two alien groups held copies of the tape, he found his voice growing harsher as he talked.

But he made no attempt to moderate it. He had failed to stop Mial. Nothing mattered now.

These were Annie's results, he thought, and they were correct and undeniable. The two alien races could ignore them only at the cost of cutting off their noses to spite their faces. Whatever else would come from Mial's scheming and actions here—this much from Annie was unarguable. No sane race could ignore it.

When he finished, he dropped the tape brusquely on top of Annie's case and looked directly at Mial. The dark-haired man's eyes met his, unreadably.

"You'll go back and wait," said Mial, barely moving his lips. The Laburti Consul glided toward Ty. Together they left and returned to the room with the baggage, where Ty had been kept earlier.

"Your device will be here in a moment," said the Laburti, leaving him. And, in fact, a moment later a mech moved into the room, deposited Annie on the floor and withdrew. Like a man staring out of a daze, Ty fell feverishly upon the side panel of the metal case and began unscrewing the wing nuts securing it.

The panel fell away in his hands and he laid it aside. He stared into the inner workings before him, tracing the connections to the power supply, the data control key, and the case that he had made earlier. There were the wires, exactly as he had fitted them in; and there had been no lack of power evident in Annie's regular working. Now, with his forefinger half an inch above the insulation of the wires, he traced them from the data control key back to the negative power lead connection, and from the case toward its connection, with the positive power lead.

He checked, motionless, with pointing finger. The connection was made to the metal case, all right; but the other end of the wire lay limply along other connections, unattached to the power lead. He had evidently, simply forgotten to make that one, final, and vital connection.

Forgotten . . . ? His finger began to tremble. He dropped down limply on the seat-surface facing Annie.

He had not forgotten. Not just . . . forgotten. A man did not forget something like that. It was a lifetime's moral training against murder that had tripped him up. And his squeamishness would, in the long run, probably cost the lives of everyone alive on Earth at this moment.

He was sitting—staring at his hands, when the sound of the door opening brought him to his feet. He whirled about to see Mial.

It was not yet too late. The thought raced through his brain as all his muscles tensed. He could still try to kill the other man with his bare hands—and that was a job where his civilized upbringing could not trip him up. He shifted his weight on to his forward foot preparatory to hurling himself at Mial's throat. But before he could act, Mial spoke.

"Well," said the dark-haired man, harshly, "we did it."

Ty froze——checked by the single small word, *we*.

"We?" He stared at Mial, "Did what?"

"What do you think? The Chedal and the Laburti are going to agree—they'll sign a pact for the equivalent of a hundred and twenty-five years of peaceful cooperation, provided matters develop according to the instrument's estimates. They've got to check with their respective governments, of course, but that's only a formality—'' he broke off, his face tightening suspiciously. "What's wrong with you?" His gaze went past Ty to the open side of Annie.

"What's wrong with the instrument?"

"Nothing," said Ty. His head was whirling and he felt an insane urge to break out laughing. "—Annie just didn't kill you, that's all."

"Kill me?" Mial's face paled, then darkened. "You were going to kill me—with that?" He pointed at Annie.

"I was going to send thirteen thousand volts through you while you were helping me with the Demonstration," said Ty, still light-headed, "—if I hadn't crossed myself up. But you tell me it's all right, anyway. You say the aliens're going to agree."

"You thought they wouldn't?" said Mial, staring at him.

"I thought you were playing some game of your own. You said you were."

"That's right," said Mial. Some of the dark color faded from his face. "I was. I had to. You couldn't be trusted."

"*I* couldn't be trusted?" Ty burst out.

"Not you—or any of your bunch!" Mial laughed, harshly. "Babes in the woods, all of you. You build a machine that proves peace pays better than war, and think that settles the problem. What would have happened without someone like me along—"

"You! How they let someone like you weasel your way in—"

"Why you don't think I was assigned to this mission through any kind of accident, do you?" Mial laughed in Ty's face. "They combed the world to find someone like me."

"Combed the world? Why?"

"Because you *had* to come, and the Laburti would

113

only allow two of us with the analyzer to make the trip," said Mial. "You were the best Operator. But you were no politician—and no actor. And there was no time to teach you the facts of life. The only way to make it plain to the aliens that you were at cross purposes with me was to pick someone to head this Mission whom you couldn't help fighting."

"Couldn't help fighting?" Ty stood torn with fury and disbelief. "Why should I have someone along I couldn't help fighting—"

"So the aliens would believe me when I told them your faction back on Earth was strong enough so that I had to carry on the real negotiations behind your back."

"What—real negotiations?"

"Negotiations," said Mial, "to decide whose side we with our Annie-machines and their Operators would be on during the hundred and twenty-five years of peace between the Great Races." Mial smiled sardonically at Ty.

"Side?" Ty stood staring at the other man. "Why should we be on anyone's side?"

"Why, because by manipulating the data fed to the analyzers, we can control the pattern of growth; so that the Chedal can gain three times as fast as the Laburti in a given period, or the Laburti gain at the same rate over the Chedal. Of course," said Mial, dryly, "I didn't ever exactly promise we could do that in so many words, but they got the idea. Of course, it was the Laburti we had to close with—but I dickered with the Chedal first to get the Laburti price up."

"What price?"

"Better relationships, more travel between the races."

"But—" Ty stammered. "It's not true! That about manipulating the data."

"Of course it's not true!" snapped Mial. "And they never would have believed it if they hadn't seen you—the neutralist—fighting me like a Kilkenny cat." Mial stared at him. "Neither alien bunch ever thought seriously about not going to war anyway. They each just considered putting it off until they could go into it with a greater advantage over the other.''

"But—they can't *prefer* war to peace!''

Mial made a disgusted noise in his throat.

"You amateur statesman!" he said. "You build a better mousetrap and you think that's all there is to it. Just because something's better for individuals, or races, doesn't mean they'll automatically go for it. The Chedal and Laburti have a reason for going to war that can't be figured on your Annie-machine.''

"What?" Ty was stung.

"It's called the emotional factor,'' said Mial, grimly. "The climate of feeling that exists between the Chedal and the Laburti races—like the climate between you and me.''

Ty found his gaze locked with the other man's. He opened his mouth to speak—then closed it again. A cold, electric shock of knowledge seemed to flow through him. Of course, if the Laburti felt about the Chedal as he felt about Mial . . .

All at once, things fell together for him, and he saw the true picture with painfully clear eyes. But the sudden knowledge was a tough pill to get down. He hesitated.

"But you've just put off war a hundred and twenty-five years!" he said. "And both alien races'll be twice as strong, then!''

"And we'll be forty times as strong as we are now,'' said Mial, dryly. "What do you think a nearly three per cent growth advantage amounts to, compounded over a hundred and twenty-five years? By that time we'll be strong enough to hold the balance of power between them and force peace, if we want it. They'd like to cut each other's throats, all right, but not at the cost of cutting their own, for sure. Besides,'' he went on, more slowly, "if your peace can prove itself in that length of time—now's its chance to do it.''

He fell silent. Ty stood, feeling betrayed and ridiculed. All the time he had been suspecting Mial, the other man had been working clear-eyed toward the goal. For if the Laburti and the Chedal felt as did he and Mial, the unemotional calm sense of Annie's forecast never would have convinced the aliens to make peace.

Ty saw Mial watching him now with a sardonic smile. He thinks I haven't got the guts to congratulate him, thought Ty.

"All right," he said, out loud. "You did a fine job—in spite of me. Good for you."

"Thanks," said Mial grimly. They looked at each other.

"But—" said Ty, after a minute, between his teeth, the instinctive venom in him against the other man rushing up behind his words, "I still hate your guts! Once I thought there was a way out of that, but you've convinced me different, as far as people like us are concerned. Once this is over, I hope to heaven I never set eyes on you again!"

Their glances met nakedly.

"Amen," said Mial softly. "Because next time *I'll* kill you."

"Unless I beat you to it," said Ty.

Mial looked at him a second longer, then turned and quit the room. From then on, and all the way back to Earth they avoided each other's company and did not speak again. For there was no need of any more talk.

They understood each other very well.

Rehabilitated

I went into a bar.

"Gimme a drink," I said to the bartender.

"Brother, don't take that drink," said a voice at my elbow. I turned and there was a skinny little guy in his fifties. Thin, yellow hair and a smile on his face. "Brother, don't take that drink," he said.

I shook him off.

"Where'd you come from?" I said. "You weren't there when I sat down here one second ago." He just grinned at me.

"Gimme a drink," I said to the bartender.

"Not for you," said the bartender. "You had enough before you came in here." A fat bartender polishing shot glasses with his little finger inside a dishtowel. "Get your friend to take you home."

"He's no friend of mine," I said.

"Brother," said the little man, "come with me."

"I want a drink," I said. An idea struck me. I turned to the little man. "Let's you and I go someplace else and have a drink," I said.

We went out of the bar together, and suddenly we were somewhere else.

After I started to get over it, it wasn't too bad. The first week was bad, but after that it got better. When I found how the little man had trapped me, I tried to get away from the mission or whatever it was he'd taken me to. But after the booze died out I was real weak and sick for a long time. And after that stage was over I got to feeling that maybe I would quit after all. And I started having long talks with the little man. His name was Peer Ambrose.

"How old are you, Jack?" he asked me.

"Twenty-six," I said.

He looked at me with tight little brown eyes in his leather face, grinning.

"Can you run an elevator, Jack?"

"I can run any damn thing!" I said, getting mad.

"Can you, Jack?" he said, not turning a hair.

"Whattayou mean, can I run an elevator?" I shouted at him. "Any flying fool can run an elevator. I can run any damn thing, and you ask me can I run an elevator. Sure I can run an elevator!"

"I have one I'd like you to run for me," he said.

"Well, all right," I said. I didn't mean to yell at him. He didn't seem to be a bad little man; but he was always grinning at me.

So I went to work running the elevator. It wasn't bad. It gave me something to do around the mission or what ever it was. But it wasn't enough to do, and I got bored. I never could understand why they didn't have one of the automatics, anyway—any elevator with an operator was a museum piece.

But we were only about half a mile from the spaceport, and when there wasn't anything doing I'd take the elevator up to the transparent weather bubble that opened on the roof garden and watch the commuters and the sky with its clouds and the big ships taking off all sharp and black like a black penpoint at the end of a long white cone of exhaust. I didn't do much—just sat and watched them. When the signal rang in the elevator, I'd press the studs and we'd float down the tube to whatever floor wanted an elevator, and that'd be that.

After a few weeks, old Peer rang for me one day on

the office level and told me to leave the elevator and come on in to his office. When I went in with him there was another man there, a young man with black hair and wearing a business cut on his jacket.

"Jack," said Peer, "this is counselor Toby Gregg. Toby, this is Jack Heimelmann. Jack's been with us for over a month now."

"Is that a fact?" said Toby. "Well, I'm glad to meet you, Jack." He put out his hand, but I didn't take it.

"What's this?" I asked, looking at Peer. "What're you cooking up for me now?"

"Jack," said Peer, putting his hand on my arm and looking up into my face, "you need help. You know that. And Gregg here has training that'll help him give it to you."

"I don't know about that," I said.

"Jack," said Peer, "you know I wouldn't recommend anything that was bad for you. Now, I'm going to ask you to talk to Gregg. Just talk to him."

Well, I gave in. Peer said he'd get somebody else for the elevator and I was to come and talk to Gregg three times a week, and meantime I was to be given some books to read.

The first time I went to see Gregg in his office on office level, he offered me a drink.

"A drink!" I said. And right away the old thirst came charging up. And then, while I stood there, it faded again, all by itself.

"I guess not," I said. Then I stared at him. "What's the idea of offering me a drink?" I asked. "What're you trying to do?"

"I'm just proving something to you, Jack," he said. We were sitting in a couple of slope-back easy chairs with a little low table between us that fitted up against one wall of the office. He reached over and pressed a stud on the table and a little panel in the wall above the table opened and a bottle and some glasses slid out on a tray. "Go ahead, you can have the drink if you want. I'm just

119

showing you that it isn't your drinking that we have to fix, but what's behind it. When we get through with you, you'll be able to take a drink without going out on a bender."

"I will?" I said. I looked at the tray. "I still guess I won't have anything."

"Cigarette?" he said, offering me one.

I took that.

"Tell me, Jack," he said, when I had the cigarette going between my lips, "how long have you been smoking, now?"

"Why," I told him, "let's see. I was smoking in general prep school when I was twelve. That'd be . . . let's see . . ."

"Fourteen years," he said. "That's a long time. You started early. You must have had a pretty rough bunch of kids around that general prep."

"Bunch of damn sissies," I told him. "Catch *them* smoking! I bet there isn't a dozen of them that smoke today."

"Most people don't, you know," said Gregg.

"My dad started at ten," I said.

"That was back a few years," he smiled. "Habits change with the years, Jack. Most of those kids you were in school with were probably looking forward to jobs where smoking wouldn't be practical."

"Yeah. Yeah, I bet they were," I said. "They sure figured to be big shots."

"All of them?" he asked.

"Most of them," I said. This talk was getting on my nerves. I didn't like to talk about general prep school. I had five years of it after I got out of secondary and I was seventeen before I cut loose. And that was plenty.

"Didn't you have a few friends?" he asked.

"Hell, yes!" I said. "D'you think I was an introvert?"

"No, Jack," he said, soothingly. "I can tell by looking at you you're not an introvert. But these friends of yours. Do you ever see any of them any more?"

I jumped up out of the chair.

"Listen, what is this?" I shouted at him. "What're you getting at? What're you trying to find out? I don't see any sense to this kind of questioning. I don't have to sit and listen to these kind of stupid questions. I'm leaving."

And I turned and headed toward the office door.

"All right, Jack," he said behind me, not irritated at all. "Come back any time you feel like it."

At the door, I turned once more to look at him. But he had his back to me. He was putting the tray with the bottles and glasses on it back into the wall.

I told Peer I had changed my mind about the counseling and went back to work on the elevator. The old man didn't seem annoyed at all. And I worked on the elevator for several weeks, riding people up and down and going up by myself to watch the sky and the people flying around and the ships. But after a while it began to wear on me.

I don't know what actually made me decide to go back to Gregg. I suppose it was because there just wasn't anything else. There was nothing much doing with the elevator, and there wasn't much sense in leaving the place and going back to the old drinking again. I really didn't want to start that all over again, but I knew if I got out by myself I would. Finally I figured I'd go back to Gregg and tell him I'd listen to just enough questions to cure me of my drinking, but nothing else.

When I went back to see him for the first time, though, he told me that wouldn't work.

"You see, Jack," he told me, "to get rid of the drinking, we have to get rid of whatever it is that's making you want to drink. And whatever that is, it's what's causing all your other troubles. So, it's up to you whether you want a complete job done or not."

I thought for a minute. Somehow talking with him made it seem easy.

"Oh, hell!" I said, finally. "Let's dig it out. I can't be any worse off, anyway."

* * *

So we went to it. And it was one rough time. Even Gregg said it was rougher than he figured. At first I was always blowing up and stamping out. But I finally got to the point where I could tell him anything. And it came out that I'd started getting a chip on my shoulder back as a kid because I thought the other kids were better than I was. Actually, Gregg said, it was my adverse environment that was hampering me. My mother was a state ward because of her unstable mental condition, and the only woman we had around the house was the housekeeper Government Service paid for. My dad was a portable-operating-room driver for a country hospital, and he was away from home on calls most of the time. He wanted me to be a driver like him when I got out of school, but by that time they had the automatic routers in, so I didn't.

But Gregg figured out that, even though I never really liked the idea, my dad wanting me to do a manual job had given me an inferiority complex. Like my driving a portable operating room, when all the other kids in school were looking forward to being Earthside deskmen, or professionals, or getting schooled for new-world trades; the sort of work that means learning half a dozen different lines that'll be needed on a new planet. Gregg figured it started hitting me as soon as I got into prep school and that was why I got into all kinds of trouble with the instructors and ran with a knify bunch and took up smoking and drinking. And he said that my inferiority complex had made me believe that I hated work; while actually, I was just taking out my dislike for my classmates on it. He said it was quite to be expected under those conditions that I would just come out of prep school and draw my social maintenance year after year without really trying to find anything to do. And then, as time went on, the drink was bound to start to get me.

Anyway we went back over all my life and he started pointing out to me where I had been wrong in thinking I wasn't as good as the other kids; and after a while I began to see it myself. And from that time on I began actually to change.

It's not easy to explain just what it was like. I had had a basically good schooling, as Gregg pointed out, and with the learning techniques used in our modern schools, the knowledge was all there, still. I had just not been using it. Now, as we talked together, he began to remind me of little odds and ends of things. My vocabulary increased and my reading speed picked up. He had me study intensively; and though at some times it was real hard, little by little I began to talk and act like someone of professional, or at least desk level.

"What you need now," Gregg said to me one day, "is to decide on some specific plan of action."

"I beg your pardon?" I said, puzzled.

"A job, or some work you can devote yourself to," said Gregg. "You've been refusing to face the fact for years, but in our modern society everyone is busy at their chosen work. Now, what would you like to do?"

I stared at him.

"Have you ever thought of emigrating, for instance?" he went on. "You're large and young and strong and—active-natured. The new-world life might suit you."

I thought about it.

"The new worlds aren't like Earth," Gregg went on. "We're overstocked here on second-raters, bogged down in a surplus of inferior talent. All the bright young men and women in each generation graduate and get off planet as quickly as they can. On a newer world, you'd be free, Jack. Your social unit would be smaller, and your personal opportunity to develop greater. It'd mean a lot of hard work, of course."

"I wouldn't mind that," I said.

While he talked, I had been thinking. I remembered the teachers teaching about the new worlds in prep school. Hitherto untouched planets, they'd told us, which in every case present a great challenge and offer a great reward to the pioneer. Twenty-four percent of our young people emigrating every year. That meant, of course, the ones who had completed their schooling and passed the physical. The more I thought of it, the better it sounded for me.

"I'd like to leave Earth," I said. "There's nothing for me here."

"Well, good," said Gregg. "If your mind's made up, then you've come a long way from the man I first met. You know you'll have to go back to school and get your certificate?"

"Sure. I know."

"Fine," said Gregg. He punched some buttons. "We'll start you tomorrow. Well, I guess that's enough for today."

He got up and went with me to the door and out into the main corridor of office level. Coming down the hall was Peer, and he had a little girl with brown hair with him. They stopped to talk with us and I got introduced to the girl. That was the first time I met Leena Tore.

I liked Leena a lot.

I had bumped into a lot of women in the past years; but either they had been no-goods, hitting the alcohol as hard as I was, or else they were stuck up and you couldn't get along with them. I'd seen them once or twice, but we wouldn't get along and that would be the limit. They all talked too much and looked down on anybody who wasn't professional level at least.

Leena wasn't like that. She didn't talk too much; and to tell the truth, she wasn't bright at all. In fact, she was stupid. But we got along very well together. She was an orphan, raised under State supervision in a private home. They found a job for her when she got old enough, but she didn't like it and finally went on social maintenance, and didn't do anything but sit around and watch shows all day. Finally Peer heard of her and brought her down to the place.

Gregg was working with her, too. But he hadn't been going on her long enough to make any real difference, and, privately, I didn't think he ever would. She was really too stupid. But she was an easy sort of person to get along with and after a while I began to think of marrying her.

Meanwhile, I was going back to school. It was hard

as hell—I'd forgotten how hard it was. But then I hadn't really worked at it before, and I'd been away from the preliminary stuff a long time.

But I'd been through it all once before, as Gregg reminded me—I'd forgotten—which helped; and they really do have good techniques and associative equipment in the schools nowadays. So after a while, I began to know my stuff and it perked me up. And when I got stuck Gregg would talk to me, and then things would come easy.

I got myself some new clothes and I began to mix with my classmates. Most of them were young kids, but by keeping my mouth shut I got along with them pretty well. And, you know, I began to feel this stuff they talk about, the sense of personal and racial destiny. I'd look around at these tall, good-looking kids talking big about the stars and the future. And then I'd look at myself in the mirror and say, "Boy, you're part of all this." And I began to see what Gregg had said my inferiority complex had cut me off from before.

They said Leena was making progress. She had been going to school too, but she was several classes behind me and she still had some time to go when I graduated. So we talked it over, all four of us, Leena and me, and Peer and Gregg, and we decided I'd go ahead and get cleared and ship out for some world. And then when Leena came along later she could just specify the same destination when she went through emigration.

Leena didn't look too pleased at having to wait. She pouted a bit, then finally gave in. But I was eager to go. These past months had gotten me thoroughly into the mood of emigration, and I was a happy man the day I went down to the big section outside the spaceport where clearing and routing went on for those who went spaceward from our city. Gregg had had a long talk with me, and I felt real good.

There wasn't to be too much to it. I presented my certificate of graduation and my credentials. The deskman glanced them over and asked me if I had any preference about examiners.

"Celt Winter," I said. This was the man Peer and Gregg had told me to ask for. They said he was a friend of Gregg's who had heard about me from Gregg and was very interested in me. It seems he didn't have much time off, ordinarily, so he never had any chance to drop around the place; and if I asked for him as my examiner, that would give us a chance to meet before I left.

The deskman ran his finger down his file and pressed a few studs. A message jumped out on the screen set in his desk.

"Celt Winter has just stepped out for a minute," he said. "Do you want to wait, or shall I give you someone else?"

I sort of hesitated. I hated to disappoint this Winter, but I was too wound up just to sit and twiddle my thumbs until he got back. I saw the deskman looking at me, waiting for my answer, and I got kind of nervous.

"Oh, anyone'll do," I said. "Just give me anybody that's free."

"Sven Coleman, then," said the deskman. "Desk four sixty-two." He gave me a little plastic tab and directed me through a door to his right.

I went through the door and came out into a big hall covered with desks at which examiners sat. Most of them had people sitting with them. I went ahead down a lane between the desks until I reached the four-sixty row, and two places off to my right I came to a desk where a tall young deskman with black hair and a long, straight nose waved me to a seat.

I handed him my credentials: my graduation certificate, my government registration card, and my physical okay sheet, for I'd taken that exam a couple of days before. He read through them.

"Well, Mr. Heimelmann," he said, smiling at me, and laying the credentials down. "You realize this is just a sort of formality. We interviewers are set up here just for the purpose of making sure that those of our people who go out to the new worlds won't want to turn back when they get there. In fact, this is just a last-minute chance for you to change your mind."

"There's no danger of that," I said.

He smiled and nodded.

"That's fine," he said. "Now perhaps you'd like to tell me, Mr. Heimelmann, what you particularly want to do when you get to your pioneer world and any preferences you might have as to location."

Gregg had told me that they'd ask me that, and I had my answer ready.

"I'd like to get out on the edge of things," I said. "I like singleton jobs. As for location, any place that's got plenty of outdoors is fine."

He laughed.

"Well, we can certainly suit those preferences," he said. "Most of our prospective emigrants are looking forward to team work in a close colony."

I laughed, too. I found myself liking this man.

"Probably afraid to get their feet wet," I said.

His smile went a little puzzled. Then he laughed again.

"I see what you mean," he said. "Too much community emphasis is a bad thing, even though the motives are good."

"Sure," I said. "If you like a crowd, you might as well stay here on Earth."

He looked puzzled again, and then serious. He picked up my credentials and went through them once more.

"You're in your late twenties, aren't you, Mr. Heimelmann?" he said.

"That's right," I answered.

"But I see that according to your graduation certificate, you just finished your trade learnings."

"Oh," I said. "Well, you see, I fooled around for a few years there. I couldn't seem to make up my mind about what I wanted to do."

"I see," he said. He put down my credentials and sat for a moment, tapping the top of the desk with his forefinger and looking as if he was thinking. "Excuse me a moment, Mr. Heimelmann."

He got up and left. After a few minutes he was back. "Will you come with me, please?" he asked.

I wondered a bit, but I got up and followed him. I didn't see any of the other interviewers doing this with the people they had at their desks. But you can't tell what the procedure is in these kind of places by just looking. Sven Coleman took me over to one side of the big room and through a door into an office where a sort of nervous older-looking man got up from a desk to greet us.

"Mr. Heimelmann," said Coleman. "This is Mr. Jos Alter. He'd like to talk to you for a moment."

"Hello," I said, shaking hands.

"How do you do, Mr. Heimelmann," answered Alter. "Sit down beside my desk here, will you? That'll be all, Sven."

"Yes, sir," said Coleman and went out. I followed Alter to the desk and sat down. He had two tired lines between his eyes and a little mustache.

"Mr. Heimelmann," he said. "I've got a little test here I want you to take. I'm going to give you a tape and I'd like you to take it over to the machine there and put it in. As the questions pop up on the screen, you press either the true stud or the false to register your choice. Will you do that? I've got to step out for a minute, but I'll be right back."

And he handed me the tape. It all seemed sort of strange to me, but as Sven himself said, this business was just a formality. I did what Alter wanted me to.

The questions were easy at first. If I have ten credits and I give two-thirds of them away, how many do I have left? If the main traffic strips are closed to children below the age of responsibility and I have a five-year-old nephew with me, can I send him home alone? But after a while they began to get harder, and I was still working when Alter came back. He took the tape and we went back to his desk, where he ran it through a scorer and set it aside. Then he just looked at me.

"Mr. Heimelmann," he said, finally. "Where've you spent the last six months or a year?"

"Why, at the place," I said. "I mean, the Freemen Independent Foundation Center."

"I see," he said. "And will you tell me briefly how you happened to go there in the first place and what you've been doing while you were there?"

I hesitated. There was something strange about all this. But I had to give him some answer, and there was no point in telling him anything but the truth when he could just press a stud on his desk and call Peer to ask him.

"Well," I said, squirming some inside, for it isn't easy to admit you've been an alcoholic, "I was drinking one day in a bar. . . ."

And I went through the whole story for him, down to the present. After I'd finished, he sat for a long while without saying anything. I didn't say anything, either. I was feeling pretty low down after admitting what I'd been. Finally he spoke.

"Blast those people!" he said, viciously. "Blast and damn them!"

I stared at him.

"Who?" I said. "Who? I don't understand."

He turned and looked me full in the face.

"Mr. Heimelmann," he said, "your friends at the Foundation—" he hesitated. "Nobody hates to tell you this more than I do, but the fact of the matter is we can't approve you for emigration."

"Can't?" I echoed. His words seemed to roar in my ears. The room tilted and I seemed to have a sudden feeling as if I was falling, falling from a great, high place. And all the time I knew I was just sitting beside his desk. I grabbed at the desk to steady myself. I had a terrible feeling then as if everybody was marching away and leaving me—all the tall young people I'd gone to classes and graduated with. But I *had* graduated. My credentials were in order.

"Listen," I said; and I had to struggle to get the words out. "I'm qualified."

"I'm sorry," he said. And he did look sorry—sorry enough to cry. "You're not, Mr. Heimelmann. You're totally unfit, and your friends at the Foundation knew it. This isn't the first time they've tried to slip somebody by us, counting on the fact that modern education can get facts into anybody."

I just looked at him. I tried to say something, but my throat was too tight and the words wouldn't come out.

"Mr. Heimelmann . . . Jack . . ." he said. "I'll try and explain it to you, though it's not my job and I really don't know how. You see, in many ways, Jack, you're much better off than your ancestors. You're in perfect physical health. You're taller and stronger. You have faster reflexes and better coordination. You're much better balanced mentally, so much so, in fact, that it would be almost impossible for you to go insane, or even to develop a severe psychosis, but—"

I tasted blood in my mouth, but there was no pain. The room was beginning to haze up around me, and I felt something like a time bomb beginning to swell and tick in the back of my brain. His voice roared at me like out of a hurricane.

"—you have an IQ of ninety-two, Jack. Once upon a time this wasn't too bad, but in our increasingly technical civilization—" he spread his hands helplessly.

The hurricane was getting worse. I could hardly hear him now and I could hardly see the room. I felt the time bomb trembling, ready to explode.

"What these people at the Foundation did to you," he was saying, "was to use certain psi techniques to excite your own latent psi talents—a procedure which isn't yet illegal, but shortly will be. This way, they were able to sensitize you to amounts and types of knowledge you wouldn't otherwise be able to absorb—in much the same way we train animals, using these psi techniques, to perform highly complicated actions. Like an animal——"

The world split wide open. When I could see again, I found little old, leather-face Peer had joined us in the room. Alter was slumped in his chair, his eyes closed.

Peer crossed over to him, looked him over, then glanced at me with a low whistle.

"Easy, Jack," he said. "Easy now. . . ." And I suddenly realized I was trembling like a leaf. But with his words, the tension began to go. Peer was shaking his head at me.

"We got a shield on Alter just in time," he said. "He's just going to wake up thinking you left and he dozed off for a while. But you don't realize what kind of a mental punch you've got, Jack. You would have killed him if I hadn't protected him."

For the first time, that came home to me. My hurricane could have killed Alter. I understood that, now. My knees weakened.

"No, it's all right. He's just out temporarily," said Peer. "Unfreeze yourself, Jack, and we'll teleport out of here. . . . What's the matter?"

"I want to know—" the words came hard from my throat. "I want to know, right now. What'd you do to me?"

Peer sighed.

"Can't it wait?—no, I guess not," he said, looking at me. "If you must know, you were an experiment. The first of your particular kind. But there'll be lots like you from now on; we'll see to that. Earth is starving, Jack; starving for the very minds and talents and skills it ships out each year. It's behind the times now and falling further every year, because the first-class young people all emigrate and the culls are left behind."

"Thanks!" I said, between my teeth and with my fists clenched. "Thanks a lot."

"Why not face facts?" said Peer cheerfully. "You're a high-grade moron, Jack—no, don't try that on me, what you did on Alter," he added, as I took a step forward. "You're not that tough, yet, Jack, though someday we hope you may be. As I was saying, you're a high-grade moron. Me, I've got an aneurysm that can't stand any kind of excitement, let alone spaceflight. Gregg, for your information, has a strong manic-depressive pattern—and so on, at the Foundation.''

''I don't know what you mean,'' I said, sullenly.

''Of course you don't. But you will, Jack, you will,'' said Peer. ''A government of second-raters were afraid to trigger your kind of talent in a high-grade moron, so they passed restrictive laws. We've just proved that triggering your abilities can not only be safe but practical. More evidence for a change that's coming here on Earth.''

''You lied to me!'' I shouted, suddenly. ''All the time you were lying to me! All of you!''

''Well, now, we had to,'' Peer said. ''It required a blockbuster of an emotional shock to break through all the years of conditioning that told you someone like yourself couldn't compete. You had to be so frustrated on a normal level that you'd go to your abnormal powers in desperation. Your desire to get off Earth to a place where life would be different was real enough. Gregg just built it up to where you couldn't face being turned down. And then we arranged the turn-down.''

I was crying.

''You shouldn't have done it!'' I said. ''You shouldn't have! For the first time, I thought I had some friends. For the first time——''

''Who says we're not your friends?'' snapped Peer. ''You think we went to all that trouble to break the law and bust you loose without figuring that you could be as close to us as anyone in the world could be? You—well, there's no use trying to explain it to you. You've got to be shown. Lock on, gang!''

And suddenly—they did lock on. For a second, I almost fell over, I was so scared. I felt Peer's mind slip into mine, then Toby Greggs's—and, without warning, there too was Leena. And she was not the same Leena I knew at all, but somebody almost as bright as Gregg. Only she was an epileptic.

All of a sudden, I knew too much. I heaved, with all the strength that was in me, trying to break loose. But the three of them held me easily.

"You just want to use me!" I shouted at them—with my mouth and my mind, both. "You just want me for what I can do for you—like a big, stupid horse." I was crying again, this time internally as well. "Just because you're all smarter than I am and you can make me do what you say!"

"Calm down, Jack," came the thought of Toby. "You've got the picture all wrong. What kind of a team is that, the three of us riding on your back? What do you think keeps Peer nicely calmed down all the time? And what do you think keeps Leena's epileptic attacks under control and me sane? Let me show you something."

And then he did something which was for me like heaven opening up and showing a rainbow in all its glory to a blind man.

"You want a few extra IQ points to think with?" said Toby. "Take mine!"

Lulungomeena

Blame Clay Harbank, if you will, for what happened at Station 563 of the Sirius Sector; or blame William Peterborough, whom we called the Kid. I blame no one. But I am a Dorsai man.

The trouble began the day the kid joined the station, with his quick hands and his gambler's mind, and found that Clay, alone of all the men there, would not gamble with him—for all that he claimed to having been a gambling man himself. And so it ran on for four years of service together.

But the beginning of the end was the day they came off shift together.

They had been out on a duty circuit of the frontier station that housed the twenty of us—searching the outer bubble for signs of blows or leaks. It's a slow two hour tramp, that duty, even outside the station on the surface of the asteroid where there's no gravity to speak of. We, in the recreation room, off duty, could tell by the sound of their voices as the inner port sucked open and the clanging clash of them removing their spacesuits came echoing to us along the metal corridor, that the Kid had been needling Clay through the whole tour.

"Another day," came the Kid's voice, "another fifty credits. And how's the piggy bank coming along, Clay?"

There was a slight pause, and I could see Clay carefully controlling his features and his voice. Then his pleasant baritone, softened by the burr of his Tarsusian accent, came smoothly to us.

"Like a gentleman, Kid," he answered. "He never overeats and so he runs no danger of indigestion."

It was a neat answer, based on the fact that the Kid's own service account was swollen with his winnings from the rest of the crew. But the Kid was too thick-skinned for rapier thrusts. He laughed; and they finished removing their equipment and came on into the recreation room.

They made a striking picture as they entered, for they were enough alike to be brothers—although father and son would have been a more likely relationship, considering the difference in their ages. Both were tall, dark, wide-shouldered men with lean faces, but experience had weathered the softer lines from Clay's face and drawn thin parentheses about the corners of his mouth. There were other differences, too; but you could see in the Kid the youth that Clay had been, and in Clay the man that the Kid would some day be.

"Hi, Clay," I said.

"Hello, Mort," he said, sitting down beside me.

"Hi, Mort," said the Kid.

I ignored him; and for a moment he tensed. I could see the anger flame up in the ebony depths of his black pupils under the heavy eyebrows. He was a big man; but I come from the Dorsai Planets and a Dorsai man fights to the death, if he fights at all. And, in consequence, among ourselves, we of Dorsai are a polite people.

But politeness was wasted on the Kid—as was Clay's delicate irony. With men like the Kid, you have to use a club.

We were in bad shape. The twenty of us at Frontier Station 563, on the periphery of the human area just beyond Sirius, had gone sour, and half the men had applications in for transfer. The trouble between Clay and the Kid was splitting the station wide open.

We were all in the Frontier Service for money; that

was the root of the trouble. Fifty credits a day is good pay—but you have to sign up for a ten year hitch. You can buy yourself out—but that costs a hundred thousand. Figure it out for yourself. Nearly six years if you saved every penny you got. So most go in with the idea of staying the full decade.

That was Clay's idea. He had gambled most of his life away. He had won and lost several fortunes. Now he was getting old and tired and he wanted to go back—to Lulungomeena, on the little planet of Tarsus, which was the place he had come from as a young man.

But he was through with gambling. He said money made that way never stuck, but ran away again like quicksilver. So he drew his pay and banked it.

But the Kid was out for a killing. Four years of play with the rest of the crew had given him more than enough to buy his way out and leave him a nice stake. And perhaps he would have done just that, if it hadn't been that the Service account of Clay's drew him like an El Dorado. He could not go off and leave it. So he stayed with the outfit, riding the older man unmercifully.

He harped continually on two themes. He pretended to disbelieve that Clay had ever been a gambler; and he derided Lulungomeena, Clay's birthplace: the older man's goal and dream, and the one thing he could be drawn into talk about. For, to Clay, Lulungomeena was beautiful, the most wonderful spot in the Universe; and with an old man's sick longing for home, he could not help saying so.

"Mort," said the Kid, ignoring the rebuff and sitting down beside us, "what's a Hixabrod like?"

My club had not worked so well, after all. Perhaps, I, too, was slipping. Next to Clay, I was the oldest man on the crew, which was why we were close friends. I scowled at the Kid.

"Why?" I asked.

"We're having one for a visitor," he said.

Immediately, all talk around the recreation room ceased and all attention was focused on the Kid. All aliens had to

137

clear through a station like ours when they crossed the frontier from one of the other great galactic power groups into human territory. But isolated as Station 563 was, it was seldom an alien came our way, and when one did, it was an occasion.

Even Clay succumbed to the general interest. "I didn't know that," he said. "How'd you find out?"

"The notice came in over the receiver when you were down checking the atmosphere plant," answered the Kid with a careless wave of his hand. "I'd already filed it when you came up. What'll he be like, Mort?"

I had knocked around more than any of them—even Clay. This was my second stretch in the Service. I remembered back about twenty years, to the Denebian Trouble.

"Stiff as a poker," I said. "Proud as Lucifer, honest as sunlight and tight as a camel on his way through the eye of a needle. Sort of a humanoid, but with a face like a collie dog. You know the Hixabrodian reputation, don't you?"

Somebody at the back of the crowd said no, although they may have been doing it just to humor me. Like Clay with his Lulungomeena, old age was making me garrulous.

"They're the first and only mercenary ambassadors in the known Universe," I said. "A Hixabrod can be hired, but he can't be influenced, bribed or forced to come up with anything but the cold truth—and, brother, it's cold the way a Hixabrod serves it up to you. That's why they're so much in demand. If any kind of political dispute comes up, from planetary to inter-alien power group levels, both sides have to hire a Hixabrod to represent them in the discussions. That way they know the other side is being honest with them. The opposing Hixabrod is a living guarantee of that."

"He sounds good," said the Kid. "What say we get together and throw him a good dinner during his twenty-four hour stop-over?"

"You won't get much in the way of thanks from him," I grunted. "They aren't built that way."

"Let's do it anyway," said the Kid. "Be a little excitement for a change."

A murmur of approval ran through the room. I was outvoted. Even Clay liked the idea.

"Hixabrods eat what we eat, don't they?" asked the Kid, making plans. "Okay, then soups, salad, meats, champagne and brandy—" he ran on, ticking the items off on his fingers. For a moment, his enthusiasm had us all with him. But then, just at the end, he couldn't resist getting in one more dig at Clay.

"Oh, yes," he finished, "and for entertainment, you can tell him about Lulungomeena, Clay."

Clay winced—not obviously, but we all saw a shadow cross his face. Lulungomeena on Tarsus, his birthplace, held the same sort of obsession for him that his Service account held for the Kid; but he could not help being aware that he was prone to let his tongue run away on the subject of its beauty. For it was where he belonged, in the stomach-twisting, throat-aching way that sometimes only talk can relieve.

I was a Dorsai man and older than the rest. I understood. No one should make fun of the bond tying a man to his home world. It is as real as it is intangible. And to joke about it is cruel.

But the Kid was too young to know that yet. He was fresh from Earth—Earth, where none of the rest of us had been, yet which, hundreds of years before, had been the origin of us all. He was eager and strong and contemptuous of emotion. He saw, as the rest of us recognized also, that Clay's tendency to let his talk wander ever to the wonder of Lulungomeena was the first slight crack in what had once been a man of unflawed steel. It was the first creeping decay of age.

But, unlike the rest of us, who hid our boredom out of sympathy, the Kid saw here a chance to break Clay and his resolution to do no more gambling. So he struck out constantly at this one spot so deeply vital that Clay's self-possession was no defense.

139

Now, at this last blow, the little fires of anger gathered in the older man's eyes.

"That's enough," he said harshly. "Leave Lulungomeena out of the discussion."

"I'm willing to," said the Kid. "But somehow you keep reminding me of it. That and the story that you once were a gambler. If you won't prove the last one, how can you expect me to believe all you say about the first?"

The veins stood out on Clay's forehead; but he controlled himself.

"I've told you a thousand times," he said between his teeth. "Money made by gambling doesn't stick. You'll find that out for yourself one of these days."

"Words," said the Kid airily. "Only words."

For a second, Clay stood staring whitely at him, not even breathing. I don't know if the Kid realized his danger or cared, but I didn't breathe, either, until Clay's chest expanded and he turned abruptly and walked out of the recreation room. We heard his bootsteps die away down the corridor toward his room in the dormitory section.

Later, I braced the Kid about it. It was his second shift time, when most of the men in the recreation room had to go on duty. I ran the Kid to the ground in the galley where he was fixing himself a sandwich. He looked up, a little startled, more than a little on the defensive, as I came in.

"Oh, hi, Mort," he said with a pretty good imitation of casualness. "What's up?"

"You," I told him. "Are you looking for a fight with Clay?"

"No," he drawled with his mouth full. "I wouldn't exactly say that."

"Well, that's what you're liable to get."

"Look, Mort," he said, and then paused until he had swallowed. "Don't you think Clay's old enough to look after himself?"

I felt a slight and not unpleasant shiver run down between my shoulder-blades and my eyes began to grow hot. It was my Dorsai blood again. It must have showed on my face, for the Kid, who had been sitting negligently on one edge of the galley table, got up in a hurry.

"Hold on, Mort," he said. "Nothing personal."

I fought the old feeling down and said as calmly as I could, "I just dropped by to tell you something. Clay has been around a lot longer than you have. I'd advise you to lay off him."

"Afraid he'll get hurt?"

"No," I answered. "I'm afraid you will."

The Kid snorted with sudden laughter, half choking on his sandwich. "Now I get it. You think I'm too young to take care of myself."

"Something like that, but not the way you think. I want to tell you something about yourself and you don't have to say whether I'm right or wrong—you'll let me know without the words."

"Hold it," he said, turning red. "I didn't come out here to get psyched."

"You'll get it just the same. And it's not for you only—it's for all of us, because men thrown together as closely as we are choose up sides whenever there's conflict, and that's as dangerous for the rest of us as it is for you."

"Then the rest of you can stay out of it."

"We can't," I said. "What affects one of us affects us all. Now I'll tell you what you're doing. You came out here expecting to find glamor and excitement. You found monotony and boredom instead, not realizing that that's what space is like almost all the time."

He picked up his coffee container. "And now you'll say I'm trying to create my own excitement at Clay's expense. Isn't that the standard line?"

"I wouldn't know; I'm not going to use it, because that's not how I see what you're doing. Clay is adult enough to stand the monotony and boredom if they'll get him what he wants. He's also learned how to live with

141

others and with himself. He doesn't have to prove himself by beating down somebody either half or twice his age."

He took a drink and set the container down on the table. "And I do "

"All youngsters do. It's their way of experimenting with their potentialities and relationships with other people. When they find that out, they can give it up—they're mature then—although some never do. I think you will, eventually. The sooner you stop doing it here, though, the better it'll be for you and us."

"And if I don't?" he challenged.

"This isn't college back on Earth or some other nice, safe home planet, where hazing can be a nuisance, but where it's possible to escape it by going somewhere else. There isn't any 'somewhere else' here. Unless the one doing the hazing sees how reckless and dangerous it is, the one getting hazed takes it as long as he can—and then something happens."

"So it's Clay you're really worried about, after all."

"Look, get it through your skull. Clay's a man and he's been through worse than this before. You haven't. If anybody's going to get hurt, it'll be you."

He laughed and headed for the corridor door. He was still laughing as it slammed behind him. I let him go. There's no use pushing a bluff after it's failed to work.

The next day, the Hixabrod came. His name was Dor Lassos. He was typical of his race, taller than the tallest of us by half a head, with a light green skin and that impassive Hixabrodian canine face.

I missed his actual arrival, being up in the observation tower checking meteor paths. The station itself was well protected, but some of the ships coming in from time to time could have gotten in trouble with a few of the larger ones that slipped by us at intervals in that particular sector. When I did get free, Dor Lassos had already been assigned to his quarters and the time of official welcoming was over.

I went down to see him anyhow on the off-chance

that we had mutual acquaintances either among his race or mine. Both of our people are few enough in number, God knows, so the possibility wasn't too far-fetched. And, like Clay, I yearned for anything connected with my home.

"*Wer velt d'hatchen, Hixabrod*—" I began, walking into his apartment—and stopped short.

The Kid was there. He looked at me with an odd expression on his face.

"Do you speak Hixabrodian?" he asked incredulously.

I nodded. I had learned it on extended duty during the Denebian Trouble. Then I remembered my manners and turned back to the Hixabrod; but he was already started on his answer.

"*En gles Ter, I tu, Dorsaiven,*" returned the collie face, expressionlessly. "*Da Tr'amgen lang. Met zurres nebent?*"

"*Em getluc. Me mi Dorsai fene. Nono ne—ves luc Les Lassos?*"

He shook his head.

Well, it had been a shot in the dark anyway. There was only the faintest chance that he had known our old interpreter at the time of the Denebian Trouble. The Hixabrods have no family system of nomenclature. They take their names from the names of older Hixabrods they admire or like. I bowed politely to him and left.

It was not until later that it occurred to me to wonder what in the Universe the Kid could find to talk about with a Hixabrod.

I actually was worried about Clay. Since my bluff with the Kid had failed, I thought I might perhaps try with Clay himself. At first I waited for an opportune moment to turn up; but following the last argument with the Kid, he'd been sticking to his quarters. I finally scrapped the casual approach and went to see him.

I found him in his quarters, reading. It was a little shocking to find that tall, still athletic figure in a dressing gown like an old man, eyes shaded by the lean fingers of one long hand, poring over the little glow of a scanner

143

with the lines unreeling before his eyes. But he looked up as I came in, and the smile on his face was the smile I had grown familiar with over four years of close living together.

"What's that?" I asked, nodding at the book scanner.

He set it down and the little light went out, the lines stopped unreeling.

"A bad novel," he said, smiling, "by a poor author. But they're both Tarsusian."

I took the chair he had indicated. "Mind if I speak straight out, Clay?"

"Go ahead," he invited.

"The Kid," I said bluntly. "And you. The two of you can't go on this way."

"Well, old fire-eater," answered Clay lightly, "what've you got to suggest?"

"Two things. And I want you to think both of them over carefully before answering. First, we see if we can't get up a nine-tenths majority here in the station and petition him out as incompatible."

Clay slowly shook his head. "We can't do that, Mort."

"I think I can get the signatures if I ask it," I said. "Everybody's pretty tired of him . . . They'd come across."

"It's not that and you know it," said Clay. "Transfer by petition isn't supposed to be prejudicial, but you and I know it is. He'd be switched to some hard-case station, get in worse trouble there, and end up in a penal post generally shot to hell. He'd know who to blame for it, and he'd hate us for the rest of his life."

"What of it? Let him hate us."

"I'm a Tarsusian. It'd bother me and I couldn't do it."

"All right," I said. "Dropping that, then, you've got nearly seven years in, total, and half the funds you need to buy out. I've got nearly enough saved, in spite of myself, to make up the rest. In addition, for your retirement, I'll sign over to you my pay for the three years I've got left.

Take that and get out of the Service. It isn't what you figured on having, but half a loaf . . ."

"And how about your homegoing?" he asked.

"Look at me."

He looked; and I knew what he was seeing—the broken nose, the scars, the lined face—the Dorsai face.

"I'll never go home," I said.

He sat looking at me for a long moment more, and I fancied I saw a little light burn deep in back of his eyes. But then the light went out and I knew that I'd lost with him, too.

"Maybe not," he said quietly. "But I'm not going to be the one that keeps you from it."

I left him to his book.

Shifts are supposed to run continuously, with someone on duty all the time. However, for special occasions, like this dinner we had arranged for the Hixabrod, it was possible, by getting work done ahead of time and picking the one four hour-stretch during the twenty-four when there were no messages or ships due in, to assemble everybody in the station on an off-duty basis.

So we were all there that evening, in the recreation room, which had been cleared and set up with a long table for the dinner. We finished our cocktails, sat down at the table and the meal began.

As it will, the talk during the various courses turned to things outside the narrow limits of our present lives. Remembrances of places visited, memories of an earlier life, and the comparison of experiences, some of them pretty weird, were the materials of which our table talk was built.

Unconsciously, all of us were trying to draw the Hixabrod out. But he sat in his place at the head of the table between Clay and myself, with the Kid a little farther down, preserving a frosty silence until the dessert had been disposed of and the subject of Media unexpectedly came up.

"—Media," said the Kid. "I've heard of Media. It's

145

a little planet, but it's supposed to have everything from soup to nuts on it in the way of life. There's one little life-form there that's claimed to contain something of value to every metabolism. It's called—let me see now—it's called—"

"It is called *nygti*," supplied Dor Lassos, suddenly, in a metallic voice. "A small quadruped with a highly complex nervous system and a good deal of fatty tissue. I visited the planet over eighty years ago, before it was actually opened up to general travel. The food stores spoiled and we had the opportunity of testing out the theory that it will provide sustenance for almost any kind of known intelligent being."

He stopped.

"Well?" demanded the Kid. "Since you're here to tell the story, I assume the animal kept you alive."

"I and the humans aboard the ship found the *nygti* quite nourishing," said Dor Lassos. "Unfortunately, we had several Micrushni from Polaris also aboard."

"And those?" asked someone.

"A highly developed but inelastic life-form," said Dor Lassos, sipping from his brandy glass. "They went into convulsions and died."

I had had some experience with Hixabrodian ways and I knew that it was not sadism, but a complete detachment that had prompted this little anecdote. But I could see a wave of distaste ripple down the room. No life-form is so universally well liked as the Micrushni, a delicate iridescent jellyfishlike race with a bent toward poetry and philosophy.

The men at the table drew away almost visibly from Dor Lassos. But that affected him no more than if they had applauded loudly. Only in very limited ways are the Hixabrod capable of empathy where other races are concerned.

"That's too bad," said Clay slowly. "I have always liked the Micrushni." He had been drinking somewhat heavily and the seemingly innocuous statement came out like a half-challenge.

Dor Lassos' cold brown eyes turned and rested on him. Whatever he saw, whatever conclusions he came to, however, were hidden behind his emotionless face.

"In general," he said flatly, "a truthful race."

That was the closest a Hixabrod could come to praise, and I expected the matter to drop there. But the Kid spoke up again.

"Not like us humans," he said. "Eh, Dor Lassos?"

I glared at him from behind Dor Lassos' head. But he went recklessly on.

"I said, 'Not like us humans, eh?' " he repeated loudly. The Kid had also apparently been drinking freely, and his voice grated on the sudden silence of the room.

"The human race varies," stated the Hixabrod emotionlessly. "You have some individuals who approach truth. Otherwise, the human race is not notably truthful."

It was a typical, deadly accurate Hixabrodian response. Dor Lassos would have answered in the same words if his throat was to have been cut for them the minute they left his mouth. Again, it should have shut the Kid up, and again it apparently failed.

"Ah, yes," said the Kid. "Some approach truth, but in general we are untruthful. But you see, Dor Lassos, a certain amount of human humor is associated with lies. Some of us tell lies just for fun."

Dor Lassos drank from his brandy glass and said nothing.

"Of course," the Kid went on, "sometimes a human thinks he's being funny with his lies when he isn't. Some lies are just boring, particularly when you're forced to hear them over and over again. But on the other hand, there are some champion liars who are so good that even you would find their untruths humorous."

Clay sat upright suddenly, and the sudden start of his movement sent the brandy slopping out over the rim of his glass and onto the white tablecloth. He stared at the Kid.

I looked at them all—at Clay, at the Kid and at Dor Lassos; and an ugly premonition began to form in my brain.

"I do not believe I should," said Dor Lassos.

"Ah, but you should listen to a real expert," said the Kid feverishly, "when he has a good subject to work on. Now, for example, take the matter of home worlds. What is your home world, Hixa, like?"

I had heard enough and more than enough to confirm the suspicion forming within me. Without drawing any undue attention to myself, I rose and left the room.

The alien made a dry sound in his throat and his voice followed me as I went swiftly down the empty corridor.

"It is very beautiful," he said in his adding machine tones. "Hixa has a diameter of thirty-eight thousand universal meters. It possesses twenty-three great mountain ranges and seventeen large bodies of salt water . . ."

The sound of his voice died away and I left it behind me.

I went directly through the empty corridors and up the ladder to the communications shack. I went in the door without pausing, without—in neglect of all duty rules—glancing at the automatic printer to see if any fresh message out of routine had arrived, without bothering to check the transmitter to see that it was keyed into the automatic location signal for approaching spacecraft.

All this I ignored and went directly to the file where the incoming messages are kept.

I flicked the tab and went back to the file of two days previous, skimming through the thick sheaf of transcripts under that dateline. And there, beneath the heading "Notices of Arrivals," I found it, the message announcing the coming of Dor Lassos. I ran my finger down past the statistics on our guest to the line of type that told me where the Hixabrod's last stop had been.

Tarsus.

Clay was my friend. And there is a limit to what a man can take without breaking. On a wall of the communications shack was a roster of the men at our station. I drew the Dorsai sign against the name of William Peterborough, and checked my gun out of the arms locker.

I examined the magazine. It was loaded. I replaced the magazine, put the gun inside my jacket, and went back to the dinner.

Dor Lassos was still talking.

". . . The flora and the fauna are maintained in such excellent natural balance that no local surplus has exceeded one per cent of the normal population for any species in the last sixty thousand years. Life on Hixa is regular and predictable. The weather is controlled within the greatest limits of feasibility."

As I took my seat, the machine voice of the Hixabrod hesitated for just a moment, then gathered itself, and went on: "One day I shall return there."

"A pretty picture," said the Kid. He was leaning forward over the table now, his eyes bright, his teeth bared in a smile. "A very attractive home world. But I regret to inform you, Dor Lassos, that I've been given to understand that it pales into insignificance when compared to one other spot in the Galaxy."

The Hixabrod are warriors, too. Dor Lassos' features remained expressionless, but his voice deepened and rang through the room.

"Your planet?"

"I wish it were," returned the Kid with the same wolfish smile. "I wish I could lay claim to it. But this place is so wonderful that I doubt if I would be allowed there. In fact," the Kid went on, "I have never seen it. But I have been hearing about it for some years now. And either it is the most wonderful place in the Universe, or else the man who has been telling me about it—"

I pushed my chair back and started to rise, but Clay's hand clamped on my arm and held me down.

"You were saying—" he said to the Kid, who had been interrupted by my movement.

"—The man who has been telling me about it," said the Kid, deliberately, "is one of those champion liars I was telling Dor Lassos about."

Once more I tried to get to my feet, but Clay was there before me. Tall and stiff, he stood at the end of the table.

"My right—" he said out of the corner of his mouth to me.

Slowly and with meaning, he picked up his brandy glass and threw the glass straight into the Kid's face. It bounced on the table in front of him and sent brandy flying over the front of the Kid's immaculate dress uniform.

"Get your gun!" ordered Clay.

Now the Kid was on his feet. In spite of the fact that I knew he had planned this, emotion had gotten the better of him at the end. His face was white with rage. He leaned on the edge of the table and fought with himself to carry it through as he had originally intended.

"Why guns?" he said. His voice was thick with restraint, as he struggled to control himself.

"You called me a liar."

"Will guns tell me if you are?" The Kid straightened up, breathing more easily; and his laugh was harsh in the room. "Why use guns when it's possible to prove the thing one way or another with complete certainty?" His gaze swept the room and came back to Clay.

"For years now you've been telling me all sorts of things," he said. "But two things you've told me more than all the rest. One was that you used to be a gambler. The other was that Lulungomeena—your precious Lulungomeena on Tarsus—was the most wonderful place in the Universe. Is either one of those the truth?"

Clay's breath came thick and slow.

"They're both the truth," he said, fighting to keep his voice steady.

"Will you back that up?"

"With my life!"

"Ah," said the Kid mockingly, holding up his forefinger, "but I'm not asking you to back those statements up with your life—but with that neat little hoard you've been accumulating these past years. You claimed you're a gambler. Will you bet that those statements are true?"

Now, for the first time, Clay seemed to see the trap.

"Bet with me," invited the Kid, almost lightly. "That will prove the first statement."

"And what about the second?" demanded Clay.

"Why—" the Kid gestured with his hand toward Dor Lassos—"what further judge do we need? We have here at our table a Hixabrod." Half-turning to the alien, the Kid made him a little bow. "Let him say whether your second statement is true or not."

Once more I tried to rise from my seat and again Clay's hand shoved me down. He turned to Dor Lassos.

"Do you think you could judge such a point, sir?" he asked.

The brown inhuman eyes met his and held for a long moment.

"I have just come from Tarsus," said the Hixabrod. "I was there as a member of the Galactic Survey Team, mapping the planet. It was my duty to certify to the truth of the map."

The choice was no choice. Clay stood staring at the Hixabrod as the room waited for his answer. Rage burning within me, I looked down the table for a sign in the faces of the others that this thing might be stopped. But where I expected to see sympathy, there was nothing. Instead, there was blankness, or cynicism, or even the wet-lipped interest of men who like their excitement written in blood or tears.

And I realized with a sudden sinking of hopes that I stood alone, after all, as Clay's friend. In my own approaching age and garrulity I had not minded his talk of Lulungomeena, hour on repetitive hour. But these others had grown weary of it. Where I saw tragedy, they saw only retribution coming to a lying bore.

And what Clay saw was what I saw. His eyes went dark and cold.

"How much will you bet?" he asked.

"All I've got," responded the Kid, leaning forward eagerly. "Enough and more than enough to match that bank roll of yours. The equivalent of eight years' pay."

Stiffly, without a word, Clay produced his savings book and a voucher pad. He wrote out a voucher for the whole amount and laid book and voucher on the table before Dor Lassos. The Kid, who had obviously come prepared, did the same, adding a thick pile of cash from his gambling of recent weeks.

"That's all of it?" asked Clay.

"All of it," said the Kid.

Clay nodded and stepped back.

"Go ahead," he said.

The Kid turned toward the alien.

"Dor Lassos," he said. "We appreciate your cooperation in this matter."

"I am glad to hear it," responded the Hixabrod, "since my cooperation will cost the winner of the bet a thousand credits."

The abrupt injection of this commercial note threw the Kid momentarily off stride. I, alone in the room, who knew the Hixabrod people, had expected it. But the rest had not, and it struck a sour note, which reflected back on the Kid. Up until now, the bet had seemed to most of the others like a cruel but at least honest game, concerning ourselves only. Suddenly it had become a little like hiring a paid bully to beat up a station-mate.

But it was too late now to stop; the bet had been made. Nevertheless, there were murmurs from different parts of the room.

The Kid hurried on, fearful of an interruption. Clay's savings were on his mind.

"You were a member of the mapping survey team?" he asked Dor Lassos.

"I was," said the Hixabrod.

"Then you know the planet?"

"I do."

"You know its geography?" insisted the Kid.

"I do not repeat myself." The eyes of the Hixabrod were chill and withdrawn, almost a little baleful, as they met those of the Kid.

"What kind of a planet is it?" The Kid licked his lips. He was beginning to recover his usual self-assurance. "Is it a large planet?"

"No."

"Is Tarsus a rich planet?"

"No."

"Is it a pretty planet?"

"I did not find it so."

"*Get to the point!*" snapped Clay with strained harshness.

The Kid glanced at him, savoring this moment. He turned back to the Hixabrod.

"Very well, Dor Lassos," he said, "we get to the meat of the matter. Have you ever heard of Lulungomeena?"

"Yes."

"Have you ever been to Lulungomeena?"

"I have."

"And do you truthfully—" for the first time, a fierce and burning anger flashed momentarily in the eyes of the Hixabrod; the insult the Kid had just unthinkingly given Dor Lassos was a deadly one—"*truthfully* say that in your considered opinion Lulungomeena is the most wonderful place in the Universe?"

Dor Lasso turned his gaze away from him and let it wander over the rest of the room. Now, at last, his contempt for all there was plain to be read on his face.

"*Yes, it is,*" said Dor Lassos.

He rose to his feet at the head of the stunned group around the table. From the pile of cash he extracted a thousand credits, then passed the remainder, along with the two account books and the vouchers, to Clay. Then he took one step toward the Kid.

He halted before him and offered his hands to the man—palms up, the tips of his fingers a scant couple of inches short of the Kid's face.

"My hands are clean," he said.

His fingers arced; and, suddenly, as we watched, stubby, gleaming claws shot smoothly from those fingertips to tremble lightly against the skin of the Kid's face.

"Do you doubt the truthfulness of a Hixabrod?" his robot voice asked.

The Kid's face was white and his cheeks hollowed in fear. The needle points of the claws were very close to his eyes. He swallowed once.

"No—" he whispered.

The claws retracted. The hands returned to their owner's sides. Once more completely withdrawn and impersonal, Dor Lassos turned and bowed to us all.

"My appreciation of your courtesy," he said, the metallic tones of his voice loud in the silence.

Then he turned and, marching like a metronome, disappeared through the doorway of the recreation room and off in the direction of his quarters.

"And so we part," said Clay Harbank as we shook hands. "I hope you find the Dorsai Planets as welcome as I intend to find Lulungomeena."

I grumbled a little. "That was plain damn foolishness. You didn't have to buy me out as well."

"There were more than enough credits for the both of us," said Clay.

It was a month after the bet and the two of us were standing in the Deneb One spaceport. For miles in every direction, the great echoing building of this central terminal stretched around us. In ten minutes I was due to board my ship for the Dorsai Planets. Clay himself still had several days to wait before one of the infrequent ships to Tarsus would be ready to leave.

"The bet itself was damn foolishness," I went on, determined to find something to complain about. We Dorsai do not enjoy these moments of emotion. But a Dorsai is a Dorsai. I am not apologizing.

"No foolishness," said Clay. For a moment a shadow crossed his face. "You forget that a real gambler bets only on a sure thing. When I looked into the Hixabrod's eyes, I was sure."

"How can you say 'a sure thing?' "

"The Hixabrod loved his home," Clay said.

I stared at him, astounded. "But you weren't betting on Hixa. Of course he would prefer Hixa to any other place in the Universe. But you were betting on Tarsus—on Lulungomeena—remember?"

The shadow was back for a moment on Clay's face. "The bet was certain. I feel a little guilty about the Kid, but I warned him that gambling money never stuck. Besides, he's young and I'm getting old. I couldn't afford to lose."

"Will you come down out of the clouds," I demanded, "and explain this thing? Why was the bet certain? What was the trick, if there was one?"

"The trick?" repeated Clay. He smiled at me. "The trick was that the Hixabrod could not be otherwise than truthful. It was all in the name of my birthplace—Lulungomeena."

He looked at my puzzled face and put a hand on my shoulder.

"You see, Mort," he said quietly, "it was the name that fooled everybody. Lulungomeena stands for something in my language. But not for any city or town or village. Everybody on Tarsus has his own Lulungomeena. Everybody in the Universe has."

"How do you figure that, Clay?"

"It's a word," he explained. "A word in the Tarsusian language. It means 'home.' "

Time Grabber

Feb. 16, 2631—Dear Diary: Do I dare do it? It's so frustrating to have to be dependent upon the whims of a physicist like Croton Myers. I'm sure the man is a sadist—to say nothing of being a pompous ass with his scientific double-talk, and selfish to boot. Otherwise, why won't he let me use the time-grapple? All that folderol about disrupting the fabric of time.

He actually patted me on the shoulder today when I swallowed my righteous indignation to the extent of pleading once more with him. "Don't take it so hard, Bugsy," he said—imagine— 'Bugsy'—to me, Philton J. Bugsomer, B.A., M.A., L.L.D., Ph,D., "in about twenty years it'll be out of the experimental stage. Then we'll see if something can't be done for you."

It's intolerable. As if a little handful of people would be missed out of the whole Roman Empire. Well, if I can't do it with his permission, I will do it without. See if I don't. My reputation as a scholar of sociomatics is at stake.

Feb. 18, 65: MEMO TO CAPTAIN OF THE POLICE: The emperor has expressed a wish for a battle between a handful of gladiators and an equal number of Christians. Have gladiators but am fresh out of Christians. Can you help me out?

(signed) Lictus,
CAPTAIN OF THE ARENA

Feb. 19, 65: MEMO TO CAPTAIN OF THE ARENA: I think I might be able to lay my hands on a few Christians for you—possibly. And then again I might not. By the way, that's a nice little villa you have out in the Falernian Hills.

(signed) Papirius,
CAPTAIN OF POLICE

Feb. 19, 65: Papirius:
All right, you robber. The villa's yours. But hurry! We've only got a few days left.
L.

Feb. 21, 65: Dear L:
Thanks for the villa. The papers just arrived. By an odd coincidence I had overlooked the fact that we already had sixteen fine, healthy Christians on hand, here. I am sending them on to you.
Love and kisses,
P.

Feb. 22, 2631: Dear Diary: Congratulate me! I knew my chance would come. Late last night I sneaked into the physics building. That fool of a Myers hadn't even had the sense to lock the door of his laboratory. I opened it and went in, pulled down the shade, turned on the light, and was able to work in complete security. Luckily, I had already played on his credulity to the extent of representing myself as overawed by the mechanical mind, and so induced him to give me a rough idea of how he operated the time-grapple (this over the lunch table in the Faculty Club) so, with a little experimenting, and—I will admit it—some luck, I was able to carry off my plans without a hitch.

I bagged sixteen young males from the period of Nero's reign—along somewhere in the last years. By great good luck they happened to be Christians taken prisoner and destined for the Roman Games. Consequently the guards had them all huddled together in a tiny cell. That's why the time-grapple was able to pick up so many at one grab. They came along quite docilely, and I have quartered them in the basement of my house where they seem to be quite comfortable and I can study them at my leisure.

Wait until the Sociomatics department here at the University sees the paper I'll write on this!

Feb. 23, 65: MEMO TO CAPTAIN OF POLICE: Where are my Christians? Don't you think you can gyp me out of my villa and then not deliver.

(signed) Lictus,
CAPTAIN OF ARENA

Feb. 23, 65: MEMO TO CAPTAIN OF THE ARENA: You got your Christians. I saw them delivered myself. Third cell on the right, beneath the stands.

(signed) Papirius,
CAPTAIN OF POLICE

Feb. 24, 65: MEMO TO CAPTAIN OF POLICE: I tell you they're not there.

(signed) Lictus,
CAPTAIN OF THE ARENA

Feb. 24, 65: MEMO TO CAPTAIN OF ARENA: And I tell you they are:

(signed) Papirius,
CAPTAIN OF POLICE

P.S. Are you calling me a liar?

Feb. 25, 65: MEMO TO CAPTAIN OF POLICE: I tell you THEY'RE NOT THERE. Come on over and look for yourself if you don't believe me.

(signed) Lictus,
CAPTAIN OF THE ARENA

Feb. 25, 65: Listen, Lictus:

I don't know what kind of a game you think you're playing, but I haven't time to bother with it right now.

Whether you know it or not, the Games load a lot of extra work on the police. I'm up to my ears in details connected with them, and I won't put up with having you on my neck, too. I've got the receipt signed by your jailer, on delivery. Any more noise from your direction and I'll turn it, together with your recent memos, over to the Emperor himself and you can straighten it out with him.

Papirius

Feb. 25, 2631: Dear Diary: What shall I do? How like that sneaky, underhanded physicist to be studying historical force lines in the Roman era, without mentioning it to me. Myers came into lunch today fairly frothing with what can only be described as childish excitement and alarm. It seems he had discovered a hole in the time fabric in the year 65, although he hasn't so far been able to place its exact time and location (this is, of course, my sixteen Christians) and he tried to frighten us all with lurid talk about a possible time collapse or distortion that might well end the human race—if the hole was not found and plugged. This is, of course, the most utter nonsense. Time collapse, indeed! But I can take no chances on his discovering what actually happened, and so I realized right away that I had to plug the hole.

The idea of putting back my Romans is, of course, unthinkable. They are beginning to respond in a most interesting manner to some spatial relationship tests I have been giving them. Therefore I cleverly sounded out Myers to find the necessary factors to plug the hole. I gather that any sixteen men would do, provided they conformed to the historically important characteristics of the Roman group. This sounded simple when he first said it, but since then the problem has been growing in my mind. For the important characteristics are clearly that they be all Christians who are willing to die for their faith. I might easily find such a group in Roman times but in order to hide the gap my replacements will make I will have to take them from some other era—one Myers is not studying. I have only a day or two at most. Oh, dear diary, what shall I do?

PHYSICIST GIVEN KNOCKOUT
DROPS

(*University News*)
(Feb. 27, 2631). When Croton Myers, outstanding physicist and professor of Physical Sciences at the university here showed a marked tendency to snore during his after-lunch classes, his students became alarmed and carried him over to the University Hospital. There, doctors discovered that the good professor had somehow been doped. There were no ill effects, however, and Dr. Myers was awake and on his feet some eighteen hours later. Authorities are investigating.

Feb. 29, 2631: Dear Diary: SUCCESS! Everything has been taken care of. I am so relieved.

Feb. 28, 1649 (From the Journal of John Stowe)—Today, by the will of the Lord, we are safely on our way from Appleby, fifteen men under the valiant leadership of Sergeant Flail-of-the-Lord Smith, having by our very presence in Appleby served to strike fear into the hearts of the papist plotters there, so that they dispersed—all of the troop in good health and spirits save only for one small trouble, of which I will relate.

It hath come to pass, that, being on our way from Appleby to Carlisle, there to join the forces of Captain Houghton, if God shall suffer such to come to pass, we have found ourselves at nightfall in a desolate section of the country, wasted by the late harrying and pillaging. We decided to pitch camp where we found ourselves rather than adventure farther in the dark.

Therefore, we made ourselves comfortable with such simple fare as contents a servant of the Lord, and our provisions supplied, and having sung a goodly hymn and given ourselves over to an hour or so of prayer for the pleasing of our souls, some among us fell to talking of the nature of the surrounding waste, recalling that from heathen times it hath had the name of being a place of most evil and supernatural resort. But our good Sergeant Flail-of-the-Lord, speaking up cheerily, rebuked those who talked so, saying "Are we not all servants of the Lord, and strong in his wrath? Therefore, gird ye up your courage and take heart."

But there were still some among us—and I do confess some sort of the same weakness in myself—who found the blackness and desolation press still heavily upon our souls, reminding us of manifold sins and wickedness whereby we had placed ourselves in danger of the Pit and the ever-present attacks of the Enemy. And our good Sergeant, seeing this, and perceiving we needed the sweet comfort and assuagement of the Word of the Lord, he bade us sit close by him, and opening his Book which was the Word of the Lord, read to us from II Kings Chapter 9, concerning the overthrow and just fate of Jezebel, whereat we were all greatly cheered and entreated him that he read more to us.

But it happened at this time that a small trouble was thrust upon us, inasmuch as it appeared to all of us that the wide and empty fields of night which surrounded us were whisked away and the appearance of a cell, stone on three sides, and a thick iron grating on the fourth, surrounded us. Whereat we were at first somewhat surprised. However, our good Sergeant, looking up from his Book, bade us mind it not, for that it was no more than a manifestation of whatever unholy spirits plagued the spot and which they had called up in jealous defiance of the sweet virtue of the Lord's word, as he had been reading it.

On hearing this, all were reassured, and, the hour being late, lay down to rest, inasmuch as we are to march at the first break of dawn. So, now, as I write these words, by God's mercy, nearly all are disposed to slumber, saving that the enchantment of the cell doth make somewhat for cramped quarters and I do confess that I, myself, am somewhat ill-at-ease, being accustomed to the good pressure of my stout sword against my side as I go to sleep. This, however, may not be helped, for, since it is the custom of our troop to lay aside all sharp tools on coming into the presence of the Lord our weapons are hidden from us by the enchantment and it would be a mark of lack of faith to pretend to search for them.

And, so, thanks be to the Lord, I will close this entry in my journal and dispose myself for a night of rest.

March 1, 65: MEMO TO CAPTAIN OF POLICE: I notice you finally got cold feet and got those Christians over here after all. But I warn you. I'm not yet altogether satisfied. They look like pretty odd-appearing Christians to me. More like barbarians. And if you've rung in something like that on me, I warn you, the Emperor will hear of it. My gladiators are too valuable to risk with a group of Goths or Vandals.

(signed) Lictus,
CAPTAIN OF THE ARENA

March 1, 65: MEMO TO CAPTAIN OF ARENA: Papirius has unfortunately been called out of the city on police business, and it is uncertain when he will be able to get back. I am sure, however, that if the Captain said that these men were Christians, they are Christians. However, if you're doubtful, there's nothing easier than to test the matter. Give any of them a pinch of incense and see if they'll sacrifice to the gods to gain their freedom. If they won't, they're Christians. You know how these things work.

(Signed) Tivernius
Acting CAPTAIN OF POLICE

(From the Journal of John Stowe) March 2, 1649: Lo! Satan is upon us and his devils do surround us. Trusting in the Lord, however, we have no fear of them.

Early this morning we awoke to find the enchantment still strong about us. Whereupon we took counsel together concerning our conduct in this strait. After several hours of discussion, it was decided that we could not necessarily be considered remiss in our military duties for not pushing on to Carlisle when bound and held by devils. This settled, it remained only to decide on our course of conduct toward these imps of Satan, and Sergeant Flail-of-the-Lord hath determined this by ordering that all present be industrious in prayer and considering of the good works of the Lord.

So it fell out that about the third or fourth hour after sunrise when we were engaged in singing that hymn of sweet comfort—

Lo! We shall crush His enemies
And drown them in their blood—that a fat, balding devil of middle age, somewhat wrapped and entwined in a sheet of bed linen approached the outer grating of our cell and did speak with us.

At first we were slow in understanding; but as it did happen that by good chance I had had some teaching in my youth in papist ways, it was not long before I realized that this devil was speaking a particularly barbarous and unnatural form of latin; and, on my conveying this information to Sergeant Flail-of-the-Lord, it was decided that I should speak with the devil for all of us.

I began by abjuring him to turn from the ways of the devil and cast himself upon the mercy of the Lord. But, so imperfect were the creature's wits and so inadequate his grasp of the tongue in which we conversed that he failed to grasp my meaning. Whereupon, I demanded of him by what right he held us and he did name several devils with Romish names and, producing several objects of strange manufacture, seemed to call on us for some kind of action.

At this point, Sergeant Flail-of-the-Lord interrupted to order me that I draw the devil out in conversation and learn whatsoever I could, that the knowledge might be a means to breaking the enchantment. Therefore, I did show interest and beseeched the devil to further explain himself.

Whereupon he did so. And it was apparent immediately that our wise Sergeant, praise the Lord, had correctly judged the state in which we were held. For after a great deal of words which I had some trouble interpreting, it became apparent that this spawn of the Devil, this creature of Satan was endeavoring by means of foul enticements and false promises of release from our enchantment, to cozen us into bowing down to graven images.

No sooner had I understood this, than I was filled with the wrath of the Lord, and, feeling His hand upon me, spoke words of fire to the lost being before me. I observed that he quailed, although odd as it seems, some of our troop claim to have noticed a slight trace of satisfaction upon his hellish visage. Whereupon he closed the interview with a question.

"Are you all Christians?" he demanded of me.

I answered, "Yes," and, rubbing his hands together with an expression of glee he hurried off.

I related all this to my comrades and the Sergeant. The Sergeant then advised us that we continue as we had before, saying that no doubt we were not alone at the mercy of the Devil, but that were being somewhat tested by the Lord, and as long as our faith in Him remained steadfast, no harm could surely come from this.

So hath the day past, very decently in praying and godly conversation. From scraps of conversation I have overheard from neighboring cells it becometh apparent that tomorrow we are to be thrown into the 'Arena,' which I take to be a devilish word for the pit. So be it. We abide the issue, all of us, with firm faith and quiet hearts. Amen.

March 2, 2631: Dear Diary: What a vexatious group! What on earth shall I do? These Romans seem to be pining away and losing interest in my tests, taking them lackadaisically, if at all. I'm sure I don't know what's wrong. I've given them the most attractive apparatus I can find, different colored little balls and pegs and objects, and brightly-lit shadow cards to study. I've piped all sorts of cheerful music into the basement and given them authentic Roman diets of the period and all they wanted to eat. They just don't seem to have any interest. I can't imagine what's wrong.

(From the notebook of Croton Myers) March 2, 2631:

11:02 P.M.—Dial settings. A-26.24, B-5.1, C-2. 73779 Calibration check, Vernier check. (Run 73)

Found it. Year 65, our calendar, Feb. 22, 10:15 P.M. (Approx). Sixteen individuals. Time scar to present date and year. Hole plugged on or about Feb. 27. Structure therefore safe middle late Roman era, disregarding minor time-thread damage which runs out anyway. However—took general check on hunch, and hunch confirmed. There's another hole even closer to our time. I can tell by the strains on the major time-threads. No time to trace it down now. We've got about five hours worth of elasticity in the present time-fabric before there'll be (a) a time collapse, or (b) an attempt by the fabric to rearrange itself to relieve the strain. Even the rearrangement could do for us. This second hole's too close to our own period.

I'm no Sherlock, but to me it adds up to only one answer— Bugsomer. I'm going over and see if I can force the information out of him.

The damn fool!

March 3, 65: TO THE CAPTAIN OF THE ARENA: Order your gladiators to stretch out this battle with the Christians. I don't want a sheep-slaughter. I want some sport. Some running around and excitement. See to it.

NERO, Imp.

March 3, 65: TO THE EMPEROR: Hail Caesar! I will do whatever I can when the time comes. But you know how uncooperative these Christians are. They won't even pick up their swords and armor. They want to be martyrs. However, I promise that the Emperor will not be disappointed.

(signed) Lictus

CAPTAIN OF THE ARENA

Dear Diary: I have no idea what the date is, so I just won't put any down. If the world goes topsy-turvy, it's not *my* fault. I'm all in a flutter. I hardly know where to begin writing.

I guess it all began when that pig-headed Myers came breaking into my house in the middle of the night. Breaking in, literally! My front door was locked, naturally, so he just kicked in a window and walked through it. I was down in the basement with my poor Romans, who hadn't been sleeping too well lately. I was trying to get them to take some barbiturates, but they seemed afraid to do so for some reason. They preferred to turn and toss on their cushions all night.

Well, at any rate I heard a noise. And then the next thing I heard was his bull voice calling, "Bugsy! Bugsy!" Before I could head him off he was at the top of the steps and clumping down. My poor Romans just stared at him.

"So here you are," he said triumphantly.

"Is that odd?" I replied. "After all, it's my house. And, while we're on the matter, I'd like to know how you got in, and by what right—"

"Oh, shut up," he said and pointed at my Romans. "Are these the sixteen you stole first?"

"I don't know what you're talking about," I answered coldly. "These are some foreign students from one of my classes. We're holding a seminar in Roman customs."

He just snorted, and ignoring me entirely, turned to the nearest Roman and started jabbering at him in barbarous high-school Latin. I even had trouble following him, but my Roman didn't. His face lit up and before I could say a word he was telling Myers all about what had happened to them, and the tests I'd been giving them. And right then and there, I learned something about Roman ingratitude. Can you believe it? Those sixteen young fellows weren't the least bit thankful for being saved from death in the Arena. All that concerned them was the fact that they were homesick. Homesick! For lions and gladiators!

I interrupted and asked my Roman whether he hadn't been well treated. And he turned on me and said—almost in those very words—that he had—he'd been too well treated. He'd been a hardworking artisan and Christian all his life and it didn't come natural to him to loll around on cushions and play with children's toys. He ended up by saying that if I gave him another test he'd ram it down my throat.

Well, after something like that, I was only too glad to get rid of them. I told Myers so and we started up the stairs. Just at that moment there was the most curious shiver—decidedly unpleasant—and we all suddenly found ourselves back at the foot of the stairs again. Myers turned white as a sheet.

He gasped. "Good God, I didn't think it would start this quickly!"—And I don't mind telling *you*, dear Diary, that for a second even I felt a touch of fear.

We hurried, all eighteen of us, across the darkened campus and up to his laboratory. Twice more those curious shivers threw us back a step or two in time, and we had to do things over.

"It's cracking faster," said Myers, and herded my Romans into an area marked off by chalk lines on the floor. Myers took me by the arm.

"Listen," he said, "and listen good, because I don't have time to say it twice. I've got the sixteen Romans waiting in a trigger area. There's a trip mechanism that will throw them back to their own time the minute there's an opening for them to fit into. I'm going to stay here and operate the machine. I want you to ride the time-grapple back to the Arena and see that the others—you said they were Roundheads?—and nobody but they get into the time-grapple for transference back to their own time."

"Me?" I said. "Into the time-grapple. I certainly will not—" Before I could finish he seized me by the shoulders and pushed me into the time-grapple area.

The moment I stumbled across the line the laboratory faded around me. I felt a moment of nausea, and then I was swinging, unsupported and apparently invisible above the royal box in the arena. When I leaned down I was right on a level with Nero himself. I took one horrified look at him, gasped and turned away.

I looked down in the arena, and saw immediately why Myers had sent me back. The time-grapple would, of course, have to get the Roundheads all on one grab and it would be impossible until they were all close together. I knew that, back in the laboratory, Myers could see me apparently standing on the floor in front of him and his devilish machine. He could also, of course, see Nero and part of the Royal box. I would have to direct him to the Roundheads when the time came.

I looked out in the arena, and groaned. The door to the cells was just opening and the Roundheads were filing out onto the field: The gladiators were already out; the Roundheads were too far dispersed for the time-grapple to grab them.

"Get together, get together!" I cried—but of course they couldn't hear me as long as I was in the time-grapple field.

Just then Nero spoke up next to my ear, and I *could* hear him, because of the auditory equipment built into the field.

"My dear," he was saying petulantly to a thickly powdered, fat-faced woman beside him. "Look at those Christians! And Lictus promised me that I shouldn't be disappointed. Look how sober and dull they are. They usually come on with their faces lit up, almost exalted."

"Perhaps," said the woman, "this group doesn't feel so much like being martyred. Maybe they'll run around a bit more."

I could stand no more of this, and signaled Myers to move the field down toward the Roundheads. The idiots were still too far apart to be picked up and were talking together in the odd, seventeenth century English.

"What think you, Sergeant," said one fresh-faced youngster, "are we to be put to trial by those armored demons, yonder?"

"It may be, John," replied the individual addressed as Sergeant.

The young man sighed. "I feel the hand of the Lord strong upon me," he said. "None the less, had I but my claymore—"

"Fie, John Stowe," reproved the Sergeant. "Let not your mind dwell upon earthly matters. Look rather upon yon armed demons, with a mind to marking their true natures. See yon demon with the chased shield, which is surely Pride. And the other beside him, whom, by his lean and envious face I clearly read as Covetousness.''

And the Sergeant went on giving names to the various gladiators, so that the other Roundheads became interested and drifted over. I was beginning to have hopes of snatching them up immediately when the Sergeant wound up his little discussion.

''And besides, John Stowe,'' he said. ''If the Lord wisheth us to have weapons, He surely will provide them.''

At this moment, an attendant of the Arena leaned over the stone parapet that encircled the field and dropped a bundle of swords and armor.

''What did I tell you?'' said the Sergeant.

So they dispersed in the process of putting on the armor, and the chance was lost.

''What's holding things up?'' boomed the voice of Myers in my ear.

''The battle,'' I snapped. ''They're supposed to fight those gladiators.''

''What!'' yelled Myers. ''Stop them. Don't let them do it. They've all got to get back alive.''

''What can I do?'' I asked bitterly. ''It's up to the Roundheads.''

And, indeed it was. There is no way of knowing how many lives were depending upon those Roundheads at that moment.

At any rate, there was a toot on a horn, or some kind of signal like that, and off they went.

''Do you take Pride, Stowe,'' said the Sergeant. ''And so each of the rest of you pick out a cardinal sin. I, myself, will take Covetousness.'' He lifted his Roman short sword over his head and shouted like a wild man.

''Now, LET GOD ARISE!'' he shouted, and the Roundheads charged toward the enemy.

''I'm moving you back to Nero,'' said Myers' voice in my ear. ''Maybe we can put pressure on him somehow.''

I was swooped back to the royal box. But by the time I got there the situation was such that neither of us could think of anything to do. Nero was bouncing around like a fat toad, squeaking at the top of his lungs.

"Why—what—what—" he was squealing. "What are they doing? You Christians, stop chasing my gladiators, do you hear me? Stop it! Stop it!"

Somebody blew that silly horn again, and the gladiators stopped, but the Roundheads went right on.

"Guard thyself, Pride!" the stentorian voice of John Stowe floated up to us in the Royal box. Beside Stowe there was a clang and a thud as the Sergeant decapitated Covetousness.

Gladiators were getting cut to pieces right and left. But not for long. Nero was ordering his own guard out of the stands, down into the Arena.

"I've got an idea," I called to Myers. "Drop me on the field."

"It better be good," he grunted. "Or you'll go the same way they're going!"

He dropped me. I came into sight of those Romans suddenly, and the shock of my appearance temporarily halted the Praetorian Guard. They looked from me to Nero and back again.

"To me!" I yelled, running over the field, waving my arms. "To me, Roundheads!"

Well, they looked up at the sound of my English voice and, to make a long story short, gathered around in short enough space for Myers to pick them up. The field faded around us . . .

March 3, 65: TO THE CAPTAIN OF THE ARENA: I thought I ordered you to produce Christians for slaughter! What devilish magic have you loosed upon Rome under the guise of Christians? I order you to capture those sixteen hell-spawned devils who murdered our gladiators. At once!

NERO, Imp.

March 3, 65: TO THE EMPEROR: My Caesar! I know not how the sixteen Christians escaped from the arena—

replacing themselves with sixteen others. I have contacted Papirius, Captain of Police, and he informs me it must be a plot on the part of the Christians for an uprising throughout the City. I believe the missing sixteen are in hiding. My Guard will be ordered out at once to apprehend them.

(signed) Lictus,

CAPTAIN OF THE ARENA

March 3, 65: TO CAPTAIN OF POLICE: I have at hand information from Lictus, Captain of the Arena, concerning the plot of the Christians to overthrow Roman rule with today's events in the Arena as a signal for insurrection. Drastic action must be taken. Burn out every festhole in Rome where the Christians are massed. At once!

NERO, IMP.

March 3, 65: TO THE EMPEROR: Hail, Caesar! Your command has been obeyed. Even now the Christians burn in their catacombs!

(sighed) Papirius,

CAPTAIN OF POLICE

March 3, 65: TO THE CAPTAIN OF POLICE: Are you mad, you fool? By whose authority have you put the torch to Rome? The flames are spreading throughout the city— underground—and already are at the arena dungeons! Send help to quench the fires!

Lictus,

CAPTAIN OF THE ARENA

March 3, 65: TO THE CAPTAIN OF THE ARENA: Don't call me a fool, you idiot! How was I to know the fire would spread through the catacombs! I can't send you any men. I'm appealing to the Emperor for help myself. The fires are getting beyond control!

Papirius,

CAPTAIN OF POLICE

March 3, 65: TO THE EMPEROR: Mighty Caesar! The

Christians have turned the fires against us and our city is in danger of being consumed. What shall we do?

(signed) Papirius,
CAPTAIN OF POLICE

March 3, 65: TO THE CAPTAIN OF POLICE: You imbecile! I order you to burn out the Christians and you set fire to the entire city! Already my palace is on fire! Consider yourself under arrest! Report to me after you have the flames under control. Or perhaps you'd prefer throwing yourself into the closest inferno and cheat me of the pleasure of roasting you alive later!

NERO, Imp.

March 3, 65: TO THE EMPEROR: The city is engulfed, my Caesar! I shall die fighting the flames. But what of you, my Emperor? I shall pray to the Gods that you be spared my fate.

(signed) Papirius,
CAPTAIN OF POLICE

March 3, 65: TO THE EX-CAPTAIN OF POLICE: The Gods be damned—I'm getting the hell out of Rome!

NERO, Imp.

April 1, 2631: Dear Diary: Myers has seen to it for my transfer. Oh, he's clever and all that to keep the fact hidden that I used the time-grapple. But I can't see what all the fuss is about. We corrected the time stress before anything critical could happen. The way he carries on you'd think we did something (I, that is) that would go down in history. A ridiculous thought, but then Myers is a physicist and you know what suspicious natures they have. . . . I often wonder though how the games did turn out that afternoon . . .

I've Been Trying to Tell You

"DO YOU think it's the end of the world?" asked the girl.

It had been a sweltering summer. And now, on a late afternoon in August, the sun seemed to hang still in a brassy sky and broil the earth beneath it. The office of the State University that Jem Allinson sat in, mentally damning the day he had ever become a reporter, had its air conditioning on the blink for some strange reason. He sat with his jacket taken off and thrown over the back of his chair; and he suspected that there were large damp spots staining the underarms of his dress T-shirt. He did not care. He knew that he stank—although the less sensitive nose of this girl could probably not catch that—clear through the deodorant with which he had anointed himself, and he did not care. Why should he, he thought? Long since he had weighed the human race in the balance of his admiration and found it lacking. For this reason the girl's remark, so much like some he had made himself from time to time, tickled him.

"What gives you the idea the world's close to ending, Miss Hansen?" he asked her. Almost immediately he regretted the question. He was not here to talk about philosophy. The day had been long; and he was tired—and thirsty. To compound the delay, she was gazing away out the office window at the 1980 skyline and did not answer immediately.

175

Miss Hansen, of course, was not a girl. She was an entomologist, a "Doctor" and a member of the University Staff. But she was extremely small and young-looking, with a round pretty face and a voice so soft that Jem seemed always on the verge of having to strain to hear it. The sort of girl, Jem thought bleakly, he might have fallen in love with once upon a time, when he had been equally young—equally innocent. Eidel Hansen, her name was, Associate Professor of Entomology. She did not look it. Jem shifted restlessly in his straight-backed chair, smoothing out the wrinkles in his jacket. He did not want to talk about the end of the world. What he wanted was some good, quotable quotes to take back to the Courier's newsoffice and write a Sunday feature article about.

"The old order of things is breaking down," she answered. "Everything's different. You—don't you feel different?"

He felt tired, Jem thought, old and tired. He looked over at the piece of white paper towelling on her desk, on which were spread out the corpses of the half-dozen odd-shaped insects that had been brought in to the Courier by people during the last two weeks. She had hardly glanced at them. She was more concerned with the end of the world and how he felt. Well, how should a man feel when he's thirty and some and has worked too hard and drunk too much for twelve years? He thought of the article to be banged out after he left here. An hour's work—and then the blessed numbing coolness of a dark bar. Anonymity and forgetfulness. Lethe. . . .

"Mr. Allinson!"

She was staring at him. He roused himself.

"I feel dead and unburied," he said. "It's the heat." He looked at her. The article didn't have to be in until tomorrow and an idea was tempting him. Well, why not? She was good-looking enough in her schoolgirl way. "Feel like a drink?" he said.

She hesitated.

"I—" the hesitation vanished. "Yes, I do. Thank you."

176

"Don't thank me," he said. "I want one myself."

He should have said it lightly. They should have smiled. But neither did. The day was too heavy for anything but plain speaking.

"Do you have a car—"

"Outside," he told her.

She got up from the desk without adding a jacket or a hat, or stopping to correct her makeup; and they walked down the summer vacation emptiness of the building's ringing stone corridors. His car, a convertible, was parked with the top up against the fierceness of the sun, in a no-parking zone before the building's steps.

The brightness of the sun on cement and concrete almost blinded them. Jem had a sudden vision of them coming out and shielding their eyes as they were doing, she small and neat, he large and untidy, his black hair damp with sweat above the heavy bones of his face. Then he was leading her down the steps and handing her into the car. He went around and got in beside her.

"Any place in particular?" he asked her.

"I'll leave it to you."

She answered almost inaudibly, leaning back against the hot brown leather of the seat, still shielding her eyes. He started the motor and drove off.

They went to Danny's—a good bar, but a little run-down, in the market area south of the town's business district. After they were seated with drinks in a high-backed plastic booth which all but cut them off from the view of the rest of the bar, a little lamp gleaming in the dimness—faint watts of light through a yellow shade on the wall beside them—Jem remembered something.

"The bugs," he said. "I left them back at your office."

"It doesn't matter," she twisted her glass around between her fingers. "I can tell you what they were. They were all *diptera*."

"Diptera?"

"Two winged insects," she looked up from the glass

to him. "In the case of the ones you brought me—flies and mosquitoes."

"Flies and mosquitoes?" He stared at her. "You sure? I never saw any like that."

"I know. Our department—" she caught herself. "They're mutations."

"Mutations?" he stared at her for a second, searching his mind for the meaning of the word. Instantly, he was all reporter again. "You mean they're freaks hatched out by ordinary bugs? Is that official?"

"Well," she said, turning her glass again, aimlessly. "We all think—yes, you could say that."

"How come?"

"No one knows," she said. "No one."

He peered at her face in the dim light. It was unhappy, lost.

"There's something here," he said. "Mutations—nobody knows—do I think the world's going to end. If you don't want to tell me about it, what're you hinting around the subject for?"

"That's all there is to it." She raised her head and met his eyes. "There's nothing but monsters being born nowadays."

He waited, but she sat silent.

"I don't get it," he said, flatly and finally.

"How do you want me to say it?" she asked. "Nine little insects out of ten. Nine little animals out of ten are coming out—different. Have been for the past year."

He stared at her.

"That's crazy," he said. He almost glared at her. So young, so—so something that it reached inside of him and twisted at him with an almost forgotten feeling of tenderness for her. So full of crazy ideas. "You're crazy. I'd have heard about it."

"Haven't you?"

He began to remember. Farmyard freaks. There had been an epidemic of them in the spring. But they'd died out. He told her so.

"Farmers stopped talking about them," she said.

"There's a scare through the upper midwest and probably the rest of the country, too. Sort of a superstition. Farmers kill the freaks and don't tell anyone. But there's government secrecy in on it, too. And the University Farm Campus has been going out of its head trying to figure out reasons for it."

"I still would have heard."

"Because you work for a newspaper," she smiled sadly.

"That's right."

"How'd you like to talk to Peter—DeWin, he's head of Zoology?" she asked. "He's worked with some of the animal mutations. You might believe him."

"All right." Jem shoved back his drink and stood up. "Let's go."

"Go?" she laughed, then stopped laughing suddenly, like someone who abruptly realizes she is at a church, or a funeral. "And leave this nice bar? Let him come to us. He could use a drink, too."

Standing, Jem considered her. Did he want somebody else barging into the party? He had planned—you could always lose yourself in a woman. For a little while. For a few hours, or a night, you could forget that there was nothing left to believe in, that all the bright, shining words and principles that people prided themselves on were cheap and fragile hollownesses inside, like Christmas tree ornaments. It all came back in the morning, of course, but meanwhile there had been a moment of rest and forgetting— and the fresh, soft youngness of her had beckoned his arid soul like an oasis.

But this was more important. This was news.

"Why not?" he said. She stood up.

"I'll go phone him," she said. He watched her walk away from him.

Professor Peter DeWin was a thin, slight man in his fifties. Both his voice and his hands shook a little and his face was tired. He called Eidel "my dear" like a stage grandfather; but Jem, listening closely, understood swiftly that it was not so much an affectation as the sort of nervous habit a shy, elderly man might fall into in trying to avoid both intimacy and formality.

"It was nice of you, my dear," he said, "to call me. And thank you, too, Mr. Allinson." He lifted the drink the waitress brought him.

"No thanks necessary," said Jem. "I got you here to pick your brains."

"There's nothing up there any longer to pick, I'm afraid," said Peter DeWin, apologetically. "Nothing but a lot of obsolete knowledge."

"Poor Peter," said Eidel, softly.

Jem frowned at him.

"Sorry," he said. "I don't get it."

"He means," Eidel answered, turning to Jem, "that all the old classifications are breaking down, now."

"Oh?" he said. He looked at Peter. "Miss Hansen said—"

"Eidel said," she corrected him.

"Eidel said, then"—he stumbled a little, awkwardly, over her first name, feeling again the same odd twisting sensation of tenderness toward her.

"That's better," she said quietly, looking at him.

"—that nine out of ten births was producing a mutation. Is it that high?"

"How can you tell?" the older man shrugged wearily. "Maybe it's ten out of ten. A mutation isn't necessarily something you see right off."

"But *all* animals and insects?" demanded Jem, incredulously.

"Perhaps," Peter drained his glass and set it down on the table. "I'd like another drink, I think."

Jem beckoned the waitress. After she had taken their order and returned with a fresh round, he turned back to his questioning.

"When did it start?"

The older man smiled.

"Sometime earlier this year," said Peter. "It's hard to tell when."

"What started it?"

"Wouldn't everyone like to know," he answered. He seemed to hesitate; and Jem—out of more than ten years' experience in interviewing people—sensed something held back.

"You wouldn't," he said, looking closely at Peter, "have some theory of your own?"

Peter looked up at him sharply for the first time. "Is this for publication?"

"Not if you don't want it to be."

"Never mind." The older man seemed to sag suddenly. He turned to Eidel. "I'm sorry—the Security men were around a month ago. They said not to let it out even to the department. It's strontium-90, of course."

"I'd guessed," she whispered.

"Strontium-90?" said Jem, leaning closer.

"I'm sorry," said Peter, turning back to him. "You'd simply call it radioactivity. There are other villains in the fall-out from the bomb tests we've been having these last thirty years. But strontium-90 seems to be our leading assassin. It's a radioactive isotope of the element strontium, capable of causing osteosarcomas, leukemias—" he gave a sad little laugh that was half a hiccup "—capable of causing genetic changes, hereditary changes in the reproductive—" his voice dwindled off into silence "—tissues," he said with a sudden final effort.

"What're you talking about?" demanded Jem, staring hard at him. "We've lived with various levels of bomb-test radiation for forty years."

"We let it get too high," said Peter. "Not war but peace has destroyed us. Now, as if passing over a valley ridge, we get the strange little insects, the strange little animals. And the children?"

"What about the children?" snapped Jem.

"I don't know," Peter said. "Has anyone checked lately? Maybe it's already started."

Jem considered them both through narrowed eyes. Then he whistled a few thin notes between his teeth, rubbed his chin and stood up.

"I can check on that," he said. Eidel got up quickly to stand beside him.

"I'll go with you," she said.

"My dear—" Peter looked up at her. "I wish you'd stay here with me and have another drink."

"We'll come back." She reached out and touched his shoulder lightly, in a little comforting gesture. "We'll be back as soon as we can. Come on, Jem."

He led the way out of the bar.

Colin Powers was an intern Jem knew at General Hospital. He was off duty and they persuaded him to come out for a cup of coffee; but he was nervous and ill at ease.

"I ought to be getting back," he said, after they had sat and talked a while.

"What's eating you?" demanded Jem with harsh suddenness. "What's going on, over there?"

"Just the usual things." Colin looked at his coffee cup.

"And some unusual, maybe?" said Jem.

Colin looked up abruptly. His brown young eyes had gone hard.

"So that's why the visit," he said. "You asked me out to pump me about something."

"Then I'm right."

"No," replied Colin, evenly, rising.

Jem slammed a large hand down on the other's arm, almost knocking him back into the little coffee-shop booth.

"Want me to write up a question about something being kept under cover at the hospital?" he said, tightly. "And see it printed with your name mentioned?"

Colin's face was pale with anger.

"A physician isn't required to violate the confid—"

"Shut up and listen to me," said Jem, fiercely, feeling for the first time a cold, uneasy stirring in his guts. "I know what's going on over there. It's happening everywhere and to everything. You've seen these freak insects we've had flying around lately. Well, it's all insects and all animals—and now all humans. Isn't it?'' He shook the younger man's arm. *''Isn't it!''*

''I've got nothing to say,'' gasped Colin.

Jem jerked his head in Eidel's direction.

''Miss Hansen here is from the Zoology Department at the U.,'' he said. ''She's been studying the animal and insect part of it for months now. So don't try to kid us!''

Colin's face wobbled toward Eidel.

''Is—are you—''

''Yes,'' she answered him. ''What Jem says, is true.''

Colin slumped, sinking back in the booth. Jem let go of his arm.

''Just tell us one thing,'' Jem said. ''When did it start?''

Colin turned a ravaged face toward him.

''All year, and getting worse and worse—.'' He buried his face in his hands.

''All the kids?''

''Most of them. Four out of five—'' the young man shuddered. ''Some were—pretty bad.''

Jem nodded, slowly.

''That's all,'' he said, soberly, getting to his feet. ''Thanks. You can go back now.''

''Are you going to print it?'' whispered Colin.

''I don't know,'' said Jem. He turned to Eidel, who rose also.

''Where're you going then?''

''We've got a date with a man named Peter,'' said Jem. ''And some drinks.''

Peter DeWin was still sitting just as they had left him, when they got back to Danny's. He had obviously been drinking steadily, but he was not completely drunk—yet.

''Hi, sport,'' said Jem, following Eidel into the booth seat across from the zoologist. ''How many's it been since we left?''

''I really don't know,'' answered Peter. His words came out a little slowly, but otherwise the alcohol in him

183

did not show. He looked over at Eidel. "How are you, my dear?"

"Fine, Peter, fine." She reached across the table and patted his hand.

"And the children?" asked Peter.

"All year and getting worse," said Jem, grimly, signaling the waitress. "Four out of five. Somebody goofed about this business." He looked at DeWin with hard eyes. "Maybe a lot of people goofed. They should have started doing something about this a long time ago."

Peter broke suddenly into a little, hiccuping laugh.

"Do something—" he echoed. Then he got control of himself. "My dear Mr. Allinson—Jem—what would you suggest doing?"

Jem stared at him for a long, hard moment. Then he stood up.

"I know some people down in Washington," he said. "I'm going to call them."

He walked away.

He was gone for a few minutes. When he returned, he was walking slowly. He sat down in the booth again.

"Well—" he said, seeing the waiting faces of the other two upon him, "It's all over. The President is going on the air tomorrow in concert with the heads of other nations." He spread his large hands on the table. "Emergency conditions—world-wide."

"Yes," said Peter, nodding and lifting his drink in a gesture.

"What I can't understand!" In sudden fury, Jem slammed his fist down on the table before them. "This has been building over a year. They saw it coming. How could they let it go like this? How could they?"

"It was too late then," said Peter. "It was too late five years ago—or ten." He looked over at Eidel and patted her hand where it lay on the table. "My dear—"

"I'm all right," she answered; but she did not look up.

"Goddamit!" exploded Jem suddenly. "Can't you

two do anything but sit there and cry? What's wrong with you, giving up like this?''

"Jem—" Peter shook his head, slurring the word a little. He signaled the waitress. "Like the dinosaurs, Jem. We had our chance."

"What're you talking about?"

"We made our own end. We had our chance to get together. We let things go—as we always let things go— even though we knew our time was shortening, that the sun was going down. Now our sun is setting." He made a little plaintive gesture with one hand. "Darkness."

"We're no bunch of lizards!" snapped Jem. "What're you talking about? That's what civilization's for—to handle things like this. We'll work out methods—some sort of radiation armor. Shield the nurseries. There'll be ways."

"No," said Peter. He shook his head slowly, and pawed among the change on the table before him. Selecting a half-dollar, he held it between thumb and forefinger while he rolled back the sleeve of his jacket. He displayed his hairy, old-man's forearm before them naked. It was thin and lumpy, with an odd swelling like a long tumor running from the base of the thumb back to disappear into the wider muscles below the elbow. "I'm in my sixties," he said. "And I was never strong. But look—" Casually, without strain, he compressed his thumb and forefinger. The half dollar crumpled between them as the odd swelling bunched and moved. "You see," said Peter and let his head sink gently to the table. It nudged a half-empty glass, spilling it. The liquid pooled silver on the dark table top. "That's why it's too late. Even me. Even us." He closed his eyes.

Eidel drew in her breath with a hiss. She sat, huddled and frozen in the booth, her eyes on the mashed coin, their pupils abnormally dilated.

"Eidel!" said Jem.

She did not respond.

Eidel!" He shook her gently by one shoulder. A little of the paralysis seemed to leak out of her slowly. She

185

turned her head to look at him; but the look of terrible, arctic fear was still there.

"Snap out of it!" said Jem. He shook her again, as if to start the watch of her life and youth again to ticking.

"You saw—" she breathed.

He felt the muscles clench in his cheek, spasmodically.

"Sure I saw!" he said harshly. "So he's a bit of a freak himself. So what's that got to do with the real mutations? And what if it did? There's no difference. The situation right now's still the same."

She did not answer, turning toward Peter.

"Look at him!" snapped Jem, giving the other man's head a push. It rolled a little on flaccid neck muscles. "Is *that* something to be afraid of? A drunk? A drunk who can do a coin trick?"

"No," she said, in so low a voice he had to strain to hear her. "There's more to it than that. You don't understand."

"I don't understand—" The waitress had come up to their table, carrying a bar towel. She mopped the wet surface before them, glancing at Peter's collapsed form.

"He out?" she asked.

"Just taking a little nap," said Jem.

"At that age they shouldn't drink." She finished and went off. Jem looked at his own hands, which were wet from the spilled drink.

"Excuse me," he said. "I want to wash. I'll be right back."

She nodded dully. He turned and went toward the washroom, cutting across a little courtyard filled with beach umbrellas and tables, now empty in the reddish light just before sunset. In the washroom, he washed automatically, his mind numbed-feeling as if by the action of some powerful anesthetic; and he shook his head angrily, to get it working again.

There was, he thought, something wrong with him. This situation was throwing him, and situations just didn't do that—to Jem Allinson. He had always had an invincible belief in his own ability to come out on top. So the world was in for a rough time. All right, what about it? He could take care of himself.

And then it hit him. Then it came home to him all at once; and he stood, dumbly watching the water flow over his hands. It was not himself he was worried about—it was her, Eidel.

Years ago, after his first wife had left him, he had cut a niche for the women in his life and kept them there. But now, suddenly with the world crumbling beneath him, he felt the tawdriness of his life and wanted something more, something real—someone small, with soft blond hair and large eyes who sat chilled by a strange, icy fear in the booth upstairs. He grinned at himself mirthlessly in the mirror.

"Well, sport," he said softly to his reflection. "What now?"

He dried his hands and left the washroom. As he stepped out into the little courtyard again, the whole western half of the sky was alive with fire; and the murky coal of the sun descending beyond the far jagged teeth of the skyline, now black in silhouette. He was reminded all at once of Peter's words about the sun setting—the sun of the human race setting—and in spite of himself little hairy feet of fear ran up his spine and nestled in the dark back of his mind. He wondered then—

In the same instant he leaped—whirled and stamped. His shoe came down on something small, dark and scuttling whose sudden scream was smashed by Jem's crushing heel. Sweating, he stood for a second, then bent over to pick it up.

Its two protruding fangs were sunk into the leather of his shoeheel and he had to break them loose. He lifted it up in front of his eyes. It was evidently something that once had possessed rodents for ancestors. It looked a little like a mouse or rat and was halfway in size between the two. Forcing its mouth open he saw the small sac behind the two broken fangs. Poisonous, almost certainly.

Holding it, he found himself suddenly wondering what had warned him of its attack—for attack it most certainly had been. A musty odor from the creature's fur came up in his nostrils and he bent to sniff at it. It was unlike any odor he had heretofore experienced and that, alone, must have set him on his guard. Unconsciously now, he flared his nostrils and searched about for scent that would warn of any similar presence in the courtyard.

He caught no other like scent, but a great wave of mingled odors washed in on him. He had been cursed with this all his life—an unduly sensitive nose, so that the ordinary smells of human life were a torture to him and he had trained himself to ignore most of what came to him in this fashion, for the sake of his own comfort. Now, for the first time in years, he opened his nose wide to the atmosphere around him; and a thousand different reeks came in—the smells of people, wood, and metal and stone—and food and drink—

He caught himself suddenly. A slow, horrible suspicion was congealing him. He stood, motionless, and the body of the dead rodent mutation in his fingers slipped from his heedless grasp and dropped to the courtyard floor. Why, something cried out inside him, why hadn't he seen it before? Peter with his abnormal fingers and he, Jem, with—.

Abruptly, he began to laugh; and his laughter scaled up until he was forced to take great, gulping breaths of air to stop it. Then he sobered. He stood swaying, a big, raw-boned man, normal in all respects, now that he had ceased to use the animal-like abilities of his nose. His nose, he thought—oh, God, his nose!

He took one last gasping breath and straightened his shoulders and went back into the bar. Peter was once again sitting up in the booth, his eyes open, but staring at nothing. Jem ignored the other man and sat down beside Eidel. Through the window he could see the sunset.

"Listen," he said urgently. She turned her face to him.

"Listen—" he said again, "we're getting out of here, you and me. The world's going smash, all right: but we can get off somewhere where it's safe. Eidel—you understand what I'm saying? You and me."

"You and me," she echoed obediently, but without feeling.

"Listen!" he closed his fingers cruelly about her arm. "There'll be people who'll keep their heads about this. As soon as we know who—who's safe, we'll join them. But to start with, we can't take the risk. Everybody's changed—mutated, probably. Even me. I've known about it all my life, but I never realized. Look!" He lifted his head, sniffing. "You've got face powder in your purse, and a little bottle of cologne, and a candy bar—look, see if I'm not right. Eidel!"

He shook her, but she did not move. She only turned her head away.

"Don't you understand?" he cried at her. "We've got to get away, so I can take care of you. Eidel, I want you—I love you. Look at me!"

She turned back to face him.

"Don't you understand me?" he said. "I—I love you. I want to protect you—"

"Too late," said Peter.

Jem turned furiously on the other man.

"What do you mean, too late? If we leave now, while there's time—"

"There is no time," said the zoologist. "There was no time yesterday, or last month, or last year, or fifty years ago. It was already too late."

"What're you talking about?" raged Jem.

"Like the dinosaur," said Peter, dully, drunkenly. "We had our chance. We didn't take it. We could have learned, we could have put an end to the old instincts of fear and hatred, and fighting and killing, each man for himself. We could have learned to like and trust each other—"

"Don't listen to him!" broke in Jem, seizing Eidel by the shoulders and turned her around to face him. "He's old. He's given up. That's no reason for us, for you and me—there's all the hope in the world for us to come through—''

"No," she whispered. There were tears in her eyes. "No, Jem. He's right."

"Right!" he cried. "He's wrong. I tell you. Wrong. Wrong!"

"No—" she shook her head. "I know." She looked up at Jem. "Don't you think I know? Didn't it occur to you that I might be a mutation, too?"

"You?" His hands dropped from her shoulders. "You changed? How?"

She whimpered a little, suddenly.

"I didn't want to tell you," she said, pitifully. "All those years in school I hid myself away from life. And now you come along, too late—too late—''

He drew back a little from her in the booth.

"What is it?" he said harshly. "What's happened to you? Tell me!"

"I can see, that's all!" she cried. "I can see it all as it's going to happen, every time I lie down to sleep, every time I close my eyes, I see it like looking through a window—all the future."

Jem sucked in breath.

"The future?" he said quietly. And when after a minute she still did not answer, "You can see the future?" Suddenly he shouted at her. "Well, tell me! Tell me, then! What do you see? What's going to happen?"

"Oh, my God!" she screamed suddenly. "I told you! I've been trying to tell you all day. The fighting and the feeding—all over, all over! The end of the world!"

Flat Tiger

I am proud and happy to announce that contact with intelligent beings other than ourselves had finally been achieved and that, as a result of that meeting, peace has come at last, with the peoples of all nations firmly united behind a shining new doctrine.

The true story of this final contact has been delayed for several months, for security reasons, which necessitated that any publication of the facts be cleared first with the Secret Service, the FBI, the Treasury Department, the ICC, the Immigration Service and Senator Bang—who, while he had no direct official connection with the matter, would have caused everybody else a lot of trouble if he hadn't been checked with first.

Also, it was necessary to clear with the opposite numbers of the above individuals and organizations in some one hundred and twenty-seven other nations, who either had representatives at the final contact aforementioned, or learned about it afterward in one way or another, and were understandably miffed at not being invited to the conference, as they called it.

The story actually begins some few months back when a spaceship landed on the lawn of the White House one morning about eight A.M. and the President, looking out the window of his bedroom, perceived it.

"A spaceship!" he ejaculated.

"*That is correct, sir,*" replied a voice inside his

head. "*The ship you see is the racing spaceabout* Sunbeam *and I am Captain Bligh. Over.*"

"Captain Bligh!" echoed the astounded President.

"*Why, yes—*" The voice broke off suddenly and the President received the impression of a chuckle of amusement. "*Oh, I see the coincidence that startles you. I read you loud and clear. Strange, isn't it, how words will sometimes duplicate themselves in a totally alien language? If you will go down to your office, you will meet me and we can talk there. Over.*"

"I'll be right down," said the President, hurriedly grabbing for his pants.

"*Right. See you then. Over and out.*"

"Over and out," replied the President mechanically.

He rushed down to his office and locked the door. A curtain by the window stirred and there stepped into view, a creature slightly shorter than himself, but much heavier, equipped with tentacles and fangs. The President, however, was pleasantly surprised to note that it—or rather he, for it later turned out that Captain Bligh was, indeed, a male—did not in the least repel him with his alienness, thus being the first human to discover that no totally unfamiliar form can arouse an emotional response.

"Captain Bligh, I presume," he said politely.

"The same," replied the captain in passable English. "I have been profiting by the interval since we last spoke to learn your language and succeeded to some degree. Two-way mental radio is a marvelous device, you know. Over."

"Roger—I mean you do very nicely," said the President, passing a hand over his damp brow. "But you know, my dear sir, that ship of yours will attract all sorts of attention."

"Not at all," answered Bligh. "The spaceabout's light-reflecting properties have been heterodyned to your personal retinal pattern only. Be assured that you are the only man on this world that can see it at the present moment."

"That's a relief. You have no idea how the papers would jump on something like this." He gestured to a chair. "Won't you sit down?"

"Thanks, but I'd rather stand. No leg joints, you see. You're probably wondering how I happen to be here."

"Well, I don't think I should commit myself by giving you a definite answer immediately on that," said the President cautiously.

"No matter," said Bligh. "I will explain anyway. I happened to be in a round-the-Galaxy race at the moment—the *Sunbeam* is a stripped-down hot-warp. Unfortunately, as I was passing your solar system, I got a flat tiger and had to pull in for repairs."

"I bet your pardon?" queried the President. "Did you say a flat tiger?"

"Excuse me," said Bligh. "I should have explained. The tiger—*Felis Tigris Longipilis* or what you know as the Siberian tiger—is a discarded mutant variform of a race which was formerly distributed everywhere throughout the Galaxy, but which has since ended its physical existence and passed on—" Captain Bligh's voice took on a reverent hush and he removed the top of his head, considerably startling the President until he realized that it was actually a cap of some sort—"to that great macro-universe up yonder to which we must all go one day."

The President cleared his throat embarrassedly. Captain Bligh put his cap back on and continued his explanation.

"Tigers are, therefore, to be found on every world and familiar to every intelligent race. Since they still possess many of the potentials of their departed master-strain, they have been bred and conditioned to a variety of uses. One of the most widespread of these is as neural governors on the feeders that meter out fuel to the warp engines. The fuel feed must be controlled with such delicacy that no mechanical process can be devised fine enough. I have four warp engines on my *Sunbeam* and therefore, naturally, four tigers; one petty tiger and three tigers second class."

"Ah—yes," the President replied. "But you said that this tiger was flat."

"Exactly. My tigers and others like them have been bred and trained for their work. It is a very exacting job, as you can imagine, since a tiger's attention must not waver for one milli-second while the ship is in operation. To aid them in their concentration, the tigers' lungs are filled with a drug in gaseous form under high pressure, which, being slowly absorbed into the bloodstream, keeps them in a state of hyper-concentration."

"Oh?" said the President. "But why a gaseous drug? I should think an injection—"

"Not at all. A gaseous drug has the great advantage that when the trip is over, or at any moment when the situation may require it, the tiger may exhale and within a few seconds be rid of the effects of the drug. No tiger of your planet, of course, could do it—but our tigers are quite capable of holding their breaths for weeks."

"Then how did this accident occur?"

"My Number One Port Tiger somehow omitted a basal metabolism test at his last physical checkup," said the Captain sadly. "I am sorry to say that he was eighteen points over normal and used up his gas ahead of schedule. There is no room on the ship to set up the gas-manufacturing apparatus and, of course, yours was the only habitable planet for us to land on in this system. I did not know it was—er—civilized."

"And when you saw it was?" prompted the President.

"I looked you up immediately," replied the Captain. "I am in no sense an official, but I could hardly wait to offer you the tentacle of friendship on behalf of the Galactic Confraternity of Intelligences."

Coughing explosively to gain a little time, the President dabbed at his mouth with his handkerchief and put it away again.

"I am only, you must understand, executive head of this one nation."

"Oh? I see—" said Captain Bligh, telepathing the equivalent of a bothered frown. "That makes it troublesome. Time is, of course, relative; but there's this little matter of my possibly losing the race if I have to spend too much time here. I can, of course, notify Exploration when I reach the finish point on Capra IV, but that will mean centuries of red tape. It would short-cut things enormously if I could carry word directly to Confraternity Headquarters that you already consider yourselves a member world."

"Oh, I see," said the President. "Tell me, just how much time can you afford to spend?"

"Well, let me see— To set up the apparatus, one of your days— To gas Number One Port Tiger, two days— To dismantle, half a day. Say, three days from this coming sunset."

"Hum," said the President thoughtfully, "I'll see what I can do."

They went outside to the spaceabout together.

"Be with you in a minute," said the Captain and dived in through the airlock of his vessel, to return a moment later, carrying—he was obviously of inhuman strength—a rather thin, helpless-looking tiger.

"Mr. President," said the Captain. "May I present my Number One Port Tiger, second class."

The Tiger extended a paw.

"*This is indeed an honor,*" it telepathed feebly.

"Not at all, not at all," said the President gingerly shaking the animal's paw.

"The poor fella's worn out," said the Captain in an aside to the President as he laid the Number One Port Tiger on the White House lawn. "The last of his gas went while we were still a number of light-years short of your system and we went the last stretch on nerve alone. Pretty well took it out of him."

Looking at Number One Port lie on the grass, looking more like a cardboard cut-out of a tiger than the real item, the President was inclined to agree.

"You're going to set up your apparatus here?" he asked, somewhat nervously.

Bligh instantly comprehended the cause of his agitation. "Don't worry," he reassured. "I guarantee complete invisibility."

"Well, if you think so—" replied the President, rather doubtfully. "I'll leave you to that and see what I can do in this other matter."

The President returned to his office and sat down at his desk, pressing a button as he did so. A few seconds later, his Special Secretary, Morion Stanchly, put in an appearance.

"Yes, Mr. President?" he said.

"Sit down, Morion," said the President. "I have something to discuss with you." And he waved his Special Secretary to a chair.

Morion Stanchly was a little administrative secret. He had been around the White House for forty years, inheriting the office from his father who had had it in turn from *his* father, and so on back to Preserved Stanchly, who had first been named to the post by General Washington, before the General became President. It was, of course, an unofficial post. Special Secretaries were always carried on the payroll under a different title and usually under a different name. Morion was, at the moment, down on the official books as a White House chauffeur named Joe Smith.

He would remain Joe Smith until some contingency required him to adopt another cover name and occupation. But he would not leave the White House; and the secret of his existence would be passed on by word of mouth as a strictly administrative secret from one President to the next. His duty was to do the impossible.

He was a tall, dark-browned capable-looking man in his early sixties and he nodded agreeably as he took his chair.

"Morion," said the President. "We have been contacted from outer space."

A true Stanchly, Morion merely raised one eyebrow quizzically. "Yes, sir?" he said. "And—"

The President told him the whole story. Morion got

up and looked out the window onto the White House lawn. But, of course, he saw nothing.

"What would you like me to do, sir?" he said, returning to his seat.

"Three days," said the President. "I know it sounds ridiculous—but would there be any possible chance of arranging a meeting of the Four of us inside of three days?" Hardly were the words out of his mouth when he realized how incongruous they sounded. "No, no, of course not," he said. "I'm thrown a little off balance by this thing, Morion. Maybe—"

"Well, now, Mr. President," said Morion judiciously. "*All Four*. Well now—"

The President looked at him with hope beginning to revive in his eyes.

"Morion!" he said. "You don't mean—"

"There is a certain possibility," said the Special Secretary. "Considering the gravity and urgency of the situation. Mark you—just a possibility. I'll have to swear you to secrecy, of course."

"Anything, Morion, anything!"

"Very well, then," said the Special Secretary.

He rose from his chair and went to one wall of the room. He pushed aside a picture of a former President that was hanging there and revealed the front of a wall safe. His fingers spun the dial, the safe opened and he removed an old-fashioned wall-phone with a handcrank, from which a long cord led back into the depths of the safe. He carried the phone to the desk and set it down.

"Would you lock the door, Mr. President?" he asked courteously.

The President went to do so, hearing behind his back the shirring ring of the phone as Morion turned the bell crank for one long ring and three shorts. There was a slight pause; and then the Special Secretary spoke into the antiquated mouthpiece.

"Hello? Boris? This is Morion . . . why, yes. A trifle chilly here. Yes, a head cold. No! You don't say. No! Is that a fact? Not really. No—'' He paused, covered the mouthpiece with his hand and turned apologetically to the President.

"If you don't mind, Mr. President," he said. "Perhaps you'd better wait outside, after all."

Bowing his head, the President unlocked the office door and went out, closing it behind him. Outside, he lit a cigarette and paced up and down nervously.

After a short while, he returned to the office door and opened it a crack. The voice of Morion came to his ear, in conversation now with a man apparently named Cecil. The President went back to his pacing for another fifteen minutes and then ventured to open the door again. Morion waved him to come back inside.

"—that's right, Raoul," he was saying into the mouthpiece. "Here tomorrow at three o'clock local time, in the afternoon. Yes . . . Yes. You may bring your man in by the north underground entrance. Yes . . . Yes, indeed. The same to you and Félice. Good-by."

He hung up, returned the phone to the safe, closed the safe and replaced the picture.

"They'll be here tomorrow, sir," he told the President.

"Morion!" said the President, delightedly. "This is miraculous."

"Part of my duties, sir," replied Morion, immovably.

"It is a miracle!" said the President. "What would I do without you? Tell me, Morion—those other men you were talking to. They wouldn't by any chance be the Special Secretaries of—"

"*Mr. President!*" interrupted Morion, deeply shocked.

"Oh, sorry," said the President. "I didn't mean to pry."

"Such information is *absolutely* restricted."

"Sorry."

"Well, now," said Morion, the stern lines of his face relaxing. "No damage was done, fortunately. You understand, though, that the strictest security is necessary in my work."

"Oh, of course," said the President. "Where shall I meet the other—the visitors, Morion?"

"I would suggest right here in your office, Mr. President," said Morion. "Leave the details to me."

"Gladly," said the President. "And now," he added a trifle nervously, "perhaps I'd better go back outside and let Captain Bligh know."

"I would advise that, sir," said Morion Stanchly, nodding soberly.

"I will be honored to attend your meeting," said Captain Bligh, waving a cheerful tentacle as he busily connected pieces of equipment together.

At three o'clock the following day, Captain Bligh and the President were ensconced in the President's office, for the meeting that would start as soon as those others due to be present had arrived. They were talking golf. Or rather the President was talking golf, and the Captain, as befitted a being strongly sports-conscious, was listening.

"The fourteenth on that particular course is a dogleg," the President was saying. "Three hundred and forty-five yards from tee to pin. I decided to take a chance—"

There was a discreet knock on the door and Morion appeared, ushering in, in that order, the Prime Minister of England, the President of France and the Secretary of a Certain Party in Russia.

The President of the United States rose to his feet.

"Gentlemen," he said warmly. "May I present Captain Bligh of the Galactic Confraternity of Intelligences—" and there was the usual bustle of hand and tentacle shaking and personal introductions, which ended with all four of the humans seated around the President's desk and Bligh standing facing them all.

"To start the ball rolling," said our President, "may I say that there is nothing official about this meeting. Just a little—er—get-together."

"Of course," said Great Britain.

"But certainly," said France.

Gordon R. Dickson

"Maybe," said the Secretary of the Certain Party, looking suspiciously at Bligh.

"Well, at any rate," said the President, hurrying along, "since the meeting's to be informal, I suggest we get right down to business. I assume that you have all been informed of the reasons for Captain Bligh's presence on Earth and his willingness to carry to the Confraternity Earth's wish to join the rest of the Galaxy in that great organization to which he belongs. The question in my mind, and I'm sure in yours, is why it would or would not be feasible for us to do so. Captain Bligh has offered to cast some light on this question for us by explaining something of what life is like as a member of the Confraternity and afterward answering any questions we may wish to put him. Captain Bligh?"

He sat down, leaving the floor to the Captain, who waved a tentacle modestly.

"Well, now," he said. "I'll see what I can do to satisfy you people about the Galaxy. As you know, there's nothing official about my visit or myself and there are many octillions of beings who could describe the situation much better than I—you'll meet some of them if you decide to join the Confraternity. But I'll do my best as an amateur and a sports-being to pinch hit for them.

"I don't happen to know the figures on how many races and inhabited worlds there are in the Confraternity. Let's just say that there are enough of both to make their exact counting a thing of merely academic interest. As for why you haven't been visited before—a question my host here asked me on the first day of my arrival—you know how it is. Most of the Galaxy has been explored; and, without any offense, you are in kind of an out-of-the-way corner here. I'd say it was inevitable that someone should come along sooner or later and find you; but not so surprising that it hasn't happened before this, though for all I know, you may have been noted down in some ship's logbook a few thousand years ago—"

"Look here," interrupted the Prime Minister, "if something like that happened, wouldn't the Confraternity have taken some measures to acquaint us with their existence? Now *wouldn't* they?"

"Well—I suppose they might have," said Bligh, a trifle embarrassed. "But a few thousand years ago, I don't imagine you would have been too much interested in interstellar travel. Plenty to keep you occupied here, then, you know. Not too much point in making a big to-do about establishing contact. Of course, I don't *know* if that's what might have happened, it's only a reasonable guess."

"Grumpf!" said the Prime Minister.

"How about these flying saucers?" demanded the President of France.

"Pardon me?" asked Bligh.

The President of France explained.

"Oh," said Bligh. "Chlorophyllsniffers. Perfectly harmless, but a slight menace to low-flying aircraft. Every planet has them flitting in occasionally. A few billion tons of soap bubbles released in your upper atmosphere will scare them off."

The President of France looked uncertain, but made a note of Bligh's answer.

"You're supposed to be telepathic," said the Prime Minister, returning to the attack. "Aren't there some telepaths in this Confraternity that would have received our—er—thought whatchamacallits? *Wouldn't* there?"

"Well, yes," said Bligh. "Bound to be, I suppose. There's some races that can hear an electron scratch its nose in the next spiral nebula. Still, maybe they didn't think it important to mention it. Different people, different ways, you know. It takes all kinds to make a universe."

"Well, dammit!" said the Prime Minister. "Isn't there any organization with the job of finding new cultures?"

"Oh, yes— Exploration," replied Bligh. "But they're mostly a bunch of hobbyists in actual fact, you understand. I mean—no great purpose in finding another new culture when there's so many around to begin with. They might be poking around here; and then they might decide to poke around there. Lots of places, you know, where a new race might pop up.''

This announcement seemed to throw the meeting temporarily into silence. Then the Secretary of the Certain Party leaned over and whispered in the ear of the President of the United States, who drew the other two into a huddle, which ended with them all resuming their places and the President facing Bligh again.

"I ask for all of us," said the President, "whether you are truly representative of the intelligence and culture of the normal member of the Confraternity?"

"Not at all, not at all," Bligh hurried to assure him. "There's every conceivable kind of intelligence and culture in the Confraternity. All kinds of life-forms. All kinds and types of intelligences."

There was a moment's silence.

"Then what—" demanded the Secretary, speaking up unexpectedly and gutturally on his own, "do they have in common between them?"

"Love," replied Bligh blissfully. "Their mutual love and affection."

There was another short silence.

"Love each other, eh?" grunted the Prime Minister.

"Yes," said Bligh, "just as they will love your humans if you become a part of the Confraternity."

All four national representatives withdrew into another conference. Little telepathic snatches of conversation reached the mind of Captain Bligh—"The U.N., of course—but the circumstances—decadent capitalistic emotion—now, my dear fellow, be reasonable—" but he very politely ignored them.

The President broke from the huddle and once more approached Bligh.

"Naturally," he said, "none of us here disparage love as a desirable acquisition, where one people are concerned with others. But—er—there is the practical side to any alliance—a question of tangibles—"

"Tangibles? Why, of course!" cried Bligh. "It's with tangibles that the United Peoples of the Confraternity will wish to express their love toward you. Grants-in-aid and rehabilitation funds from the Galactic Treasury—donations of up-to-date equipment and supplies. Technical assistance, of course."

"Of course?" said four voices at once.

"For little things. Merely to raise your standard of living to average Confraternity level," said Captain Bligh. "Electronic power plants—am I correct in assuming you have not yet cracked the electron?—force shields, weather control units, drugs to conquer all your diseases and reverse the process of aging—all these little home comforts will be donated to you as a matter of course."

The four humans looked at each other.

"And—" continued Bligh, "you will want to hook on to the absolutely free Galaxy-wide transportation system. A terminal will be set up on your Moon immediately. You will find," said Captain Bligh with a roguish telepathic twinkle, "many pleasant vacation spots in the Galaxy with all conveniences furnished free of charge by the local life-form."

He stopped speaking. For a moment, nobody said anything. Then the President cleared his throat and spoke.

"And what kind of tangibles," he said, "would the Confraternity expect us to express our love with?"

"Tangibles? From you? My dear human!" cried Bligh. "What are material things compared to the pure emotion of love? Tangibles can't buy happiness. After all, it's love that makes the Universe go around." He telepathed a quick shake of the head. "No. No. You people will give in return only the rare quality of your affection."

The four men looked doubtful.

"Believe me," went on Captain Bligh, earnestly, "out in the Universe, material things are nothing and less than nothing. With so many differing races, how could a material standard be set up common to all? Useless and less than useless. That is why, among the stars, the common currency is love and a people are rated on the quantity and quality of their capability for affection.'' He beamed at them. ''Permit me to say that you people strike me as having great capabilities along that line. I've only had a chance to glance at things here, but judging from your movies, your books and magazines—''

''Ahem!'' said the President, clearing his throat abruptly. ''Well, now, I must admit you paint an attractive picture, Captain. If you'll excuse us again for a minute—''

Captain Bligh waved a gracefully assenting tentacle, and the four humans withdrew into another huddle. After a few moments of animated conversation, they returned to Bligh.

''I have been deputed to say, for all of us,'' said the President of the United States, ''that while, as I have mentioned before, there is nothing official about this little meeting or ourselves, certainly there seems to be no conceivable reason why we humans should not respond with affection to affection freely given by others.''

''My dear sir!'' cried Bligh, delighted. ''How well you put it. I was sure you would agree.'' His gaze took in all. ''It was inevitable. While I'm not a particularly perceptive being, as beings go, it seemed to me that I could see Love and Affection hovering around you all like an aura. How right I was. Gentlemen, the Universe is yours, just as soon as you make your adjustment.''

''Adjustment?'' said the Prime Minister.

''Of course. But a mere bagatelle. A nothing,'' said Captain Bligh. ''A mere matter of love extended logically to include all living creatures. A moment's adjustment by a metabolic ordinator, completely painless. Clicksnap and it's over and you are all energy eaters.''

''Eaters of what?'' said the President of France.

''Energy. My dear sirs,'' said Captain Bligh. ''You surely would not wish to continue with your present diets. How could you eat something you love? And love, like charity, begins at home. Moreover—'' he went on—''how could you expect the rest of the Universe to accept you otherwise? Consider the similarity of shapes. For example, what a Red-eyed Inchos would think on arriving to set up a modern weather control system for your planet, if he should see one of you sitting down to—'' the Captain shuddered—''a roast turkey, except for a slight difference in size, the exact image of himself. Similarly with a Lullar and a barbecued pig, or a Brvandig and a baked sturgeon.''

After a moment, the President of the United States cleared his throat.

''Perhaps—'' he suggested, ''a strictly vegetarian—''

''Mr. President,'' said Bligh, interrupting with dignity, ''I am myself only one of uncounted myriads, but some of my best friends are plants.'' He fixed the President with a stern eye. ''I hate to think what a Snurlop would say if he happened to see a loaf of your bread and imagined a child of his own being harvested, threshed, ground and even *baked*!''

''But now—'' interposed the President of France hastily, ''certainly liquids such as wine—''

''Please!'' choked Bligh, turning green. He staggered and leaned against the desk beside him. Hastily the President of the United States fanned the Captain's face with a major-general's appointment that happened to be lying close at hand. Slowly, the color returned to Bligh's gums.

''Please,'' he repeated feebly, ''amputation, crushing, fermentation—horrible.'' He shook his head. ''No—no liquids.''

''Water,'' said the Prime Minister.

Bligh looked at him. ''Think,'' he said, ''just think of the minute organisms that must die, either through being boiled alive, poisoned with chlorine, or digested living, to provide you with ordinary drinking water. Why, the Fellibriks of—''

''Yes, yes,'' interrupted the President hastily, ''I'm sure your little friends would be shocked. If you will excuse us just once more—''

"Certainly," replied Bligh, faintly, sagging against the desk.

Stout sports-being as he was, the images just conjured up by the recent conversation had turned him pale inside (he was incapable of turning pale outside). As he breathed heavily and tried to recover, little bits of conversation reached him.

"Borscht—civet de lapin—rare steak—roast beef and Yorkshire pudding—sacrifice—solidarity—"

Slowly, but with the look of men who have been through the fire and emerged triumphant, the four representatives of humanity turned back to the representative of the Galactic Confederation of Races.

So that is how peace has come to the world. We are united at last as we have never before been in history, united as one people behind what has come to be known as the UnBligh Doctrine, and which is now emblazoned in letters of gold over the front doors of the U.N. Building.

No government or individual or collection of individuals shall have the power at any time to come between any other individual and the due and lawful exercise of his appetite.

Let the Galactic Confederation of Races beware!

The Rebels

"Well, gentlemen?" said Dr. Stanhope Turner, in jagged, ice-like tones. "Well, gentlemen, what have you got to say for yourselves?"

Peter Stoddard and Ridgley Barr stared defiantly back at the president of Garibaldi College. William Winkely blushed and dropped his eyes. He was a timid soul, Winkely.

Indeed, he was the first to admit his own timidity. And, in general, his archaeological colleagues did not hold the fact against him. Not but that there had been one dark moment in the field trip from which the three had just returned; a moment when a gang of desert Arabs had attempted to use the tent in which they had stored a priceless find of early Egyptian pottery for target practice. Stoddard, it was, and Barr, who had rushed from the dinner table and routed the barbarians with only the table knives they held in their hands.

Winkely had hesitated.

It was a hesitation which no true archaeologist could ever condone. True, Winkely did not have a table knife in his hand at the moment, like his companions. Only a fork. But that should have made no difference. Definitely, beyond the shadow of a doubt, his spirit had been tried and found lacking.

But there was an additional reason for Winkely's present agony. It was he who had got the three into their present predicament. Stoddard and Barr were covering up for him at the immediate moment. He knew it and appreciated it; but did not have the nerve to face Dr. Turner alone.

For it was Winkely who, with the best intentions in the world, had cultivated the acquaintance of a local mystic living near their excavation. The mystic (he was an apostatic Yeziri) had taught Winkely simple telekinesis, which, roughly speaking, is the ability to move material objects by power of mind alone, in order that the archaeologists could do a more thorough job of excavation. And Winkely had, in turn, passed the skill on to Stoddard and Barr. Shortly, the three could leave the shovels and whisk brooms to work by themselves and devote their time exclusively to the fascinating business of classifying their finds.

Again, it was Winkely, who, when the three returned to the States, let fall the information about their telekinetic methods of excavation. He had even demonstrated it to a reporter by lifting the nearest taxicab six feet into the air by mental power alone. Winkely had conceived the demonstration as an interesting parlor trick. It turned out to be the material for nation-wide publicity.

Bad publicity, in the eyes of Dr. Stanhope Turner.

"What are we here, at Garibaldi College?" he had asked, with some reason. "Sideshow barkers?" And summoned the three immediately to his office.

"Well, gentlemen?" he inquired, when they were assembled. "Well, gentlemen, what have you got to say for yourselves?"

"Dr. Turner," replied Stoddard with some asperity, "Your question seems to imply that we need to defend some reprehensible action. I consider it unjust."

"And so do I," added Barr, stoutly.

Winkely shuddered. Stoddard and Barr were young men. As for Winkely, his forehead had made two large, v-shaped sallies into his hairline and, barring a new medical miracle (probably not to be hoped for in the near future) would hold the territory gained. He, alone, would never have replied so brashly.

Dr. Turner's respectable stomach swelled with wrath. Challenged, to his face, and by mere instructors who were not even related to outstanding alumni!

"If you please," he snorted. "I will be the judge of the justness of your actions where this college is concerned. Garibaldi has been held up to public ridicule by your charlatanism, your display of kitchen magic."

Stoddard's black hair flopped rebelliously forward over his eyes. Barr's jaw crept pugnaciously out. Into both their attitudes was creeping the same wild battle-light which had sent the desert Arabs flying from their table knives. But Dr. Turner was no armed nomad. He was opening his mouth to utter further thunders when Winkely meekly interrupted.

"But it really works," said Winkely, appeasingly.

"*Mr.* Winkely," snapped Dr. Turner, turning on the little man with fine sarcasm. "What on earth has that got to do with it?"

"I only thought—" began Winkely. But Dr. Turner steamrollered over him.

"It is not *accepted*!" he roared, pounding his desk with one large fist. "Telekinesis may be as pure a science as—as—physics, for all I know—or care. But as long as I'm President, it will not be treated with other than contempt, here at Garibaldi. Possibly, when ninety percent of the other outstanding institutions in this country have accepted it, we may consider recognizing the subject here. But even then, even then, gentlemen, I promise you it's chance will be a slim one."

There was a momentary space of deathly stillness in the office following his awful statement. Dr. Turner allowed the anger to fade slowly from his massive face.

"What do you want us to do about it?" demanded Stoddard with youthful rashness.

Dr. Turner's white brows drew together into a forest of inexpressible grandeur.

"Gentlemen," he said solemnly, looking in each of their faces in turn. "You must issue a public retraction to the papers."

"What!" cried Barr.

"Retract!" thundered Dr. Turner, drawing himself up to his full height.

"Never!" replied Stoddard and Barr with one voice.

Winkley gave an ambiguous squeak which could be taken whichever way a listener might feel inclined to take it.

"What!" said Dr. Turner in his turn. "Consider what this means, gentlemen. You will be cast out of your positions here at Garibaldi. You will be unable to get another post at any other respectable institution. Think it over."

"Never," repeated Barr. "I don't know about men from other departments—" Dr. Turner, who was originally from History, started angrily—"but an archaeologist never retracts."

"Then," roared Dr. Turner, "Garibaldi will disown you."

"Oh, will it?" said Stoddard, nastily. "Then I resign."

"And I resign," said Barr.

Winkely gave another ambiguous squeak.

"You can't resign!" said Dr. Turner in a towering rage. "You're already discharged, all three of you!"

Sadly, the three archaeologists stood on the steps of the college Administration Building, watching the sun go down. Already they seemed to be intruders in the place where they had studied and worked for years. Behind them the academic world was locked and barred, forever shut to them, who up to this time, had been like fragile, scholarly children, kindly sheltered by its stout walls from the crude world outside.

"What are your plans, Barr?" Stoddard asked his friend.

"I don't know," said Barr. "I don't know at all."

"How about you, Wink?" Stoddard asked. Winkely sighed wistfully.

"I am not completely without friends," he said in a sad voice. "One of my former pupils has gotten me a position as night janitor in the Grisley Office Building downtown—for old time's sake.''

"Well, as for me," said Stoddard, in a strong voice, fire lighting up his rugged face, ''I'm through with all this, forever.'' He indicated the campus with a wide sweep of his arm.

"Society has cast me out!'' he cried in a ringing voice. "Let Society beware! I am not made to vegetate in some crass job. I will take to the road and become a bindlestiff.''

"And I, too!'' echoed Barr, with sudden enthusiasm. "I turn my face against them.''

"Right!'' said Stoddard. "Two human wolves, outlaws of their kind. Put 'er there, pardner.''

They shook hands with grim purpose.

"Come with us, Winkely,'' Barr begged. But Winkely shook his head.

"It isn't for me,'' he said, resignedly. ''I'm not as young as you two. I don't have the spirit for open defiance and my physical weaknesses would probably hold you back. Thanks anyway.''

"Trust us,'' said Stoddard, taking the older man's hand in his own. "We won't forget you, Wink.''

Touched, Winkely shook hands with each of them in turn.

"Good-by,'' he said. "If you ever need me, you know where to reach me. Grisley Office Building, between six P.M. and six A.M. Daytimes, you will probably find me feeding pigeons in the park.''

"Good-by,'' echoed Stoddard, and Barr. And, with a last handshake, they turned away from him and set out together across the campus, into the rays of the setting sun. Winkely watched the two dark figures, like shadows in a dream, dwindle in the distance. A tear ran down his tanned cheek. From now on he would be completely alone in the world.

Winkely could never afterward remember with precision just how he slipped into his new job, like a hermit crab into a new shell. It was an imperceptible change, but a profound one. Night after night, he grew more at home in the long, dim corridors and the empty offices; and gradually an affection for his inanimate surrounding began to creep over him as the months went by.

He did his cleaning by telekinesis; and, as he sat watching the mop scurry along the halls, mopping, and the wastebaskets emptying themselves, it was not surprising that he should come to personify the animated tools of his new trade. Indeed, if anything, they seemed to respond to the affection his lonely little heart gave so freely. There was one dust rag which appeared to love to sit on his knee for hours at a time, while he stroked its grey cloth and told it stories of his field trips.

And it was this storytelling to the dust rag that gave him the idea of finally clearing his name.

Winkely had no hope of changing the minds of his contemporaries. No, innocent of the passions of men as he was, the little archaeologist knew enough to be sure there was no hope of that. But, one night after he fell silent with the dust rag on his knee, the thought occurred to him that he might at least set the story before Posterity, and that Posterity, judging and understanding him, would not then hold him cowardly in refusing to follow the ways of the open road as his companions had done.

At this thought, he fell into an absent, musing state, in which he looked back on the days of that last fatal field trip. How happy he had been then. Even—yes—even in the moment following his disgrace in shirking combat with the Arab vandals, he had been happy. For then life stretched out before him, smooth and uninterrupted; teaching, with luck, a few more field trips, retirement, and then, perhaps a modest pamphlet or two in which he discussed recent discoveries or argued the relative age of North American pottery invention. And now, all this had been put forever beyond his reach. Future archaeologists would sneer at his name. If only he could prove the innocence of his motives in using telekinesis for excavational purposes.

In this dreamy mood, he scarcely noticed the stray

impulse that made him send a piece of paper skittering across a desk in the large insurance office in which he now sat. He watched it idly as it slipped into position in the typewriter, was rolled up by the platen and indented by the tab button.

His lips moved thoughtfully.

"I begin this book," said Winkely, half to himself. The typewriter keys commenced to click busily, "with many misgivings. Above all, I am conscious of my own inability to relate the discovery and use of telekinesis in Archaeology, in that manner best calculated to inform my readers. I feel myself, at this moment, desperately unworthy of putting before the world exactly what took place on that field trip and afterward, on the return of myself and my two colleagues, Peter Stoddard and Ridgely Barr, to this country."

The dust rag slid unheeded to the floor as Winkely rose to his feet and began to pace the room, up and down the long rows of typewriter laden desks. Occasionally he would stop and peer at his own machine to see how it was doing. It typed with remarkable neatness and a minimum of errors.

"Perhaps some of you who read this may know," Winkely continued, "what our purpose was in making that particular field trip. We were investigating a recent field of glazed pottery in the lower Nile area. . . ."

As he talked, the room seemed to fade about him. Imperceptibly, its outlines were replaced by those of his old classroom at Garibaldi. The mops, the buckets, the brooms, the cleaning compound, went on with their work in all parts of the building, lonely, automatically, and all but completely forgotten.

The months slipped by. Now, in the long insurance office, it was not one, but ten typewriters that clicked busily, as Winkely, with a skill born of long practice, dictated mentally at a speed that no one machine could sustain. He paced the room with short, jerky strides, occasionally pausing to glance out the tall office windows at the roofs of the dark buildings around him, on the rooftops which were already beginning to be capped by the white snow that fell steadily and softly upon them, covering their dark, sooty surfaces like white, sugary frosting on a chocolate cake.

"—after proving to me," Winkely was dictating, "that neither he nor I existed, Murad Ali was going on to prove that nothing else existed either, when he perceived that my intelligence was not adapted to taking such a great step in one jump. So he picked up a stick by way of illustration, and, placing it in the air between us, some six inches above the ground—where it stayed—told me to try and move it—"

The door to the insurance office swung suddenly open and two rough-looking figures charged into the room.

"—this I was unable to do—" Winkely continued to dictate automatically. Then comprehension struck him.

"Stoddard!" he cried. "Barr!" And hurled himself joyfully forward upon his two young friends. They surrounded him gleefully, slapping him on the back and shaking his hand so energetically that it was a moot point whether it would be torn off or not.

The hubbub of greeting over, Winkely had time to stand back and take a square look at his friends. Both were looking remarkably healthy, but then they always had, so that was not too telling a detail. The greatest difference was in their voices. Both had acquired deep, carrying tones well adapted to shouting down arguments and threatening people. They moved with a loose swagger that captured Winkely's attention at once. No one could look squarely at them and fail to recognize at once that they were rugged sorts of characters.

"We've been kicked out of twelve towns," Barr informed Winkely, happily.

"Thirteen, wasn't it?" said Stoddard deprecatingly.

"You're right," said Barr. "It was thirteen. I wasn't going to count Las Vegas."

"Oh, Las Vegas," said Stoddard, with a slight sneer. "That's where we broke jail."

"*Broke jail!*" gasped Winkely.

"Nothing to it," said Barr. "They were trying to hold us for a sanity hearing. 'What nonsense!' I said to Stoddard, and we telekineticized our way out."

"Did you get hurt?" inquired Winkely, round-eyed.

"With only steel, concrete and twenty armed guards to stop us?" said Stoddard. "Of course not. I haven't done a day's work since I left," he added proudly.

"Neither have I," said Barr.

"But how did you eat?" asked Winkely.

"Oh, handouts," said Stoddard, casually. "We never went more than three or four days without something. And I needn't tell you that shelter was no problem, since camping out in a howling blizzard at forty below zero is child's play for any archaeologist with experience in fieldtrips."

Winkely was struck speechless.

Then a sudden thought galvanized him. "How did you get in here?" he asked. "I must have forgotten to lock the street door." And he started to hurry from the room. Stoddard restrained him with one strong hand.

"Telekinesis, of course," said Stoddard. "We used it to unlock the door and quiet the burglar alarm, too."

"Of course," said Winkely, relieved. "How stupid of me." He struck his brow apologetically as if to punish it for containing insufficient brains.

"And what have you been doing?" asked Stoddard.

"Oh, the same old thing," said Winkely, deprecatingly. "Mopping, dusting, nightwatching. By telekinesis, of course. Nothing interesting like your breaking jail and being kicked out of towns."

"Oh well," Stoddard consoled him. "We can't all lead interesting lives—"

"Hey!" interrupted Barr, suddenly, pulling a sheet of paper out of the nearest typewriter. "What's this?"

Winkely blushed.

"Oh, that," he said.

"Yes, this," said Barr, waving a sheet of paper in the air. "What is it?"

"Oh, *that*!" said Winkely, with the energetic air of someone who has just had some knotty problem explained to him. "Nothing."

"What *kind* of a nothing?" asked Stoddard.

"Well—" Winkely coughed a little, deprecatingly. "It's just something I thought I'd leave to be published after my death. Memoirs, of a sort. About our last field trip."

"It is?" cried Stoddard. He reached hurriedly for the pile of completed manuscript and began to skim through it. Barr joined him.

Winkely watched them, standing nervously first on one foot and then on the other. He hummed a few bars of "Sweet Adeline." He wandered to the window, stared out for a while, and then came back to stand watching them in an agony of embarrassment and suspense.

"It's nothing," he hastily assured them, as they put the last pages down. "Nothing at all. Really."

Stoddard and Barr looked at each other.

"Stoddard," said Barr. "I'm ashamed of myself."

"And so am I," said Stoddard. "Here we've been charging around the country, breaking out of jails, heedlessly enjoying ourselves, while Wink here put his nose to the grindstone and went quietly to work at clearing our reputations." He turned to the older man and held out his hand.

"You're a better man than I am, William Winkely," he said simply and impressively.

Somewhat bemused—but touched, nonetheless—Winkely shook hands solemnly with each of his erstwhile colleagues.

"Oh, it's all right," he said shyly, "I was just filling in my spare time. I don't know what you could have done to help, anyway."

Barr brought his fist down with a crash on a nearby desktop.

"What we could have done—hah!" he cried, his eyes flashing fire.

"What we can still do," echoed Stoddard enthusiastically. "We're still in time to get the story properly published for you, Wink."

"I thought," said Winkely timorously, "of paying the publication costs out of my life savings as a janitor. Sort of a private printing of a limited edition of a hundred and fifty or two hundred copies."

"Hundred!" snorted Stoddard. "A hundred thousand. And they'll pay you. Just leave all that end of the business to Barr and myself."

"Thanks," said Winkely.

"Think nothing of it," said Stoddard, magnanimously. And Barr nodded to show his agreement.

It was Christmas before the manuscript was finished, spring before it was sold, and fall before it was published. Its sales zoomed almost immediately to unprecedented heights. Stoddard and Barr returned from New York to find Winkely surrounded by huge piles of mail and feverishly opening letters.

"Success!" cried Stoddard in ringing tones, as they closed the door to Winkely's apartment behind them.

"Winkely," said Barr affectionately to the little archaeologist, "you're famous."

Winkely rolled tortured eyes up from his correspondence.

"What am I going to do?" he inquired frantically. "They all want something or other from me. Listen—" he reached into the pile in front of him and picked out a letter at random.

Acme Wrecking Co.
Tuglo, Penn.

Dear Mr. Winkely:
    I have read your book with a great deal of pleasure; and it occurs to me that an arrangement might be

worked out between yourself and my firm which would be of great advantage to both of us.

Would you care to drop down to Tuglo at my expense and talk the matter over further?

Very truly yours,
Gus Hammerstall, Pres.

"Well—that one isn't so bad," said Winkely. "They only want to offer me a job or something. Where's one of the other kind? Oh yes—"

Dear Mr. Wankly:

Three yrs. ago Granpa come in from the farm for a short visit and moved in the front bedroom. It has been three years now and he is out getting drunk on corn likker and chasing the girls every night the old rip. Like I say, it has been three yrs, and I can't look the nehbors in the face. I would take it kindly if you telephoned him back to the farm.

Much obliged,

Doris Mae Leona Wilters (Mrs.)

"Not that I could do anything about that one even if I wanted to," said Winkely. "There's no return address. Still—"

Barr had been pawing through the stack of unopened mail. Suddenly he interrupted, holding up an envelope.

"Here's one from Garibaldi!" he exclaimed.

Winkely's face lit up. Eagerly he snatched the letter from Barr. There was a suspicious tremble to his fingers as he tore it open. But as he read the brief message inside his face fell.

"What is it, Wink?" demanded Stoddard.

"I thought it might be from Turner," he said. "But it's only from one of the College Trustees." He sighed deeply and read it to them.

Dear Dr. Winkely:

I and several other of the Trustees at Garibaldi College were very sorry to see you and Mr. Stoddard and Mr. Barr leave when you did. As a matter of fact, we protested the matter to Dr. Turner, but were overruled.

It has occurred to us that the gratifying success of your recent book gives good grounds for reopening the matter of your reinstatement. There is a regular Trustee's meeting next Thursday, at which Dr. Turner will be present, and we intend to confront him with the question at that time. Assuming that you, Mr. Stoddard and Mr. Barr, are still interested in reappointment, would you do us the favor of appearing at that meeting to say a few words on your own behalf?

Sincerely yours,
Thomas Melham
Secy. Board of Trustees
Garibaldi College.

"Humph!" said Stoddard. "That won't do any good. The Trustees at Garibaldi are just a rubber stamp for the President. Everyone knows that."

"That's right," said Barr. He looked sympathetically at the older man. "Might as well forget about it, Wink."

But Winkely's lips were unexpectedly set in a thin line and there was a gritty look of determination in his eye.

"After all," he said, suddenly. "What have we got to lose?"

Stoddard and Barr stared at him in surprise.

"Why, Wink," said Stoddard. "What's gotten into you?"

"The alternative," said Winkely. He cast a look at the pile of mail and shuddered. "The Acme Wrecking Company and Mrs. Wilters. It just came home to me." He looked at his two friends. "How would you like to spend the rest of your life tearing down houses and moving grandparents?"

"But you don't have to—" began Barr.

"Never mind," said Winkely, with a firmness entirely foreign to his usual gentle nature. "This is at least a chance and we're going to take it."

The following Thursday was a bright autumn day.

Much to Winkely's surprise, as they rode to the Administration Building by taxi, he noted a large number of students and other people milling around the campus. He pointed them out to Stoddard and Barr. His two young friends looked serious.

"The students are in an ugly frame of mind," said Barr.

"That's right," agreed Stoddard, solemnly, "by and large the students are for you. You have become something of a popular hero. I'm afraid that if Turner doesn't reinstate *you*, at least, blood will be spilt."

"Over me?" said Winkely, astonished.

"I'm afraid so," said Stoddard. He hesitated, and then went on. "Didn't you even notice the large number of students in your *Introduction to Geology* course?"

"Why, yes," said Winkely, "now that you mention it—"

"And tell me, Wink," said Barr. "When was the last time you flunked a student?"

"Well—er—" said Winkely, embarrassed. "I—er—well now—"

"I'll tell you," said Barr. "Everyone on campus knows, since it was a historic occasion. It was five years ago, and the man was that bank robber who was masquerading as a student to hide from the FBI."

"But—" stammered Winkely.

"No buts about it, Wink," Stoddard said, firmly. "For years now, the majority of students at Garibaldi have been taking Geology from you to satisfy their requirements in science for graduation. You have become an institution and those students out there are desperate. Seventy-three point five per cent of them are facing a dismal future in which they remain undergraduates forever. If Turner should refuse to reinstate you now, they may well tear him limb from limb. In which case the three of us will be guilty of murder."

Winkely gasped.

"Can't we talk them out of it?" he cried. Barr looked thoughtful.

"The students—possibly, yes," he said. "But you noticed the other, older people on campus, too?"

"Yes," quavered Winkely, his heart palpitating.

"Those are parents," said Barr. "If the students remain undergraduates, the parents will have to support them for the rest of their lives. I doubt if we could talk them out of anything."

Winkely shuddered.

"If only Dr. Turner weren't so stubborn," he said, unhappily.

Thomas Melham, the slight, dark-haired trustee who had written Winkely the letter, met them in the outer office of the board room, where Trustee meetings were held. He was mopping his brow.

"Word has gotten out," he said as Winkely, Stoddard and Barr came up.

"We know," answered Stoddard in low tones. "The students and their parents outside know all about this meeting."

"So does Dr. Turner," said Melham. He motioned them to the closed door that separated the office from the board room.

"Charlatans—hogwash—coercion—never give in—" muffled by the heavy door, but understandable enough, a few words in Turner's angry basso came filtering through to them. Melham shook his head sadly.

"I'm afraid it's no use," he said. "The student-parent threat has merely got his back up. Listen to him a minute!"

From the Board Room a sudden bellow of rage took cognizance of a thousand-voiced chant which had begun under the administration windows.

"We want Winkely!" roared the voices outside. "WE WANT WINKELY!"

The three friends looked at each other. Winkely took a deep breath.

"Come on!" he said—and before any of the others could stop him, he had pulled open the door and gone striding into the Board Room.

221

His appearance struck Turner momentarily dumb. Winkely profited by the moment's respite to walk the length of the Board Room.

"Well Viper?" inquired Turner furiously from the far end of the room. "Don't you think you can intimidate me!"

Winkely faced the enraged College President. His face was pale, but his voice was firm.

"I have a few words to say," he said. "Will you listen!"

"Never!" roared Turner. A babble of pleas and protests rose immediately from the board members.

"Very well!" shouted Turner, flinging himself down in his chair at the head of the table and folding his arms implacably. "For five minutes!"

Winkely opened his mouth to speak, but at that moment a new sound began to well up from the crowd of students outside. For a moment, none of them in the room could identify it. But then the words came sharp and clear, even through the third story window. The crowd was singing; and the song was *"We'll Hang Dr. Turner From a Sour Apple Tree."*

His face purpling, Dr. Turner leaped back to his feet. "No!" he roared. "After that I won't—"

"Turner!" The sudden command in Winkely's voice rang through the Board Room. Dr. Turner froze, his arm upraised. Slowly, he lowered it and sank stiffly back into his seat.

"Dr. Turner!" said Winkely huskily. "You made a promise and I expect you to keep it. With your permission, I will go on with what I was going to say."

Turner's face flushed and his lips trembled slightly. But he said nothing.

"Er—" Winkely looked around desperately.

"The quality of mercy is not strained," he babbled. "It droppeth as the gentle rain from heaven—"

The Trustees looked at Winkely in surprise. Then they looked at each other. Finally they looked at Turner,

222

but the College President only nodded as if encouraging Winkely to go on.

"It is twice blessed—" continued Winkely, and with a few errors and transposed lines he struggled through the rest of the famous quotation from Shakespeare's *Merchant of Venice* in which Portia attempts to soften Shylock's bitter heart.

To the surprise of everyone present, Dr. Turner made no move to interrupt.

"Everyone has the right of free speech," Winkely went on somewhat wildly. The perspiration was standing out on his forehead. "Why not the right of free telekinesis?"

Dr. Turner nodded.

"Ah, you agree," cried Winkely. "I knew you would. Consider that we—er—stand at the threshold of a new science. Will you be the one to hold it back?"

Dr. Turner shook his head.

"Listen!" said Winkely, with sudden inspiration. "I heard the voice of the future outside that window—" he paused to let the yells of the students outside come floating into them—"do you recognize it for what it is?"

Dr. Turner nodded.

"Then may I ask once more," said Winkely, "that you reconsider the case of Stoddard, Barr and myself. Do what your heart impels you, but let me ask once more that you reinstate us."

A long moment of awful stillness, followed. A terrific struggle seemed to be going on within Dr. Turner. His face became even more ruddy than usual and his large body shook with inner emotion. Finally, slowly, he nodded his head.

The Trustees burst into cheers. They leaped up from their chairs. Reappointment papers for Winkely, Stoddard and Barr were pushed in front of him, and, slowly, ponderously, he signed them. Melham, the Secretary to the Board, rushed up to Winkely.

"Marvelous—uh—speech," he said, shaking the little archaeologist. "Tell me, how—"

He was interrupted by the heavy form of Dr. Turner, pushing his way through the crowd. Having signed the papers, he had risen, and was now headed out of the room. He nodded absently to those board members who attempted to speak to him, brushed past them and went out the door.

"Excuse me—" said Winkely, tearing himself away from Melham and diving after the College President. Stoddard and Barr followed him. Melham stared after them for a second, then turned away and hurried to the open window, where he leaned out, waving papers and telling the students below all about the happy conclusion of the meeting.

The students cheered. The parents cheered louder. Happiness reigned supreme on the campus.

"Viper!" snarled the President of Garibaldi College, between his teeth.

"But Dr. Turner!" pleaded Winkely, "I did it for your own good."

The four of them—Dr. Turner, Winkley, Stoddard and Barr, were standing in a little park some three blocks away from the campus. Distant cheers still drifted to their ears.

"For my good!" echoed Turner. "*Ha!*" And he laughed a cold, sarcastic laugh.

"For your good," maintained Winkely stoutly. "The students and their parents were up in arms. I was given to understand that if you refused to reinstate us you would never leave the campus in one piece. I took the only course I could perceive. Using telekinesis, I held your body and vocal chords in a paralyzing grip and made you nod your head at the appropriate moments."

Turner snorted.

"I know what you're thinking," Winkely went on, gathering strength as he spoke. "You think I wasn't interested in you—I just saw a way to get our jobs back. Just to disabuse you of that notion," said Winkely determinedly, "I resign."

Stoddard and Barr opened their mouths to resign also, but Turner was before them.

"Oh no, you don't!" he snapped. "Try to get out of

that appointment and I'll sue you for everything you ever hope to own. You—" he said, shaking a heavy forefinger under Winkely's nose—"have made a fool out of me for the last time. Making me sit there and nod my head like a—like a—nincompoop! No indeed, you will not resign! You will remain on the staff of Garibaldi as an employee: and as an employee you will take orders—from me." Dr. Turner laughed with a harsh note of triumph. "I know you, Winkely. After a few days back in your old position you will obey my slightest whim rather than risk losing it again. And why?" he thrust his face close to Winkely. "Because you are a scholar, and to scholars their work means more than anything else in the world. No," finished Turner, throwing back his shoulders and surveying him with unconcealed glee, "your day is over, Winkely. I shall never be made a fool of again!"

And with that, the President of Garibaldi College, turned on his heel and strode off. So flushed was he with his victory that he failed entirely to notice that only the toes of his black, well-polished shoes were contacting the pavement. His heels trod thin air; and the general impression he unconsciously gave as he disappeared down the block in the direction of the campus, was that of a fat and elderly ballet dancer prancing like a balloon into the distance.

"Stoddard," said Winkely, in a tone of mild reproach, "You shouldn't have—really!"

The Mousetrap

There was nothing to do. There was no place to go. He swam up to consciousness on the sleepy languor of that thought. Nothing to do, no place to go, tomorrow is forever. Could sleep, but body wants to wake up. His body was a cork floating up from deep water, up, up, to the surface.

He opened his eyes. Sunlight and blue sky; sky so blue that if you looked at it long enough you could begin to imagine yourself falling into it. No clouds; just blue, blue sky.

He felt as if he had slept the clock of eternity around and back again until the hands of time were in the same position they had held when he went to sleep. When had that been? It was a long time ago, too far back to remember. He stopped worrying about it.

He lay supine, his arms flung wide, his legs asprawl. He became conscious of short blades of grass tickling the backs of his hands. There was a tiny breeze from somewhere that now and again brushed his face with its cool wing. And an edge of white cloud was creeping into the patch of blue that gradually filled his field of vision.

Slowly, physical awareness crept back to him. He felt smooth, loose clothing lying lightly against his skin, the expansion and contraction of his chest, the hard ground pressure against the long length of his back. And suddenly he was complete. The thousand disconnected sensations flowed together and became one. He was aware of himself as a single united entity, alive and alone, lying stretched out, exposed and vulnerable in an unknown place.

Brain pulsed, nerves tensed, muscles leaped.

He sat up.

"Where am I?"

He sat on a carpet of green turf that dipped gradually away ahead and on either side of him to a ridiculously close horizon. He twisted his head and looked over his shoulder. Behind him was a gravel walk leading to a small building that looked very airy and light. The front, beneath a thick ivory roof that soared flat out, apparently unsupported for several yards beyond the front itself, was one large window. He could see, like looking into the cool dimness of a cave, big, comfortable chairs, low tables, and what might possibly be a viseo.

Hesitantly, he rose to his feet and approached the building.

At the entrance he paused. There was no door, only a variable force-curtain to keep the breezes out; and he pushed his hand through it carefully, as if to test the atmosphere inside. But there was only the elastic stretch and sudden yield that was like pushing your fist through the wall of a huge soap bubble, and then a pleasant coolness beyond, so he withdrew his hand and, somewhat timidly, entered.

The room illuminated itself. He looked around. The chairs, the tables, everything was just as he had seen it from outside, through the window. And the thing that looked like a viseo *was* a viseo.

He walked over to it and examined it curiously. It was one of the large models, receiver and record-player, with its own built-in library of tapes. He left it and went on through an interior doorway into the back of the house.

Here were two more rooms, a bedroom and a kitchen. The bed was another force-field—expensive and luxurious. The kitchen had a table and storage lockers through whose transparent windows he could see enough eatables and drinkables stored there to last one man a hundred years.

At the thought of one man living in this lap of luxury for a hundred years, the earlier realization that he was alone came back to him. This was not his place. It did not belong to him. The owner could not be far off.

He went hurriedly back through the living room and out into the sunlight. The green turf stretched away on every side of him, empty, unrelieved by any other living figure.

"Hello!" he called.

His voice went out and died, without echoes, without answer. He called again, his voice going a trifle shrill.

"Hello? Anybody here? Hello! *Hello!*"

There was no answer. He looked down the gravel path to his right, to the short horizon. He looked down the path to his left and his breath caught in his throat.

He began to run in a senseless, brain-numbing, chest-constricting panic.

The grass streamed silently by on both sides of him, and his feet pounded on the gravel of the path. He ran until his lungs heaved with exhaustion and the pounding of his heart seemed to shake his thin body, when at last fatigue forced him to a halt. He stood and looked around him.

The building was out of sight now, and he found himself on the edge of a forest of tall flowers. Ten feet high or more, they lay like a belt across his way, and the path led through them. Green-stemmed, with long oval leaves gracefully reaching out, with flat, broad-petaled blue blossoms spread to the bright sky, they looked like the graceful creations of a lost dream. There was no odor, but his head seemed to whirl when he looked at them.

Somehow they frightened him; their height and their multitude seemed to look down on him as an intruder. He hesitated at that point where the path began to wind among them, no longer straight and direct as it had been through the grass. He felt irrational fear at the thought of pushing by them—but the loneliness behind him was worse.

He went on.

Once among the flowers, he lost all sense of time and distance. There was nothing but the gravel beneath his feet, a patch of blue sky overhead and the flowers, only the flowers. For a while he walked; and then, panic taking him again at the apparent endlessness of the green stems, he burst into a fear-stricken run which ended only when exhaustion once more forced him to walk. After that, he plodded hopelessly, his desire to escape fighting a dull battle with increasing weariness.

He came out of it suddenly. One moment the flowers were all around him; then the path took an abrupt twist to the right and he was standing on the edge of a new patch of turf through which the path ran straight as ever.

He stopped, half disbelieving what he saw. With a little inarticulate grunt of relief, he stepped free of the flower-shadowed pathway and went forward between new fields of grass.

He did not have much farther to go. In a few minutes he topped a small rise and his walk came to an end.

There, in front of him, was the building.

The very same building he had run away from earlier.

He approached it slowly, trying to cling to the hope that it was not the same building, that he had somehow gone somewhere else, rather than that he had traveled in a circle. But the identity was too complete. There was the large window, the chairs, the viseo. There was the door to the bedroom and the one to the kitchen.

Moving like a man in a dream, he walked forward and into the house.

He knew where he was going now. He remembered what he had seen before—a bottle of light, amber-colored liquid among the stores in the kitchen. He found it among a thickly crowded bank of others of its kind and took off the cap humbly. He put the bottle to his lips.

The liquor burned his throat. Tears sprang to his eyes at the fire of it and he was glad, for the sensation gave him a feeling of reality that he had not yet had among the dreamlike emptiness of his surroundings.

Taking the bottle, he went outside to the grass in front of the building.

"This is good," he thought, taking another drink, and sitting down on the grass. "This is here and now, a departure point from which to figure out the situation. *I drink, therefore I am.* The beginning of a philosophy."

He drank again.

"But where do I go from there? Where is this? Who am I?"

He frowned suddenly. Well, who was he? The question went groping back and lost itself in a maze of shadows where his memory should have been. Almost, but not quite, he knew. He shook his head impatiently.

"Never mind that now. Plenty of time to figure that out later. The thing is to discover where I am, first."

Where was he, then? The drink was beginning to push soft fingers of numbness into his mind. The grass was Earth grass and the building was a human-type structure. But the flowers weren't like anything on Earth. Were they like anything on any other planet he'd ever been on?

He wrinkled his forehead in a frown, trying to remember. If only he could recall where he had been before he woke up! He thought he had been on Earth, but he wasn't sure. The things he wanted to remember seemed to skitter away from his recollection just before he touched them.

He lay back on the grass.

Where was he? He was in a place where one walked in circles. He was in a place where things were too perfect to be natural. The grass looked like a lawn and there were acres of it. There were acres of flowers, too. But the grass was real grass; and from what he'd seen of the flowers, they were real and natural as well.

Yet there was something wrong. He felt it. There was a strange air of artificiality about it all.

He lay back on the grass, staring at the sky and taking

occasional drinks from the bottle. Without realizing it, he was getting very drunk.

His mind cast about like the nose of a hunting dog. Something about the place in which he found himself was wrong, but the something continued to elude him. Maybe it had to do with the fact that he couldn't seem to remember things. Whatever it was, it was something that told him clearly and unarguably that he wasn't on Earth or any of the planets he'd ever known or heard of.

He looked to the right and he looked to the left. He looked down and he looked up, and realization came smashing through the drunken fog in his mind.

There was no Sun in the sky.

He rose to his feet, the bottle in his hand, for a horrible suspicion was forming in his mind. He turned away from the house, looked at the chronometer on his wrist and began to walk.

When he got back to the house, the bottle in his hand was empty. But all the alcohol inside him could not shut out the truth from his mind. He was alone, on a tiny world that was half green grass and half great blue flowers. A pretty world, a silent, dreaming world beneath a bright, eternal sky. An empty world, and he was on it—

Alone.

He went away from the world, as far as drink would take him. And for many days—or was it weeks?—reality became a hazy thing, until the poor, starved body could take no more and so collapsed. Then there was no remembrance, but when he came back to himself at last, he found a little miracle had happened during that blank period.

Memory of a part of his life had come back to him.

Born and raised on Earth, in Greater Los Angeles, he had been pitched neck and crop off his native planet at the age of twenty-one, along with some other twenty million youngsters for which overcrowded Earth had no room. Overpopulation was a problem. Those without jobs were deported when they reached the age of maturity. And what chance had a poor young man to get an Earthside job when rich colonials wanted them? For Earth was the center of government and trade.

He was spared the indignity of deportation. His family scraped up the money for passage to Rigel IV and arranged a job in a typographers' office for him there. They would continue to pull strings, they said, and he was to work hard and save as much as he could in the hope of being able eventually to buy his way back—although this was a forlorn hope; the necessary bribes for citizenship would run to several million credits. They saw him off with a minimum of tears; Father, Mother, and a younger sister, who herself would be leaving in a couple of years.

He went on to Rigel IV, filled with the determination of youth to conquer all obstacles; to make his fortune in the approved fashion and return, trailing clouds of glory, to his astounded and delighted parents.

But Rigel IV proved strangely indifferent to his enthusiasm. The earlier colonists had seen his kind before. They resented his Earth-pride, they laughed at his squeamishness where the local aliens were concerned, and they played upon his exaggerated fears of the *Devils*, as the yet-unknown alien races beyond the spatial frontier were called. They had only contempt for his job in the typographers' office and no one liked him well enough to offer him any other occupation.

So he sat at his desk, turning out an occasional map copy on his desk duplicator for the stray customers that wandered in. He stared out the window at the red dust in the streets and in the air, calculating over and over again how many hundreds of years of hoarding his salary would be required to save up the bribe money for citizenship, and dreaming of the lost beauty of the cool white moonlight of Earth.

Above all else, he remembered and yearned for moonlight. It became to him the symbol of all that he wished for and could not have. And he began to seek it—more and more often—in the contents of a bottle.

And so the breakup came. Though there was little to

do at his job, a time came when he could not even do that, but sprawled on his bed in the hotel, dreaming of moonlight, while the days merged one into the other endlessly.

Termination came in the form of a note from his office and two months' salary.

Further than that, his recovered memory would not go. He lay for the equivalent of some days, recuperating; and when he was able to move around again, he discovered to his relief that he was now able to leave the remaining bottles in the liquor section alone.

Shortly after, he discovered that the house walls were honeycombed with equipment and control panels, behind sliding doors. He gazed at these with wonder, but for some reason could not bring himself to touch them.

One in particular drew him and repelled him even more than the rest. It was by far the simplest of the lot, having only four plain switches on it. The largest one, a knife switch with a red handle, exerted the strongest influence over him. The urge to pull it was so strong that he could not bear to stand staring at it for more than a few minutes, without reaching out his hand toward it. But no sooner did his fingertips approach the red handle than a reaction set in. A paralysis rooted him to the spot, his heart pounded violently, and sweat oozed coldly from his pores. He would be forced then to close the panel and not go back to it for several hours. Finally, he compromised with his compulsion. There were three smaller switches: and finally, gingerly, he reached out his hand to the first of these, one time when he had been staring at it, and pulled it.

The light went out.

He screamed in blind animal fear and slapped wildly at the panel. The switch moved again beneath his hand and the light came back on. Sobbing, he leaned against the panel, gazing in overwhelming relief out through the big front window at the good green grass and brightness of the sky beyond.

It was some time before he could bring himself to

touch that switch again. Finally he summoned up the nerve to pull it once more and stood a long while in the darkness, with thudding heart, letting his eyes grow accustomed to it.

Eventually he found he could see again, but faintly. He groped his way through the gloom of the front room and lifted his face to the sky outside, from which the faint glow came.

And this time he did not cry out.

The night sky was all around him and filled with stars. It was the bright shine of them that illuminated his little world with a sort of ghostly brilliance. Stars, stars, in every quarter of the heavens, stars. But it was not just their presence alone that struck him rigid with horror.

Like all of his generation, he knew how the stars looked from every planet owned by man. What schoolchild did not? He could glance at the stars from a position in any quarter of the human sector of space and tell roughly from the arrangement overhead where that position was. Consequently, his sight of the stars told him where he was not; and it was this knowledge that gripped him with mind-freezing terror.

He was adrift, alone on a little, self-contained world, ten miles in diameter, a pitiful little bubble of matter, in the territory of the *Devils*, in the unknown regions *beyond the farthest frontier*.

He could not remember what happened immediately after that. Somehow, he must have gotten back inside and closed the light switch, for when he woke again to sanity, the light had hidden the stars once more. But fear had come to live with him. He knew now that malice or chance had cut him irrevocably off from his own kind and thrust him forth to be the prey or sport of whatever beings held this unknown space.

But from that moment, memory of his adult life began to return. Bit by bit, from the further past, and working closer in time, it came. And at first he welcomed almost sardonically the life-story it told. Now that he knew where he was, whatever his history turned out to be, it could make no difference.

As time went on, though, interest in the man he had been obsessed him, and he seized on each individual recollection as it emerged from the mist, grasping at it almost frantically. The viseo that he kept running, purely for the sake of human-seeming companionship, played unheeded while he hunted desperately through the hazy corridor of his mind.

He remembered his name now. It was Helmut Perran.

Helmut Perran had gone from despondency to hopelessness after his dismissal from the job at the typographers. He was a confirmed alcoholic now, and with labor shortage common on an expanding planet, he had no trouble finding enough occasional work to keep himself in liquor. He nearly succeeded in killing himself off, but his youth and health saved him.

They dragged him back to existence in the snake ward of the local hospital, and psychoed a temporary cure on him. Helmut had gone downhill socially until he reached rock bottom, until there was no further for him to go. He began to come back up again, but by a different route.

He came up in the shadowy no-man's-land just across the border of the law. He was passer, pimp and come-on man. He fronted for a gambling outfit. He made some money and went into business for himself as a promoter of crooked money-making schemes, and he ended as advance agent for a professional smuggling outfit.

Oddly enough, the business was only technically illegal. With the mushroom growth of the worlds, dirty politics and graft had mushroomed as well. Tariffs were passed often for the sole purpose of putting money in the pockets of customs officials. Unnecessary red tape served the same purpose. The upshot was that graft became an integral part of interstellar business. The big firms had their own agents to cut through these difficulties with the golden knife of credits. The smaller firms, or those who could less afford the direct graft, did business with smuggling outfits.

These did not actually smuggle; they merely saw to it that the proper men and machines were blind when a shipment that had been arranged for came through regular channels. They dealt with the little men—the spaceport guard, the berthing agent, the customs agent who checked the invoice—where the big firms made direct deals with the customs house head, or the political appointee in charge of that governmental section. It was more risky than the way of the big firms, but also much less expensive.

Helmut Perran, as advance agent, made the initial contacts. It was his job to determine who were the men who would have to be fixed, to take the risk of approaching them cold, and either to bribe them into cooperation or make sure that another man who would be bribed took their place at the proper time.

It was a job that paid well. But by this time, Helmut was ambitious. He was sick of illegality and he thought he saw a way back to Earth and the moonlight. He shot for a job as fixer with one of the big firms that dealt directly with the head men in Customs—and got it.

It was as simple as that. He was now respectable, wealthy, and his chance would come.

He worked for the big firm faithfully for five years before it did. Then there came along a transfer of goods so large and involved that he was authorized to arrange for bribes of more than three million credits. He made the arrangement, took the credits, and skipped to Earth, where, with more than enough money to cover it, he at last bought his coveted Earth citizenship.

After that, they came and got him, as he knew they would. They got him a penal sentence of ten years, but they couldn't manage revocation of the citizenship. Through the hell of the little question room and the long trial, he carried a miniature picture in his mind of the broad white streets of Los Angeles in the moonlight and the years ahead.

But there the memory ended. He had a vague recollection of days in some penal institution, and then the mists were thick again. He beat hard knuckles against his head in a furious rage to remember.

What had happened?

They couldn't have touched him while he was serving his sentence. And once he had put in his ten years, he would be a free man with the full rights of his Earth citizenship. Then let them try anything. They were a firm of colossal power, but Earth was filled with such colossi; and the Earth laws bore impartially on all. What, then, had gone wrong?

He groaned, rocking himself in his chair like a child, in his misery. But he was close to the answer, so close. Give him just a bit more time—

But he was not allowed the time. Before he could bring the answer to the front of his mind, the *Devils* came.

Their coming was heralded by the high-pitched screaming of a siren, which cut off abruptly as the spaceship came through the bright opaqueness of the sky, like the Sun through a cloud, and dropped gently toward the ground, its bright metal sides gleaming as if they had been freshly buffed. It landed not fifty feet from him. The weight of it sank its rounded bottom deep beneath the surface of the sod, so that it looked like a huge metal bowl turned face-down on the grass.

A port opened in its side and two bipedal, upright creatures stepped out of it and came toward him.

As they approached him, time seemed to slip a cog and move very slowly. He had a chance to notice small individual differences between them. They were both shorter than he by at least a head, although the one on Helmut's left was slightly taller. They were covered with what seemed to be white fur, all but two little black buttons of eyes apiece. And they seemed to have more than the ordinary number of joints in their legs and arms, for these limbs bent like rubber hose when they walked or gesticulated. They were carrying a square box between them.

Helmut stood still, waiting for them. The only thought in his mind was that now he would never get to know how he had happened to be here, and he was sorry, for he had grown fond of the man he had once been, not the one he later turned out to be, as you might be fond of a distant relative. Meanwhile, he could feel his breath coming with great difficulty and his heart thumping inside him as it had thumped that time he had first tried the switch that turned off the light.

He watched them come up to a few feet from him and set the box down.

As soon as it was resting on the grass, it began to vibrate and a hum came from it that was pitched at about middle C. It went up in volume until it was about as loud as a man saying "aaahh" when a doctor holds down his tongue with a depressor to look at his throat. When it had reached this point, it broke suddenly from a steady sound into a series of short, intermittent hums that gradually resolved themselves into syllables. He realized that the box was talking to him, one syllable at a time.

"Do not be afraid," it said. "We wish to talk to you."

Helmut said nothing. He wanted to hear what the box had to say, but, at the same time, a compulsion was mounting within him. It screamed that these others were horrible and unnatural and dangerous, that nothing they said was true, that he must turn and run to safety before it was too late.

They had been watching him for a long time, the box went on to tell him. They had listened from a safe distance to the viseo tapes he had run on the machine and finally translated his language. They had done their best to understand him from a distance and had failed, for he seemed to be unhappy and to dislike being where he was and what he was doing. And if this was so, why was he doing it? They did not understand. Where had he come from and who was he? Why was he here?

Helmut looked at the four little black eyes that gazed at him like the puzzled, half-friendly eyes of a bear he had seen in a zoo while he was a boy back on Earth. There was no possible way for white-furred faces to have shown expression, but he thought he read kindness in them, and the long loneliness of his stay on the sphere rose up and almost choked him with a desire to answer them. But that savage irrational corner of his mind surged forward to combat the impulse toward friendliness.

He opened his mouth. Only a garbled croak came out. He turned and ran.

He raced to the building and burst through the entrance. He threw himself at the panel that hid the switches, pulling it open and sliding aside the door that covered them. He reached for the red-handled switch, hesitated, and looked over his shoulder at the two creatures. They stood as he had left them. For the last time, he wavered under the urge to go back to them, to tell them his story, at least to listen to their side once—first.

But they were Devils!

The fear and anger inside him surged up, beating down everything else. He grasped the red switch firmly and threw it home.

What followed after that was nightmare.

He had been sitting for a long time in the cold hall and nobody had paid any attention to him. Occasionally, men in Space Guard uniforms or the white coats of laboratory workers would go past him into the Warden's office, and come out again a little later. But all of these went past him as if he did not exist.

He shifted uncomfortably in the chair they had given him. They had outfitted him in fresh civilian clothes, which felt clinging and uncomfortable after the long months of running around on the sphere half-naked. The clothes, like the stiff waiting-room chair, the hall, and the parade of passing men all chafed on him and shrieked at him that he did not belong. He hated them.

The parade in and out of the office went on.

Finally, the door to the office opened and a young Guardsman stuck his head out.

"You can come in now," he said.

Helmut got to his feet. He did it awkwardly, the unaccustomed clothing seeming to stick to him, his legs half-asleep from the long wait in the chair.

He walked through the door and the young Guard shut it behind him. The Warden, a space man of Helmut's age, with a military stiffness in his bearing and noncommittal mouth and eyes, looked up from his desk.

"You can go, Price," he said to the Guard; and, to Helmut, "Sit down, Perran."

Helmut lowered himself clumsily into the armchair across the desk from the Warden as the young Guardsman went out the door. The Warden stared at him for a moment.

"Well, Perran," he said, "you deserve to congratulate yourself. You're one of our lucky ones."

Helmut stared back at him, numbly, for a long time. Then, abruptly, it was like being sick. Without warning, a sob came choking up in his throat and he laid his head on the desk in front of him and began to cry.

The Warden lit a cigarette and smoked it for a while, staring out the window. The sound of Helmut's sobs was strained in the silence of the office. When they had dwindled somewhat, the Warden spoke again to Helmut.

"You'll get over it," he said. "That's just the conditioning wearing off. If you didn't break down and cry, you'd have been in serious psychological trouble. You'll be all right now."

Helmut lifted his head from the desk.

"What happened to me?" he asked, his throat hoarse. "What happened?"

The Warden puffed on his cigarette. "You were assigned to one of our Mousetraps," he answered. "It's a particularly hazardous duty for which criminals can volunteer. Normally, we only get men under death sentence or those with life terms. You're an exception."

"But I *didn't* volunteer!"

"In your case,' said the Warden, "there may have been some dirty work along the line. We are investigating. Of course, if that turns out to be the case, you'll be entitled to reparation. I don't suppose you remember how you came to be on the Mousetrap, do you?"

Helmut shook his head.

"It's not surprising," said the Warden. "Few do, although, theoretically, the conditioning is supposed to disappear after you capture a specimen. Briefly, you were given psychological treatment in order to fit you for existence alone in the Mousetrap. It's necessary, because usually our Baits live their life out on the sphere without attracting any alien life. You were one of the lucky ones, Perran."

"But what is it?" asked Helmut. "What is it for?"

"The Mousetrap system?" the Warden answered. "It's our first step in the investigation of alien races with a view to integrating them into human economy. We take a sphere like the one you were on, put a conditioned criminal on it, and shove it off into unexplored territory where we have reason to suspect the presence of new races. With luck, the alien investigates the sphere and our conditioned Bait snaps the trap shut on him. Lacking luck, the Mousetrap is either not investigated or the aliens aren't properly trapped. Our conditioned man, in that case, blows it up—and himself along with it.

"As I say, you were lucky. You're back here safe on Kronbar, and we've got a fine couple of hitherto undiscovered specimens for our laboratory to investigate. What if those creatures had beaten you to the switch?"

Helmut shuddered and covered his eyes, as if, by doing so, he could shut the memory from his mind.

"The Guard Ship was so long coming," he muttered. "So long! Days. And I had to watch them all that time caught in a force-field like flies in a spider web. I couldn't go away without stepping out of the building and being caught myself. And they kept talking to me with that little box of theirs. They couldn't understand why I did it. They kept asking me over and over again why I did it. But they got weaker and weaker and finally they died. Then they just hung there because the force-field wouldn't let them fall over."

His voice dwindled away.

The Warden cleared his throat with a short rasp. "A trying time, I'm sure," he said. "But you have the consolation of knowing that you have performed a very useful duty for the human race." He stood up. "And now, unless you have some more questions—"

"When can I go home?" asked Helmut. "Back to Earth."

The Warden looked a trifle embarrassed. "Your capture of the aliens entitles you to a pardon; and of course you have Earth Citizenship—but I'm afraid we won't be able to let you leave Kronbar."

Helmut stared at him from a face that seemed to have gone entirely wooden. His lips moved stiffly.

"Why not?" he croaked.

"Well, you see," said the Warden, leading the way to a different door than the one through which Helmut had entered, "these specimens you brought back seem to be harmless, and inside of a month or two we'll probably have a task force out there to put them completely under our thumb. But we've had a little trouble before, when we'd release a Bait and it would turn out later that the aliens had in some way *infected* him. So there happens to be a blanket rule that successful Baits have to live out the rest of their life on Kronbar." He opened the door invitingly. "You can go out this way, if you want. Private entrance. It leads directly to the street."

Slowly, Helmut rose to his feet and shambled over to the door. For one last time a vision of moonlight on the bay at Santa Monica mocked him. A wild scheme flashed through his head in which he overpowered the Warden, stole his uniform and bluffed his way to a Guard Patrol ship, where he forced the crew to take him either to Earth, or, failing that, out beyond the Frontier to warn the white-furred kin of the two alien beings he had killed.

Then the scheme faded from his mind. It was no use. The odds were too great. There were too many like the Warden. There were always too many of them for Helmut and those like him. He turned away from the Warden, ignoring the Warden's outstretched hand.

He went out the door and down the steps into the brilliant daylight of Kronbar.

Kronbar, the Bright Planet, so-called because, since it winds an eccentric orbit around the twin stars of a binary system, there is neither dark nor moonlight, and the Sun is always shining.

GORDON R. DICKSON

THE BEST IN SCIENCE FICTION

THE CIRCLE EIGHT

MATTHEW

THE CIRCLE EIGHT

MATTHEW
EMMA LANG

KENSINGTON PUBLISHING CORP.
www.kensingtonbooks.com

PROLOGUE

March 1836

The back of Matthew Graham's neck prickled, the little hairs standing up like tiny soldiers. He turned his head slowly to look around without appearing as though he was. His instincts told him something wasn't right and he had learned to trust those instincts.

"Matt, what's wrong?" His brother Caleb stepped up beside him on the wood-planked sidewalk. The gentle early spring breeze ruffled his chocolate brown hair under his battered hat.

"Dunno." Matthew didn't notice anything out of the ordinary in town. It looked as it always did—like a small town in eastern Texas. Nothing seemed out of place, yet he knew something was.

His other brothers and sisters were gathered around the front of the mercantile. Two of his sisters, Olivia and Elizabeth, played checkers while the youngest, Catherine, sat on Livy's lap. Rebecca and Nicholas played marbles in the dirt.

Matthew had performed a supply trip every Saturday for the last four years, always bringing the brood with him to give his parents time alone. Today had been no different, until now.

"Go see what's keeping Joseph with the nails. We need to get home." Matthew didn't wait to see if Caleb did as he was bade. The Graham children fought and competed daily, but when they needed to, they closed ranks and became a formidable force.

"Livy." He caught his sister's attention. She glanced up at him, her blue eyes alert. "Get 'em ready."

Again, she didn't question his order, she just acted. If only that could happen daily instead of once in a blue moon. They were all in the wagon within ten minutes, which at any other time would have been an incredible feat. Today it was nine minutes too long.

All of them seemed to sense Matthew's urgency because their usual banter, bickering, and general noise were tucked away. The two-hour ride back to the ranch grew tenser with each passing minute.

His parents were home alone with five-year-old Benjamin, the youngest of the Grahams' eight siblings. Even their cook Eva Vasquez, and her two sons, Javier and Lorenzo, were gone until tomorrow. Matthew could not have explained his urgency if anyone had asked him.

He just knew he had to get home.

The first sign something was wrong was the smoke. It curled into the bright blue sky like a black snake. Matthew's heart ceased beating for a second, then it pounded harder than the horses' hooves.

He snapped the reins, standing up in the wagon to shout at the team. "Hiya, boys, hiya!" Sweat ran into his eyes and his arm muscles ached as he controlled the two racing bays. Dirt and rocks kicked up by their hooves stung his skin, but he didn't pay them any attention.

The younger children started crying and clung to Olivia. Caleb held on to the seat beside him with a tight jaw and panic in his gaze.

No one spoke even as Matthew drove the team at breakneck speed. The clouds of smoke billowed higher and his throat grew tighter. He could see the fire was near his mother's garden.

Their ranch was only six hundred acres, enough to make a living raising cattle, but just barely. Any loss would be devastating, and a fire could be catastrophic. He prayed it was just a small fire.

But then he saw the front porch of the house.

And his mother's body lying in the dirt beside it.

CHAPTER ONE

May 1836

Matthew rose before the sun, finding his way outside into the gray predawn light. He walked as silently as the air around him, his early morning sojourn a habit born of necessity.

It was the only time of the day he could find quiet.

The noise of his brothers and sisters constantly rang in his ears. There was no way to escape all of them except when they were sleeping. Matt had taken to getting up at four-thirty each day to go for a ride. At first he was so sleepy he nearly fell out of the saddle, but now it had become a pleasure he never missed, even during bad weather.

As he entered the barn, he picked up a bridle from a nail on the wall. The tinkle of the metal was met with a soft whinny from the last stall. His gelding, Winston, was a quarter horse with a crooked blaze down his nose. His parents had given the animal to Matt for his twelfth birthday. Although Winston was at least fifteen years old, he was a good, solid ranch horse.

Matt stepped into Winston's stall and the horse immediately pushed his head toward him, sniffing at his coat pockets.

"Easy, boy. I've got something for you, just don't tell Olivia or she'll have my hide." He spoke low and soft, careful not to disturb any of the other horses or livestock. Matt pulled a cloth from his pocket and poured a half cup of sugar into his hand. Winston lapped at the sweet treat until every last morsel was gone. Matt had to push his mouth away. "That's it, boy."

The quarter horse seemed reluctant to stop, but smacked his lips as Matt saddled him quickly. Their routine was as familiar as breathing, and within ten minutes, Matt walked the gelding outside into the cool early morning air.

He took a deep breath and then another. They rode their standard route, stopping only for Winston to take a drink in a nearby creek. Matt found that he needed this time alone more and more. Each passing day reminded him of their difficult situation, how much responsibility he'd had to take on, and how heavily it weighed on his shoulders.

Their ranch wasn't as big as others, but was large enough to get lost in for an hour each morning. The sun was turning the sky pink when he started back toward home.

When he returned, the lights in the house were on, and he knew the rest of the Grahams were stirring. Life on a ranch started early every day. Although their lives had taken a hard right turn two months ago, chores still needed to be done. After he took care of Winston, he walked toward the house with slower steps than when he'd left. As he reached the door, Matt took a deep breath and stepped in.

*   *   *

"You have to go claim it." Olivia crossed her arms and glared at Matt, her blue gaze cold as an icicle. "Pa would have wanted us to get those acres. He wanted this ranch to be something."

Sometimes Matt wished he didn't have siblings. Like today. The seven of them were in the kitchen sitting at the enormous table their father had built after Matthew was born. It was their standard meeting place when they discussed family business. Unfortunately, this wasn't a discussion. It was a flat-out argument.

Lately all they seemed to do was bicker, fight, and argue everything to death. Matthew wanted to *do* something, not just talk about it until his ears bled.

Pa had intended to claim four thousand acres offered by the Republic of Texas to residents. It was going to make their little six-hundred-acre ranch six times bigger. He knew it had been Pa's dream to create a legacy for his children, but his murder had turned that dream to ashes.

Now the burden fell on Matt to decide what to do. Of course, the rest of the Graham children thought they had to tell him exactly how they felt about the decision. For days, even weeks on end. As much as he loved them, his siblings were driving him loco. His father had usually taken his side, but circumstances had taken his father instead.

"Elizabeth, take Catherine and Rebecca outside to play." Matthew didn't need the younger girls clouding the issue. They didn't understand and were still recovering from the loss of their parents.

"I don't want to go outside." At nine Rebecca could be incredibly stubborn. She pouted her lip and flung her caramel colored braids back over her shoulders.

"That's too bad because you're going anyway." He

gave them his best big brother glare and Rebecca sniffled dramatically.

Little Catherine rose and took her sister's hands. She was a peacemaker like Mama had been, although Benjamin's disappearance had affected her deeply. Sometimes he heard her at night talking to Benjamin although their five-year-old brother had not been found in the two months since their parents' deaths.

"Let's go play." She was the only blond girl in the family, the others having varying shades of brown hair. Rebecca and Elizabeth both walked out haughtily, but they went outside as he ordered.

"You know, they have every right to be here." Nicholas was fifteen and had an opinion about everything. He and Olivia were his biggest problems in that regard.

"Right now I don't need the little ones here. They're not going to help." Matthew sipped at his coffee, which was now cold.

"They're Grahams, too." Olivia sat beside her brother, staring him down.

"Right now we don't need to fight. We need to agree on something." Matthew's heart still ached at the way he'd been thrust into the role of parent. At twenty-five, he was too young to be responsible for his entire family and their ranch, but he accepted the role. He loved his family and the Circle Eight.

"Matt's right." Caleb was seventeen, the third oldest in the family. He had wavy dark brown hair and his father's brown eyes. "Let's stop fighting and start talking."

"I've been trying to do that all morning," Olivia said harshly. She had been bitter ever since she'd spurned her young man. Just when she needed his understanding most, the fool had tried to make her leave the ranch and forget about the unsolved murders of her parents.

Matthew was secretly glad the man had been tossed out on his ass, literally, by him and his brothers. He thought perhaps her bruised heart had closed in on itself after that. She was harder than she'd ever been, rarely giving an inch, and her smile had become a rarity.

"We have the papers Pa had ready to claim the acres. Now you just need to go to Houston and file them. You're the oldest Graham now and you're an adult." She pointed at him. "I don't see what there is to argue about."

"Four thousand acres is six times the size of what we have now. Lorenzo and Javier are crack hands, but even so we don't have enough men to handle that much land." Matthew's fingers tightened on his cup. He wanted to roar at the unfairness of their situation, to run screaming into the field and let loose the grief he had locked away inside.

"Then we claim it and add cattle as we can. If we ride the line to check on the land every week, we can do it." Caleb shrugged. "I think Pa wouldn't want us to miss our chance to take it because we were scared."

"I'm not scared. I'm practical." Matthew felt stung by his brother's reversal.

"Practical is okay, but we need to do what's right." Nicholas fiddled with the rest of his biscuit, the crumbs littering his plate.

This decision would affect all the siblings and their families for generations. It wasn't to be made lightly and the weight of it forced almost all the air out of Matthew. He considered everything his brothers and sister had said, and realized they were right. He was scared. But he had to get past that. This family was everything to him, and if he made the wrong decision, they'd all suffer. He was practical enough to know that he, his brothers and their two ranch hands could take care of four thousand acres. Caleb's idea to build slowly was a good one.

Thoughts whirled around in Matthew's head until he slammed his fist on the table, startling everyone. He closed his eyes and took a deep breath. The only thought left in his head was, *what would Pa do?*

"I'm going to Houston."

Caleb and Nicholas smiled while Olivia nodded at him. The Grahams were going to take a chance.

Houston was so much larger than he had expected. Matthew felt like an ant on a hill. There were so many people he could hardly walk down the street without bumping into someone. Olivia had stayed behind to take care of the ranch, but Nicholas accompanied Matthew. They were both goggle-eyed at the big city.

They had found the land grant office after a few wrong turns, then waited for nearly two hours before the name "Graham" was called. Matthew wouldn't admit it to Nicholas, but a passel of frogs were currently jumping in his stomach.

The man behind the desk was bald with round spectacles. He was also plump, and if Matthew had to venture a guess, the fellow hadn't done a lick of hard labor in his life. His pasty white hands thumbed through their papers. With each passing moment, Matthew thought he might lose his breakfast. To his surprise, Nicholas appeared calm, even studying the stranger with curiosity.

"Your father died then, did he?" The man peered at them through his thick spectacles.

"Yes, sir, Mr. Prentiss. He died in March. I'm twenty-five and control the ranch and property now." Matthew managed to swallow the lump in his throat. He was not comfortable in a place like this, in a situation like this. Put him on a horse and he was unstoppable, but here he felt useless.

"Of course you do. I'm sure you're doing a fine job, too." He picked up his pen and dipped it in the inkwell. "Just tell me the name of your wife and we can finalize the land claim."

Time seemed to stand still as the dust particles floated in midair in the small office. Matthew managed not to sound like a complete idiot although he had to choke back the word that immediately danced on his tongue. *Wife?*

"You need my wife's name?" His voice sounded far away to his ears.

"Yes, we do, Mr. Graham. This land grant is for a family. That includes a husband and wife, current and future children. Now I realize the children are your brothers and sisters, so we'll overlook that particular. All we need is your wife's name for the deed." His pen was poised atop the paper.

Matthew knew if he lied, he would be putting his family and the ranch in jeopardy. If he didn't lie, they would lose the land grant they were entitled to. It was an untenable position, and he only had seconds to decide what to do.

"Hannah. Her name is Hannah." He managed a weak smile.

Nicholas started in the chair next to him, but blessedly kept his mouth quiet. Thank God Matt hadn't brought Livy or Caleb. They'd likely have called him on the lie—he couldn't lie worth a damn.

"Fine then. I'll just write her name down here." Mr.

Prentiss fussed a bit more with the papers, then looked up at Matt again. "Is your wife here in Houston with you?"

"Uh, no, she stayed home to help take care of the children." The lies were just rolling off his tongue now. His mother would have taken a switch to him.

"I see. Well, because you seem like honest boys and have had such a tragedy in your lives, I will grant you a thirty-day extension." He stacked the papers neatly. "Until then I will hold your land for you."

Matt had no idea what the man was talking about. "What is an extension?"

"It means that within the next thirty days, you must bring your wife with you to Houston to sign the papers. It doesn't matter if she doesn't know how to write; an *X* will do just fine. I can't turn over the grant until then." Mr. Prentiss pushed up his glasses with one pudgy finger. "I hope you understand, Mr. Graham."

Oh, he understood all right. He had just lied to a Texas official, to the *law,* and now he had thirty days to find a wife named Hannah or they would lose their land grant.

His family would tan his hide.

"What do you mean, you lied?" Caleb looked more shocked than anyone. "You never lie."

Matthew continued taking the saddle off his horse as his brother hopped around like grease on a hot griddle. It was time to be calm because if anyone knew how many knots his stomach was in, there'd be no end to the dramatics.

"I had to." Matthew stopped and stared at the three of them, Olivia, Caleb, and Nicholas. "Nick was there. He'll tell you I'm right. If I wasn't married, then we wouldn't get the land."

"All right, you lied to them. What happens now?" Olivia got the words out through gritted teeth. Matthew noted she had started to put her hair in a bun like Mama used to, making her look forty instead of nineteen.

"He has to find a wife in thirty days and her name has to be Hannah." The words jumped out of Nicholas's mouth so fast and loud, Matt actually winced.

"What?" Olivia's hands clenched into fists. "Are you plumb loco, Matt? How are you going to find a wife in thirty days and one named Hannah to boot? There is no one in this county who would marry you. You're ornery, a liar, and bad company." Her cheeks flushed as red as the sunset behind her. "You've just cost us that land."

Matt endured his sister's insults even though he wanted to yell right back at her. She was plenty ornery herself.

"Matt did what he had to." Nicholas took the blanket off his own horse. "I almost believed him when he told the man he had a wife named Hannah."

"Yes, but he doesn't." Caleb slapped his hat on his leg, a cloud of dust rising from the worn trousers.

"What if you buy a wife? I heard tell of folks getting a mail-order woman to marry 'em." Nicholas started currying the horse as the bay placidly munched on feed.

"No time. I have to be there in thirty days and no woman in her right mind would move to Texas to live on a small ranch with the six of you. I sure as hell wouldn't." Matthew couldn't count on finding a wife in a newspaper advertisement, much less one willing to take on an entire family.

"I wouldn't either, but unfortunately we don't have a choice, do we?" Olivia stomped out of the barn. He could almost see the waves of fury coming off her body.

"Livy sure likes to be mad at me. It helps keep things normal for her." Matt took off his hat and wiped his brow. "I am in a pickle though, and it's of my own making."

"What are you going to do?" Caleb frowned at him.

Matthew leaned against the stable door. "I don't have much of a choice. I'm going to find a wife named Hannah in thirty days."

CHAPTER TWO

Hannah Foley hated doing dishes. There was no worse chore, in her opinion, than scrubbing greasy food off plates and forks. She hated the feel of it, the way her fingers pruned up, and especially the way her back ached after standing at the sink for an hour. There were more dishes to wash at a boarding-house than a regular household, which made it even worse.

She wiped her forehead on her sleeve and tried to focus on one dish at a time, rather than the mound still waiting for her attention. It would be nice if there was someone to help her, but with Granny's arthritis, and no money to pay any help, it was up to Hannah alone.

Sometimes while she washed dishes, she imagined being somewhere and someone else. It was a little game of "what if" she played with herself. Of course she never told Granny about it—she didn't want her to think she wasn't grateful for the place to live and food to eat. Orphans couldn't exactly be choosy.

She had one particular daydream that recurred each time she allowed her mind to drift. She was at a picnic by the river in town, and she was dressed in a lovely new blue dress and pretty new shoes. Her hair was braided and the sun shone on its hidden red and gold strands. Her large family surrounded her, but she was also with a beau, a handsome man with a big smile and a booming laugh. Around them she heard the sounds of the water gurgling in a nearby stream, her family laughing and chatting, but most of all, she heard the beating of her heart. And she felt peace and happiness.

A silly daydream of course. At twenty-three, she wasn't the youngest or even remotely the prettiest girl in town. There weren't likely going to be any beaus, since there hadn't been any yet. No, she would live at the boardinghouse with Granny and that would be that.

Her silly heart, however, could not help but keep bringing the daydream back at every opportunity. Some days she didn't like being a woman at all. Truthfully, she knew she wasn't very attractive. Hannah was what her granny called "sturdy." The word made her wince, but she couldn't deny it described her.

She had thick brown hair that she could barely wrangle into a braid, mud brown eyes, big breasts, and a plumpness to her behind she was unsuccessful at wishing away. Plain as toast for sure. There were many other pretty girls in town worthy of a beau or even multiple beaus, but not Hannah.

She wasn't bitter about it, just wishful. That darned heart of hers had a mind of its own. Perhaps one day she could ignore those daydreams about a family, a man, a future other than chapped hands and serving strangers.

A realization hit her with the force of a mule kick. Hannah stopped so suddenly, she splashed water all over her chest. She had been wallowing in self-pity, like some crazy old spinster. That was not what she wanted, ever.

She had a good life, and she was grateful for it. This silly behavior had to stop. There were things she could change and things she couldn't. Her looks and her family were set in stone; her attitude was not.

Hannah knew she'd given herself a brain slap and was glad for it. Somebody had to, might as well be her.

After tamping down on her mental meanderings, she finished the dishes and moved on to the task of making a stew for dinner.

"Hannah?" her grandmother called from the parlor.

"Yes, Granny?" Hannah's hands were covered with the flour she was currently rolling the stew meat in. She hoped her grandmother didn't need anything immediately.

"I need you."

Hannah blew out a breath so hard her hair moved off her forehead. "Can it wait about ten minutes? I'm fixing the stew."

There was a brief pause. "I s'pose."

Hannah's chin fell to her chest and she counted to ten. Twice. "I'll be right there."

She cleaned her hands as best she could on the rag and headed into the parlor. Granny had bad pain in her joints and sometimes needed help getting up from bed and chairs. She was a tough old bird though, insisted on making the beds and tidying every day. Hannah worried Granny was doing too much, but there was no one else to do it, and there was only so much Hannah could do with the time she had.

Within a year, Granny might not be able to do anything, which would leave all the work to Hannah. They'd have to close off half of the eight rooms they rented to folks in the huge house her great-grand-father had built. It would mean their income would be cut in half, and they barely made ends meet as it was. Hannah dismissed the thought for now. There was nothing she could do and fussing about it would do her no good.

Hannah walked into the parlor and found Granny on her knees beside the settee. Panic coursed through her as she raced toward her grandmother.

"What happened? Are you all right?" She crouched down and peered at Granny's face. "Did you break anything? How did you fall?"

"For pity's sake, child, stop your caterwauling." Granny flapped her hand in the air as if Hannah were a pesky fly. "I dropped my needle while I was doing some darning. I picked it up but couldn't quite make it back onto my seat. Now you can help me."

Granny wasn't a small woman, but she was smaller than Hannah. In fact, when she lifted her grand-mother up by the armpits, she was shocked to find just how light the older woman had become. It was as if old age was stealing her body inch by inch, turning her into a shell of the robust woman she had been.

"Have you been eating?"

"Not as much as I should." Granny let out a sigh of relief when her behind connected with the settee cushion. "My stomach's been feeling poorly for a while now. I eat enough to get by and it ain't like I'm gonna starve to death. We Foleys are bred to survive and built to have babies." She turned a frown on Han-nah. "Speaking of which . . ."

"Do we have to talk about this again?" Hannah wanted to run from the house, heck, from the entire town, rather than talk about her lack of a husband *again*. It had become a nearly daily conversation with

Granny, and she was tired of it. Bad enough her own heart kept returning again and again to a fantasy it could never have.

"Don't sass me, child. I raised you better than that." Sometimes Granny still treated her as a seven-year-old orphan.

"I'm not a child, Granny. I am a grown woman and if I don't want to talk about my obvious lack of a husband, then I damn well won't." Hannah almost slapped her hand across her mouth for not only back-talking but cussing, too. Yet she didn't. It was time she stopped hiding behind a sink full of dirty dishes.

Granny smiled at her and wagged her finger. "Now you sound like me."

They both broke out laughing and Hannah sat down beside her, pulling her grandmother into a hug.

A surge of love and concern for Granny flooded through Hannah. Her grandmother was getting old— heck, she *was* old at sixty-two, which meant she would be getting sick more often. They couldn't afford a doctor and that meant Granny wouldn't even tell Hannah if she felt sick.

Shaking off her disturbing thoughts, Hannah got to her feet. "Everything okay now?"

"Pshaw. On with you now, young'un. You'd better get to making that stew or we won't eat dinner until supper."

Hannah went back to the kitchen, shaking her head and hoping she was that much of a curmudgeon at sixty-two.

Making the stew brought some order back into her scattered thoughts. She cut up the carrots and onions, then pulled out the sack of turnips from the pantry.

"Damn." The curse was under her breath so she wouldn't have to endure any reprimand.

There were only three turnips to feed twelve people. Hannah vaguely remembered telling herself to get more at the store, but she had forgotten to add it to her list. And now she didn't have enough to make dinner for everyone. She had a little bit of time, perhaps a half hour, to get to the store and then get back.

Hannah dried her hands quickly, then took off her apron. "I'm going to the store, Granny. Be right back." Luckily she had a dollar in her reticule, which she grabbed from beneath the sink.

As she headed out the door, she tripped and fell down the two steps, landing squarely on her knees in a mud puddle. She cursed again, this time a bit more loudly, then got to her feet and looked down at her mud-spattered skirt.

It wasn't her best garment, but it had been clean. Until now. She would change later. For now she'd just have to endure people staring and possibly pointing at her. It wasn't the ideal situation but there was no help for it.

She hurried down the street, nodding at folks who glanced her way. Who cared if she had flour on her blouse, mud on her skirt, and a grimace on her face? It had already been a bit of an unlucky day for her. Things couldn't possibly get any worse.

Matthew stared at the collection of rifles for sale. He had his father's to use, and had given his old one to Nicholas, but Caleb needed a gun. They were so doggone expensive though. He didn't want to choose between food and a weapon, although with a rifle he could get food.

It was Saturday again, and he'd had three days to

mull over the pickle he was in. So far, he hadn't come up with any solution other than finding a wife named Hannah in the next twenty-seven days. Easier said than done. Most of the women in town were married, and the ones who weren't were either too young or too old. And he didn't know of one named Hannah who wasn't married.

The bell over the door to the store tinkled and he heard a muffled curse, then a slam. Matthew peered around the display to see Caleb sprawled on the floor while a woman bent over with her hand outstretched to help him up.

"I don't need no help," his little brother snapped.

"I'm sorry about that, mister. I'm in a bit of a hurry." Her voice was like whiskey, husky and rich. The sound of it intrigued him.

He must have made a noise because she straightened up and his gaze locked with hers. His first thought was that she was plain as prairie wheat; brown hair, brown mud on her skirt, with a round bosom to match her round behind.

Yet she had that voice. He still felt a tingle from it.

With a nod, she stepped around Caleb, who was just getting to his feet. "Stupid cow."

"Caleb. Apologize to the lady."

"I don't see no lady." Caleb stuck out his lip like a five-year-old.

"What you will see is my fist when you get knocked on your ass again." Matt towered over him. "Now apologize."

"Sorry." The word was flung without grace or sincerity.

Matt met the woman's gaze again. She shrugged and turned away, but not before he saw a glimmer of pain in the depths of her eyes.

He should just go about his business and not worry about a woman he didn't know. Yet something told him to make peace with her. It was what his mother would have wanted. That thought alone made his feet move.

Matt found her by the turnips, empty sack in hand.

"Excuse me, ma'am?" He was surprised to see her start. "I didn't mean to scare you."

"You didn't. I'm just, well, never mind. It's been a bad day." She didn't even look up from examining the vegetables.

It gave him the opportunity to study her. She smelled of flour and fresh bread, with just a hint of onions. Her hands were long-fingered and although she obviously worked with them, they were elegant. Her skirt had mud on it and was as plain as the potato sack in her hand.

Her hair, which looked like light brown from far away, had bits of gold and red in it. Curls were stuffed into a fat braid that swung with each movement. He wondered what that hair would feel like in his hands.

Matt almost choked on his own spit. First her voice woke up his body into imaginings, and now his imagination was getting into the act. What he needed to do was stop thinking about this stranger and focus on his more immediate problem with the land grant.

"I just wanted to apologize for my brother."

"Don't fuss over it. He's a boy." She had the sack half full by then, picking turnips faster with each word out of his mouth.

Matt reached out and took her wrist to stop her, wanting to explain why Caleb acted so foolish. He never got the chance. A jolt of something like lightning raced through him, hitting him square in the stomach. He dropped her arm and jumped back a foot, much to his embarrassment.

She stared at him, her brown gaze wide. "What was that?"

"I have no idea."

"Why did you touch me?" She clutched the potato sack to her chest and inched her way toward the counter.

"I don't know. I was trying to apologize."

"You already did that." She bumped into the counter, never taking her gaze off him.

"I know. I'm sorry." He was tripping over his own tongue, trying to figure out what the hell was wrong with him.

She put a dollar on the counter. "I only got half a sack, Frank. I'll be back tomorrow for the other half."

With that, she almost flew out the window, like a muddy brown bird running from an eagle who had threatened her.

Matt wanted to slap his forehead. He didn't have a huge amount of experience with women, but he had some. Enough to know he had just acted like a bigger jackass than Caleb.

Frank, the mercantile owner with eyebrows that had a life of their own, eyeballed him with a frown. "What did you say to Hannah to make her run like that?"

A second jolt of lightning smashed into him. "Did you say her name was Hannah?"

"Yes, you young fool. Hannah Foley is one of my best customers. Doesn't usually come in on Saturday and you done run her off." Frank wagged his finger at Matt. "You had no call to be rude to her."

"I wasn't rude. Jesus, did you say her name was Hannah?" He surely sounded like a young fool.

"Are you deaf, boy? I done told you that already." Frank leaned forward. "Are you tetched in the head or somethin'?"

Matt shook his head. "No, just a huge fool. Is she new in town?"

"She's lived here all her life at the boardinghouse with her granny. You and your kin are the new ones in town." Frank humphed.

"I really didn't mean to scare her. I was just trying to apologize." Matt knew he might have just made another big mistake by letting Hannah leave the store. Not only did she have the right name, but there was a bizarre connection between them.

He turned and glared at Caleb, who was back to staring at the rifles. "I ought to kick your ass six ways to Sunday."

Caleb's eyes widened at the ferocity in Matt's tone. "What did I do?"

"You just insulted my future wife."

CHAPTER THREE

Hannah walked as fast as she could with the sack of turnips clutched in her hands. Something had happened at the mercantile and she had no idea what. There was a man there and *something had happened*.

Her stomach jumped as if a dozen frogs had taken up residence in it. If she wasn't walking so fast, her knees would be knocking. Her experience with handsome men could fit into a thimble, and she had just met the most beautiful man she'd ever seen.

Nothing about him was ordinary, including his incredible blue-green eyes, strong jaw, and wide shoulders. She'd never forget his hands. When he'd touched her wrist, it was as if something had traveled between them, making every small hair on her body stand up. She was sure he'd felt it, too.

It was extraordinary.

Hannah refused to let her imagination loose, but it was damn hard. For the first time in her life, something romantic had happened to her. Muddy, disheveled, and so very plain, she had caught his attention. What did it mean? She should talk to

Granny about it, but first she wanted to relive every moment as she cut up the turnips.

This time, her fantasy wasn't something she made up. Hannah had a real man to daydream about. Hannah wanted to chide herself for dwelling on the handsome blue-eyed man. Perhaps if there hadn't been an instant spark between them it would have been easy to dismiss him, but there had been and so she couldn't.

"Hannah, what are you doing?" Granny's voice yanked her out of her reverie like a bucket of cold water.

"What?" She looked down and realized she was standing in the kitchen clutching the potato sack while the stew bubbled merrily on the stove.

"It looks like you're touched in the head, child." Granny's cane thumped on the wooden floor as she walked toward the small table and chairs. "I've been calling you the last five minutes."

Hannah's cheeks heated. "I'm sorry. I had to go buy turnips at the general store and I, uh, was wool-gathering a bit."

With more fervor than necessary, she got busy washing more turnips for the stew. She cut them into smaller pieces since they should have been in the pot thirty minutes ago. Granny sat there, staring a hole in Hannah's back until she was about ready to scream.

"Why are you staring at me?" she finally asked, keeping her voice as steady as she could.

"I'm trying to puzzle out what is wrong with you." Granny was too observant.

"There's nothing wrong with *me*. But lots of other things have gone wrong today." Just then the knife slipped and she sliced open her thumb. "Dammit to hell."

"Hannah Josephine Foley! Who taught you how to

cuss?" Granny had shot to her feet, her face flushed, her jowels swinging with each word, her finger wagging. "I ought to wash your mouth out with soap."

"I'm not a little girl. I can cuss if I want to." Hannah was embarrassed to have cursed in front of her grandmother, but her thumb pulsed with pain. She wrapped a towel around it and held her arm up. For a time about five years ago, the town doctor had lived at the boardinghouse and he taught Hannah a lot about taking care of wounds and sickness. She'd had dreams of marrying him, but he was thirty and a widower. Within six months there were more young women buzzing around the boardinghouse than flies. He'd been married by the end of the year, leaving Hannah with nothing but some medical knowledge. It did prove useful though. She knew the bleeding would stop faster if she applied pressure to the cut.

"Not in this house you won't." Granny had moved on to true anger.

Hannah moved right along with her. "Then maybe I won't live here anymore."

"Where do you think you're going?" Granny thumped her cane hard this time. "You have a beau I don't know about?"

Granny was too close to the mark for Hannah's comfort. She had met a man, or sort of met a man, this morning, and perhaps he was the beau she had been dreaming of. Granny's tone assured her the older woman was being as sarcastic as she could be.

"Now you're just being mean, Granny. I don't need a feeble old widow like you cutting me down." With that, she stomped out the back door.

The air outside felt good on her skin, which was sweaty from the heat of the stew and her own emotions. She plopped down on an upended log and tried to calm herself. Her heart raced with the events of the day, culminating in yelling at her grandmother. The woman who'd raised her and loved her. The woman who was probably too hurt to follow Hannah out the door to demand an apology.

They had both been unkind to each other, but Hannah was definitely meaner. She had actually called her granny old and feeble. Completely true, but remarks more fitting to a harridan than a grand-daughter. Hannah sighed and pressed her forehead against her arm. What a mess she'd made of things.

"I'm sorry, child." Granny appeared on the steps. "I didn't know."

Hannah stared at the ground. "Know what?"

"That you had met a beau. I didn't mean nothing by what I said. Just an old woman mouthing off like an old fool." She shook her head, one gray curl bouncing in the breeze.

Hannah's laugh was more like a strangled chuckle. "I didn't meet a beau. I met a man who made me act like a fool. I could hardly speak to the fellow." She finally met her grandmother's gaze, and saw understanding clearly shining in her wise eyes.

"That's what we do. Act like fools around them until they get up the nerve to come courting." Granny waved at her. "Come on back in and let's take a look at your thumb. And we can talk about your young man."

"He's not my young man." Hannah got to her feet and almost dragged herself toward the back door. Granny would ask so many questions she didn't want to answer, or perhaps couldn't answer. It would be awkward, but it was also exactly what she'd been hoping for. Someone to talk to who would understand and maybe give her the advice she needed.

One thing she did know. Something had happened and she owed it to herself to find out what.

After wrapping her thumb in a strip of cloth, she got all the turnips in the stew. Within twenty minutes, she'd started the gravy with some fat from the meat. The work gave her time to stop thinking about everything. Granny hummed as she snapped peas from her perch at the table. Things felt normal again.

Matthew had paced outside the boardinghouse for a good thirty minutes before Olivia found him. She put her hands on her hips and narrowed her gaze. The afternoon sun cast a shadow beneath the rim of her bonnet so he couldn't see just how annoyed she was. Good thing, too.

"What are you doing? We've been looking for you." She tapped her foot, raising a cloud of dust with each movement of her boot.

The last thing he needed was Livy sticking her nose into his business again. She needed to let him be head of the household without following him around like an angry hen. He wanted to talk to this Hannah Foley.

And he needed to do it on his own or not at all.

"Go back and make sure the young'uns are all doing what they're supposed to."

"You cannot talk to me like that, Matthew Bodine Graham." She pinched her lips together so tight, they were nearly bloodless.

"Yes, I can, Olivia Mae Graham. I run this family and make the decisions that best suit everyone." He gave her a hard stare. "Now go back to the store and make sure everyone does what they're told."

"But—"

"No, I'm done talking, Livy. This is important." He pointed. "Go."

She glared at him, letting him know he would hear all about how unhappy she was later. She was strong like Mama, but unlike their mother, Livy did not want to listen to what anyone else had to say. After she turned and stomped away, he turned and strode up the steps of the boardinghouse.

The paint on the door was peeling, but the porch was well-swept and tidy with four rocking chairs, which were also showing wear. He swallowed and knocked on the door.

Voices sounded from within, two females if he wasn't mistaken, and they were getting louder by the second. The door was flung open and Hannah stood there with a surprised expression.

And a big glob of gravy on her cheek.

"Good morning, Miss Foley, my name is Matthew Graham. I, uh, hope you don't mind me dropping by like this." He tried not to sound like a stuttering fool, but his tongue had other ideas. "I, uh, did I interrupt something, Miss Foley?"

"No. I was making—oh never mind." She flapped her hand, which reminded him of a small bird. "Why are you here?" Her cheeks colored and she slapped her hand across her mouth. When her fingers came in contact with the gravy, she pulled her hand away to look. Her eyes widened.

"Oh shit."

With that, she disappeared into the house and slammed the door behind her.

He stared at the door, blinking and trying to figure out what had just happened. When he heard a wail from inside, he knew he needed to follow her in. This was a boardinghouse so it wasn't as if he was walking into someone's private home. Strangers walked in all the time. Besides he had introduced himself so he wasn't a stranger anymore.

"Miss Foley?" He opened the door and poked his head in. Voices echoed from deeper in the house, but no one answered him. Matt stepped in and left the door open behind him.

The house was neat as a pin, but everything he could see was very worn. The upholstery on the chairs was a bit tattered, the wood floors dull and scuffed by years of use. However it was the smell of cooking food that hit him the hardest. It was the most heavenly scent he'd smelled for quite some time. If he wasn't mistaken, it was stew or pot roast.

"Miss Foley?"

He walked deeper into the house, following a hallway toward the voices. And the smell.

"I can't believe that just happened, Granny. Not only am I perspiring, but I have grease, flour, and gravy on me. On my face!" It was Miss Foley, talking to her grandmother obviously. "Never in my life have I been so embarrassed."

"Ain't no never mind, Hannah. Done is done." The older woman's voice was gravelly and rough.

"Yes, I know. Done." Miss Foley sounded so defeated, it pinched at his conscience. After all, he'd been the one to show up on her doorstep without being invited. He owed her an apology.

Matt cleared his throat and shuffled his feet as he approached the open door to what he assumed was the kitchen. "Miss Foley?" Complete silence met his words. When he finally stepped into the kitchen, both women were staring at him.

Miss Foley's face was even redder and the older woman, a gray-haired version of her granddaughter, chuckled when she saw him.

"Well, ain't that a hoot." She slapped her knee, spilling a bowl of snap peas across the table.

"Granny!" Miss Foley exclaimed, but kept her gaze on him. He realized in the bright sunlight of the kitchen that her brown eyes weren't a singular color. They had shades of amber and whiskey in them.

He shook himself mentally to stop forgetting why he was there. Miss Foley didn't have to be pretty or smart or a good cook, she just had to be willing to marry him. If she happened to be any of those things, too, well, so much the better.

Matt took off his hat and nodded at the older woman. "Ma'am, my name is Matthew Graham. I'm pleased to make your acquaintance."

"Just call me Granny Foley, Matthew. Everybody does." She snorted another laugh, while her granddaughter shot her daggers from her eyes.

"Why are you in my kitchen? I mean, I'm sorry, Mr. Graham. I don't understand why you're here, and I really don't know why you came into the house." Her voice sounded all breathy and even huskier than before. It sent a line of chill bumps down his back.

"If we can sit down, I will explain." Of course, he didn't know how he would explain what he was doing. It was a fool's errand but he was fast running out of time.

"Sit down, child." Granny pulled out one of the mismatched chairs. "Let the man speak." She gestured to the other chair and winked at him.

Winked! Oh boy, now he really had to contend with something. Granny Foley obviously thought he was there as a beau. This situation just kept getting stickier.

After they all sat, Matt realized just how difficult it would be to explain his proposal.

"I don't know if you knew my parents, Granny, but we own a ranch about an hour outside town. Stuart and Meredith Graham?"

Granny nodded. "I remember them a bit. Nice folks, lots of young'uns."

"Yes, ma'am, there are eight of us."

She leaned forward and peered at him, and the sharpness of her gaze was not lost on him. "Something bad happened back a piece, didn't it?"

This time he had to swallow the lump in his throat. Twice. "My parents were murdered and my youngest brother, Benjamin, disappeared."

"Cryin' shame that is. Why would anyone kill good folks like that? And steal a boy? Sounds like Injuns to me." Granny shook her head. "You young'uns are running the ranch then?"

"Yes, ma'am. We have a couple of ranch hands too and our housekeeper, Eva. I'm the oldest, so I take care of the business end of things." He glanced at Miss Foley, who was staring at him with her hands clasped in her lap. "We, uh, that is, my father had applied for the land grant from Texas. It's six thousand acres to every resident."

"Six thousand? I can't even imagine how big that is." The younger woman finally spoke again.

"Miss Foley, it's as far as the eye can see, and then some. It's going to make our ranch ten times its original size."

"Hannah." Her voice had slid down into a near whisper.

"Pardon?" He leaned toward her and got a whiff of her scent again.

"My name is Hannah." She caught her lip with her

teeth. They were straight and white, contrasting sharply with the dark pink of her lips.

Matt told himself to stop acting stupid.

"Hannah." The name fit her perfectly, slightly feminine but strong. "My Pa didn't have a chance to claim the land grant before he died. I went to Houston to claim it, but it seems there's a requirement I don't meet."

"Spit it out, boy." Granny was obviously not shy.

"I, uh, need to be married. The wording on the land grant means the Graham who claims it must be married." He let that piece of information sink in before speaking again. "While I was in the land grant office, I did something I shouldn't have and now I'm, well, truly stuck between a rock and a hard place."

"What did you do?" Hannah leaned forward, her whiskey eyes wide.

"I told them I was already married." He paused and couldn't even muster up enough spit to swallow. "And that my wife's name was Hannah."

The only sound in the room was the burbling of whatever smelled so good on the stove. Granny's gaze narrowed while Hannah's eyes just kept growing wider.

"And you're here because my Hannah isn't married and you need a wife named Hannah to get your land." The older woman's tone was not very warm.

"I didn't want there to be any misunderstanding about my intentions." He turned to Hannah. "I can offer you a good home, a faithful marriage, and a promise that I'll always take care of you the best I can." There, he'd finally gotten it all out. Funny thing was, he didn't feel any better.

"A-are you asking me to *marry* you?" Hannah's mouth was slightly open.

"Yes, yes I am." He slid off the chair and onto one knee. "I know you don't know me from the next person. Please don't say no right away. Take a week to get to know me before you make a decision." He took her hand, ignoring the rush of lightning that again hit him as soon as they touched. "Please."

She stared at him, her hand trembling in his. "I, uh . . ." Hannah glanced at her grandmother while he waited, his stomach somewhere near his throat. "Okay."

"Okay, you'll take a week to get to know me?" Now his voice sounded almost as breathy as hers.

She shook her head. "No, okay, I'll marry you."

There was a rushing sound in his ears as he realized he'd found a woman named Hannah, one he was already attracted to, *and* she was a good cook. Best of all, she'd agreed to marry him. A surge of joy hit him and he leaned forward and kissed her hard.

He didn't know who was more surprised, he or Hannah. She put her fingers to her lips while he sat back in his chair. The silence hung between them, low and heavy.

"I guess we're having a weddin'," Granny cackled merrily from her perch.

Matthew managed to make it back to the store without making a fool of himself, but his knees were still knocking an hour later. He'd actually asked a stranger to marry him, invited her into his home, to share his name and likely have children with him.

His stomach turned over once, then twice, leaving a coating of bile in the back of his throat.

Olivia waited by the wagon, fussing over the younger ones like baby chicks, as was her way. She didn't bother to look at Matt, but started to shoo the Graham brood onto the wagon. He knew she'd seen him and that she was still fuming about his dismissal thirty minutes earlier.

Now he would have to deal with her wrath. He had a moment to wonder what it would be like when Hannah moved in and had to fight for control of the house with his sister. No doubt it would be more than interesting. Hannah seemed a bit shy, but she also appeared to be strong. All she had to do was stand up to Livy and she'd be all right.

Matt nodded to Caleb, who stood next to the wagon smoking a cheroot. "Let's go."

The ride back to the ranch was quiet except for the melodic voice of Rebecca reading a story in the back of the wagon. Livy rode between him and Caleb, speaking not a word, her ramrod straight back never bending even a smidge.

Her silence was okay by Matt since it gave him time to think about what he had done and what was in store for him in a week's time. He'd first have to tell everyone about Hannah, and that included Eva and her sons. It gave them only one week to ready the house for a wedding and a new mistress.

It also meant he would have to move into his parents' bedroom. He'd avoided it since their deaths, but he couldn't expect Hannah to sleep on a narrow bed in the same room with Nick and Caleb. That left the biggest bedroom, which stood empty, full of ghosts and memories.

It was a chore he had put off as long as possible. Who wanted to go through the things that had belonged to their parents? It was a weakness he'd tried to overcome but hadn't been able to. Neither had Livy or Caleb for that matter. The room had become a sanctuary of sorts, an area they didn't go into for fear they'd lose something, or perhaps destroy the memories of their parents.

It was silly to think or feel that way, but there it was. He didn't know how to deal with losing his parents so abruptly and violently. So he avoided thinking about it at all. There were so many other things to occupy his mind, after all. Excuses, of course.

Perhaps marrying Hannah would let him confront the painful task of letting his parents go.

Hannah was not a small girl, thank God, so perhaps his mother's things would fit her. Most of the Graham children had taken after their father in height and slenderness, except Rebecca and Catherine. Matt knew his mother would approve of someone like Hannah wearing her clothes. She'd always altered clothes for the next sibling down, eking out every last possible use from a garment before it was cut up into rags to be used for cleaning. Very rarely was anything thrown away.

They were within ten minutes of the house when Livy finally decided to speak.

"Are you going to tell me why you acted like such a jackass?" Olivia demanded.

"I wasn't acting like a jackass." Matt kept his temper under control. He wouldn't give her the satisfaction of seeing that she had riled him. "I was acting like the head of the family."

"Humph. That'll be the day."

He turned to look at her. "Whether or not you like it, I am head of this family. Ma and Pa are gone and I'm the oldest. Sometimes you might not like what I have to say or do, but that's just too bad."

Her brows drew together as he spoke, forming a brown caterpillar of annoyance. "I won't accept that."

"Find yourself a husband then."

Caleb snickered while Nicholas sucked in a breath. Livy punched him in the arm. Hard.

"Now don't start something you can't finish, sis." His arm smarted from her knuckles.

"I'll finish it, all right. You can't tell me what to do, and that's that."

Matt's sleeping temper rose and he pulled on the reins, stopping the wagon in the middle of the road. He turned to her. "No, you are wrong, Livy. I do have the right. I have to make hard decisions and our family can't turn into an anthill of insanity every time I do. I just asked a perfect stranger to marry me for this family. Don't think for a second you have the right to do whatever you want. I certainly don't have that right and neither do you."

The only sounds were the drone of bees nearby and the occasional chirp of a bird. Olivia's mouth had fallen open. Everyone else stared at him with wide eyes.

"What did you say?" Livy whispered.

"You heard me. I found myself a wife." He leveled a fierce stare at all of them. "Now shut up until we get home and I'll tell you about her."

To his surprise, they did just that. He sat back to enjoy the minutes of peace before they reached home. The next week, hell, the next month, would be a whirlwind of chaos.

Hannah's hands shook so hard, she burned herself three times just trying to get the biscuits out of the oven. The day had started so badly, and now it seemed as though she had stepped into a dream, or perhaps a nightmare.

A man she barely knew had asked to marry her. He was handsome, had a ranch and nice teeth. Yet the only reason he wanted to marry her was to make his ranch bigger and to hide his own lie.

It wasn't an especially good start to a marriage, by any stretch of the imagination. She should have said no, for that matter, she shouldn't have even listened to what he had to say. He'd had the audacity to walk into the boardinghouse without being invited. But she hadn't said no; instead, she had agreed to marry him.

What was wrong with her? Was she that desperate for a husband she'd accept a total stranger? *Something* had compelled her to accept his sideways proposal and she didn't know what.

Granny had gone upstairs to take a nap, so Hannah was left alone with her whirling thoughts. Hours later, she poured herself a cup of coffee and sat down heavily in the chair to watch the setting sun paint the back of the kitchen shades of orange and pink.

He'd kissed her. That was what was running through her mind over and over, even more than the impending marriage. It was her first kiss, such as it was, though of course he couldn't know that. His lips were soft but firm, and she tasted a bit of sweetness like he'd been eating a peppermint.

She had stopped breathing for a moment afterward, dumbstruck by not only the kiss, but the idea that she would be married in one week's time.

Married!

Aside from changing the course of her life irrevocably, the agreement meant Hannah would be leaving the boardinghouse and Granny. That didn't sit too well with her. It was a dark cloud on what could be a bright horizon. She couldn't leave her grandmother alone to run the boardinghouse, which left her two choices. One, they must hire someone to cook and clean, which they couldn't afford. Two, Granny must close the boardinghouse, which would leave her with no income. Either option would be tough.

She sipped the bitter brew and thought about how selfish she had been not to have considered how her leaving would affect Granny. For the last ten years, Hannah had been the one running the boarding-house. Her grandmother socialized with the boarders, kept them happy, and collected their rent. Hannah did everything else.

As the reality of her decision hit her, Hannah knew she'd made the wrong choice. No matter how hand-some or appealing Matthew was, he was not more im-portant than Granny. She would have to tell him she couldn't marry him. The thought made her heart pinch, but it had to be done.

"Don't you think about changing your mind, child." Granny's voice made her jump a country mile.

"How did you—" She stared at her grandmother, amazed by the woman's perceptiveness.

"Now that you've had time to think about it, you remembered the boardinghouse." Granny pointed at her with one bony finger. "Don't you dare be giving up this chance for a husband and family because of it."

Hannah opened her mouth to refute the accusa-tion, but closed it, knowing Granny was absolutely right. This was her chance and obviously she was meant to have it, but that didn't make it any easier to contemplate Granny's fate. She refused to put her own happiness in front of her grandmother's entirely.

"What will you do?"

Granny shrugged. "I'm too old to run this place anyway. Have been for some time. You been running it, child. It's high time I sell it and live out my days watching sunsets and sunrises. Been thinking about doing that for a while now but I didn't know what you would do. Now God saw fit to solve both problems."

Hannah had never considered that her grand-mother wanted to sell the boardinghouse. What a strange twist of fate to have Matthew Graham need a wife named Hannah, and Hannah needing a way to fulfill her fondest wish for a family of her own.

"Then I guess I'm getting married."

Granny grinned and pulled her into a robust hug. "Then we'd best get busy selling this house and mak-ing you a weddin' dress."

Hannah was scared to death.

CHAPTER FOUR

The day of the wedding dawned full of clouds with a misty rain in the air. The steel gray of the sky loomed overhead as Hannah and her grandmother walked toward the church. She wore Granny's old shoes, the ones she'd worn at her own wedding fifty years earlier. They were old, dusty, and a little too small, but they were better than clumpy boots, the only footwear Hannah had.

Hannah had thought she wouldn't be nervous, but she was. With each footstep, her stomach twisted tighter. She was about to be married! For the last few years, that had seemed like an impossible dream. The unreality of the situation was not lost on her.

She felt like a different person, and she wore a pretty dress for the occasion. It was light blue, made from Granny's own wedding dress as well. Fitting because it was borrowed, old, and blue, if they were to follow the rhyme. Granny was a genius with a sewing needle and, within four days, had altered the dress to fit Hannah's rounder, shorter figure.

For the first time in her life, Hannah felt pretty. Too bad she also felt like she wanted to vomit.

They were to meet the groom at ten o'clock at the small church and although it was only nine-thirty, they headed over. Sometimes the cold weather made it difficult for Granny to walk and Hannah didn't want her grandmother to have to rush. That could lead to an injury, the very last thing they needed.

Hannah had actually spent time fixing her hair that morning, another unusual occurrence. She normally put it in a braid or in a knot and never thought twice about it. Of course, she had wasted her time attempting to look pretty, for the rain had already turned her hair into a mass of kinky curls. It had been the first time she'd tried ironing it, too. She hoped her new husband didn't notice the burn mark on her neck.

The door to the church was slightly ajar. Perhaps the preacher was already there, waiting or preparing for the ceremony. Matthew had told her he would make the arrangements. She hadn't heard anything from him except a cryptic note three days earlier to meet him at the church at ten.

That time had almost arrived.

"Stop pinching my arm, child." Granny pulled her to a stop. "There's no need to be scared. He's a good man."

"I'm not scared, Granny. I'm, um, well, I'm not scared." Her stomach told another story, but she wasn't about to admit it. "I'm just worried is all. Nobody's bought the boardinghouse yet."

"That fella from Eagle Creek might. He came back twice already. Said he was gonna bring his missus next week." Granny waved her free hand in dismissal. "I ain't worried, so you don't need to be."

"But I—"

"We're done jawing about it." The older woman started walking again and Hannah had no choice but to keep up. "You are trying to slow down time and it won't work."

Was that what she was doing? Trying to hold onto her maiden status just a few minutes longer? Granny was probably right. Hannah held her head high and straightened her shoulders. At least she could maintain her dignity and show her new husband just how much of a lady she was.

She pulled the church door open and held it for Granny. When they stepped inside the gloom of the foyer, the church was totally silent. Then as Hannah walked into the light, she realized that although it was quiet, the church was not empty by any means.

There were seven of them, all standing together at the altar. The tallest was Matthew, but there were two other young men beside him, and four girls. Hannah recognized the oldest girl from long ago when she had attended school, but couldn't remember her name. They were all of varying sizes, some with brown straight hair, some with brown wavy hair, even one with blond hair. Their eyes, however, were very similar, all shades of the same bluish green, all blinking at her like a family of owls.

Hannah's heart slammed into her throat and she couldn't have made a sound if she'd tried. Granny must have sensed Hannah's panic and the old woman saved her again.

"Well, howdy. I didn't know we'd have a passel of folks here." Granny stepped forward, peering at each of them in turn. "I'm Martha Dolan. You can call me Granny. This here is my granddaughter, Hannah Foley."

Hannah was able to catch her breath and murmur a hello. Not a great first impression to make with her new family, but there it was.

"She's tall." The smallest of the bunch, a blond-haired girl, peered up at Hannah. "Almost as tall as Matt."

Matt. It suited him better than Matthew. One was formal while the other matched him, at least what she knew of him. She felt as if she'd stepped back in time and had an arranged marriage. But instead of the marriage being arranged by their parents, they'd done it themselves. Many marriages still started out that way, where the bride and groom barely knew each other.

"Hush now, Catherine. Let me introduce you proper." Matt nodded at Hannah. "Miss Foley, Mrs. Dolan, may I present Olivia, Caleb, Nicholas, Elizabeth, Rebecca, and Catherine Graham." Each sibling in turn either nodded or curtseyed toward them. They were obviously a well-mannered family.

"It's very nice to meet you all." Hannah winced to hear how breathy she sounded. "I knew you had a big family but didn't realize how big." She smiled shakily at Olivia. "I remember you from Miss Green's classroom when I was seven."

Olivia's brows drew together. "Now that you mention it, yes, I do remember you. You left after that year, didn't you?"

The memory of not going back to school hit Hannah. Her parents had died of a fever within two days of each other, leaving Hannah an orphan, and in her grandmother's care. It was the darkest time of her life, one she was sorry she had brought up.

"I did, that's right." Hannah turned her attention to Matthew, trying to close the door on her ancient pain. "Is the preacher here?"

"Uh, not yet. We got here early."

"We had to get up before the sun," the young girl

said. "That was really eeeearly. I had to eat in the wagon, and I dropped a piece of my biscuit." She looked very unhappy about that biscuit.

"Catherine, hush up," Olivia snapped. "Miss Foley doesn't need to hear any of that from you."

"Don't tell her to hush up." Another sister, possibly Rebecca, stuck her chin up in the air.

"Don't think you can just do whatever you please." Olivia put her hands on her hips. "I am still—"

"Enough." Matt's hand cut through the air. "Now is not the time for bickering." He turned his gaze to Hannah and in the depths of his pretty eyes, she saw exhaustion and stress. "Can I talk to you?"

Hannah's heart did a little flip. She wondered if he'd changed his mind before they even saw the preacher. It wasn't as if she would blame him for changing his mind, but oh, how it would hurt.

He took her elbow lightly, leading her toward the back of the small church and away from the big ears of his family. Granny started talking to the Grahams, distracting them so Hannah and Matt could speak privately.

He stopped in the shadowy corner by the door. After blowing out a breath, he took off his hat and met her gaze. "I just want to make sure you still want to marry me. I wouldn't blame you if you didn't. I surprised you and now that you've had a week to think about it, I thought you might have changed your mind."

She looked at him in astonishment. He thought *she* might change her mind? The very idea almost made her laugh but she kept it inside through sheer force of will.

"No, I haven't changed my mind." She clasped her hands together so he wouldn't see them shaking.

"What about your grandmother?"

Hannah blinked. "What about her?"

"Will she want to live with us at the ranch?"

"Um, I'm not sure. All the boarders moved out this week, but we need to sell the boardinghouse. There is no way she can run it without me. Then she has to decide what she wants to do." She and Granny had talked about it each night, speculating what she might want to do.

"We have a housekeeper and cook, Eva, but she's lonely, always talking about visiting in town with other women." He spun his hat on his hand. "I just wanted to tell you your granny is welcome to live with us. We can find room for her."

At that very moment, Hannah fell a little in love with Matt. He had worried about her grandmother, which told her a lot about his character. She smiled at him, the first genuine smile she'd felt since meeting him.

"That's very kind of you. I think she might accept." She glanced at her grandmother, knee deep in little girls. "Granny loves to tell stories and be around young'uns."

"There's plenty of those around the ranch." He put his hat back on his head and held out his arm.

Matt might be a cowboy but he was a gentleman. Hannah nestled her arm in his and took the first step toward her new life.

Matt had never felt so out of control in his life. Hannah and her grandmother weren't making him nervous; his stomach was. He was about to marry someone and spend the rest of his life with her, and he didn't even know her middle name. It was loco and the stupidest thing he'd ever done, yet he wasn't going to stop now. He'd made sure she was still going to go through with it and that reassurance was all he needed. It was too important to his family that he go through with this quick marriage.

Too bad nobody had told his stomach. He hoped he didn't embarrass himself and vomit all over his intended.

The preacher appeared through the back door, scowling at all of them. They were being loud, as always, but most of them were crowded around Mrs. Dolan as she spun a yarn about a chicken and a full moon.

"This is a house of God, children. You must show the proper respect." Reverend Beechum was not his favorite person. In fact, Matt had never liked him, and neither had his father. They didn't go to church much because of the gray-haired bible-thumper. He made children feel like sinners if they lied about sneaking a cookie, but he was the only preacher in town. That left Matt with no choice.

The children hushed up, frightened by the preacher's surly visage. Matt felt Hannah tighten up beside him and he didn't blame her a whit. This church was not a happy place.

"Mr. Graham, do you have my fee?" Another reason Matt didn't want to be here. They were paying the man *five* dollars to perform a marriage ceremony. It stuck in Matt's craw to even give the man the time of day, much less a chunk of their money. However, he handed it over, albeit grudgingly.

"Excellent." The money disappeared into the voluminous trousers the preacher wore. "Now, are we ready to begin?"

Matt swallowed the huge lump in his throat. "Yes, we are."

He stepped forward with Hannah at his side and knew the course of his life had just taken a sharp right turn. He was stepping into his future.

The preacher spoke his words quickly, a simple ceremony that could have been done by a judge. The only time the man showed a glimmer of emotion was when Matt told him he didn't have a ring.

"No ring?" His disapproval was almost palpable.

"No, sir. I didn't have money for one." He turned to Hannah. "I promise I'll get you one someday."

She shook her head. "I don't mind waiting. It's okay."

Matt was lying to both his new wife and the obnoxious minister marrying them. He had a ring—his mother's. She'd hardly worn it because she did so much work with her hands that she was always afraid of losing it. The ring sat in a small pouch in the chest of drawers her husband had made for her, beneath the clothes she'd never wear again. Matt had found it when he had cleaned their room.

He had stared at the ring in his palm, knowing he should give it to Hannah. It was what his mother would have wanted, but he couldn't do it. The ring was now safely tucked away beneath his own clothes in the chest of drawers in his parents' room, the room that was now his.

"It's not proper, but I understand the need to conserve funds with so many children in the family." The preacher made it sound as if having children was a bad idea. Didn't the church promote being fruitful?

"Ain't nothing wrong with lots of young'uns," Granny piped up. Matt decided he really liked

Martha. If she were a man, he'd say she had brass balls.

With a disapproving look at the older woman, the preacher finished the ceremony within a minute or two. "I now pronounce you man and wife."

Without preamble, he led them to a table in the corner to sign the marriage certificate. Matt had forgotten to ask Hannah if she could write, and was glad to see her sign her name, even if it was with a shaking hand.

"Congratulations, Mr. Graham. Mrs. Graham. Now if you'll excuse me, I have other duties to attend to."

Reverend Beechum herded all of them out of the church and they found themselves outside in the rain, the door firmly shut behind them.

"He didn't do the kiss the bride part." Catherine always had something to say. "Does that mean you're not married?"

Matt looked at his new wife and saw a glint of amusement in her gaze. "No, we're married, sprite. True and proper."

He was about to ask Hannah if she wanted to head back to the ranch after dinner when the heavens opened up and the mist turned into a downpour. The young ones squealed while the older ones scrambled to cover everyone up.

"Let's head to the boardinghouse. We can get dry there." Hannah took Catherine's and Rebecca's hands and started running, heedless of the rain or the mud.

He scooped up Granny, who squealed in his ear, and ran after his new wife.

"Jehoshaphat, boy! What in tarnation are you doing?"

Matt didn't bother to see if the rest of his siblings followed. Either they did or they would spend the af-

ternoon in the rain without shelter. It took only minutes to reach the boardinghouse but he was soaking
wet by the time he arrived.

Hannah had left the door open, and he skimmed in
sideways with the older woman still hooting in his
arms. Giggling echoed from the kitchen so he followed the sound. He found the girls sitting at the table
and Hannah handing them each a towel.

She glanced up at him, then at her grandmother. A
smile spread across her face and a laugh burst from
her. It wasn't a little tinkling laugh, but a full-fledged
belly laugh. Matt was so surprised by the way she
looked and sounded, he stopped in his tracks.

Hannah was lovely.

"Well, put me down then, young man. I need a
towel, too."

Matt broke out of his momentary stupor and managed to get Mrs. Dolan into a chair without dropping
her. It really had been the strangest day and it still
wasn't over yet. In fact, it had only just begun.

The rest of his family tromped in, dripping and
complaining. Hannah handled the situation with a
quiet grace, handing out dry towels and rags, even arranging the shoes by the stove to dry. After stoking up
the fire, she put on a pot of coffee. She obviously
worked hard at the boardinghouse—not a big surprise—but he was amazed by how well she did it all.

"You don't have to serve us." Matt stood by the back
door, watching her flit around like a bumblebee in a
field of flowers.

"I'm used to it," was her only response.

The young ones took to her right away. Catherine
in particular seemed to be attached to Hannah's hip.
She missed Mama the most and her new sister-in-law
represented a mother figure. Besides, Hannah was

obviously comfortable in the kitchen and accommodating of big groups of people. Even if she wasn't being as social as his mother had been, she made everyone feel at ease by taking care of them.

He noted she hadn't taken care of herself. She still wore her wet clothes and shoes. Her hair hung in kinky curls, framing her face, making the paleness of her skin that much more prominent.

During all the hubbub, Livy was the only one who stood apart. She didn't take off her shoes and only accepted a small rag to wipe her face. Matt's sister was not happy about the marriage and he would try to find out why later. For now he'd have to ignore her unfriendly behavior and hope Hannah didn't take it personally.

They were, after all, family now, for better or for worse.

Hannah had gotten everyone comfortable and warm. The kitchen was cozy with so many folks gathered around. It was different from the boarders, these folks weren't there for ten minutes of food only to run off again. Her relationships with the former residents of the building had always been cordial, but a little impersonal. She was almost glad of the rain since it gave her a chance to meet the Grahams in the comfort of her home.

She'd spent countless hours in the last week wondering what Matt's family would be like. They'd surprised her and scared her. Olivia was seething with dislike or annoyance, she couldn't tell which. The younger three girls, however, were charming children. So bright and full of life. Hannah thought perhaps she would feel better about moving to the Graham ranch now that she'd met them.

Matt's brothers eyed her with curiosity, but kept their distance. They accepted coffee and spent their time murmuring to each other. She didn't sense bad intentions from them, more curiosity than anything.

She tried not to pay attention to Matt though. He watched her as she worked, making her more nervous than she already was. Hannah knew if she looked at him, it would only make her nervousness worse.

Thunder rumbled in the distance, bringing all conversation to a stop.

"Damn." Matt's soft curse sounded loud in the quiet room.

"Does that mean we're stuck here?" Elizabeth appeared to be about twelve, and she seemed to take care of Catherine and Rebecca well.

"Yes, at least until the storm passes. We can't be out in the wagon if there's lightning." Matt snagged Hannah's gaze. "I know we've already invaded your house."

Hannah gave a nervous chuckle. "It's Granny's house, not mine. Besides we're used to feeding at least eight boarders at a time." She shrugged. "You're welcome to stay here as long as you like."

"We don't want to put you out." Matt's brows drew together. "Besides, Eva was planning on a big feast for supper."

She knew Eva was their housekeeper and cook. Another person Hannah was nervous about meeting. No woman liked another moving into her territory. It would be a relationship that would take time, of that she was certain.

"If it's thundering outside, she won't expect you." Granny slurped her coffee noisily.

"Do you think?" Matt glanced outside. "She'd started making bread this morning before we left."

"I met Eva a few times, knew your Mama, too. Eva can put the bread up and keep the supper for tomorrow." Granny belched more loudly than her slurp. The young girls giggled. "Excuse me, y'all. Things don't work right much anymore."

Hannah felt her cheeks heat. Granny kept on drinking her coffee. Next thing, she'd probably fart.

"We've got plenty of food and rooms for everyone." Hannah realized she could spend her wedding night here, in her own bed, rather than at the Graham ranch. Once she thought of the possibility, she couldn't get it out of her head.

"I don't think the storm will last that long." Olivia finally spoke. "I certainly don't plan on staying here all night."

Matt frowned in her direction, then turned to Hannah. "I appreciate the offer. Let's just wait and see what happens." He nodded at his brother, Caleb. "Stay here and make sure they behave."

Before Hannah knew it, he'd taken her by the elbow and led her to the front of the house with a lantern in hand from the kitchen. The parlor was empty now; the boarders had been gone for a couple days. Matt gestured to the settee and Hannah perched on the edge. When he sat across from her in a chair, she felt herself relax a little.

"I wanted to talk to you alone without our families stirring things up." He rested his elbows on his knees and captured her gaze.

Lord above, the man was handsome as sin.

The ghost of whiskers had started to appear on his

cheeks and chin. His eyes looked very green in the meager light of the parlor. She found herself falling into their depths. His scent surrounded her, a combination of man and clean soap. Quite heady.

"I know this marriage isn't starting in the best circumstances. I just wanted to say thank you." He held her gaze while she digested what he'd just said.

Thank you? That's what he wanted to say?

It felt like a slap. She wanted to be insulted and tell him to go to hell, but she didn't. Hannah had no illusions this was a marriage of love. He had been honest with her when he'd proposed. She really had no right to react emotionally.

Yet her heart could not be convinced otherwise.

"You're welcome, Matthew. I, um, hope I won't disappoint you." She didn't want him to have illusions either. "Believe it or not, I don't have a lot of experience with men." She wanted to look away, but she didn't. If this marriage was going to have a chance, she had to be herself.

To her relief, he smiled. "Disappoint me? I don't think that will ever happen."

"I won't hold you to that."

He chuffed a laugh. "You have a sense of humor."

She gave him a small smile, but inside she was grinning widely. "I guess I do."

That's when a small kernel of hope blossomed within her. Perhaps her marriage would be more than she expected.

The rain continued as if it would never cease. The road turned into a river of mud while the trees swayed with each gust of wind. It was the storm of the season, and on Matt and Hannah's wedding day.

Hannah didn't know if she should take it as a bad omen or a sign of good things to come, a cleansing of the earth. Either way, they were well and truly stuck at the boardinghouse. Even if it stopped raining, by some small miracle, the mud would prohibit travel for a while. How long depended on when the sun came out.

Hannah was making beds for the Grahams, absurdly glad she had done the laundry the day before. The boarders had left something of a mess in each room so she was finishing up the cleaning as she went from room to room.

When Hannah finished, she ended up in her own room, staring at the narrow bed. There was no way a man Matt's size could share that bed with a woman of her size. That would make their wedding night more than awkward.

She had to put someone else in her room and take one of the two rooms with a larger bed. There was no help for it—she knew the consummation of the vows was important to start a marriage. Without a proper bed, it would be a disaster in the making. After the nearly hostile preacher and the rain, she couldn't allow the actual wedding night to go haywire as well.

"He only married you for the land, you know."

Hannah jumped at the sound of her new sister-in-law's voice. Olivia stood in the doorway, arms crossed, lips pinched shut.

"I know that." Hannah was glad of the fact Matt had been completely honest with her. "Matthew told me everything."

"And you were so desperate for a husband you said yes?" Olivia's tone became knife sharp.

Hannah weighed her options. If she got into an argument with Olivia, it would set a precedent. But if she backed down, that would let her sister-in-law know Hannah could be intimidated. It was a narrow path to navigate.

"No, I was not desperate, but I recognized a good man and a good offer when I heard it." Hannah met the other woman's gaze. "You and I were friends when we were young'uns. I don't expect you to hug me or nothing, but I want a chance to fit in."

There, that sounded reasonable, and she wasn't shouting, although she was on the inside. Hannah had a bad habit of reacting to insults by biting the head off the insulter, but nobody liked a young woman with a temper.

"You won't get that chance from me." Olivia's eyes flashed. "My brother got us into this mess by lying and now we all have to live with the consequences. But that doesn't mean I have to like them."

"What put the bee in your bonnet?" Hannah now sounded just as annoyed as her new sister-in-law. "You've no call to blame me for any of this."

Olivia's laugh was humorless. "Then who do I blame? The people who murdered my parents? The incompetent sheriff who couldn't catch them? Or maybe the bastard who took my little brother?" She straightened her shoulders. "All I know is you are a reminder of everything that went wrong in our lives and now my brother is saddled with a cow he never wanted."

Hannah felt every word as if she'd been punched in the gut. She pressed her hand to her stomach and leaned over. The Graham family had been through so much, but that didn't give Olivia a reason to be so dang vicious.

"You've no call to be like this to me."

"I have every right. This is my family." Olivia turned and disappeared from view.

"It's my family now, too." The walls were the only witness to Hannah's whisper.

It wasn't as if everything Olivia had said wasn't true, even though her words had a knife-sharp edge. Her new sister-in-law had just ripped her to shreds on her wedding day. Hannah realized words had more power to hurt than the biggest stick in the world.

It took her ten minutes before she felt in control again. She didn't check to see if the sheets were on sideways or were even tucked in. Completely unlike her, but so was the fact she was now married. Her world was topsy-turvy.

After she finished making the last bed, she sat down on the window seat in her room. She pressed her forehead against the cool glass and stared out into the nearly unrecognizable street.

The rain was coming down in sheets outside. Hannah was trapped in her own home with her new family who didn't want her and a husband who'd married her because her name was Hannah.

The storm had definitely not been a good sign.

She didn't know how long she sat there before she noticed the rain had stopped and someone was calling her name. Getting to her feet, she realized she must have fallen asleep. Her feet and legs prickled as she stood up. Her hair was a mess of curls sticking every which way.

"Hannah?" A voice echoed down the hallway.

She rubbed her eyes and tried to remember what had happened and why she was asleep on her window seat. A yawn grabbed hold of her and wouldn't let go.

That's how her new husband found her. The day could get worse, but she couldn't possibly think how.

CHAPTER FIVE

The rain had turned the street into a lake. There was no chance the Grahams would be able to leave for home. Hell, Matt probably couldn't even make it to the livery for the wagon and horses without drowning.

After he had surprised Hannah, she'd disappeared into the kitchen, mumbling an excuse about preparing supper. Of course, that was hours before that particular meal was usually served, so he didn't know what she was doing except avoiding him.

Olivia had been upstairs, and he'd bet a nickel she'd said something to Hannah. Something not very nice. It was no secret Livy did not want Matt to marry Hannah, but she'd never given him any valid reasons why.

They were all in the parlor except for Catherine, who remained in the kitchen with Hannah and her grandmother. Livy sat in the corner, barely acknowledging anyone while the younger kids played checkers and jacks. The games must have been Hannah's when she was younger because they were well used, but well maintained. Like everything else in the house.

Matt watched the clouds break up just in time for the sun to set. Fortunately they could stay at the boardinghouse for the night and not have to pay for a hotel or a restaurant. With seven of them, that could get awfully expensive. After paying Reverend Beechum five dollars, there wasn't any extra money to throw around.

"Mattie?" Catherine snuck up next to him, cuddling against his side as she'd done since she was a little girl.

"Hey there, sprite." He hugged her close, her blond curls tickling his chin.

"Don't squish me." She pushed at his arms. "I came to tell you it's time for supper."

Matt got to his feet and tossed Catherine on his shoulder. She squealed, as she always did, and he tickled her with each step. The rest of the Grahams followed him into the dining room. It had been set up for the boarders, so there were plenty of chairs, although mismatched, for everyone.

Hannah stood at the table with a bowl of steaming mashed turnips. Two thoughts flew through his mind.

Turnips were the reason they'd met; and her expression was so full of longing it made his breath catch. She was watching the play between him and Catherine. With Mrs. Dolan as her only family, he knew right then Hannah had never really known the affection of siblings as his brothers and sisters did.

He turned away, uncomfortable with the personal knowledge she'd given him and unsure of what to do with it. Catherine dropped to her feet and scrambled around to one of the chairs.

"This is my seat." She climbed onto the chair and pointed at the chair across from her. "That's your seat."

Matt sat down where she'd indicated while the others awkwardly found a place to perch. Hannah waited until everyone had found a spot before she put the food on the table. It was simple fare, but it smelled delicious.

With the Grahams filling the dining room, there was only one chair empty. Matt started to rise but Hannah shook her head.

"Don't worry about us. Granny and I always eat in the kitchen. Eating in here would feel strange." She shrugged. "I don't mind, really."

He didn't know how to respond so he let her leave the room without saying a word. Caleb frowned at him and Catherine kicked him in the shin.

"Ow, why are you kicking me?" He rubbed his leg and scowled at his youngest sister.

"You let Granny and Hannah eat in the kitchen. That's not very nice." She crossed her little arms like a forty-year-old schoolteacher.

"Heck, Matt, we could have taken turns." Caleb joined the blame party.

"I didn't tell them to eat in the kitchen."

"She's your wife. You tell her where she eats." Nicholas wasn't prepared for the punch in his arm Olivia landed.

"I'm hitting you because that's a stupid thing to say. Men don't have the right to tell women where to eat." She reached for the food and started filling the younger children's plates.

"You'd best do something," Caleb added. "I think Nick is right. She's your wife."

Matt pondered what they'd said and realized this

was one of the first tests of their marriage. He couldn't possibly let his wife eat in the kitchen on their wedding day. How was he going to stop her though? He didn't want to just tell her what to do, but he also didn't want her to think he wasn't the head of their new family.

He got to his feet and all six pairs of eyes watched him, some judgmental, others curious, and one downright hostile. Livy and he would have to have a talk when they got back to the ranch. He couldn't live with that kind of hostility from his sister.

Hannah and her grandmother sat at the kitchen table, talking quietly. When he walked in, they both looked up at him with identical expressions of surprise.

"Are you out of food already?" Hannah started to rise.

"No, nothing like that." Matt knew there wasn't room for both of them in the dining room, and he couldn't leave Mrs. Dolan in the kitchen by herself. Likely Hannah wouldn't let her eat alone either. He was in a tight situation again and this time it was over something as minor as a meal.

"I'll be right back." He went back into the dining room.

All six of them started talking at once but he ignored them and took the empty chair. Then the noise stopped and he allowed himself to snort at the fact that he'd shut them up.

When he returned to the kitchen with the chair, the two women were still watching him. Hannah stared at the chair, then returned her gaze to his.

"You don't have to eat in the kitchen with us." She shook her head. "It's not proper for a guest to be in here for a meal."

He chuckled. "I'm not a guest. I'm your husband."

Her eyes widened at the word, and sure enough it made him pause, too. Husband. It almost fell out of his mouth like a stone into a still pond.

"That you are." Mrs. Dolan pointed at the chair. "Then you'd best sit a spell and have some vittles."

Matt felt awkward, but he did just that. Hannah hopped up and fixed him a plate from the pots on the stove. She set his plate down on the narrow table and sat back down.

The silence remained as they ate. The only sounds were those of chewing. Mrs. Dolan mostly gummed her food, since apparently a good deal of her teeth were missing.

It was never quiet at meals at the Graham ranch, and he hadn't realized just how much noise people made when they chewed. He tried to think of something to say to break the silence but the longer it went on, the worse it got. He probably should have stayed in the dining room.

"You two need to sleep in the room at the top of the stairs tonight," Mrs. Dolan announced as she noisily smacked her lips on the last bite. "It's got the biggest bed." She winked at Matt.

His stomach flipped at the idea that she wanted them to use a big bed and flipped a second time when she winked at him. Matt was no fool—he knew Hannah and he needed to live as man and wife in all ways, but he sure as hell hadn't expected her grandmother to think about their having sex.

Matt made the mistake of meeting Hannah's gaze and saw all of what he was feeling, as well as something he'd hoped not to see, panic and fear.

It had been a long wedding day, and he knew it would be a very long wedding night.

*   *   *

Hannah wanted a hole to open up right there in the floor and swallow her. She knew she was blushing and looked like a complete fool, but she couldn't help it. Granny had no business talking about the bedroom or the size of the bed. She knew Hannah had next to no knowledge about men or bedding them.

It would be a disaster. What was she thinking? It already was a disaster. And she'd wondered how her wedding day could get worse.

After meeting Matt's gaze and seeing the same discomfort in his face, she wanted to weep. It would be bad enough to share a bed with the stranger who was now her husband, but to know he didn't want to be in the bed . . . that was ten times worse.

He obviously didn't want to share a bed with her. Yet he'd married her, for better or for worse. Apparently the worse would be arriving right around bedtime.

She didn't taste her food but mechanically chewed it anyway. Granny had taught her never to waste food so she did as she had always done—obeyed. Matthew ate heartily, finishing off what was left in the pots and peering around for more. She didn't want to tell him again to go back to the dining room, but any remaining food would be in there.

Actually, they were lucky to have the food supplies they did. Making two meals for the Grahams had practically used up all of the food stores they had left. Somehow Hannah would have to find a way to restock the food before she left for her new home, or convince her grandmother to come with them. Coffee, some dried jerky, and a few biscuits were not going to last long.

Hannah got to her feet, ready to do something where she didn't have to think so hard. She started to clear the dishes and Matthew stood up.

"Oh, no, you are not going to clean up after us." He took her by the elbow and walked into the dining room. His hand felt warm even through the material of the dress—it was an odd but very pleasant feeling. "Who's on dishes today?"

To Hannah's surprise, his brother Nicholas got up.

"Who's on water duty?"

Rebecca got to her feet.

"Good. Both of you will clean up just like if you were at home. Becca, they have a pump in the sink so you don't have to go outside, but you should get to heating the water now." He turned his attention to Nicholas. "Don't break anything."

It was astonishing to think all of these children, including the boys, took turns at chores such as dishes and fetching water. Hannah truly hated doing dishes and to have that particular chore done by someone else lifted her spirits entirely. The Grahams were a unique family, that was for certain.

"You have five minutes." Matthew shepherded Hannah out into the hallway. "When they're ready, show them where everything is."

Hannah wasn't used to men who took charge. After all, she'd lived with her grandmother. There were no strong male figures in her life. She wasn't sure if she should enjoy someone else taking control so she didn't have to, or if she should wrestle it back from him. This was their wedding day, after all, and it would likely set the tone for the rest of their marriage.

"Matthew, I um, want to say something." She met his gaze, then immediately looked down. It was hard to believe she had a husband who was so tall and so doggone handsome. She couldn't be assertive with that gorgeous visage in front of her. "Um, I wanted to thank you for asking your, well, telling your family to help with chores."

Not exactly what she'd planned to say but Hannah was tripping over her own tongue.

"They're your family now, too." He continued to stare down at her. She could feel his gaze as if it were a physical touch.

"Yes, but I don't know how I fit in with all of them. I hope they won't think I'm lazy because I'm not doing the dishes." God knew her relationship with Olivia was off to a bad start.

He chuckled and put his finger under her chin until she met his gaze. "I don't think there's a person in the world who could say you were lazy. You've been working nonstop since we arrived."

She felt herself falling into his eyes. They were very green in the low light of the hall. It was as if they'd stepped into another place, without their entire noisy family only feet away. His thumb grazed her lips and a skitter of heat slid down her body. Her stomach felt funny and her woman place grew warm and tingly. Hannah could hardly catch her breath.

"Are you going to kiss me?" she blurted.

He smiled and leaned down, his lips slowly approaching hers. She didn't want to close her eyes and miss it, but the closer he got, the more she fell into a whirlpool of unfamiliar sensations. His lips were softer than anything she'd felt before. Just a brush against hers, and then the second pass was a true kiss.

A small moan sighed from her throat as the second kiss turned into a third. Her body was throbbing to the frantic beating of her heart. Hannah didn't want to even take a breath for fear of interrupting the most erotic moment of her life.

His arms closed around her and she was pressed up against him. Oh my. He was hard from head to foot, harder than she'd expected. Matthew was a man who worked for a living, covered in muscle, with callused hands and a firm grip.

"Oh, yuck. Kissing already?" Nicholas's voice broke the spell between them.

Hannah jumped back, her hand pressed to her lips, still wet from her new husband's kisses. Her heart was about to jump right out of her chest, and he appeared completely unruffled.

"What do you want, Nick?" Matthew's voice was as controlled as the rest of him.

"Don't know where the soap is."

"I'll show him." Hannah didn't run, but she walked as quickly as possible out of the hallway, away from an amazing experience she'd been completely unprepared for. No one had told her that a kiss could turn her into a quivering pile of foolish. No one said her entire body would catch fire just by touching his, with clothes on even!

She was beyond flustered, and needed a few minutes away from the man who obviously knew now how to control his wife. Hannah wanted a moment to catch her breath and figure out how she could survive being Mrs. Matthew Graham.

"Nice timing, squirt." Matt tugged on Nick's hair. "I was enjoying myself with my wife."

"Kissing doesn't look fun. Lots of swapping spit is what it is." At fifteen, he admitted that he liked girls, but also admitted he wasn't quite sure he wanted to touch them yet.

"Well, it is fun. Now get on in the kitchen and get the dishes done before Hannah does them instead. We've imposed on her hospitality enough for one day."

After Nick scurried into the kitchen, Matt took a deep breath. Then he had to lean over and put his hands on his knees. That kiss was nearly his undoing. He'd never expected to have such a strong physical reaction to kissing Hannah.

She was attractive in an unconventional way. Her lips were incredibly soft and plump. Hell's bells, he'd completely lost control because of them. He was still hard as a hammer in his trousers. He wondered if she understood exactly what went on between a man and a woman.

If she didn't, their wedding night would be disastrous. He wasn't as experienced as many men, but he had been with women before, mostly away from home on trips with his father.

Now he would have a permanent woman in his bed. Matt was going to have to find some measure of control around her or she could lead him around by the dumb stick between his legs. No man in his right mind wanted to be controlled by a woman or his urges for that woman.

On the other hand, his father had loved his mother so deeply, so completely, his world had revolved around her and, as the product of that love, their children. Matt had always wanted to ask his father why he let his mother control everything. He'd never had the courage though and now, of course, it was too late.

Matt knew how incredible a marriage could be, but he also knew how dangerous it could be. He couldn't let Hannah realize just how much she affected him.

* * *

Hannah sat on the edge of the bed wringing her hands. The lamp was turned down so low it was barely a flicker in the darkness of the room. She heard footfalls on the stairs and knew Matthew was nearly there. The rest of the family was settled in their beds, which left only one person who could be walking up the steps.

Her husband.

Oh, she'd thought she was ready for this but she'd been sorely mistaken. Perhaps if she hadn't kissed him before, she might not have been so nervous. Now that she'd had a taste of him, of what it felt like to be in his arms, just how soft his lips were, she was a mass of quivering nerves.

The door slid open with barely a whisper and Matthew's form filled the doorway. Hannah's heart lodged in her throat while every small hair on her body stood up at attention.

"Good evening, Hannah." His soft voice was probably meant to calm her, but it didn't. In fact it was as if he had whispered in her ear, heightening the tension within her.

"Matthew." Her voice was not her own, huskier and deeper than normal.

He shut the door and she started, nearly falling off the bed. She certainly didn't present an air of sophistication.

"Matt, please call me Matt. The only time someone calls me Matthew is if I'm in trouble." He smiled and she was again reminded just how handsome her husband was.

"Matt." This time she whispered and his smile disappeared.

"I want to thank you for—"

She held up her hand to stop him. "Please do not thank me for marrying you. I don't think I could stay in this room if you did that."

He sat down beside her, dwarfing the bed. Lord, the man really was big. When he took her hand in his, his warmth had a calming effect on her frazzled nerves.

"I wasn't going to thank you for that." He kissed her knuckles. "I was going to thank you for cooking. We're a big crew and it takes a lot to satisfy us."

Hannah's heart decided to pick that moment to start racing like a thoroughbred. She could barely hear him over the rushing sound of the blood passing her ears.

"Y-you're welcome."

He reached up and cupped her cheek, his callused thumb sliding lazily across it. "Don't be scared, Hannah. I promise to always take care of you and keep you safe."

In the semi-darkness of the room, hearing the soft tones of his deep voice, she fell a little bit more in love with her new husband.

"I promise to be the best wife I can be, although I haven't had any practice."

He smiled and pressed his forehead against hers. His warm breath mingled with hers. Although they were barely touching, it was an incredibly erotic moment. For the first time in her life, she was sharing part of herself, her very breath, with someone else. She'd never been that close to anyone before, not even Granny.

She felt she could not have picked a better husband and although she'd only known him a week, Hannah trusted Matt. He would keep his promise. When his mouth moved close to hers, she shut her eyes and let the moment take over.

His lips were almost hot on hers, moving slowly across from one side to the other, nibbling and kissing. She was lightheaded from the sensations bombarding her, but it didn't matter.

Before she realized what was happening, he laid her back on the bed and they were pressed together again. This time the sensation didn't frighten her— it excited her. He was as hard as he'd been before, a sharp contrast to the soft plumpness of her own form.

His hands moved down her neck to her chest. She should have been frightened but she wasn't. When his hand closed around her breast, her nipple immediately popped against his palm. She groaned and he echoed the sound. Her nightdress was nothing but a thin layer of cotton between them. He pinched the nipple right through the cloth and she felt an answering thrill between her thighs.

Matt made quick work of the buttons and soon the cool night air caressed her heated skin. He kissed his way down her neck, moving closer to her aching breasts. She didn't know what she wanted, just that she needed him to do something. And he did.

His mouth closed around one turgid peak. The hot wetness of his mouth made her back arch toward him. His tongue swirled around while his teeth nipped at her. She had never known the pleasure to be had from the plump breasts she had always wished away. What a fool she'd been.

As his mouth feasted on one breast, then the other, his hand crept down her body to the aching core between her legs. Although she was inexperienced, Hannah opened her legs, eager for some relief. He inched up the nightdress until the darkness caressed her bare flesh.

His fingers touched her gently. "You're already wet."

Hannah had no idea what that meant, but didn't much care either because he started touching her. Her nipples had proved to be an exciting place when she was in bed with her husband. The place he had his hand now proved to be ten times more intense. Bolts of pleasure shot through her entire body as his nimble fingers rubbed and teased her.

She couldn't get a breath in as sensations bombarded her. A coil wound tight within her. His thumb pressed against the magic spot as his fingers moved lower. When they entered her, she almost sighed with relief. That was what she wanted.

He moved in and out, inching deeper with each thrust of his fingers. She pushed against him, needing more.

"Hang on, darlin'." He stood up, leaving her in the cold air alone. She could have wept for the loss of sensation, of the ecstasy found with just his hands and mouth. Hannah didn't even feel like herself anymore. She was someone else, a wanton woman aching, throbbing, and pulsing for more of what a man could give her.

It was probably only seconds, but it felt like hours before he joined her on the bed, and this time, he was nude. She wished she had been smart enough to leave the light on so she could see him. Yet alas, it was too dark to make out anything but his general shape. But oh, her hands found his warm skin, the crinkly hairs on his chest. She touched him because she had to.

He kissed her from above as he positioned himself between her legs. When his thumb found the hooded button of pleasure again and his mouth closed around her nipple, Hannah closed her eyes and leapt into the abyss.

His cock nudged her entrance and she opened her legs even wider. As he slid in, he felt enormous, but strangely good. The slow slide turned into a friction that sent sparks through her. She wanted to tell him to go faster, but thought he would wonder why. Perhaps she truly was a wanton.

When he was finally embedded deep within her, Hannah took a breath and realized this was the closest she'd been to anyone. It was amazing, it was life altering.

He kissed her. "Okay?"

She murmured a yes and tugged a bit on his back. Hannah needed him to move and joyfully, he did. At first his pace was slow, giving her time to adjust to the sheer size of him. Then she raised her knees and he groaned above her.

Hannah knew he was holding himself up with one arm as he pleasured her and thrust his cock within her. She wanted to kiss him but couldn't. She whimpered as the coil within her wound so tight, she couldn't even think.

Then something crashed over her, stealing her breath and stopping her heart. The wave spread out from her center and through her body, an ecstasy that was almost unbearable. She thought she shouted his name, but realized she couldn't tell for the ringing in her ears.

He leaned down and kissed her then, his body finally covering hers completely. She clenched around him as he thrust faster and faster, his breath coming in grunts against her cheek. She opened her mouth to his questing tongue, just as her body was open to his staff.

Matt's fingers bunched the coverlet beneath them as he thrust in so deep, she saw stars. The pleasure that had been ebbing within her began again. She held him close as he whispered her name in her ear, filling her with his seed.

Tears formed in her eyes so she shut them tightly. She had never known what it meant to be close to someone, to have a mate. *She'd never known.*

Hannah had become Mrs. Matthew Graham.

Matt stared at the ceiling, his mind a jumble of thoughts. What he'd intended as a simple introduction to the ways of men and women had turned into something completely different. He'd lost control.

Again.

Hannah wasn't anything special. She was an ordinary woman with plain features. He had never noticed her before even if they had been in town at the same time. It was only through sheer coincidence they'd met in the store a week ago.

Then why? Why did he fall into some kind of spell every time he touched her?

He sure as hell didn't understand it, and if he were honest with himself, he didn't like it. Matt was the oldest, the one who had to be in charge and in control at all times. Hannah threw him off kilter, made his body react in ways it never had. And he lost the ability to think when he was with her.

It was disconcerting and maddening. It was also frightening.

Matt knew his parents' marriage had been one based on love. They were affectionate and had always respected each other. That wasn't a bad thing, but his father had also kowtowed to his mother's wishes. Matt wanted his marriage to be based on mutual respect and not this loco physical reaction he was wholly unprepared for.

Of course, at this point they were well and truly married, and there was no way to reverse that particular event. He still didn't know exactly what had happened after that first kiss. It was as if his mind took a nap while his body thoroughly tasted, teased, and joined with hers.

Just thinking about what they'd done made his cock hard again. It twitched beneath the covers at the memory of being with Hannah. Hungry again for her only minutes after their first time together.

She couldn't know how much she affected him. Ever. Matt wanted to hold the reins in their marriage and if Hannah knew she could control him with her body, he'd never touch those reins again.

He finally closed his eyes, the grit in them uncomfortable. Perhaps he would sleep or perhaps not. His wedding day had not turned out as he'd expected, that was for sure. As Matt began to drift off, he was vaguely aware Hannah had snuggled up beside him, her touch giving him the extra comfort he needed to finally sleep.

CHAPTER SIX

Hannah was awake and out of bed long before the sunrise. She could hardly put two thoughts together but she managed to make coffee. The first mouthful of the strong hot brew helped make her feel a bit more grounded.

Yesterday morning she'd drank coffee from the same cup in the same room. Today she was a completely different person, wedded and bedded, a girl no more. She was a little sore, but ignored the discomfort. After all, it was probably normal. She had other things to worry about.

She had made a batch of biscuits and still had jerky. That and coffee would have to do for breakfast. Now she had to convince Granny to come with them to the Graham ranch. Hannah could not allow her to stay at the boardinghouse alone.

"Good morning." Matt appeared in the doorway, wearing the same clothes he'd worn the day before.

Memories of the night's activities flooded her thoughts. She was suddenly hotter than the coffee and distinctly tingly between her legs. Was this supposed to happen when she saw her husband?

"Morning." Hannah jumped up and poured him a cup of coffee. She couldn't sit still for more than a few moments. If she did, she might grab him and kiss him until neither one of them could see straight.

He sat at the table and reached for a biscuit. When she set the coffee down, he smiled up at her. "Thank you, Hannah."

Her tongue had ceased to function so she just nodded and stepped back. To her relief, the rest of the Grahams started filing into the room, each of them quiet and sleepy-looking.

"Caleb, you and Nick go get the team hitched up. The road is still muddy but it ain't a lake anymore." Matt took a bite of his biscuit. "Girls, make the beds upstairs and make sure everything is clean."

This time when Matt glanced at Hannah, the smiling seductiveness of last night was gone. He was as serious as she'd ever seen him.

"How soon can you have everything packed so we can leave?"

"Um, I'm already packed. I need to talk to Granny though." She had to do more than talk to her—she had to convince her.

"Then get to it. I want to be on our way in fifteen minutes." He finished his biscuit and rose with a piece of jerky in his hand. "I'll make sure the outside of the house is secure."

There it was again. That bossiness she'd noticed the night before. He had been in charge at the ranch only a few months so it must be something he'd always done. That didn't mean she had to like it though.

She left the Grahams to eat what they wanted of the humble meal. The hallway was deserted as she walked to her grandmother's room. She heard her talking aloud as Hannah knocked.

"Who is it?" her grandmother called from inside.

"It's me, Granny. It's time to go."

"So go." She sounded as grumpy as normal.

"I mean both of us need to leave with the Grahams," she said through the closed door.

"I ain't leaving until this place is sold. That's that."

Hannah waited a minute before speaking again. She needed to find a way for her grandmother to think it was her own idea to leave.

"I need your help, Granny. I . . . I can't go to the ranch with all of those strangers. At least one of them doesn't like me already." She pressed her forehead on the door, feeling every word for the truth it was. "I feel lost and I need you with me. Please."

The door opened so suddenly Hannah fell in the room. She landed on her hands and knees with a painful thud. At least she didn't land on her face.

"What are you doing, child?"

Hannah's wrists throbbed as she got back to her feet. "Trying to break my arms, apparently."

"Well, get up then. We've got to pack my things, I reckon." Granny grinned at her. "How much time did that handsome husband give you?"

"Fifteen minutes." Hannah knew her wrists would hurt like the dickens later, but for now she had no time to think about it.

"Best get crackin' then." Granny pointed at her traveling bag, open on the bed. "I already started."

Hannah hugged her grandmother so hard, she felt her own bones creak. "Thank you."

"Don't thank me yet. I may fight so much with Eva, you will send me back here on a mule."

They both laughed as they made quick work of packing Granny's belongings. There wasn't much, most of it sentimental pieces from her parents, husband, and daughter.

Hannah started when she saw Matt standing in the doorway, hat on his head and a scowl on his face.

"We were just, uh, finishing up in here." She took her grandmother's hand. "Granny is going to come with us."

"Fine then. We need to get back to the ranch. There's a lot of chores and animals that need tending to." He gestured to her traveling bag. "I took your things to the wagon already, Hannah. Is that everything you need, Mrs. Dolan?"

"Yep. I'm leaving everything else here for now. Maybe whoever buys the old place will want the furnishings." Granny tucked Hannah's elbow in her own.

Matt picked up the bag and led them out of the room. Hannah didn't know what to think of his brusque behavior other than that he was worried about the ranch. He hadn't acted like this with her before. Maybe now that they were married, he had dropped the kind and soft-spoken mask. She hoped not because that would make fifty years seem like an eternity.

As they walked toward the front door, Hannah found her steps slowing. This boardinghouse was the only home she knew. Her parents had died when she was young enough that she'd forgotten their small farmhouse almost completely. When they reached the front door, she stopped.

Granny patted her arm. "I know how you feel, child. It's time to go to your new home though. No use looking back." She pointed at Matt, who was currently putting the bag in the back of the wagon. "Look instead at what's ahead."

Matt bent down, giving them an unobstructed view of his behind. It was a very nicely shaped rear end, something she hadn't noticed before. Staring at it made her cheeks flush and a hint of memory from last night whipped through her.

"Are you ready?"

The sound of Granny's voice cut through Hannah's distracted thoughts. "Um, yes, I'm ready now." No need to let her grandmother know exactly what she had been thinking about.

They walked outside, the sound of the door closing behind them a final thump on the first chapter of Hannah's life. She wouldn't dwell on what could be or she'd drive herself loco. The truth was, she had no idea what waited for them at the Graham ranch. There was only one way to find out.

The wagon was full of the Grahams, all staring at her and Granny. Hannah didn't know whether to be scared or excited.

"We made you a seat, Mrs. Dolan." Catherine jumped up and down beside them. "Matt said you can't ride like we do so we made you a special seat."

"Is that so? How thoughtful of him." Granny allowed Matt and Caleb to help her up into the wagon.

Catherine hopped up beside her and took her hand, leading her to the front. "Right here, Mrs. Granny."

Hannah smiled as her grandmother settled down on the seat made of what appeared to be blankets draped over something, perhaps a couple crates. Catherine perched beside her, her hand firmly clasped with Granny's.

"You want to ride up front with me?" Matt asked from behind her, his warm breath gusting past her cheek.

She closed her eyes for a moment at the unfamiliar sensation. "Do you want me to?" she blurted. "I mean, yes, I'd like to."

Matt took her elbow again. This was a familiar touch and she found herself enjoying it. A lot. In that moment, it was as if they were a regular married couple sharing casual touches, with no boundaries between them.

Hannah couldn't help the smile that spread across her face at the thought. Perhaps there was a future for the two of them, regardless of the challenges coming their way. If they were as compatible emotionally as they were physically, then it was going to be a good life.

Then she caught sight of Olivia in the corner of the wagon. Her gaze was full of dark emotions and anger, all directed at Hannah. She had no idea what would make her new sister-in-law treat her as if she had committed a crime. It destroyed her good mood, wiped the smile off her face, and made her lose her footing.

Matt grabbed her arm, his grip tight on her wrist. She winced at the pain, sucking in a breath.

He sighed. "Are you okay?"

"Oh, I'm fine. Sorry about that. I, uh, can be clumsy." Avoiding her new husband's gaze, Hannah put her foot on the wheel and hauled herself up into the wagon.

When she got herself settled, she realized Caleb was waiting for her to move to the center. It appeared she would ride between Matt and his brother. They were both big men and their shoulders and legs touched hers. Another new and decidedly strange sensation.

When the ranch came into view, her stomach quivered and her heart followed suit. She was about to arrive at her new home.

*   *   *

Matt squirmed in the wagon seat. He had woken up that morning expecting Hannah to be next to him, but she had left him alone in the bed. For a reason he could not understand, it had put him in a foul mood. He should be ecstatic. After all, he was married and could now claim the acreage from Texas.

He was far from being happy though, bordering on downright grumpy. The ride out to the ranch took twice as long as usual because of the muddy condition of the ground. The horses pulled them through, albeit slowly, and they arrived by late morning.

Everything looked fine, and he knew there was no reason to worry about the ranch. Yet as soon as the wagon stopped in front of the house, he tossed the reins to Caleb and jumped down.

"I'm going to check on things. Take care of the wagon." Without a word to Hannah or Mrs. Dolan, he walked to the barn.

"That wasn't very nice." Catherine's voice followed him across the still muddy ground. She was right, of course, but he wasn't about to change his mind.

Matt needed to be alone for a bit. He missed his morning rides, that peaceful time when he could be completely by himself. It would be harder to do that with a wife, he realized. Now was the time he truly could not stop himself from escaping. Later he would explain why if Hannah asked.

Obviously Javier or Lorenzo had already cleaned the stalls that morning. It was usually Nick's job, but the ranch hands did what they had to. They were good people, as was their mother, Eva. Without her helping with the young'uns, Matt didn't think they would have survived after their parents' deaths and

Ben's disappearance. The Vasquez family was linked with the Grahams, and he hoped when they did get the land, to give some of it to them. He knew it was the right thing to do, and his father would have approved wholeheartedly.

Matt walked farther into the barn and the familiar surroundings made him feel better immediately. Winston poked his head out of the stall and nickered when he caught sight of Matt. With a grin, Matt scratched the big gelding behind his ears and endured the snuffling of his pockets for treats he didn't have.

"Sorry, boy, I'm just back from town. Later I'll bring you something." He leaned his forehead against the horse's neck and tried to calm down.

Something was making him so tense, his teeth were beginning to ache from clenching them. He thought it might have to do with bringing Hannah home and moving into his parents' room. It was also a significant adjustment to suddenly have someone who was legally bound to him, and yet another person he was responsible for keeping safe.

It wasn't her fault, of course. He had to place all the blame right where it belonged, on his own shoulders. Hannah was a good person. She'd accepted his loco proposal although she should have kicked him out of the boardinghouse. Now she was not only married but bedded, and there was no turning back.

His stomach did a funny flip at the thought of sleeping with her every night for the rest of his life. He was not prepared for that kind of intimacy, especially sharing everything with her. Even though he was part of such a big family, Matt knew he was something of a loner. He spent time with his family, but most times he kept his thoughts and feelings to himself. Maybe it was because he was the oldest, but no matter the reason, he kept himself to himself. Hannah might put a kink in that whole approach to life.

Matt wasn't looking forward to that. There was a reason he was a loner, it kept him solid and focused. A wife would be a completely new element in an already complex situation. Too many siblings, too much tragedy, and a ranch to run. A ranch that was about to grow ten times bigger. He would also never give up the quest to find his parents' murderer and locate his youngest brother. There was a big goddamn hole in his heart and it wouldn't be filled until he accomplished both those tasks.

As he brooded over the significant changes in his life, Matt saddled Winston and then led him out the back of the barn. He mounted the horse, briefly considering the idea of showing Hannah around the ranch, introducing her to Eva, Lorenzo, and Javier, but then he dismissed it. His sisters and brothers could take care of that. Matt needed to think.

Hannah didn't let the hurt show on her face after Matt walked away from the wagon. He had dismissed her as if she were just another one of his siblings, no one of consequence or importance. Caleb didn't say anything as he helped her down. The rest of the Grahams dispersed like a swarm of bees, going every which way. Nicholas at least brought their bags inside the house before disappearing.

That left Granny and her standing on the doorstep of the Graham ranch house. Hannah felt like crying and screaming at the same time. Was this treatment what she must accept for the rest of her life? To be an afterthought, not even warranting the attention of a guest? It was heartbreaking to know she was so unimportant to every Graham, particularly the one she had pledged her life to.

"Are you ready to meet Eva?" Catherine appeared beside them, her gap-toothed grin wide on her pixie face.

Hannah could have cried for the sweetness of the child. Instead she hugged her and took her hand. As natural as could be, Catherine wrapped her hand around Hannah's.

"I'm ready," Hannah said.

"Okay, then let me show you everything." Catherine pointed at the house. "This is our home and our front porch. We live here."

With a lighter heart, Hannah took her grandmother's arm and they walked into the house with little Catherine. It had already been a long day, and the most difficult part still awaited them.

The interior of the house smelled of wood and bread. They were comfortable scents, almost welcoming. The front part of the house was a big room with furniture and a rag rug positioned in front of a large fireplace. There were nails in the wood to the left of the door with a few coats hanging on them. Several pairs of muddy boots sat beneath them. At least Eva had them trained to keep dirty shoes out of the house.

The room was obviously where they gathered as a family, with well-worn pillows and an afghan dotting the sofa. She liked this room and all it represented.

"This is the parlor. We have fires over yonder in the fireplace when it's cold and Matt reads to me at night on the sofa. At Christmas we even sing 'round the fire." Catherine's interpretation of everything was so refreshing. She didn't see the room's practical functions, but rather the memories of good times she'd had in it.

"It's lovely." Hannah smiled at her. "I like it a lot."

"Me, too." Catherine tugged at her hand. "Now let's go to the kitchen. That's where we eat."

Hannah heard Granny chuckle as they both walked through a large archway into the very spacious kitchen. Sitting in the middle of it was the biggest table she'd ever seen, a necessity no doubt with a big family like the Grahams.

"This is the table my Pa built." Catherine pointed to a diminutive woman Hannah hadn't noticed. "Eva, this is my new sister."

The woman turned, her dark chocolate eyes assessing and incredibly sharp. This was the person who ran the house. The one Hannah would have to win over or she would never be at home in the house.

Hannah managed to smile. "Hello, Mrs. Vasquez. I'm Hannah."

There was a pause before the other woman spoke. *"Buenos dias, señora."*

Hannah knew some Spanish but not enough. "It's wonderful to meet you."

Eva's gaze moved to beyond Hannah's shoulder and her expression changed to surprise. "Martha!"

"Eva Vasquez. How long has it been?" Granny pulled the other woman into a hug. "I can't believe I had to ride all the way out here to see you again."

Eva chuckled. "You are still a *mujer loca*. *¿Es la señora su nieta?*"

"Yes, she is. Joanna's girl." Granny gave Hannah a wink. "She's been running the boardinghouse for the last five years. Lord knows I ain't worth a damn anymore."

"Si, es la verdad." Eva turned to Hannah, and after

a moment, took her hands. "Welcome to our home. *Bienvenidos.*"

Hannah couldn't have been happier to feel the small woman's callused palms against her own. She'd had no idea what to expect at the Graham ranch, and was doubly glad Granny had come with them. Without Granny's friendship with Eva, she sensed the greeting would have been very different.

Catherine must have grown bored with the adults' conversation. She stood in the doorway and did a little dance. "Let's go now. I need to show you the rest of the house."

"*Hija,* you need to be patient." Eva didn't raise her voice, but her tone made the little girl stop fidgeting.

"Yes, ma'am." The sigh was small but dramatic nonetheless. "May I please show Hannah the rest of the house now?" Catherine twirled her braids around her fingers. "Please?"

"*Uno momento, hija.*" Eva squeezed Hannah's hands. "Come back after your journey with Catarina. We will talk."

"I'm gonna stay here and chat a spell with Eva. You go on, child." Granny lowered herself into a chair.

"I look forward to it." Hannah smiled at Eva. The housekeeper could definitely be a good source of information about her new husband. He certainly didn't appear to be very forthcoming and had acted as if he didn't even want her at the ranch. Perhaps his motives were as he said, simply to get a wife so he could secure the land for the ranch. She had hoped for more, much more, but no one could ever know that.

Hannah kissed her grandmother's forehead, then walked over to Catherine and took her hand.

"Oh good, now I can show you the room you will sleep in. My Mama and Papa used to sleep there, but they went to Heaven to be with Jesus." Catherine's tone spoke of much more than a simple seven-year-old's understanding. "Their bedroom is empty and it makes me sad when I see it."

She led Hannah to an open door down the hallway, one of five that must lead to other bedrooms. Bright sunshine spilled through a window with white lace curtains hanging on either side. Hannah knew that someone had decorated the room with love. She saw not only the intricate lace curtains, but a beautiful quilt on a bed with a headboard of carved wooden flowers. A chest of drawers sat in one corner, one drawer askew. There was a fresh smell in the air, as if it had been newly cleaned.

Hannah couldn't have explained it well, but the room made her feel safe. The Grahams had loved each other; she'd understood that right away. They had died together, violently from what she knew. Yet instead of their horrific end, Hannah sensed the good life they had lived.

"Do you like it? It's an awful big bed." Catherine climbed up and bounced on it.

"Yes, I like it very much. It's lovely." She ran her hand along the tight stitches on the quilt and wondered who had made it. Her first instinct was that Matt's mother had made it while preparing for her own wedding. The romantic notion made her smile.

"Now let's see my room." Catherine jumped down and pulled Hannah from the room.

As she followed the girl around the house, Hannah's thoughts remained in her new room, and what the night held in store.

CHAPTER SEVEN

Matt rode Winston until the horse was lathered and breathing hard. When he finally realized his horse was exhausted, he gentled his movements until he saw the creek up ahead. After he climbed down off the horse, he realized his knees were sore from gripping the saddle.

What the hell was he doing running away and almost killing his horse in the process? Stupid and foolhardy. Something a boy ten years younger would do, not a man who was responsible for almost a dozen people's lives. He had to remain strong and keep hold of his emotions. Outbursts would not help anything and certainly couldn't happen again.

He let his horse drink his fill and graze on the sweet grass on the bank. Matt looked east, toward where the house was, and his future. His wife. He needed to talk to someone about how to act around her. It was awkward and downright uncomfortable between them, mostly due to his own behavior.

Knowing he'd been a coward, and angry at himself, Matt threw himself up into Winston's saddle. He rode back toward the ranch, toward Hannah. He had to find a way to accept his new life and his new wife.

No matter how much he told himself to go into the house, Matt spent an inordinate amount of time rubbing down, then currying Winston. The gelding would have been smiling if he could have.

"Are you hiding?" Nicholas appeared with Javier in the stall doorway. The younger Vasquez was sixteen, the same age as Nick, but he was as big as his brother, Lorenzo. Both Vasquez men were natural horsemen and miracle workers with ornery cattle. Each of them was devoted to their mother, and had the same olive-toned skin, chocolate eyes, and thick black hair.

"Yes." Matt didn't think lying to his brother would work, so he just blurted the truth.

"She seems nice." Nick stepped in and leaned against the wall.

"Yeah, she's nice. I just . . . Hell, I don't know what to do with a wife." Even after watching his parents all his life, he found the relationship between them a mystery. He just didn't understand it.

Javier shook his head, a grin splitting his face. "You don't know what do with your new *esposa*?"

Matt realized what he'd said, and to his annoyance, felt his cheeks heat. "That's not what I meant. I don't know what else to do with her."

"You could start by talking to her. Maybe even have a meal with her." Nick snorted at his not-so-funny quips and Javier laughed out loud.

"Both of you get the hell out of here. Don't you have work to do? Some cattle to take care of?" Matt snapped.

"Nope, we're done for now. We came back for supper." Nick turned to leave, still chuckling under his breath.

"Supper?" Matt repeated. It couldn't possibly be that late, could it?

"It's five o'clock, Matt. You disappeared six hours ago. I think Eva is ready to kick your ass." With that Nick and Javier left Matt alone.

It was five in the afternoon? He had been gone half the day, and not only had he left Hannah alone all that time, but he'd spent a second day doing no work around the ranch. Irresponsible didn't even begin to cover his behavior and no doubt Eva would tan his hide for it, not to mention what Mrs. Dolan would do. And dammit, he was hungry since he'd obviously missed dinner.

He finally left the barn, this time with a bit of speed in his step. Everything appeared to be normal as he walked into the house. Then he heard the laughter.

Hannah.

He'd heard her laugh once before, but nothing like this. The sound was full of joy that echoed around him and through him. Damned if it didn't make him smile. Whatever had happened while he'd been off on his own must have been better than he'd expected.

He took off his boots and hung up his hat, then headed into the kitchen. Not knowing what to expect, he trod lightly, peering around the corner so they wouldn't know he was there. Eva and Hannah stood beside each other at the counter. One tall and curvy, the other short and round. One dark, one light. They were a study in opposites, but they appeared to be in harmony.

The kitchen had an air of happiness he hadn't experienced in months. He wondered if it was Hannah's presence that had lifted the cloud of doom that had hung over the ranch for so long. When he'd met her in the store one week ago, Matt had had no idea how entwined their lives would become.

Perhaps he was foolish to stay away from her, to be afraid of being married. If Eva liked her, then he knew he'd made a good choice. He trusted the housekeeper implicitly—she'd been a second mother to him for the last fifteen years. Maybe later he'd get some time with her. No doubt he'd have to endure a dressing-down, but he'd also have a chance to talk to her about Hannah. That's what he should have done when he'd arrived instead of running away. He'd probably feel the repercussions of his behavior for a while.

Mrs. Dolan sat at the table with a cup. She was the first to spot him. "And the prodigal son returns. You'd best get on in here and get it over with. I'm thinking you have some groveling to do." Hannah's grandmother was definitely not one to keep a thought to herself.

Hannah and Eva turned to look at him as he walked into the kitchen. One woman was wary, the other most assuredly annoyed. They both had flour all over the aprons they wore and their hands.

"Eva is teaching me how to make tortillas," Hannah blurted before she turned back to the counter.

Eva shook her head at him, and he felt the force of that stare all the way to his toes. She could embarrass him further by scolding him right then and there. He sure as hell hoped she wouldn't.

"She is a fast learner." When Eva finally let her gaze move away from his, Matt took a deep breath. "Go ring the bell and wash up. Supper will be ready in fifteen minutes."

"Yes, ma'am."

Matt bolted out of the kitchen to ring the dinner

bell. No need to tempt fate by giving Eva another opportunity to yell at him. He owed Hannah an apology but he couldn't seem to form the words. Maybe later when they went to bed, he'd feel more relaxed and be able to speak to her without tripping over his tongue.

Hannah hardly saw the tortilla in her hand for the pounding in her head and her heart. Matt had spent hours away from the house, and he didn't even say a word to her. She managed to swallow the lump of hurt in her throat, but just barely. Eva must have sensed Hannah's discomfort because she took her hand.

"*No te preocupes, hija.* He does not know yet who he is."

Hannah didn't understand the Spanish but she recognized the message just the same. She nodded and managed to make some semblance of a tortilla.

"Why don't you stir the beans and then set the table. I will finish." Eva gently turned Hannah toward the stove.

After wiping her hands on a towel, she found the act of making dinner gave her back some normalcy on the strangest day of her life. She set the table for the twelve of them. Mr. Graham obviously knew what he'd been doing when he built a table with benches on either side. The two chairs had been for the parents and Hannah wondered who would sit there during this meal.

Within ten minutes, the Grahams started filing in and sat on the bench, including Matt. He did not meet her gaze, again, as she and Eva put the food on the table. A pot of beans with a bit of meat, tortillas, and pitchers of water comprised the simple fare.

Matt rose from the bench and went to the chair at one end of the table. He finally glanced up at her. His expression was unreadable, but he gestured her toward the chair at the other end. It was a small peace offering, and she was stupidly grateful for it.

"Sit, *hija*, sit." Eva pulled the chair out for her and helped Hannah sit. It was something a gentleman would do, but she had already realized her new husband wasn't necessarily trained to act as a gentleman should.

After they all sat, everyone dug in, filling fresh tortillas with beans. Hannah hadn't had such delicious food before and hoped Eva would show her the secrets of the spices. The flavorful beans danced on her tongue, while at the same time filling her belly quickly.

The family chatted throughout the meal, mostly about things to do with the ranch. Hannah was an observer, not really part of the conversation. No one spoke directly to her and Olivia continued to treat Hannah as a very unwelcome visitor. At least she was safe and warm, and accepted by two members of the family.

Catherine sat beside her, her legs swinging on the bench as she gobbled up her supper. With a bite still in her mouth, she looked at Eva. "May I be excused please?"

"Yes, *hija*, you go wash up and get your schooling books ready." Eva appeared to be the person who kept everyone on schedule.

"Can I read to Hannah tonight instead of you?" Catherine directed her question at Matt. It surprised both him and Hannah.

"You want to read with her?" Olivia snorted. "We don't even know if she can read."

Hannah flinched at the animosity in her sister-in-law's voice. "I can read. As you know, I went to school until I was seven. Afterward, Granny taught me at home."

"No need to be like that, Livy." Matt's tone was not very firm, even if he said the right words. "Are you sure, Catherine?"

Hannah didn't know whether he didn't trust her or whether he was jealous that Catherine had changed their routine. Either way it wasn't good for such emotions to be between them.

"It's okay. We can do it another time together, okay?" Hannah wanted to avoid the conflict and try to find a compromise with Matt.

"I don't want to do it another time." Catherine pouted her lip. "I want Hannah." She pointed at Matt. "Besides, you were mean to her today."

"I was not mean." Matt's brows slammed together. "I had chores to do after being away for more than a day."

"Is that why you went riding on Winston all afternoon?" Nicholas smirked at him.

"If you didn't want to marry her, you shouldn't have." Olivia apparently couldn't keep quiet any longer.

"Jesus please us, will you all just shut up?" Matt's face was flushed with anger.

"Don't use the Lord's name like that, Mateo." Eva sounded as mad as he was.

The supper that had started with the fun of making tortillas had turned into a family argument. And Hannah was squarely in the center of it.

"Listen, all of you, Hannah and I are married now, and you all have to accept that. You're embarrassing me and yourselves in front of her." He glared at each of them in turn. "This is hard enough without all of you acting like spoiled idiots."

Hannah could not bear one more second of the arguing. She got to her feet. "I'll start heating water for the dishes." The water could never be as hot as her cheeks felt.

Her departure seemed to defuse the situation, because the Grahams were suddenly quiet. All she heard as she pumped water into a bucket was chewing and breathing. Eva appeared at her elbow and touched her shoulder. It was a wordless gesture that meant a lot.

After the pail was nearly full, she picked up the handle and swung it over to the stove. She stoked up the fire and got the blaze glowing bright with a few pokes of a stick. When she turned to get another pail heated, she ran smack into Matt's chest. He felt as hard as he had the two times she'd touched him before, and her traitorous body reacted with a jolt of pure pleasure.

She stepped back and glanced around, eager to avoid his gaze and his touch. To her surprise, everyone else was gone, and he had apparently been left to clear the plates.

"They don't normally behave like that." He set a stack of plates in the sink.

"I don't know if I believe that." Hannah wanted to slap her hand across her mouth but it was the truth. "I mean, I think you are all painfully honest with each other."

He made a face but didn't disagree with her. "They feel things deeply and this year has been more than hard." He leaned against the sink. "Once we get the ranch expanded, solve some things, and settle down a bit, things will be better."

She certainly hoped so or she would have a lot of trouble fitting in with them. "I didn't know Catherine would ask for me, I mean, for her reading."

"She misses Mama."

Hannah knew he didn't mean to say she was a substitute mother, but it sure felt that way. She pushed
aside the silly notion that everything revolved around
her. The Grahams had suffered a lot and she needed
to stop thinking of herself.

"I won't ever be able to take your mother's place,
but I hope I can be part of this family."

He looked surprised. "You already are."

She shook her head. "No, I'm not, but I'm trying."
With that, she turned to the sink and busied herself
filling another bucket. When she turned around a few
minutes later, he was gone.

At least the day was nearly over.

Matt stood outside on the porch with Caleb at his
side. The night air was cool on his skin, a much
needed sensation after the supper that had turned
into a fiasco.

"That could have gone better," Caleb said drily.

"Thanks for helping out there, brother."

"Livy has a bee in her bonnet about your wife,
Catherine is stuck to her like a cocklebur, and Eva
seems to like her." Caleb held up his hands. "I'm not
getting in the middle of all that."

"I'm living in it. Knee deep in it." No matter what
Matt did, it was the wrong thing. "I need to get to
Houston with her to sign those papers. If it ain't raining, we'll go on Monday. I don't want to wait any
longer."

"I don't blame you. You want me to come?"

"No, not this time. I need you here." Matt figured
the trip alone with Hannah might help fix things between them, too.

The brothers went to the barn and checked the

animals, making sure they were settled for the night. The darkness surrounded them as the night creatures began to sing. It was peaceful, at least temporarily. Caleb disappeared with Lorenzo, leaving Matt to return to the house alone.

It was time to go to his new bedroom and his new wife. He took a deep breath and headed back into the house.

The kitchen was empty, everything cleaned and put away. He walked down the hallway, feeling his heart thump with each step. The door was closed without any light shining beneath it. Matt took a deep breath and opened the door.

In a splash of moonlight coming through the curtains, he could see she was curled up in a corner of the bed, only her hair visible above the quilt. Since it was barely nine o'clock, he didn't know if she was truly sleeping or just avoiding him.

Either way, he didn't think he would be enjoying his marriage bed that night. As he began to undress, the reality of sleeping in this room hit him. The room wasn't his and neither was the bed. The only thing in the room he could claim was currently hiding or sleeping under the covers.

He closed his eyes and thought about how important it was to his family to expand the ranch, to do what his father had intended to do. Reminding himself this was just a room, and his parents were never going to use it again, didn't really help. Matt stood there with his shirt untucked and his fists clenched, unable to proceed or retreat.

What had started as a simple act of preparing for bed turned into a battle between his heart and his head. The unexpectedness of life shouldn't surprise him, but it always did.

"Matt?" Hannah's soft voice was like an angel's whisper.

He sucked in a breath and was finally able to move. "Sorry if I woke you, Hannah." Even his voice sounded odd.

"I was just dozing. Are you okay? You were just standing there like a statue." She must not be too angry with him; at least she was concerned about him and actually speaking to him.

"Yeah, I'm fine. It's just this room. I haven't slept in it before." He couldn't quite tell her how he'd been overcome with emotion and unable to take off his shirt. He'd been embarrassed enough for the day. He fumbled with the buttons on his shirt.

"You haven't?" There was a pause and then she spoke again. "Oh, Matt, I didn't realize."

The covers rustled and her hand pressed against the center of his back. Heat flowed from her into him and within seconds, he wasn't frozen any longer. In fact, he was too hot.

He turned around to face her and although she was only a shadow in the night, he could smell her, would have known it was Hannah even if he hadn't heard her voice. When he pulled her flush against him, her softness melded with his hardness. Matt knew he needed to talk to her, to find some peace between them after the crazy antics of supper, but at that moment, nothing could have stopped him from kissing her.

Her lips were as soft as the rest of her, pliant beneath his, moving with them as he explored her mouth. His cock turned into a hammer, pounding at her stomach, wanting to be let out and satisfied. Matt should have gone slower, he should have taken care of seducing her, but he didn't.

Within seconds, his clothes were on the floor along with her cotton nightdress and their skin was touching head to toe. It was incredible, indescribably wonderful.

"Oh my." Her breathy whisper skittered across his neck, raising gooseflesh.

He scooped her up and set her on the bed, then climbed on top of her. If he thought standing naked near her felt good, lying on her was enough to make him come immediately. It was only through sheer force of will that he didn't.

Matt wanted to savor every second with Hannah in bed. It was the first time for them in their new room and he wanted this first memory to be a good one.

He kissed her jaw, making his way to her neck. She trembled as he nibbled and kissed a path down her neck to her collarbone. For some reason he found the hollow there interesting and spent time exploring the expanse of skin. She must've grown restless because she shifted beneath him and made a sighing noise.

Reminding himself to go back to that sweet spot later, he moved to her breasts. Ah, what a treasure they had been to discover. He'd had no idea what had been hidden behind her plain dress. They were the perfect size for his hand, and her nipples grew instantly hard when touched. She was obviously made for loving, so inherently passionate, he counted his lucky stars her name was Hannah and that she was his.

While he cupped her left breast, his mouth closed around the right. This time she moaned and then squeaked when he nipped at her. Hannah was a treasure and she didn't even know it. He switched breasts, pleasuring her and himself until he could wait no longer. His cock throbbed with each beat of his heart, wanting and needing more.

He raised himself up and kissed her, spreading her legs with his knees. She opened up to him like a flower waiting to be pollinated. As his cock touched those hidden petals, he groaned at the wetness and heat that greeted him. Hannah pulled at his shoulders when he paused. If he didn't think he'd explode, he might have laughed at how impatient she was.

He sank into her softness and shook with the raw pleasure coursing through him. She'd been made for him, the perfect size, the perfect fit, the perfect everything. She might not know it yet, but Matt did. He almost lost control once he was fully sheathed inside her.

After a moment's pause to regain his wits, Matt began to move, slowly at first. She picked up his rhythm and pushed up as he thrust down. As natural as could be, she was in tune with everything he did. It was astonishing, and if he had a thought in his head, he would have been frightened by the implications.

She tugged on his shoulders again and he picked up his pace. Her channel grew tighter with each thrust. His balls tingled as his release grew closer. He wanted her to experience pleasure, too, so he lifted himself up in order to reach between them. Her clit was swollen, begging for his touch.

At the first flick of his fingers, she arched her back and gasped. He thrust faster and faster, pleasuring her clit as her tightness pleasured his cock. She was so slippery he couldn't hold back any longer.

"Come on, honey, come fly with me." The guttural voice didn't even sound like his.

She arched again, squeezing around him like a vise. "Matthew." Her whispered scream went straight to his balls and the world exploded around him.

Pure ecstasy flooded him as he pumped into her

again and again. He held onto the bed for fear he'd truly fly away from the pleasure, the likes of which he'd never experienced.

His teeth buzzed in his head, every limb tingled, and he was still hard, buried deep inside her. He pressed his forehead to hers and caught his breath.

When he could finally form a coherent thought, he rolled off her, almost groaning when he left the warmth of her body. Matt pulled her close until they were spooned together on the bed. He was asleep within minutes, his new wife's heart beating against his.

The best laid plans never come to fruition if Mother Nature has her way. Although Hannah knew the land grant deadline was approaching, they hadn't been able to get away from the ranch because of problems. First there were missing cattle, which took nearly half a day to find in a secluded valley on their neighbor's property. Then, two of the new calves got sick, and Matt seemed to have a magic touch with the tiny bovines.

Before Hannah knew it, four days had flown past and things were still unsaid between them. After their first night at the ranch, she had been asleep before Matt even came to bed; then he was up before the sun. They hadn't been close again, at least no closer than sleeping beside each other.

Thank God Eva had taken her under her wing. The things she'd learned in the kitchen, what people on a ranch ate, how to make things like tamales, filled her days. She helped to clean, do laundry, and tried to lend a hand with the children.

Yet she didn't feel at home yet. Perhaps it was Olivia's ongoing hostility, the fact that Nicholas and

Rebecca ignored her, or maybe it was that she couldn't find her place. No matter what she did or didn't do, nothing was quite right.

Granny was there to talk to but she'd taken to spending a great deal of time in the kitchen with Eva. They obviously had a lot in common and Hannah didn't begrudge them their friendship. Truthfully, without the boarders to take care of or Granny's company, Hannah was lonely.

She woke up Thursday morning without her husband. Again. She dragged her feet a bit washing up and getting dressed. Breakfast was likely just getting started, judging by the gray light of dawn coming through the window. Matt hadn't slept in their bed the night before, which just made her feel worse. Hannah knew he'd been taking care of a sick calf, but that didn't make the situation better. She couldn't help thinking he cared more for the animal than his wife.

Self-pity didn't become her and she tried to stop it from creeping into her thoughts. Hannah needed to find something to do, so she would feel useful.

When she arrived in the kitchen, Rebecca and Elizabeth were already there. Both of them murmured a greeting and then returned to their chores of making breakfast. Eva was nowhere to be seen, but the girls were busy making cornpone and some kind of hash.

"Anything I can do to help?" Hannah noted the shoulder on Elizabeth's dress was missing a few stitches.

"No." Rebecca looked at her sister. "Thank you anyway."

At least they weren't hostile like Olivia, but they were not nearly as friendly as Catherine. Hannah went over to the stove and checked the coffeepot. It was nearly ready so she replaced the top and turned to the sink to get some cold water to settle the grounds.

Elizabeth stood there, pinning her with those same greenish blue eyes Matt had. "Eva don't want you messing with the coffee."

"I was just taking a peek." Hannah managed a weak smile. "I'm good with a needle. I can fix your dress for you."

Elizabeth's expression softened with surprise and she fingered her shoulder. "Really? Eva can't sew worth a darn. Mama always—well, none of us learned how."

Rebecca stared at her. "You can sew?"

This time, Hannah genuinely smiled. "Yes, I can. Granny taught me from the time I was a little girl. I have my sewing box with me."

Rebecca disappeared down the hallway at a run. She reappeared moments later with a large basket in her hands. It was obviously well used but in good shape. When she grinned, Elizabeth did, too.

Rebecca set the basket on the big table. "She can sew!"

They danced around the table chanting a silly song about sewing. Hannah laughed along with them, her heart so much lighter than it had been five minutes earlier.

"*¿Que pasa, hijas?*" Eva walked into the kitchen, her brow furrowed.

"Hannah can sew." Rebecca pointed at the basket.

Eva's gaze snapped to hers. "Truly?"

"Yes, I'm right handy with a needle." Hannah almost wanted to do a dance herself.

"*Dios mio,* Hannah. I've got a pile almost as high as Catherine that needs fixing." Eva took her hand. "You stay right there. Girls, get back to cooking."

Elizabeth and Rebecca jumped to do their duties while Hannah took the large sewing basket and started looking through it. By the time breakfast was ready, Hannah had already fixed two shirts and darned a pair of socks.

The mood was high and the laughter abundant until Olivia walked in. She carried a basket of eggs and a scowl.

"Livy, Hannah can sew." Rebecca seemed to be the most pleased by the newfound knowledge.

"Does that call for a holiday?" Olivia set the basket on the counter.

Eva cracked the eggs into the readied pan, and a sizzling sound filled the room. "*Sí*, it does call for a holiday. We have much sewing with so many people."

Olivia shrugged. "I sew."

Elizabeth snorted. "Like a bull dances."

"Shut up." Olivia speared her younger sister with a fierce glare. "At least I tried. More than you did."

"I know I can't sew, but at least I can cook. All you can do is scrub floors and clothes." Elizabeth stuck her nose in the air.

Olivia nearly leapt across the room at her sister. Eva stopped her with one look. The rest of the Grahams came in, no doubt after hearing the commotion between the girls.

Nicholas and Caleb stood by the door while Catherine rushed in with her braids flying.

"What happened? You didn't yell at Hannah again, did you, Livy?" Catherine was her protector of sorts.

"No, she didn't." Hannah gestured to the basket. "I was getting some sewing done and everybody got excited." It sounded foolish to her ears, but her explanation seemed to appease everyone.

Then Matt stepped in, pushing his brothers aside.

He surveyed the room quickly before his gaze settled on Hannah. With a nod, he came into the room and sat down at the other end of the table.

The tension dissipated and they all sat down to eat. Hannah finally had an appetite, after days of an upset stomach and an upset heart. The food was delicious, and she almost thought Olivia had softened just a smidge toward her. Hannah could have been imagining it, but she had a small bit of hope their relationship might be getting better.

"Hannah and I are going to Houston to sign the papers," Matt announced without any preamble, and without talking to Hannah about it first.

Everyone stopped eating and stared at him, then turned to look at Hannah. After she had finally found a way to fit in at the ranch, Matt was taking her away.

"For how long?" She was surprised her voice didn't shake.

"Two days at the most." Matt glanced at her. "After breakfast, pack what we need, including food."

Just like that, her husband had taken that goodness away from her. She wanted to tell him no. She wanted to tell him to ask her to do things instead of ordering her. Anger mixed with hurt, churning in her stomach. She lost her appetite for the delicious breakfast.

Hannah got to her feet. "I'm going to go check on Granny."

Most mornings Granny had trouble getting up because of pain in her joints. She usually made it up after the sun rose, but today Hannah wasn't going to wait. Today she needed her grandmother.

CHAPTER EIGHT

Eva's stare nearly burned a hole in Matthew's head. She was obviously angry with him, but he wasn't about to invite her to tell him why. The rest of his siblings were a barrier he was glad was there.

He had handled delivering the news about the trip to Houston badly. Truth was he was tired and his thoughts were a bit jumbled. He'd rehearsed talking to Hannah about it in his head numerous times during the night while he was taking care of the calf. Then somehow he thought he had done it already. Judging by the look on Hannah's face, he sure as hell hadn't.

Damn.

After that first night in the bedroom, he thought they had started to understand each other. At least the sex had been incredible. Damn, he spent half his time thinking about going to bed with her now. Unfortunately his tiredness and his big mouth had put a dent in that possibility.

Matt knew he'd have to talk to her, he just wanted to avoid it until they were on the trail together. It was a long ride to Houston. Plenty of time to talk.

Now all he had to do was avoid Eva until they left.

* * *

"He's a man, child. That's all I can say." Granny slowly buttoned her dress with gnarled hands. Hannah knew if she offered to help the older woman would be insulted. "Men can bully you around if you let them."

"I don't want him to bully me around." Hannah frowned. "But it seems he only wants me for the land."

Granny snorted. "Well, he told you that the minute he proposed. Why is it a surprise to you?"

It wasn't a surprise; it was a disappointment. Hannah had let her romantic side wreak havoc with her practical side, and it had resulted in misery.

"It's not. I just, well, I wanted more." She sighed and sat on the bed beside her grandmother, whose familiar scent helped calm her.

"Then you gotta earn it." Granny held out her hand and Hannah helped her to her feet. "Ain't no call to sit around whining."

Hannah's mouth dropped open. "I'm not whining."

"Land sakes, you've done nothing but whine since we got here." Granny speared her with one of those looks that always made Hannah squirm.

"I didn't think I was whining." She thought back over the four days since her wedding and realized Granny was right. She had been just accepting what was given to her rather than asking for what she wanted. That caused resentment, and obviously, whining.

"It's only natural that you feel out of place, Hannah. They're a big family." Granny patted her knee. "What you need to do is stake your claim, let them know who you really are."

Hannah didn't want to admit she didn't know who she was, and couldn't tell anyone anything. "What if they don't like me then?" Her voice dropped to a whisper. "What if Matt doesn't?"

"Get a backbone, child. There ain't no guarantees in this world. You got to take what you want and fight for what you need." Granny pointed at the chest in the corner. "Fetch me my reticule from that chest."

After some searching, Hannah found the ancient looking reticule, oft-mended and tattered as it was. She handed it to her grandmother.

"Now when I first got married, your grandfather was a fool. He was a terrible husband. My mama saw that and told me the same thing I'm telling you. Stand up for yourself and don't let nobody step on you." Granny fished around in the reticule and pulled out a handkerchief yellowed with age. As she unfolded it, Hannah found herself leaning forward, trying to see. "This here was my mama's wedding band."

Granny held up a thin band of silver. "I don't know what it's made of, but it's worth something. She gave it to me and said to keep it hidden. It was mine to do with as I chose." She put it in Hannah's palm and closed her fingers around it. "It's now yours. If you need to, sell it for money, but only if it's for you. This whole ranch is your husband's, but now you have something of value, too."

The slight weight of the ring in her hand didn't compare to the significance of what her grandmother had given her. It might not be a treasure, but it was something she could keep and call her own. She hugged her grandmother, so happy to have her there, to have her support and her love.

"Thank you. I will keep it safe."

"A'course you will. That's a legacy, that is. Not much

of one, but it's what I have to give you." Granny got to her feet.

She had given Hannah so much more than a ring. Without her grandmother's love and support, Hannah would have ended up in an orphanage or worse. Granny meant the world to Hannah.

"Now quit your whining. Go get what you want and fight for what you need." Granny shuffled toward the door. "I need some vittles and you'd best get packing." She glanced back at Hannah. "I've got faith in you, child. Go get him."

With that, her cackling grandmother had left her alone with her thoughts whirling. Hannah didn't think she'd been whining, but what Granny said did make sense. Matt had told her up front exactly what he wanted from her, and she had turned their marriage into a fairy tale of epic proportions. Foolish girl.

It was time Hannah actually started building the foundation for her marriage instead of waiting for someone to open the door for her. She would find a way to earn Matt's love and respect, instead of simply being his roommate. Hannah got to her feet and marched to her bedroom, ready to do battle.

He arrived in the bedroom five minutes later. She had begun packing her own bag, not knowing where his was. Without turning, she knew he was in the doorway watching her.

"I packed what appeared to be your Sunday clothes, along with mine. I brought the boot polish and brush, and my hairbrush." She looked down at her outfit. "I have a split riding skirt that used to be my mother's. What will the temperature be like at night? Do I need to bring my wool cape?"

He stared at her, surprise clearly written in his expression. "You're packing my things?"

"Of course. Isn't it a wife's job?" She had no idea what a wife's job was, but maybe he didn't either.

"I guess." He nodded. "I reckon I'll say thank you." He glanced at the bag. "We ought to get moving soon."

Hannah went back to packing as if she'd had ample experience doing it, which was far from the truth. She'd only packed twice in her life, once to move to the boardinghouse after her parents' deaths, and once when she got married. There had been no trips any-where for her. The one to Houston would be the first time she'd left their little town.

A glimmer of excitement tickled her chest. Perhaps she'd not only be able to get closer to her new hus-band but also have an adventure to one day tell her children. With an even lighter heart, she finished packing and changed into the butter-soft leather rid-ing skirt. It had been her mother's. Although Hannah remembered her as being tall, she must've been short. The skirt was at least six inches too short. It wasn't as if Hannah could make it longer now, so it would have to do.

As she carried the bag toward the kitchen, voices echoed down the hallway, two of them unfamiliar. Her feet faltered for a second, but she kept going. As soon as she stepped into the kitchen, she wanted to run back to the bedroom.

In front of her stood the most beautiful woman she'd ever seen. She had porcelain skin, auburn hair, cornflower blue eyes, and ruby red lips. The woman wore an elegant green dress in some fancy fabric with a matching hat. She was smiling at Matt, her pearly white teeth shining against her plump lips.

Holy Mary, the woman was simply stunning.

"That's right kind of you to stop by, Margaret, but

I'm about to leave. You and Jeb are welcome to stay and visit, a'course." Matt hadn't even noticed Hannah.

Jeb was almost as good-looking as the woman, with the same auburn hair and blue eyes. No doubt the woman's brother. He spotted Hannah and smiled.

"Good morning, madam." He tipped his hat, his smile almost blinding. "Jeb Stinson. And you are?"

Matt swung around and his jaw tightened. "This is Hannah."

Margaret turned, smiling, with her hand outstretched.

"My wife."

The other woman's smile disappeared and shock rippled across her perfect features. "Wife?"

"You got married?" Jeb smiled and clapped Matt on the back. "I didn't know you were even courting anyone."

"Wife?" Margaret whirled around to face Matt. "Matthew Graham. I cannot believe my ears. You, well I thought, I'd never considered you would marry and not tell me."

Hannah's heart dropped to her feet. Obviously the woman had set her cap for Matt, and Hannah had destroyed that particular dream. She couldn't possibly feel more awkward than she did at that moment. If only there was a hole in the ground in front of her to drop into.

Matt frowned at Margaret. "You and me, we never courted. I know Mama had hopes, but you're a thoroughbred and I'm a cow pony."

The redhead put her gloved hand on his chest. "Matthew, I don't consider you beneath me. Just because Daddy has the biggest ranch in eastern Texas does not mean I wouldn't marry for love." Her lip quivered and her eyes grew moist.

Hannah dropped the bag and left the house, running after she cleared the front door. It didn't matter what they thought of her. She could not stand by and watch a perfect, beautiful woman throw herself at Matt.

Nicholas, Caleb, and the Vasquez boys were in the corral looking at a horse when she ran past. They all stopped to stare at her, but no one spoke. She didn't stop until she reached the crest of the hill just beyond the barn. By then she was out of breath and shaking.

She bent over and put her hands on her knees. Hannah tried to calm her breathing and her heart, which was about to break a rib it was beating so hard. There had been no way she could have stayed in the house a second longer. The last thing she'd expected was a woman who had obviously been waiting to marry Matt. Why had he married Hannah instead?

"Hannah." Matt walked up the hill toward her. "What are you doing?"

The laugh that burst from her throat was more like a pitiful cry. She straightened up and met his gaze, knowing her pain and confusion shone in her eyes. "Why? Why did you marry me?"

"Hannah, I told you why." Matt put his hands on his hips and scowled. "I had to marry to get the land from Texas."

"Why didn't you marry her? She's beautiful, obviously rich, and she was expecting it from what I can tell." Hannah felt as if her heart was just pouring out of her mouth in a steady stream. No matter what, she had to get everything out or she would choke on it.

"Margaret?" He looked back toward the house. "I meant what I told her, a cow pony doesn't belong with a thoroughbred. She flirted with me, but I never took it seriously. She flirts with every man."

"She obviously wanted you to ask her to marry you. Now you've painted yourself into a corner and had to marry someone named Hannah." Hannah's hurt had turned to rage and she let the angry words fly. "You've made me into a second choice and saddled yourself with an ugly cow instead of a beautiful butterfly. You settled for me, and worst of all, I settled for you."

"Hannah." Matt's mouth opened in surprise. "You are not my second choice. I never even thought of Margaret when I needed a wife."

"Ha. I don't believe that." Hannah's face was likely redder than a beet from shouting at him.

"It's true. We don't suit, never have." He reached for her hand but she backed away.

"She's exquisitely beautiful." Her voice began to fade, as did her anger. Her pain began to seep back up, stealing her breath.

"On the outside." Matt moved closer until he backed her into a huge tree. The bark scratched at her back. "I didn't marry her because I didn't want to."

Hannah stared into his eyes, wanting so desperately to see honesty, but she didn't know him well enough to tell for sure. His tone conveyed the truth, but she couldn't believe him entirely. Her head overruled her heart again.

"I don't believe you."

For a split second, she saw hurt in his gaze, and some evil little part of her was glad of it. He'd hurt her enough already.

"I can understand that, but I don't like it." He took her hands and pressed his forehead to hers. His breath gusted across her mouth and she breathed him in, his anger and hurt mingled with hers.

"Maybe one day, I'll change my mind," she whispered. "But right now I can't."

"You're my wife, Hannah, for now and always." He kissed her lightly. "Now let's get back to the house so we can start out."

She nodded and took his proffered arm. Hannah was exhausted, as if she had run from one end of Texas to the other. Her knees shook as they made their way down the hill and across the ground to the house. Jeb stood outside with Caleb, smoking a cigar.

"There you are, Mrs. Graham. I was worried we'd offended you." His accent was as smooth as his sister's, but he didn't set off any warning bells in Hannah's heart. He appeared to be just who he was, a good-natured young man.

"I'm sorry. I felt a little sick to my stomach." She gave him a weak smile and tightened her grip on Matt's arm.

"Caleb, can you get Winston and Buttercup saddled?" Matt spoke to his brother. "We're leaving in just a few minutes."

"Sure thing, Matt." He frowned at both of them, but the younger Graham set off on his chore.

"You're leaving?" Jeb looked between them. "Nothing we said, is it?"

"No, we were heading to Houston to sign some papers." Matt opened the front door. "We can plan a visit after we get back."

"Margaret is already hatching a gathering to celebrate your wedding. No need for you to plan anything." Jeb followed them into the house.

Hannah looked around and realized so many things made sense, she wondered why she hadn't seen it before. Olivia sat beside Margaret, smiling and laughing, thick as thieves with the woman who wanted to be Mrs. Graham. It explained why Olivia didn't like her, why she was so hostile. Her sister-in-law expected her best friend to be Matt's wife, not a plump stranger plainer than prairie grass.

Eva stood at the stove, arms crossed, watching the young women. Granny sat at the table, also watching them. If she hadn't felt so awful, Hannah might have laughed at them. The sheer annoyance on the older women's faces was clear as day. Hannah realized nobody but Olivia tolerated Margaret.

"There you are, *hija*." Eva spotted them and smiled at Hannah. That simple gesture helped her feel ten times better. "I made you some food to take with you."

There on the counter was a large basket with a handle that would fit nicely on a saddle horn.

"*Gracias, Eva.*"

"*Hija*? Your housekeeper is already speaking Spanish to her?" Margaret's voice was nowhere near a whisper.

Olivia glanced at Eva, a smidge of guilt in her gaze. "She's not just a housekeeper, and she talks Spanish to everyone."

"Well, we are in Texas, and we speak English. She should learn the words she needs to know." Margaret finally looked at Matt and Hannah. "I see you found your wayward wife. She should be careful. Accidents happen on ranches all the time."

Matt held Hannah tight when she surged forward. She wanted to punch the woman and possibly chip one of those perfect teeth.

"Easy," he said under his breath. "Let's just get our things and go."

Hannah breathed through her nose until the urge to do harm passed. Margaret turned a sparkling smile on Matt.

"I want to plan the biggest party in the state to celebrate your wedding. Livy will help me." Margaret patted Livy's shoulder. "Although she's apparently not happy with your marriage. I've convinced her it's for the best."

What nonsense was this woman spouting? She didn't know Hannah well enough to know anything about her marriage or whether it was for the best. The woman had a motive that was yet to be determined. Hannah knew she'd just found a reason to be on her guard.

"Why thank you, Margaret. That's right kind of you." Matt grabbed the basket and the traveling bag. "If you'll excuse us, we'll be on our way. Eva, we'll be back in two days."

"*Vaya con dios, hijos. Buen viaje.*" She smiled at Hannah. "Take care of him, *hija.*"

Hannah wasn't sure what that meant exactly but she did know she already loved Eva. The older woman could see right through someone to their soul. She was a person to be trusted, and she'd proved to be Hannah's first friend at the Graham ranch.

"You come back now, y'hear?" Granny speared her with her gaze. "Do what you need to, child."

Hannah almost blushed at the reminder of her conversation earlier with Granny, but managed to keep the heat from her cheeks.

"We'll see you in two days."

Matt shook Jeb's hand and they walked out of the house. When she and Matt finally walked into the barn, she let out the breath she'd been holding. It had been such a long day, and it was only nine o'clock in the morning.

Caleb had the horses saddled and ready, handing the reins to his brother. He nodded at them and disappeared back into the barn. The gelding was incredibly tall and broad, a perfect match for Matt. The mare was a dainty buckskin almost the color of buttermilk. Hannah thought the horse looked nice but she wasn't sure. Her experience with horses was extremely limited.

"Can you ride?" Matt murmured to her.

"A little."

He groaned. "I should have asked."

"It's okay. I rode some when I was younger, mostly on ponies, but I remember how." She approached the mare slowly.

"Let her get to know you first." Matt took her hand. "Breathe into her nostrils so she can get your scent."

Hannah thought that was about the strangest thing she'd heard all day, but she did it just the same. The horse whickered and pressed her big snout into Hannah's chest.

"Now pet the side of her neck. Let her feel your touch." He took her hand and flattened it on the horse's warm flesh. The combination of his callused fingers and touching the mare made tears prick her eyes, this time for the right reason.

"She likes you."

Hannah let a bit of joy into her heart. "I like her, too."

"Are you ready?" He was close enough she could almost count the thick eyelashes gracing his eyelids. He was so beautiful she could hardly believe he was really her husband.

"I'm ready."

CHAPTER NINE

Matt did not know exactly what had happened at the ranch, but as they rode away, he was damn glad to be leaving. Margaret had arrived and thrown everyone into a snit, as she usually did. Damn woman knew just how to stir the pot and she did a good job. Made Hannah think they were supposed to be married.

That was so far from the truth, it was laughable. Oh, maybe when he was fifteen, he'd followed her around. But he learned his lesson when she humiliated him in front of her family at a barbecue. Matt might have dreamed about her ten years ago, but now she'd turned into something more like a nightmare.

Jeb was good folk and Matt liked him a lot. The rest of the Stinsons were more like snakes in the grass, eager to show everyone just how much they had. Margaret was a product of her mother's demanding nature and her father's pride. Jeb was somehow different from the rest. If he hadn't looked exactly like his sister, Matt would have guessed he'd been adopted.

Shaking off his thoughts of the Stinsons, he concentrated instead on Hannah's childish wonder at the horse she rode. He could see she had some amount of skill but wasn't at all confident in her abilities. That seemed to be the case with most everything she did, except for cooking and sewing. She was a puzzle he had yet to figure out.

Hannah bounced a bit in the saddle, but she had a natural seat. With some practice, she'd do fine. He'd tucked some horse liniment in his bag just in case the long ride caused her discomfort later. No reason to embarrass her, but he knew just how sore a hind end and thighs could get.

The bright blue sky above them was dotted with a few white, puffy clouds. The day was warm with only a gentle breeze. It was a perfect day for a trip, and although the purpose was enough to make him quake in his boots, he focused instead on the sheer pleasure of the ride.

"How do you feel?"

Hannah shifted in the saddle. "Good so far. Don't know about later."

"I've got liniment in case you're sore." The idea of rubbing it into her skin, of the soft downy skin between her thighs, made his entire body harden at once. Particularly his cock, which thumped against his trouser buttons.

"Oh, good. Granny usually has a good remedy but I haven't gotten the knack of making a good poultice yet." She glanced back at him, then her gaze fell between his legs. Like a bullet, her gaze snapped back to his. She obviously saw his state and was probably wondering exactly why riding a horse had made him hard.

"I, uh, started thinking about you." Maybe telling her the bare truth was the right thing to do.

"Me?" Her eyes widened. "Really?"

His grin felt more like a wolf's leer. "Yes, you, Mrs. Graham."

She giggled and the sound went straight to his throbbing staff. It was going to be a long ride.

With Margaret and the troubles at the ranch behind them, the rest of the morning passed by mostly in silence. As if they were comfortable with each other, at ease with silence.

"I hear you're a real hand at sewing." Matt tripped over his own tongue with that one.

"Oh, I know how to do basic things. I, uh, enjoy it." She looked down, as he discovered she always did when talking about herself. He realized it was embarrassment.

"That's a good thing. I mean, enjoying something that most folks think of as a chore." Matt kept his gaze on hers, willing her to look up. "I like taking care of my horse."

She finally lifted her lashes and looked at him out of the corner of her eyes. "Taking care of your horse?"

"Currying him, picking rocks out of his shoes, even using the hoof knife to keep his hooves healthy. It might be a chore to my brothers, but I like it." He patted Winston's neck. "He's, well, my friend. Stupid I know." Now it was his turn to be embarrassed.

To his surprise, Hannah raised her head. "It's not stupid. I think it's sweet." She smiled at him, and he found himself smiling back.

"Don't tell anyone else that. I won't hear the end of it."

This time, she laughed, that amazingly rich sound that always surprised him. As he watched, her freckled face lit up brighter than the sun. Hannah laughed with her entire being, the most genuine thing he'd ever seen.

After that, the ride was not silent. He found himself talking to Hannah about things he hadn't told anyone else. Not even Caleb, who was closest to him.

The conversation continued as they feasted on Eva's

ham and tortillas. They'd found a shaded spot to sit down, with a creek and sweet grass for the horses. The cool water in their canteens washed everything down. It was a simple meal, but the first one he'd truly enjoyed in six months, since his parents were taken from him.

She cleaned everything up efficiently while he retrieved the horses from the tree they were tied to. Hannah might not think much of herself, but Matt already did. He'd not admit to her that he hadn't expected much from their marriage, but he was damn glad to be proven wrong.

"You never told me the story of the land grant." She hung the basket on her horse's saddle horn.

Her question hit Matt like a punch to the gut. It was true he'd only given her the barest information about the reason behind the land grant. The entire story was painful for him and he hadn't known her well enough to tell it when he'd married her.

"I am curious, but if you don't want to tell me, that's okay." She put her foot in the stirrup and tried to boost herself into the saddle.

Matt put his hands on her behind and pushed her up.

"Oh shit!" The curse popped out of her mouth fast and hard. Matt barely had time to react before she did it again as she landed on the saddle. "Son of a bitch."

She turned to look at him, this time not hiding her pinkened cheeks. "Oh my God."

Matt did the only thing he could think of. He threw back his head and laughed. "Hannah, I can't even begin to tell you how glad I am you married me."

"I, uh, do tend to cuss sometimes," she confessed.

"Me, too." He patted her thigh. "We're going to be just fine, Hannah Graham."

Matt meant every word of it. He'd found a hidden

treasure in his wife and he intended to hang onto her, come hell or high water.

They spent the night in a sheltered area just outside Houston, surrounded by rocks and the protection of the horses. Although it wasn't an ideal place to make love, they did spoon together all night. Hannah felt safe in his arms, comfortable sleeping with him for the first time since they'd married.

In the morning, he rolled over and kissed her. The heat from his lips traveled down her body, leaving tingles in its wake. He kissed her again, this time slowly, nibbling her lips until she opened them.

She moaned in her throat and he swallowed the sound into his own. His kiss deepened and grew more demanding. His body became hard as an oak against hers and she found herself wishing they weren't on the ground, lying between two blankets. She wanted to touch him, feel his skin, and make love.

Hannah scooted closer, pressing her aching breasts into his chest. He reached between them and squeezed one nipple, drawing a gasp from deep within her. A throb of pure desire echoed through her and she knew she was already wet, again. She didn't want to admit to herself that she was falling in love with her husband, but she knew she was. Whether he would return her love had yet to be determined.

"Ah, excuse me, folks." A stranger's voice sounded from nearby. "I'm just passing through."

Hannah tucked her head into Matt's shoulder and tried not to die of embarrassment. Matt kissed her forehead and chuckled, a painful sound.

"I guess it's time to get going." He extricated himself from the blankets and held out his hand for her.

She glanced around and saw the stranger who had spoken walking down the road. The last thing she wanted to do was leave the cocoon she'd shared with Matt, but he was right. It was time to get going.

After a cold breakfast, they rode into the city. When they arrived in Houston proper, Hannah was goggle-eyed at the number of people, horses, carriages, wagons, and buildings. She could hardly take it all in without hurting her neck craning it this way and that. Good thing he knew where he was going. She would never have been able to find her way without him.

He stabled the horses and led her out of the livery. Hannah hung onto his arm as they navigated the streets. Two people bumped into her and one wagon nearly ran her down. It truly made her miss home and the quiet pace of the life she didn't realize she loved so much.

Matt took them straight to the land grant office. An officious looking man in a navy suit made them sit down in the most uncomfortable chairs she'd ever had the misfortune of sitting in. Matt stared straight ahead, stoic-faced and silent. Hannah wondered if he was nervous. Judging by the way he fidgeted as they waited, he definitely was.

"What's wrong?" she whispered.

"Nothing. Just don't like being in places like this." He glanced down at his callused hands. "I'm a rancher, not a banker or an office man."

Hannah understood what he meant and felt the same level of discomfort being there, but it was important to the ranch. She had married Matt so he could get this land grant. There was no reason to be a coward now, even if her stomach was twittering as if a bird was trapped inside.

"Mr. and Mrs. Graham?" A short, round bald man

with thick spectacles peered at them. He wore a dark gray suit and vest, which looked as if it would bust a button if he breathed too hard.

"Mr. Prentiss." Matt stood and held out his hand to help Hannah to her feet. It was a gentlemanly gesture, one she could get used to.

"I'm glad to see you back to finalize the paperwork." He turned his gaze to Hannah. "This must be your wife, Hannah."

"Yes, sir, this is my Hannah."

My Hannah. Oh, her stupid heart did a pittypat at the reference.

She nodded at him. "Pleased to meet you, sir."

"And you as well, Mrs. Graham. Why don't you both come into my office?" He led them through a frosted glass door and into a room with a large wooden desk and two of the same uncomfortable chairs in front of it. Were there no comfortable places to sit?

Hannah perched on the chair and tried to look the way she thought a respectable wife should. Her back was straight, her hands folded in her lap.

"I have papers for Mrs. Graham to sign, since you've already signed them, Mr. Graham." He pulled out a sheaf of papers and presented them to her with a fountain pen.

She'd worn her best white gloves, really the only good pair she had. As she took them off, she noted Mr. Prentiss glance at her bare ring finger. Her stomach dropped and panic danced on her neck. She forced herself to smile at Mr. Prentiss.

"My ring always gets caught on my glove." Hiding her shaking hands, she reached into her reticule and pulled out the ancient handkerchief with her great-grandmother's silver ring. She had no time to hope that it would fit. If it didn't, it would make the situation worse.

Her Grandma Peters must've been smiling down on her like a guardian angel. The ring slid onto her finger as if it were made for her, and not another woman seventy-five years earlier. Matt made a noise in his throat, which she assumed was surprise.

Mr. Prentiss gave her a small smile. "Very nice. Now if you'll sign these papers, we can complete the land grant process."

The next thirty minutes were a blur of papers, legal terms she couldn't possibly follow, and a great deal of ink. Her signature was shaky on a few of the papers, but it didn't seem to matter to the clerk.

Mr. Prentiss pulled out a large map and spread it on his desk. "Now let me show you the property lines so you are well aware of where your new property lies."

Matt and Hannah leaned forward. It was the first time she'd seen a land map, and it had lots of squiggles and symbols on it she didn't understand.

"This is your current ranch here. To the east and south is the Stinson ranch, and to the west is the McRae ranch." He pointed to a pie-shaped squiggle. "This is your new acreage. Note there is approximately two miles of land between the old property and the new."

Matt traced the property lines with one blunt-edged fingernail. "Who owns this?"

"Frederick Stinson."

Matt's jaw tightened as he continued to study the map. "Two miles, hmm? And how long does it take to get through this two miles?"

"You'd have to go around the McRaes' through this canyon. Rough estimate is thirty-five or forty miles." Mr. Stinson pushed his glasses up his nose.

Matt traced the swath of land with his finger. "How is it possible that he owns just this piece?"

"Oh, he doesn't own just this piece. His land grant was rather unusual. You see his property extended out to here." Mr. Stinson pointed to another line. "He requested the additional ten thousand acres directly adjoining his, but that wasn't possible given your father's claim. Instead he took the ragged land between."

"So what you're saying is that he deliberately took the land that separated our current property from the new property?" Matt sounded so calm, but she heard the steel in his voice.

"It appears so." Mr. Stinson pushed up his glasses again.

"Why would the Republic do that? Stinson obviously wanted to prevent my father from using both tracts of land." Matt's hand curled into a fist. "How is that fair?"

"Mr. Graham, if a legal resident of Texas has a claim to land, we grant it to them. It's not up to the Republic to determine what's fair." Mr. Stinson spoke the words, but not very convincingly. He probably hadn't realized what had been done, but now that he did, he was in the unenviable position of explaining it to her and Matt.

Hannah was flabbergasted by the implications of what they'd discovered. She didn't know much about cattle, but making a forty-mile loop around a two-mile piece of land was ludicrous. It couldn't possibly be good for the animals to walk that far on a regular basis.

"That's a load of horseshit, pardon my language." Matt sat back in the chair. "I either move my entire ranch forty miles, including my house, or I deal with Stinson for easement rights."

"Well, I'm sorry about that, Mr. Graham, but it's out of my hands." Mr. Stinson folded his hands in

front of him on the desk and gave Matt and Hannah
an apologetic, weak look.

"Just give me my papers and we'll be on our way."
Matt snatched the papers the other man held out to
him. "Good day, sir."

He took Hannah's elbow with force, not enough to
hurt her, but enough that she hurried along to leave
the land grant office. She'd seen him annoyed but
never so angry. However, she didn't blame him one
bit. Hannah was angry, too. The very idea that someone had deliberately put himself between the two
tracts of land was horrible.

"Why did he do it?" Hannah asked when they were
out on the street.

"Stinson? He's a jackass with a big mouth and an
even bigger ego. My father never liked him, for good
reason apparently." Matt almost marched down the
street, his boots slamming into the hard-packed dirt.

"What will we do?" She was glad she had long legs
to keep with him.

"Go home."

"And after that?"

He stopped and turned to meet her gaze. "I don't
know, Hannah. I just don't know."

The ride back to the ranch was considerably less
enjoyable than the trip to Houston. Matt pushed them
and the horses until deep into the night. He didn't
want to stop until he reached home. Hannah tried
talking to him, but he wasn't in any mood to hold a
conversation.

He was furious, more so than he'd ever been in his
life. The legacy left by his father was now in jeopardy
because of one man's greed. His family would join

him in the anger, but the burden to find a solution to the situation was on his shoulders.

Hannah was strong, he knew that, but that long fifteen hours in the saddle proved to him she was stronger than he'd thought. A lesser woman would have complained or insisted they stop, yet she didn't. He was used to being in the saddle for long days, but she wasn't even much of a rider.

Now she'd spent the better part of two days on a horse. For him. It was humbling.

By the time they rode into the ranch, he was about to fall out of the saddle. Matt stopped at the barn and slid to the ground, his legs barely able to straighten. He made it to Hannah's horse and saw the lines cut into her face by sheer exhaustion.

"Come here, honey." He plucked her off the saddle and into his arms. The horses' heads hung down as they waited patiently for him to take care of them. First he had to take care of his wife.

Matt carried her toward the house and she shifted in his arms.

"What are you doing? Put me down. I'm too heavy for you." She sounded so weak he could have mistaken her for a kitten.

"Hush now. We're home." He laid her on the bed gently. Then he took off her shoes and pulled up the quilt to cover her. He kissed her forehead, then returned to take care of the horses.

By the time he made it back to Hannah, she was snoring softly. After he removed his own boots, he crawled in beside her, never so glad to be home.

In the morning, he would talk to his family about what he'd learned. For now, he snuggled up beside Hannah and closed his eyes.

CHAPTER TEN

Hannah's thighs and behind were on fire. The burning sensation yanked her out of a deep sleep. She gasped as she came into full consciousness and the soreness slammed into her. The two days spent riding had taken their toll on her unprepared hindquarters. She opened her eyes and recognized their bedroom at the ranch. A hazy memory of Matt carrying her flitted through her mind. It must have really happened because she certainly hadn't walked in there on her own. Heck, she wasn't sure if she could walk.

She groaned and turned on her side. Her husband was there, fast asleep, with dark smudges of exhaustion beneath his eyes. It was the first time she'd been able to study him without his knowing. He looked so much younger asleep, as though slumber had washed away all the stresses of the ranch.

He had dark lashes, not overly long but thick. A bump on the bridge of his nose spoke of an injury earlier in his life. Another scar marred his skin just above his left eyebrow, perhaps an inch long and whitened with age. The stubble that graced his chin and cheeks was darker than the hair on his head. Unable to resist, she reached out and touched one fingertip to his chin. He was a beautiful man, even in sleep.

His eyes popped open and she froze in place. Her heart thumped hard as she waited for him to do something.

"Hannah." The rasp of his voice sent a skitter across her skin.

"Matthew."

Their gazes were locked and the air between them crackled. She wanted so badly to kiss him, but hesitated. They'd only been married a few short days, and although they'd been intimate, she was absolutely shy around him. Now she'd been caught ogling and fondling him. Perhaps what she'd done might not be considered fondling, she had been touching him.

"Where did you get the ring?"

She wasn't expecting the question. "The ring?" She held up her left hand, just now noticing she still wore it. "Granny gave it to me. It belonged to her mother."

"It fits you." He touched the ring with one finger.

"Like I was supposed to wear it."

His gaze snapped to hers and the moment stretched out. She leaned toward him and her muscles reminded her of just how much pain she was in. Hannah hissed in a breath and moved back to her side of the bed.

"Are you sore?" He shifted to a sitting position and the tension between them broke.

Hannah cursed her own foolishness and wondered if she would ever be strong enough to be a normal wife.

"Yes, a bit. Mostly on my, ah, the parts that rest on the saddle." Those parts were currently throbbing with more than soreness from the ride.

"I've got some liniment. Thought we'd use it when

we were on our trip, but I didn't think we'd ride straight back either." He rose from bed and Hannah was startled to see his erection clearly evident in his drawers. Was it like that every morning?

He fished around in the saddlebags on the floor before pulling out a tin. "Found it."

She didn't know what would happen when he rubbed the liniment on her, but she was filled with anticipation.

"Roll over and pull up your nightdress, Hannah."

It didn't sound sexy, but it sure made her feel naughty as she managed to do what he asked. Her muscles were in sorry shape, but it was the idea that his bare hands would be rubbing her that was foremost in her mind.

"My hands are a little rough." He opened the tin and put some liniment on his hands.

"I don't mind," she confessed into the pillow. "I like your hands."

He chuckled softly. "I'm glad to hear it. Just try to relax."

Now that would be quite a challenge. She wanted to enjoy the experience, but her anxiety was warring with her need.

Matt touched her behind her knees, making circles as he worked his way up to her thighs. Although his fingers were strong, his touch wasn't rough. She closed her eyes and focused on how good it felt.

Her sore muscles slowly unknotted under his hands. Matt's thumbs swiped her inner thighs, so close to her pussy that she clenched her muscles. A jolt of pain slammed up her body at the sudden movement.

He stopped, his hands still touching her. "Easy, Hannah. I'm not going to hurt you. I promise."

"I know. I, um, I'm not used to people touching me there." She sounded foolish to her own ears.

"I'm not people. I'm your husband."

Hannah was glad he couldn't see her blushing. "Please keep going."

After a moment, he started again. She wanted to show him how much she trusted him, truly she did, so she spread her legs wider.

He made a funny noise and his hands momentarily stopped. "You, ah, surprise me."

"I hope so." She spoke into her pillow but she hoped he heard her.

His thumbs traveled upward again, nearing her pulsing core, then slid past to her behind. He spread her cheeks with each circle, allowing cold air to land on her heated center. Cold. Hot. Cold. Hot.

When he kissed the nape of her neck, a moan popped out of her mouth. The massage had turned into something much more. His hardened staff brushed against her thigh.

"Hannah, I need you."

"I need you, too. Please, Matt." She pushed up against him until he was cradled right where she needed him most.

He jumped off the bed and shucked his drawers so quickly, her skin didn't even cool in the time he was gone. His now naked cock brushed her thighs, raising goose bumps in its wake.

The head teased her opening. She pushed up against him again, and he slid in further. She raised her behind up even further until he was fully sheathed inside her. Hannah gasped at the feeling of rightness. This was where she belonged, where he belonged.

His arms shook beside her as he began to thrust in

and out. With each movement, their joining made a soft, wet noise that was strangely exciting.

Hannah didn't know people could make love back to front. The sensation was different, more intense. He slid deeper within her, joining them together in a profound way.

Her stomach fluttered as the pleasure burned low and deep in her belly. She gripped the bed, the scent of their lovemaking filling her nose. Her body recognized his, reached for the ultimate peak it would find only with Matt.

"Now, Hannah, now." His arms shook harder as his pace grew faster. He slammed into her, tugging her into a whirl of sensations.

She gave herself over, falling into blinding ecstasy that raced through her. A thousand points of light echoed through her, bringing her to another realm. Matt whispered her name as he found his own peak.

They both shook with the power of their joining. Hannah didn't know he had the power to bring her to such a place. She couldn't imagine a more beautiful experience and knew she would eagerly await the next time.

He kissed her neck again, then rolled off her with a groan. "Remind me to rub liniment on you more often."

Hannah giggled. In the privacy of their bedroom, Matt softened and became the man she had always dreamed of marrying. Outside the bedroom, he was the head of the ranch, bossy, and not at all the same person. She wouldn't admit this to him, but her heart was becoming Matthew's and she was helpless to stop it.

*   *   *

The silence in the kitchen was broken only by Catherine's slurping of her milk. The rest of the Grahams and Eva stared at Matt with expressions of disbelief, anger, and confusion.

Matt's anger had not truly dissipated. It had smoldered deep within him all the way back to the ranch. Making love to Hannah had allowed him to escape while they had been together. Yet reality came crashing down the moment he spread the map on the table and explained their problem.

"What does this all mean?" Olivia's face was pale. "We have to move?"

"It means we have a two-mile gap between this ranch and our new land. We have a choice to make." He looked at all of them in turn. "We can negotiate with Stinson to run our herd back and forth across his two-mile tract. We can try to buy it from him, or we can move everything we have to the new property and abandon this one."

"That bastard." Caleb slammed his fist into the table. "He did this on purpose."

"I think so, too, but that doesn't change the fact we have to make a decision." Matt wanted to tear the map to pieces and make Stinson eat every piece. "We probably have a fight on our hands."

"Damn right we have a fight on our hands." Nicholas's expression matched Caleb's. "If Pa were alive, he would fight that son of a bitch."

"Nicholas, *hijo,* your language," Eva scolded.

"He is a son of a bitch," Nicholas mumbled under his breath.

Matt stared at the map, at the two miles standing between their dream and reality. Stinson had done it deliberately, there wasn't a doubt about that, or the fact he was a bastard. Nick had that right.

"First thing we need to do is talk to him." Olivia was still pale but calm. "Mr. Stinson is a reasonable man, and I'm sure Margaret can convince him to work with us." Olivia cast a sideways glance at Hannah. "Too bad she didn't marry you when you asked."

Perhaps no one else saw it, but Matt did. Hannah flinched at Olivia's nastiness.

"That's enough, Livy. I was five years old. Ancient history. We don't have money to buy the land straight out obviously. I want to offer Stinson a share of profits our first year to buy the land." Matt had considered a great many possibilities on their return from Houston. The first one he discarded, since murder would only garner him a noose, not a ranch.

"Give him our profit?" Caleb shook his head.

"It's logical."

"It's *loco*."

"Papa would whoop his behind."

"I'll whoop yours if you don't stop pushing me off the bench."

"We can't give him our hard-earned money."

"That's our blood, sweat, and tears, Matt."

"I don't sweat. I'm a lady."

"You sweat and you stink."

"Shut up."

"Enough, all of you!" Matt had no patience for their bickering today. "Sometimes life doesn't give you a good choice, but it does give you choices. We have to decide if it's the best one."

They all stopped yelling but there were glares around the table.

"What does Hannah think?" Catherine looked up at them, a milk mustache on her lip.

Everyone turned to look at Hannah. She'd been

sipping her coffee quietly and paused with the cup halfway to her mouth.

"Me? I don't have a say in this."

"Yes, you do," Rebecca piped up. "You're a Graham now."

Matt caught her gaze and held it, telling her with his eyes the girls were right. Regardless of Livy's attitude, the rest of the family had accepted her. She was a Graham.

Hannah glanced at her grandmother, sitting in the corner on what was now "her stool." The older woman nodded.

"The best way to catch flies is with honey, not vinegar. If you sweeten the pot, he just might accept the offer." Hannah was a born diplomat if he ever met one.

"Hannah is right. We have to approach him as a neighbor with an offer." He stared hard at Olivia. "Hannah and I will head over there in the morning."

Matt walked out of the house because he didn't want to listen to the yelling as it began again. He knew Olivia would be angry and likely Caleb would want to be part of the trip to the Stinsons' ranch. Yet another family discussion stuck in the mire of too many opinions. He had too much on his mind to take grief from his siblings.

Winston was waiting in his stall for Matt. It was too late in the day for a ride, but he could spend time spoiling the gelding. After all, he'd been ridden hard on the trip to Houston. The least he could do was give the horse something back.

He didn't admit to himself he was hiding. After all, he was a rancher, a man, and a landowner. He had no reason to hide.

*   *   *

Hannah checked her reflection in the tiny mirror for the tenth time, trying to smooth down the wayward curls that would not behave. They were leaving for the Stinsons', riding over together as an old married couple would.

She didn't have any fancy outfit, but her clothes were clean and pressed. Perhaps one day she'd get some fabric and make herself something new. Today she had to make do with what she had.

"Are you ready yet?" Matt's voice sounded from the hallway, impatience evident in his tone.

"Yes, I'm ready." She smoothed her blouse one more time, then opened the bedroom door.

He was dressed as he normally would on any other day, in a shirt and trousers, but at least his boots were clean. She suddenly felt overdressed.

"Should I change?"

"For God's sake, no. Let's just go. You've wasted enough time already." He turned away to walk down the hall.

Something inside her snapped and a surge of pure anger hit her square between the eyes. "This is my first visit with the neighbors. I wanted to make a good impression."

He stopped and turned to look at her. "What are you talking about?"

"I'm new to this whole marriage, rancher's wife thing. And ignoring me or talking to me as if I'm an annoyance is not helping." Her cheeks grew warm but this time it wasn't with embarrassment. "I need your respect outside the bedroom."

Hannah wanted to slap her hand over her mouth but she held herself firm and didn't drop her gaze.

He'd been the one to ask her opinion on what to do. Now he was back to snapping at her, but she wanted, needed, to be treated as his wife and not as an unwanted guest.

"Hannah. I, uh, was . . . I'm sorry." He ran his hands down his face. "Can you please come with me to the Stinsons now?"

Hannah nodded and walked down the hallway, her head held high. She'd taken Granny's advice for the first time. Although she was mortified by some of the things she'd said, for the first time, she was proud of herself. Hannah had stood on her own two feet.

It took them about half an hour to ride over to the Stinsons' ranch. A silent ride, much different from their previous trip to Houston. Matt was either angry with her or didn't know what to say.

Neither did Hannah.

Matt was the first man she'd spent significant time with, and obviously the first man she'd lain with. He was teaching her how to be a woman in more ways than one, even if he didn't want to.

The Stinsons' house was larger than anything she'd ever seen. It was so wide, there were at least ten rocking chairs on the front porch, and room for ten more. A barn two stories high towered over the trees. Everything was simply enormous.

They dismounted at the hitching post to the right of the front porch. Matt helped her down, silently of course, then held her elbow as they walked toward the front door. Surprisingly no one came out to greet them. The large house seemed to be deserted. Most ranch hands were likely out working, but she'd thought there would always be at least a few folks around. Someone to take care of such a big house.

Their boots echoed on the very well swept porch.

There didn't seem to be a speck of dirt anywhere on the Stinson ranch. Perhaps dirt was as intimidated by the place as Hannah was.

Matt knocked on the door. Within seconds it was opened by a plump Mexican woman wearing a fancy black maid's outfit and a spotless white apron. She nodded at Matt.

"*Buenos dias, Señor Graham.*"

"*Buenos dias, Carmen. ¿Donde esta Señor Stinson?*"

"*Esta en la jardin alla.*" The woman opened the door wider and gestured them in.

"*Gracias.*" Matt took Hannah's arm again as they walked through the ranch house.

Hannah tried not to stare, but it was hard. Everywhere, she saw fancy furniture, paintings on the walls, elaborate vases, shiny crystals on an enormous chandelier, and rugs softer than anything she'd ever felt under her feet. It was a palace fit for a king.

That king was currently sitting on a bench in a beautiful garden, filled with blossoms and the drone of bees. He was as big as she'd expected, with broad shoulders and chest, black hair liberally sprinkled with silver, and gray eyes. He watched them approach but did not rise until they had nearly reached him.

"Graham." He rose to his full height, just a smidge shorter than Matt. "Didn't expect to see you today."

His gray gaze flickered to her, then back to Matt. She'd thought Matt treated her impolitely but this man just ignored her as if she didn't exist.

Their visit hadn't started well at all. Hannah didn't want to ruin their chances of getting the land they needed, but she had to do something. Hannah's new-found courage reared its head again.

"Good morning, Mr. Stinson." She smiled broadly. "I'm Hannah Graham. I'm so pleased to meet you."

"Good day, madam." He turned his head slightly in her direction. "What brings you by, Matthew?"

"We are planning a barbecue to celebrate our marriage," Hannah blurted, surprising herself. "Matt wanted to come by to invite you and your family personally."

"That so?" Stinson rocked back on his heels and studied Matt.

"Sure is. Hannah and Eva are planning it. I just need to slaughter the steer." Matt's smile was tight.

"When is this grand event taking place?" Unbelievably, Stinson seemed to relax a little at the invitation.

"Saturday." Hannah squeezed Matt's arm. "I thought perhaps you might have someone at the ranch who plays music, too." The words were pouring out of her mouth as if someone else were controlling her voice.

"I'll see what I can do." He studied Hannah with a stare as sharp as any knife. "You got gumption, girl. I like that."

Matt cleared his throat, but she didn't know if it was because of surprise or dismay.

"Thank you, sir." Hannah managed to smile again. "Will you be able to come to the barbecue?"

"I wouldn't miss it for the world." Mr. Stinson didn't smile but she saw the amusement in his gaze. He was a formidable man.

"It was a pleasure to meet you, sir. We'll see you on Saturday then." She sketched an awkward curtsy, then turned to Matt.

He was likely wrestling with whether or not to ask about the land tract. Hannah had given him the opportunity to get Mr. Stinson on the Graham ranch. Perhaps that was a better place to talk about an offer. She had taken a chance and hoped like mad it was the right one to take.

"Of course. I'll bring Margaret and Jeb." He tipped his hat to Matt. "You've got an interesting wife there, Graham. I look forward to the barbecue."

With that, he turned and left them alone in the garden. She was afraid Matt would be angry at her, but honestly she had done it for him, for the Grahams' future.

Matt wanted to throttle his wife at the same time he wanted to kiss her. Hannah had suddenly found her voice, along with a healthy dose of sass, and she seemed to be out of control. Not only had she told him exactly how she felt, but she'd told Stinson they were having a barbecue.

Even if they had been planning a barbecue, he sure as hell wouldn't have invited the Stinsons to it. Yet Hannah had thrown out the invitation as if they were all friends. His father had had nothing but disrespect for his neighbor. The rancher had been a pain in the ass ever since his father had settled on the property. To invite the man to a gathering at Circle Eight was almost an insult to his father's memory.

Hannah hadn't known the history between the Grahams and Stinsons. He could have told her but he hadn't. She could have asked him about the barbecue but she hadn't. Matt realized he shouldn't be too angry with her because they were both to blame.

He was still annoyed though.

As they walked out of the house and onto the porch, they were both quiet. Hannah marched to Buttercup and got herself up in the saddle with very little grace. She looked down at him, her jaw set and her gaze calm. He didn't know her well enough to know what her demeanor meant.

He untied her reins from the hitching rail and handed them to her. She looked sheepish for a moment, then took them. Matt mounted Winston and they started back toward home.

After they rode for ten minutes, out of range of the house, Matt couldn't keep quiet any longer.

"Did you plan on asking my permission for the barbecue before the neighbors arrived?"

She frowned at him. "I know it came as a surprise to you, but I didn't think I had to ask permission to celebrate our wedding. I didn't want Margaret to plan it."

Matt felt the sting of her tone and her words. Though it was true they hadn't done anything to celebrate their wedding, he wasn't sure he liked being taken to task by his wife.

"A barbecue costs money, Hannah. Did you think of that?"

She huffed out a breath. "Folks bring a covered dish; the only cost is the steer for you to cook. Everything else will come from the garden. Maybe we can even do some hunting for hares and small game."

He had to admit, silently, she was right. He had no argument that would stand against her logic. However, it stuck in his craw that she'd made the decision and he had to live with it.

"There's not enough time to get ready."

She didn't respond, which irked him even further. Matt stewed for a while as they rode. If he told Stinson there was not going to be a barbecue, he'd have to hear about it every time they saw each other for the rest of his life. If he allowed the barbecue to happen, he'd have to accept that his wife had made a big decision on her own. That would set a precedent for their marriage he wasn't sure he wanted to accept.

Damned if he wasn't stuck between a rock and a hard place. The first week of his marriage was turning out to be a lot harder than he'd expected. His parents had made it look so easy to be married. He hadn't agreed with the way his father had kowtowed to his mother, but he couldn't argue the fact they had loved each other.

He wasn't in love with Hannah, but his body was damn sure in lust. Every time he saw the curve of her breast or watched her ass in the saddle, or even smelled her scent, his damn cock took over his brain.

The longer his mind whirled with thoughts, the more frustrated he got. He needed to talk to Hannah but he didn't know how. When the house was within sight, he pulled on the reins and stopped. It was time to do something.

"What's wrong?" Hannah pulled her horse to a stop with a bit more difficulty. She was still learning how to ride, but she'd come far after only a few days of practice.

"We need to go back and tell Stinson there is no barbecue."

Hannah rode over to him, her frown firmly in place. "Why would we do that?"

"I don't want him at my house."

She flapped her hand. "It's the perfect place to offer to buy his land. There will be lots of neighbors to witness it."

Matt wanted to argue with her, but dammit, she was right. Stinson loved to posture in front of people and if he was made to look like a greedy bastard, he might give in and accept the offer.

"You are the most aggravating wife I've ever had," he blurted out.

She flinched and then a mask seemed to fall over her expression. "I'm the only wife you've ever had."

At that moment, Matt saw only her; the rest of the world fell away. His breathing sharpened and his heart raced. He leaned forward and grabbed the back of her neck. As his lips slammed down on hers, she gasped. His hand tangled in her curls, knocking her hat off.

Her untutored kisses made his blood run hot. He kissed her hard, a bruising kiss meant to intimidate and to punish. He needed to show her he was the man in their relationship, in charge of their marriage.

The kisses turned into much more than a lesson in power. The softness of her lips, her eagerness to return his ardor, drew him into a dark whirl of passion so sharp, it was his turn to gasp.

Her tongue rasped against his tentatively, then with more confidence. He forgot where they were. He forgot why he was angry. He wanted only to keep kissing her until his desire was quenched.

One of the horses shifted, pulling their mouths apart. Hannah looked dazed as she put her fingers to her swollen lips. She looked as sexy as any woman who had just been thoroughly kissed.

Matt was able to pull in a breath and almost cleared his head. What the hell was he doing? They were in the middle of nowhere and he might have taken her right there if the horses hadn't interrupted them.

"Dammit, Hannah, I-I don't know what just happened." His voice was shaking as much as his hands.

"I, uh, neither do I." She looked down and saw her hat on the dusty ground. It looked like the horse had stepped on it.

"I'm sorry." He jumped down and picked it up.

The hat was probably older than she was, and the horse's hoof had put a final note on its usefulness. "I think we need to get you a new hat."

She looked stricken and he felt even worse. "It was my father's."

That explained a lot about why it was so beaten up. Matt hadn't wanted to make her feel bad by telling her the hat was pitiful. Now he had to replace it and without a lot of money, that might be difficult.

"We'll get you a new one." He didn't want his wife wearing her dead father's hat anyway. A woman should wear a female's hat. Somehow he'd find a way to get her a new one. After all, he had kissed her and distracted both of them.

"It's okay. I can wear Granny's old poke bonnet." She made a face. He'd seen that bonnet and it was as ugly as a dog's ass.

He made a silent vow to buy her a new hat. Although it seemed a minor problem, it was a promise he intended to keep.

The kiss, the hat, and the confusion diffused his anger. Matt had an abundance of pride, one of his major downfalls. He had to accept she was right about the barbecue and move on.

"Who gets to tell Eva about the barbecue?"

She smiled as the wind caressed the curls swaying back and forth against her cheeks. "I'll race you. Loser has to tell her."

With a whoop, she spurred her horse into action, leaving him standing there, a stupid grin on his face. He watched her ride, amazed by the natural seat she had. Then he noted she was getting farther away, leaving him with the chore of telling Eva she had to plan a barbecue.

"Shit!"

Matt threw himself into the saddle and chased after his wife. He didn't remember the last time he had smiled and laughed, but he did both as he raced Hannah home.

Hannah didn't recognize herself. She'd not only talked to the intimidating Mr. Stinson, but she'd also invited him to a nonexistent barbecue. Matt had been angry with her, and not because she'd made up the barbecue, but because she hadn't asked his permission before doing it.

That fact alone had made her angry enough to speak her mind. She hadn't even considered any consequences and amazingly enough, after yelling at her, he'd kissed her so deeply, it made her toes curl. There were definite advantages to being married. She could get used to the random kisses and the wildfires that erupted when their lips met. It was an amazing, thrilling experience.

As they took care of their horses, she kept sneaking peeks at him across the stalls. He was as handsome sweaty as he was clean. She'd never noticed men that way before. She wasn't sure if it was normal or not, but her body certainly recognized the attraction. As though the elemental connection they had drove them to be together again and again.

And hopefully again.

She finished with Buttercup and stepped outside the stall to rinse her hands in the water bucket. As she bent over to scoop up some water, a groan sounded from behind her.

"Woman, you're gonna kill me."

She glanced up at Matt. "I was just washing my hands."

His gaze landed on her behind. "I don't care if you're rubbing mud on your face, I wasn't looking at anything but your ass."

"Matthew!" Her cheeks heated at the bald statement.

"I can't help it, Hannah. After that kiss, I'm just not thinking straight." One large hand smacked her on the behind.

She yelped and straightened up, water flying every which way. He grinned and ran for the door.

"Remember, loser has to tell Eva."

"Cheater!" Hannah wiped her hands on her skirt and ran after him.

His long legs gave him a significant advantage. There was no way she could beat him to the house. So she decided to cheat, too.

Hannah threw herself to the ground. "Oh, my ankle!"

He skidded to a stop and turned to look at her. "Are you hurt?"

"I think I wrenched my ankle, Matt." She touched it and moaned in pain.

Matt came back and knelt beside her. "Damn, Hannah, I seem to keep apologizing to you today. Let me help you up."

His solicitousness was sweet, but she was playing to win. As soon as she was standing, she kissed him hard.

"Race ya." She picked up her skirt and ran as fast as she could toward the house.

Matt cursed behind her and she heard his footsteps slamming on the hard-packed dirt. He was nearly on her so she dug deep for another burst of energy, reaching the door a split second before he did.

They slammed into the house, laughing and breathing hard. Joy suffused her, bubbled up inside as if it were a font. She'd never felt so happy in her life. How could a simple game of teasing with her husband bring such a gift? Hannah couldn't help the wide grin on her face as Eva and Granny looked up in surprise from a game of checkers at the table.

"Looks like they had a good visit." Granny cackled.

Hannah couldn't disagree, even though Matt was probably still annoyed with her about the barbecue.

"Hannah has some news." Matt's eyes dared her to challenge him.

"I got to the door first."

"No, you didn't. My boot hit the bottom of the door before your hand hit the handle." He crossed his arms over his chest. "Besides this was your idea, honey."

Honey?

She was momentarily nonplussed by the casual way he called her "honey." It was an endearment she'd heard a few times in her life, but never in regard to herself, of course.

"Oh, yes, the news."

Granny and Eva watched her expectantly. She smiled and decided it would be good for her and for the Grahams to celebrate.

"We're going to have a barbecue next Saturday."

Granny's brows went up toward her hairline. Eva nodded and gestured with her hand for Hannah to continue.

"I thought it would be good for two reasons. First, to celebrate the wedding and such. I want to meet the neighbors, too." She glanced at Matt. "I know there hasn't been much to celebrate this year, so I'm hoping we can change that."

Matt's gaze locked with hers and warmth seeped

through her at what she saw. It wasn't love, but it was respect and definite affection. She fell deeper into his beautiful eyes and even swayed toward him.

"What's the second reason?" Eva's voice yanked Hannah back from the spell she had fallen under.

"Oh, the second reason. After I met Mr. Stinson, I decided he wouldn't be, ah, willing to sell the two-mile land belt. I thought at a barbecue with lots of folks around, he might be more willing." She saw Olivia standing in the hallway listening.

"*Sí, es la verdad.*" Eva nodded her head, then turned to Matt. "*Tu esposa es muy inteligente.*"

Hannah looked to Matt to translate. He grinned. "She said you are one smart lady."

Considering the amount of fussing Matt had done after she'd suggested the barbecue, it surprised her to see him smile. It was a small victory in the battle for her role in his life.

"I don't think it's smart at all." Olivia walked in, her arms crossed and the perpetual scowl on her face. "We have hardly any money and you let her plan to waste it on a party? What about Margaret?"

"Won't cost us nothing but a steer." Matt scowled at his sister. "Folks will bring food. Margaret can be a guest."

"He's right. They always do." Eva watched the two siblings carefully.

"Doesn't seem right throwing a party so soon after Ma and Pa were murdered." Olivia's words were laced with anger but also with anguish.

Hannah felt Olivia's pain in her own heart and understood now why her new sister-in-law was so resentful. As Matt's new wife, she represented moving on after losing their parents, a substitute mother for the young ones, and a new head of the household.

Olivia was angry at her loss, and she took it out on the likeliest target, Hannah.

"They would have been happy with Matt's choice," Eva said with a calm expression. "They wouldn't want you to grieve forever."

"You don't know what they would want, Eva. You're the goddamn housekeeper." A red-faced Olivia turned her wrath on Hannah. "And you're an ignorant orphan who dares to think she can walk in here and take over our family. You're an outsider and you always will be."

Hannah noted the tears on the other woman's face as Olivia fled the room. Her heart ached for everything the Graham family had gone through; they were now orphans, too.

"Don't feel sorry for her." Matt appeared at her side. "Livy was angry before our parents died and now it's worse. She can't allow herself to be happy and she doesn't want anyone else to be either."

"*Pobrecita*." Eva rose to her feet. "I will go find her."

The joy and happiness Hannah had been feeling were now gone, and her stomach twisted back up into a knot. Life as a Graham was proving to be a daily challenge.

"I'm going to get to work." Matt glanced at her lips and she couldn't help hoping he would kiss her, but he didn't. "I'll see you at dinner."

Hannah looked at her grandmother, who didn't appear worried at all.

"You've got yourself an interesting situation here, child."

It was an understatement of course. Hannah had a mountain to climb.

CHAPTER ELEVEN

Shuffling sounds pulled Hannah out of her slumber. She'd gone to bed early, exhausted, and was still alone in the bed. She cracked one eye and realized there was a small figure standing beside the bed.

"Catherine?"

The little girl leaned down to whisper in her ear. "We need you in our room, Hannah. Um, Rebecca needs help."

Hannah was on her feet in seconds, wiping the sleep from her eyes. "Is she okay?"

Catherine took her hand. "Yeah, she's okay. She just . . . needs help."

The two younger girls shared a small bedroom with two narrow cots. The two boys slept in a room at the end of the hall, while the two older girls had a room next to the master bedroom. Eva rounded out the house in the room across from the master. Matt's old bedroom stood empty.

When Hannah walked into the girls' room, she recognized the smell of urine immediately and understood why Rebecca needed help.

"I brought Hannah."

"Aw, Catherine, why'd you do that?" Rebecca sat on the edge of the bed, clutching her white nightdress.

"I can help." Hannah felt bad for the girl. Wetting the bed at the age of nine was embarrassing, especially when her seven-year-old sister knew about it. "I promise I won't tell anyone."

Rebecca fiddled with the fabric bunched in her hands for a few moments. "Okay. I'm not a baby though."

Hannah sat beside her. "No, I don't think you're a baby. You and your brothers and sisters had a bad thing happen to your family. Sometimes that makes people do things they normally don't."

"I don't wet the bed. Never." Rebecca sniffed.

Hannah squeezed her shoulder, remembering how it felt to wet the bed. The cold wetness and the stench were unforgettable.

"Then let's get you cleaned up so you can go back to sleep." She turned to Catherine. "Are there extra sheets?"

"Uh-huh. Eva keeps 'em in the chest in her room." Catherine seemed to know everything.

"Can you get in there without her knowing?" The last thing Hannah wanted to do was betray her promise to Rebecca.

Catherine nodded. "A'course. I'm good at sneaking."

"Not a big surprise." Hannah pointed her toward the door. "You get the sheets while I go get some warm water."

Catherine scampered out of the room, leaving Hannah alone with Rebecca. "I'm going to get some water to wash you up. Do you have another nightdress?"

Rebecca shook her head.

"I have something that will work. Stay here and I'll be right back." Hannah went into her own room first and found an old blouse that didn't fit her bosom any longer. She had planned on making handkerchiefs with it, but now she had another use.

There was a hot water reservoir in the big stove in the kitchen. Hannah quietly filled a bowl with water and took a bar of soap and a clean towel with her to the girls' room.

She had almost made it to the door when a big shadow appeared, scaring the life out of her. Part of the water spilled down the front of her own night-dress when she jumped. Matt's scent washed over her and she let out a shaky breath.

"Hell's bells, Matt, you scared the life out of me."

"What did you say?" He sounded more than surprised.

"I mean, you startled me." She now had the same problem as Rebecca with a wet nightdress. The cool night air immediately made her shiver.

"What are you doing up? And with a bowl of water?" He looked tired in the shaft of moonlight.

"I'm, um, the girls forgot to wash up before bed." It sounded like a lie, and it was.

"Oookay. . . . That's sort of odd." He touched her cheek. "Don't be long."

With that, he turned and went into their room. Hannah's body had tightened at the mere brush of his fingers. She wanted to follow him into the darkened room and feel his body pressed against hers, the rasp of his whiskers against her neck, her breasts. Lord, she wanted to touch him.

"Hannah?"

Catherine almost scared her into spilling the water a second time.

"I'm coming."

They crept back into the girls' room. Rebecca sat exactly where she'd been. Catherine set the sheets on her own bed and waited.

"Rebecca, we'll get you cleaned up. Catherine, you take the sheets off the bed while I help your sister." Hannah set the bowl on the floor and waited for the girl to remove her wet nightdress.

After an efficient wash and brisk dry, Rebecca was in the old shirt that hung to her knees. It would do for the night.

"Better?"

Rebecca nodded and hugged her quickly. The fresh scent of soap and little girl enveloped her. She had grown to love these children; they were so easy to be with. They expected nothing but love in return.

The sheets were wet, but not soaked. It appeared that Rebecca had woken up when she started peeing. Hannah checked the straw-filled mattress and found it slightly damp. She used a corner of the towel with a little soap to wipe it down.

When she opened the clean sheet the girls stood on either side of her, holding up their little hands to help make the bed. It took twice as long to finish, but turned out to be a bonding experience between them. A secret to be shared.

Hannah bundled up the soiled sheet and nightdress. She would wash them out right away, to keep Rebecca's privacy. The girls climbed back into bed and watched her expectantly.

Hannah sat down on Catherine's bed first, tucking the blanket around her slim frame. As she bent down to kiss her forehead, Catherine squirmed out and hugged her neck.

"Thank you, Hannah. I knew you'd fix it up."

Hannah smiled and moved over to Rebecca's bed. She looked so small in the bed, her eyes wide in the lamplight. Hannah tucked her in, too, and received another hug in return. She was glad to have helped Rebecca when she needed someone.

"You girls get back to sleep now. It's very late." They both nodded like little owls from their beds. "Goodnight."

Hannah took the soiled linens out of the room and closed the door as quietly as she could. She walked through the darkened house with a familiarity she hadn't had a week earlier. It was beginning to feel like home to her. She navigated her way into the kitchen and found a bucket.

"What are you doing?" Matthew's quiet question didn't startle her this time.

"Keeping a promise."

He sat at the table and watched her. Perhaps it was a dream because she wanted him there. The house was so quiet, every move she made seemed to echo. She filled the bucket with warm water, then submerged the nightdress, soaped it up, and rinsed it thoroughly. As she squeezed out the water, Matt made a strange noise.

Hannah peered at him through the darkened room and realized he was shirtless. Her stomach flipped and her core throbbed once, hard and fast. He watched her and groaned over what he saw. What did that mean?

She set the nightdress aside and cleaned the small area on the sheets that had been soiled. The soap was slippery in her hands as she worked. She also kept glancing at her husband out of the corner of her eye.

After rinsing off the sheet, she picked up the bucket

and the clean laundry. "I'll be right back. I need to hang these on the line so they'll be dry by morning."

He simply nodded, a hazy figure in the gloom. She hurried outside and dumped the bucket, then hung up the nightdress and sheet on the line with shaking hands. The moon was bright, illuminating everything for her.

Something was going to happen; she just didn't know what it was. Hannah stepped back inside and waited for her eyes to adjust. Matt sat where she'd left him in the chair. Her heart thumped as she approached him, anticipation making her mouth dry and her body tingle.

He wore only a pair of drawers, his hand inside the front of them, moving up and down. She stared, fascinated by what he was doing. Her body seemed to recognize the motion because her pussy grew damp and her nipples hard.

"Come here." His husky whisper sent a shiver down her spine.

She moved closer, his scent filling her nose, ripening her need to kiss him, touch him, be part of whatever he was doing. He took her hand and kissed it, then tugged until she was right in front of him.

Hannah couldn't take her gaze off the movement in his drawers. He unbuttoned them completely and exposed his cock to her prying eyes. His hand moved up and down the shaft, squeezing and pulling.

"Ride me, honey."

Hannah had no idea what he meant. "Help me."

"Spread your legs and lift your nightdress."

She felt naughtier than she ever had in her life, but at the same time, more excited, too. It was that excitement that drove her to lift her nightdress and straddle him. The coolness of the night air felt good on the heat from her center. As she lowered herself, he took her hips and guided her toward his cock.

The head touched her entrance and they both groaned.

"We need to be quiet." His eyes glittered in the semi-darkness as she slid down on his shaft.

She gasped at the feeling of fullness, of rightness. He was deep within her and this time she was in control of their joining. Matt unbuttoned her nightdress as far as he could, then pulled it down to expose her left breast.

As soon as his hot mouth closed around her nipple, she clenched, everywhere.

"Oh God, do that again."

She used the foot railing on the chair to push herself up and down, while his mouth remained firmly latched on her breast, biting, licking, and sucking. Streaks of pure pleasure traveled from her nipple to her center, pulsing and tingling outward. She managed to find a rhythm; he pushed up and she pushed down.

It was so erotic, Hannah completely forgot where she was, only that she was with Matt and they were making love. She closed her eyes and reveled in it.

"I'm close, honey, so close." He pulled down the fabric to expose her other breast. "I need you to come, too."

She knew what he meant but she didn't know how to get there. One of his hands crept between them and started rubbing circles on her nubbin of pleasure. The other hand tweaked the now damp nipple. She clenched again hard as a wave began within her.

"Matt, I think I'm coming."

"That's it, honey, ride me." His movements became

fiercer as she slammed up and down his shaft. His cock filled her, touched her womb, drove her to heights she never knew existed.

The storm of ecstasy slammed into her like a thunderbolt, stealing her breath, stopping her heart. She gripped the chair so hard, she heard it groan, right along with her. Hannah bit her lip to keep from crying out as her body convulsed with the most powerful pleasure it had ever felt.

Matt buried his head between her breasts, gripping her hips until his knuckles cracked. She felt his pleasure mingle with hers, his seed spill into her body. The heat between them could have melted iron.

She sucked in a shaky breath and opened her eyes. Matt stared at her, his expression unreadable in the moonlight. Before she could say a word, he got to his feet, arms firmly wrapped around her behind. He carried her to bed that way, his cock still hard, gently moving in and out of her.

When they got to the bed, she was disappointed when his cock slipped out of her. She wanted more.

To her surprise, he slid right back inside.

"Oh my." Hannah spread her legs, reveling in the slow, gentle glide. Their first joining had been fast and furious; now he took his time. She loved it.

If she wasn't careful, she might love him.

"Your hair. Spread out your hair for me." His husky words made her do as he bade.

To Hannah, they were making love. This was what she thought married people did. If her mind wasn't so scrambled, she might even admit she'd enjoyed the episode in the kitchen more. However without the frantic pace, he took his time touching her. He ran his hands up and down her thighs and stomach, up to her pouting nipples, then down to her thighs.

She watched him, the bright moonlight illuminating his every move as though he was bathed in silver. Matt appeared ethereal, not of the earth, a god of lore come to life. She threw her arms out and gloried in the amazing sensation of being with her husband.

Finally his pace quickened and his staff thrust harder, faster. His hand found her clit and flicked it as she was hoping he would. It didn't take long to recall her pleasure, to bring it forth again until she exploded into a thousand stars for her silver moonlight man.

He called her name softly as he found his own ultimate pleasure, his hands tightening on her thighs. She clenched around him, pulling him deeper into her core until he touched her womb. Hannah wanted his baby and she truly hoped his seed would find fertile ground.

Matt groaned and rolled over to lie on the bed beside her. The only sound in the room was their breathing and Hannah's heart thumping madly.

"Your hair. I'd never seen it unbound before, wild and free. It did something to me." His soft confession made her smile.

"Then I'll leave it down every night."

He rose and poured water into the basin, then used a soft rag to clean them both up. Hannah was boneless, completely drained of energy by two incredible rounds of lovemaking. By the time she crawled under the covers, she could hardly keep her eyes open. Matt lay beside her, spooning against her as had become his habit.

Hannah fell asleep almost immediately, more content than she'd ever been in her life.

* * *

The impending barbecue energized the ranch. Eva sent Javier and Lorenzo to the neighboring ranches with invitations. Within a few days, Eva told Hannah they expected at least seventy-five people to come.

It was an intimidating number, but Hannah was used to organizing meals for large groups at the boardinghouse. This was the biggest challenge she'd ever faced though. Fortunately she, Granny, and Eva worked together.

Hannah used all the scraps she could find to make a huge tablecloth while the boys put together a table from leftover wood. Eva cleaned like a madwoman and Granny was put in charge of watching the three youngest Grahams. Together, the four of them made decorations out of whatever they could find.

Olivia was the only one not helping. She sulked most days, not bothering to talk to anyone. Hannah wanted to get her sister-in-law to talk, but didn't have much success.

It was Friday, the day before the barbecue. The tables were built, the patchwork tablecloth ready. Granny was outside with Eva supervising the hanging of the girls' decorations. The men were digging the pit and preparing the steer. Hannah worked on some mending to relax.

The time between dinner and supper was usually the quietest in the house. Hannah had a cup of coffee she sipped as she worked and hummed under her breath.

"Oh, I didn't know you were in here." Olivia stood at the entrance to the kitchen, nearly hidden in the shadows of the hallway.

"I'm just doing some mending. The room is big enough for both of us." Hannah offered a smile.

"This whole ranch isn't big enough for both of us."

Olivia walked toward the stove. "What is Eva planning for supper?"

"I don't know. She's outside helping the girls with the decorations."

Olivia sighed and speared Hannah with an accusing glare. "This whole barbecue fiasco is your fault. You've turned everything upside down."

"I don't mean to." Hannah set the mending down and gestured to the chair across from her. "Will you sit and talk to me?"

"No."

Hannah threw her hands in the air. "I don't know what I did to make you hate me so much, Olivia. But Matt and I are well and truly married. Your anger isn't going to change that one bit."

"He was supposed to marry Margaret. Did you know that?"

Olivia had mentioned it before, but Hannah had ignored her revelation for fear of learning something she didn't want to hear.

"No, and it doesn't matter. He married me."

"Because your name was Hannah." Olivia might not have wanted to talk, but the words gushed from her mouth now.

"I know that. I knew that from the second he proposed." Hannah understood that the reason for her marriage was unconventional, but she had come to enjoy being married.

Olivia paced back and forth, her body fairly vibrating with energy. "You very nearly prostituted yourself for a husband."

That one stung. "There are many reasons why folks get married. I had no prospects for a husband and he needed a wife."

"No prospects? There isn't anyone out here to

marry. You took the most eligible bachelor in the county." Olivia's voice had risen. "Margaret was my ticket out of here. We were going to travel together. Maybe even go to New York. You took that from me."

Hannah's mouth dropped open. "I did no such thing."

"I had a beau once, sure I did. What girl didn't besides you? After some bastard killed my parents and Benjy disappeared, he didn't like my crying. My grief was too much for him." Her words were running into each other. "He ran off with that awful bitch Mary Walker. Then Margaret decided I wasn't good enough for her anymore. She expected us to fail without my parents. Last week was the first time she spoke to me in months."

Olivia shook her head, staring off into what Hannah could only assume was a gaping maw of grief. "I lost everything. *Everything*."

Hannah's heart ached for what the Grahams had suffered. She had hoped the new land would bring them the fresh start they needed. However, Stinson had made sure their fresh start was soured before it truly began.

"I'm so sorry, Olivia. So very sorry." Hannah got to her feet and pulled her sister-in-law into a hug. At first Olivia was stiff and unyielding, but then she softened, shaking as she wept buckets of tears. Hannah just let her cry, wondering if the young woman had ever let herself grieve for what she'd lost. It likely had been bottled up inside her all this time.

After a few minutes, Olivia's sobs began to fade. She pulled away, accepting the handkerchief Hannah offered. The moment stretched out, sliding into an awkward silence.

"Would you like some coffee?"

Olivia nodded and sat down in her chair at the table with a sigh. "I don't like who I am anymore. I'm downright mean no matter how much I try to stop myself."

Hannah poured the coffee, then set the steaming mug in front of the other woman. She sat down and waited, hoping like hell Olivia would continue talking to her.

"Grief makes us do things we normally wouldn't." She sipped her own coffee. "I don't pretend to know how it feels to have gone through what you did but I can listen if you want to talk."

Olivia wiped her eyes with a corner of the handkerchief. She narrowed her watery gaze. "I've been nothing but a bitch to you. Why are you being so nice?"

Hannah shrugged, unwilling to blame Olivia for her anger. It wasn't truly directed at Hannah, but more at the world. "I take some blame for that, too."

Olivia seemed to accept the peace offering and turned her attention back to her coffee. The silence was comfortable as they both sipped. Hannah felt relieved they were talking and being civil.

"I feel like Matt set this whole ranch on its ear when he lied about having a wife." Olivia's gaze rose to meet hers. "He's spent so much time thinking about you, he forgot about us. Forgot about Mama and Pa, and about Benjy. I was angry with him and with God."

"Tell me about them." Hannah needed to know more about the elder Grahams and the youngest child, the boy who'd vanished like a puff of smoke.

Olivia was quiet for a few minutes; then, to Hannah's relief, she started talking.

"Benjamin was Matt's shadow. He was the spitting image of him, too. Walked like him, swagger and all."

Olivia smiled. "Mama never worried about Benjy because wherever Matt was, he was always right behind him. Except for the day we were—"

The day the Grahams were killed and the barn burned. An unsolved murder in such a small town was bound to garner a lot of talk. Folks speculated it had been Indians, but there was no evidence of that. Others thought it was a couple of drifters or maybe Mexicans who were loyal to their country, trying to drive Texans off land that once belonged to them.

The oddest thing about the crime was the disappearance of the youngest sibling. There hadn't been a sign of Benjamin, dead or alive, since the Grahams had died. Hannah had heard the search had gone on for days, fanning out for miles. There had been no tracks, no trace.

"What about your parents? What were they like?" Hannah didn't want Olivia to bog down in her grief again.

"Pa loved Mama to distraction. Whatever she wanted, he made happen for her. They kissed and hugged a lot. He wasn't wishy-washy though. He was big like Matt, worked hard for everything he had. When Pa came back from the war, he was quieter than he had been. I remember when I was little, his laugh used to vibrate through my chest it was so loud. He wasn't like that anymore." Olivia paused to stare off into the distance again. "Mama kept us all together while he and Matt fought in the war. She was stronger than both of them put together. She managed eight children and this ranch and did a right fine job of it, too. Eva was here, but she was more of a housekeeper and cook than a mother figure. It was only after Mama was gone that Eva stepped in to help the young'uns."

Hannah digested all of the information, which answered quite a few questions she'd had. Matt was trying to be like his father, as most men would, but there was something else there she still hadn't pinned down. Later, she would try to find out what was driving him so hard, and what secrets he was hiding. She might not have any success but she had to try.

"I wish I had known them."

Olivia's gaze probed Hannah's until she finally nodded. "I think you mean that."

"I do. I lost my parents when I was seven. I don't remember much about them, just snatches of memories. Mama always smelled like roses and Papa like wood." Hannah had a hole where a girl's memories of a mother and father should have been. It didn't necessarily make her sad, but it sure made her lonely.

"No brothers or sisters?"

Hannah shook her head. "Nobody but Granny."

"She's your father's mother?" Olivia had begun to relax in earnest.

"No, my mother's mother. She and my grandfather took me in, but he died shortly after that. Granny has had more tragedy in her life than I have. I think she had two sons who died as children, too." Hannah stared into her coffee, realizing for the first time just how much her grandmother had been through.

"That why she opened the boardinghouse?"

"Yep. It was a big house and she had no money to speak of. I only did simple chores at first, but I grew up cleaning and cooking for large groups." Hannah smiled at her sister-in-law. "All along I was in training to join the Graham clan."

"I won't say congratulations. Some days I wish them all away. They're loud, pushy, greedy, and stomp on my last nerve." Olivia's gaze softened. "Then I think of life without all of them and know it doesn't matter how crazy they make me. They're my family."

Hannah ached for that kind of family and wished until her teeth hurt that she would be accepted as part of theirs. Good, bad, and ugly, the Grahams were everything she'd ever wanted. Matt had given her the gift of a family when he'd proposed to her. Hannah was marrying them as much as she was marrying their brother.

"I haven't made it very easy for you to join us." Olivia ran her finger around the rim of the mug. "I was protecting me and mine, making sure no one would hurt us."

"And now?" Hannah held her breath, hoping to hear Olivia was finally past her anger.

"Now I can see we have a lot more in common than I thought. I knew you disappeared out of school, but didn't think anything of it." Olivia shook her head. "You know how Catherine feels because she's seven and she just lost her parents."

Hannah hadn't even recognized the truth right in front of her face. Olivia just put her finger on the very reason Hannah had found her place so easily with the two youngest Grahams. They reminded her of her own orphaned self thirteen years earlier. She was glad to be there for the girls, to brush their hair, mend their clothes, and even wash their sheets in the dead of night.

"Yes, I know how you all feel. It's not an easy thing to lose one parent, much less two." Hannah actually felt the connection between them blossoming. "I don't want to replace anyone, or even drive your brother to distraction. I just want to be part of your family, be a wife to Matt, and maybe one day, a mother to his children."

Olivia was silent for a few moments, then lifted her gaze to Hannah's. Her eyes were so much like Matt's, Hannah's heart did a little hiccup. She really was falling in love with her husband.

"I think that's a right fine idea." This time when Olivia smiled, it was genuine.

Hannah got to her feet at the same time as her sister-in-law. They hugged briefly, then sat back down.

"Would you show me how to sew?" Olivia pointed at the pile of mending. "With so many folks in the house, that pile has grown as big as Catherine. I always refused to learn, telling Mama I'd marry a rich man and never have to mend a thing. Too bad the one man I wanted to marry found a girl without tears in her eyes."

"Then he wasn't the man for you. I never even had a beau, so I knew Matt was the one for me. Yours is out there somewhere. He just hasn't found his way to the Circle Eight yet." Hannah patted the chair next to her. "Come on over and I'll teach you the basics."

Hannah spent the next hour with Olivia, showing her how to use a needle and thread. It was the most relaxing, enjoyable time she'd spent with her sister-in-law. By the time the hour was over, Olivia was mending a ripped seam in one of Caleb's shirts.

Catherine came running into the house, her pigtails flying. She stopped so suddenly she nearly fell over, pinwheeling her little arms to stop her fall. "Jehosophat! You're both smiling."

"It's been known to happen," Olivia said with a wink.

"You two were fighting like barn cats last I knew." Catherine put her fists on her hips. "About time you two became friends. I was tired of the bickering."

She sounded so much like Olivia in that moment,

Hannah burst out laughing, earning identical, puzzled looks from both of them. Hannah waved her hand at them, trying to distract them from watching her embarrass herself.

"Did you need something, Cat?" Olivia asked.

"Oh, yep, I did. Strangers coming in a horse and buggy. Matt sent me to fetch you."

Strangers? Hannah's mirth disappeared in a blink. She looked at Olivia and they both got to their feet. Strangers on the ranch had been a deadly occurrence once before. The three of them left the house quickly and went outside to find out what was going on.

CHAPTER TWELVE

Matt had taken to wearing a pistol on his hip. It had been his Pa's from the war, now his, and he felt safer with it close by. Even though they were simply getting ready for the barbecue, he was armed. And with good reason apparently. A fancy horse and buggy was approaching the house.

He immediately sent Catherine inside, but she came right back out with Hannah and Olivia. Matt wanted to yell at all of them to get inside the house, but didn't want to be distracted by the inevitable bickering that would ensue. Instead he stood his ground, hand on his pistol.

Behind him, he knew Lorenzo, Nick, and Caleb had retrieved rifles and were standing there like a well-armed line of defense. He'd sent Javier into the barn to watch the horses. They'd lost half a dozen the last time strangers had come to the Circle Eight. Several had perished in the fire, and others had been taken by the murdering sons-of-bitches who had dared defile the ground with Graham blood.

The air crackled with anticipation as the buggy drew closer. It had fringe around the top like a fancy decoration in a rich man's house. He didn't recognize the rig or the horses and therefore wouldn't relax his guard.

He smelled Hannah's scent before she even spoke. She'd walked up directly behind him.

"Who is it?"

"I don't know. Now get back in the house with the girls."

He could almost hear her cursing him silently.

"I'll do no such thing. I'm your wife and I will stand by your side no matter what."

She reminded him of his mother, so strong and fierce. It surprised the hell out of him. Initially, Hannah had been so meek and soft-spoken. Two weeks of marriage had shown him she was merely hiding her lioness inside. While it made him proud to be married to such a woman, at the same time he wanted to spank her. She was distracting him just as he'd feared.

"Step back now," he growled under his breath.

To his shock, she appeared beside him, holding a rifle. His mouth dropped open.

"Before you ask, I know how to shoot it. Don't order me around anymore, Matthew Graham." She gripped the rifle in the right places, her hands so tight the knuckles were white. "I will protect this family with you."

Matt's brain was spinning. Hannah probably didn't even realize just how much she had turned him on his ear. Was there a day that she wouldn't surprise him?

He was going to yell at her again to get inside but the buggy had arrived, and he had no time to spend on chastising his wife. Not that she would listen to him anyway.

A man and a woman rode in the buggy. They were

unfamiliar and Matt cursed under his breath to have all the children out in plain view.

The buggy stopped in front of them and the man hopped out. He was dressed in black trousers and a black coat, white shirt with a silver string tie. His face was marked with a jagged scar on his jaw and a pair of cold blue eyes Matt could see fifteen feet away. On the man's head sat a flat-brimmed black hat to match the black, dusty boots on his feet. The shirt and his eyes were the only break in the darkness of the stranger. His gaze flickered to the pistol in Matt's hand.

He stepped around to the other side of the buggy and helped the woman down. She was older than the man, probably around Eva's age, with her salt and pepper hair in a tight bun beneath a straw hat. Her clothing was of good quality, a gray traveling suit with shiny brass buttons.

When her gaze found Matt's, a tremor shook him from head to foot. Something told him the woman was the bearer of bad news and he didn't want to hear it.

"Good afternoon." The woman's voice was tense. Her syllables were as sharp as her gaze. "I'm looking for Matthew Graham."

"That'd be me." Matt didn't move his hand from the pistol.

"I'm Mrs. Leticia Markum. I've been asked to investigate a claim of fraud by the land claim office."

His gut twisted and the taste of bile coated his throat. Fraud? Hannah sucked in an audible breath beside him.

"Fraud with regard to what?" Hannah sounded so much smarter than he was.

"And you are?" Mrs. Markum speared Hannah with her fierce gaze.

"I'm Hannah Graham, Matthew's wife."

Mrs. Markum's grin was not at all friendly. "Fraud with regard to being married as he purported to be on the land claim form."

"I assure you, Mrs. Markum, we are well and truly married." Hannah nodded to the buggy. "There's no reason for any investigation."

"We received a letter stating you had not been truthful on your land claim." Mrs. Markum remained as stiff as a board. "I must investigate."

"And your driver?" Matt watched the man. He didn't appear to be armed, but he could have a weapon hidden anywhere on him.

"Ranger Brody Armstrong. He's here for my protection and to ensure my investigation proceeds as it should." Mrs. Markum nodded to the man.

Matt wondered why a Texas Ranger was minding this bitch when he could have been fighting at the frontier. It wasn't a wise move to ask, but he sure as hell wanted to. He had noticed a hitch in the man's step, so perhaps he'd been wounded in the war.

"What do you want, Mrs. Markum?" Matt asked impatiently.

"I need to verify that your marriage is legal and valid. This is a formal investigation, Mr. Graham. While the government of the Republic of Texas is in its infancy, we will follow the laws or slide into anarchy." She somehow straightened her already impossibly straight shoulders. "My husband serves in the government and I assist him in this capacity. Wives often do that for their husbands."

It was damn odd to have a woman investigator, but maybe her husband was one of Sam Houston's friends. Mrs. Markum liked to push people around, that was obvious. Matt recognized the look of annoyance on the ranger's face and his opinion of the man went up.

"What exactly does that entail?" Hannah hadn't relaxed her stance either. She was definitely not the meek girl he thought he'd married.

"I need to see your marriage certificate, examine your sleeping quarters, and question others on your supposed marriage." Mrs. Markum gestured to the house. "With your permission, we can begin in the house."

Matt's teeth ground together. "There's no way I'm letting you in my house, lady. I don't even know who you are or what you really want, but it ain't happening."

"Mr. Graham, if you do not cooperate, I can only report that the claim of fraud is true." Her teeth shone like a wolf's in the bright sunlight.

"First of all, we need proof you are who you say you are," Hannah challenged. "This ranch has suffered at the hands of strangers."

Matt should have realized he was reacting with his heart instead of his head. Hannah was absolutely right. They didn't trust strangers, and for good reason.

"Is that so?" Mrs. Markum frowned.

"Yes, it's so. My parents were murdered and my brother disappeared this spring." Matt almost spat the words, his jaw beginning to ache from clenching it so hard.

"I assume this was reported to the authorities?"

Matt almost leapt at her, but the ranger must've seen something in his gaze because he spoke up quickly.

"It's true, ma'am. I read the report myself." Armstrong's voice was deep and dark.

"I see. Well, I have no nefarious intentions."

"That remains to be seen." Hannah sounded as angry as he felt. "Do you have any kind of verification of your investigation?"

Matt watched as Mrs. Markum's steely expression faltered. "Verification?"

"Yes, ma'am. Papers that prove you are who you say you are. You must have something." As Hannah kept after the other woman, Matt wanted to cheer for her.

"Of course I do. In my reticule. Mr. Armstrong, will you fetch it for me from the buggy?"

Ranger Armstrong shook his head and a chuckle threatened to pop out of Matt's mouth. "Ma'am, I'm not an errand boy. I'm a Texas Ranger."

Mrs. Markum huffed an impatient breath and walked back to the buggy herself. She fiddled around inside for a few minutes, then emerged with a sheaf of papers. Matt's heart lodged in his throat.

"Here is the verification. I have a letter alleging the fraud and the original deed signed last week for the land grant." Mrs. Markum shook the papers in the air.

"I will read them before we go any further." Hannah stepped toward her. Matt wanted to yank her back but didn't. His wife was a match for the other woman, and he was proud of her, even if it scared him to death to watch her walk toward the strangers.

Hannah took the papers in one hand, the rifle still in the other. She tucked the rifle under her arm, the barrel pointed at Mrs. Markum's chest. After Hannah read through the documents, she handed them back.

"That's my signature on that deed and my husband's. I don't know who wrote that letter, but it's a pack of lies." Hannah walked backward until she was beside Matt again.

"Then let me complete my investigation and I can be on my way."

Matt wanted to tell the woman no and get her off the ranch right away. Yet his gut told him to finish this so the woman could get back to whatever hole she'd crawled out of.

"Then let's get this done."

Hannah led Mrs. Markum into the house while the ranger stayed outside by the buggy. Matt decided to remain with the man rather than follow the women. Something told him it would be a good idea for him to talk to Ranger Armstrong. For once his brothers and sisters were quiet and watchful.

"I don't cotton to what Mrs. Markum is doing, but the Republic has to act like a government." Armstrong lit up a cheroot. "That means making sure folks are following the law."

"She's a bitch." Matt ignored the gasps behind him. His little sisters had heard worse, but no doubt Catherine and Olivia would chastise him later for his language.

"That she is." The ranger puffed on his cheroot. "This your family?"

"Yep."

"Look like a good group of folks." Armstrong gestured to Matt. "I wanted to talk to you about something."

Matt hesitated, not willing to be close enough to give the ranger room to outmaneuver him.

Armstrong held up his hands. "I'm unarmed. Left my weapons in the buggy."

"Okay then, let's talk." Matt stepped toward him and they walked toward the back of the buggy.

"I wasn't lying when I said I saw the report about

your parents." Armstrong's eyes were a startling blue up close. "I think I can help."

Hannah led the woman through the house, showing her each room and telling her who slept where. When they entered the master bedroom, she showed the woman her clothes hanging on the nails as well as the drawers in the chest with her meager possessions.

"How long have you lived here?"

"We've been married two weeks, but engaged for longer. I moved in here after we were officially married." Hannah knew Matt had started the land grant claim before he had proposed. A little white lie about being engaged wouldn't hurt.

"Do you have your marriage certificate?" Mrs. Markum's gaze settled on Hannah's ring.

"Yes, of course." Hannah retrieved it from the small chest she kept her most prized possessions in. Her parents' marriage certificate, her own hastily scribbled birth certificate, and the letter she'd written to God at age seven. Someday she would read it again and perhaps even share it with Matt. Today she just wanted this nasty woman out of her life.

Mrs. Markum perused the document, then handed it back to Hannah. "You were married after Mr. Graham filed for the land grant."

Hannah folded the paper carefully. "Yes, but we were planning on getting married. I didn't have any family to speak of, but his was still recovering from their parents' murder. We were going to wait, but we didn't want to lose the land grant."

She hoped she sounded truthful. Her fantasies around the man she would one day marry had become so real in her dreams, she almost believed her own white lies.

"I see. Legally the grant was not signed until after the marriage, which means you either are telling me the truth or a spinster like you saw a chance to marry a handsome rancher about to become land rich." Mrs. Markum's gaze was more disconcerting than her words.

"Is your investigation complete?" Hannah kept the angry words she wanted to say behind her teeth but oh, how they wanted to escape.

Mrs. Markum stared at her for a few beats before she nodded tightly. "Yes, I believe the land grant is valid, however sideways your marriage came to be. The letter, however, will remain with the grant along with my report on what I found."

Hannah gestured to the door and walked behind the officious woman, towering over her tiny stature. "Who wrote the letter?"

"Excuse me?" Mrs. Markum paused with her hand on the knob.

"Who wrote the letter claiming Matt had committed fraud?" Hannah didn't recognize the handwriting and it wasn't signed. However, it was written in a distinctly feminine hand.

"I don't know, Mrs. Graham, and frankly I don't care." Mrs. Markum left the house without a backward glance.

Hannah took a moment to catch her breath before she followed. She had to find out who had been so vicious as to claim Matt had come by the land through fraud. The letter was a cruel ploy written by a coward who lurked in the shadows.

She promised herself to find out who had done it and protect her new husband and her new family.

When Hannah emerged from the house, Matt was deep in conversation with the ranger. Mrs. Markum had climbed into the buggy and was currently shooting daggers with her eyes at her escort.

To Hannah's surprise, Matt shook the ranger's hand. After turning the buggy around, the two strangers left the Circle Eight. Everyone seemed to breathe a collective sigh of relief.

The three younger girls crowded around her, all chattering at once like a flock of magpies. She wanted to go ask Matt what he and the ranger had been discussing, but couldn't. He'd gone over to Caleb, Nick, and Lorenzo, and the four of them had disappeared into the barn.

Granny walked over with Eva and they both looked at her expectantly. Olivia watched from the newly created table. Hannah extricated herself from the girls and held up her hands.

"Okay, everyone. I showed her the house, the marriage certificate, and answered her questions. She said the land grant was valid and the investigation was over."

"*Dios mio*, that woman was a *bruja*." Eva made a strange sign with her hands at the retreating buggy.

"You did good, Hannah." Granny grinned. "I thought you were going to take a swing at her."

The younger girls all looked confused while Eva chuckled. Hannah felt her cheeks heat, but decided she had to be honest. This was her family after all.

"I thought about it, but I didn't want to give her any reason to stay a second longer."

This time everyone laughed and Hannah felt an enormous sense of relief. She gazed around and realized that she finally felt like a Graham.

"Let's get ready for the barbecue."

* * *

Matt could hardly focus on the pit. His mind whirled with the events of the day, particularly with what Ranger Armstrong had told him. He hadn't shared the information with anyone yet, so it was his burden to carry until he decided to tell someone.

Lorenzo and Javier were butchering the steer, which left the three Graham boys to finish the pit. They had to get the coals hot enough so the steer would cook the entire day. If they didn't put it in on time, it wouldn't be tender as he liked it.

Eva would appear with the rub any minute, so they picked up the pace. The heat made his skin feel tight and his eyes dry. It had been years since they had attended a barbecue, and they'd never hosted one. His parents had been more concerned with keeping the family safe and fed.

Eva had been the one to tell him what he needed to do to cook the steer. Any barbecue was a big event in itself, but this was also the first time the Grahams would welcome their neighbors to the Circle Eight. They would show everyone they were not only surviving their parents' deaths, but celebrating their new beginning with his marriage.

It sounded stupid to him, but Eva insisted that was what they had to do. That left him and his brothers sweating over a pit big enough to hold the steer. Lorenzo and Javier brought half the butchered steer. The brothers obviously had experience with this sort of thing and Matt deferred to their knowledge, learning as he helped them get everything done.

He looked up to find Hannah watching him. Her gaze was questioning and he could guess what she wanted to know. Matt shook his head, unwilling to talk to her, and turned his attention back to the pit. Her frustration was probably hotter than the coals he was currently stoking. Matt didn't want to talk to her and there was no way he'd let her push him into it.

A wife was important to a man, but Hannah had to understand no matter what, he was the head of the house. The bedroom was their private domain. What happened there did not give her license to tell him what to do elsewhere.

By the time they had covered the pit and decided on a shift to watch it, Matt was exhausted. The sun had set, and his body was covered with sweat, dirt, and soot. The barbecue was the next day, which meant his rest would be short because there was so much to do. Hannah had been wrong, it wasn't just a simple matter of nailing a few tables together and cooking a steer. There was a hell of a lot of work involved in feeding seventy-five people, even if there wasn't a lot of money spent.

Matt walked in to find Hannah sitting in the kitchen with a cup of steaming liquid in her hand. She wore a shawl over her white nightdress. The memory of exactly what had happened the last time she wore that nightdress made his body stir to life.

"Hungry?" Her voice sounded as tired as he felt.

"Yes, but I think I'm too tired to eat." He sat down heavily in the chair across from her. "More than anything, I want to get clean."

She smiled. "I heated water for a bath."

Matt couldn't help smiling back. Somehow she knew exactly what he needed before he did. He should be scared by that fact, but he didn't want to think about it. In fact, he didn't want to think at all.

Hannah pulled the tub in from the back porch and filled it with three buckets of hot water, then added two buckets of cold. She already had soap and a towel waiting for him along with a clean pair of drawers.

"Need help getting clean?"

Her question shocked him. She had been such a quiet, soft-spoken woman, even shy, and now she was a seductress. He couldn't quite reconcile the two and trying to do so made his head hurt. Matt didn't answer her and after a few moments of watching him undress, she sat down and picked up her mug again.

He climbed into the tub, trying to ignore the fact he was naked and his wife was five feet away. At least his cock appeared to be as tired as he was. As he sank into the water, which was the perfect temperature, he sighed with relief.

"You spent some time with that ranger." It wasn't a question, but she was fishing for information.

Matt closed his eyes and leaned his head against the back of the tub. "I don't want to talk about it right now."

"Then I won't tell you what Mrs. Markum said."

Matt sighed. "Fine." He really didn't want to think about the conversation anymore but Hannah hadn't given him a choice. "Armstrong read the report on the murders and Benjy's disappearance. He told me there had been ten other ranches within a hundred miles that had been attacked, folks killed and children taken."

She gasped. "Ten?"

"Ten. Armstrong didn't give me much but I do know he's investigating five of them himself." Matt tried not to picture what happened to the other ranchers, wives, or children. He could hardly get the image of his parents' bodies out of his head.

"Did he have any information on what happened here?" Her voice had softened.

"He knows as much as I do." Matt planned on meeting up with Armstrong next week to talk to the man more. The ranger was tight-lipped and hid secrets behind his cold blue eyes.

"It's good that a ranger is working on it, right? I've heard they are very tough lawmen."

"I hear the same thing. Whether or not he comes through remains to be seen." Matt didn't expect her touch, but it didn't startle him either. She dipped a rag in the water, wrung it out, then soaped it up. As Hannah washed the grime from his body, he felt he'd died and gone to heaven—her touch was nearly perfect.

"Mrs. Markum told me someone wrote a letter accusing you of fraud, that you lied about the land grant." Hannah started soaping up his hair.

"Who?" He managed to keep his calm although the idea that someone would accuse him of anything illegal made him want to punch something.

"She said the letter was unsigned. I showed her the house and our marriage certificate." Hannah scrubbed his scalp, her strong fingernails earning a moan from his throat. "I did tell a white lie though."

Matt's eyes popped open. "What did you lie about?"

"I told her we were engaged before you went to file for the land grant the first time." She sighed, and he hated the fact that she'd been put in the position to have to lie to save him. "I don't have much family, so I told her we were waiting for the grieving to pass before we got married. Then with the land grant requiring you to be married, we went ahead and tied the knot."

She sounded so matter of fact, as if she hadn't lied to a government person. *For him.* Matt had done it for his family, for his father, but she had done it for *him*.

Hannah had showed him with her simple gesture just what it meant to be first in someone else's heart. Matt's stomach thumped so hard against his ribs, it vibrated his bones. Could her heart be involved already? They'd known each other only two weeks. Matt didn't pretend to understand how women thought and he sure as hell wasn't going to ask. He wasn't ready to hear the answer.

"Thank you for that, Hannah. I didn't mean for you to tell any kind of lie for me." He dunked his head and rinsed the soap from his hair. When he emerged, she sat beside the tub watching him. Her gaze was pensive.

"Mrs. Markum said she was keeping the letter with the land grant." Hannah shook her head. "I don't know that we've seen the last of her. I think she's some important man's wife."

"I don't care who she is. She's a bitch." Matt was rewarded with a chuckle from Hannah, although most women would have chastised him for cussing.

"I won't argue that. I didn't like her at all." Hannah reached out and touched his cheek.

He wanted to melt into her, pull her into his arms, and make love to her until neither one of them could see straight. Matt was teetering on the edge of falling in love with his wife and it scared him witless. He didn't want to be a man who was led around by a woman. He needed to stop his feelings from going any further.

"Can I have a towel?"

"Oh, I'm sorry." Hannah got to her feet, her large breasts at eye level for a moment, which made his traitorous cock jump. Thank God the water hid the movement.

She held the towel open, waiting for him to step

from the tub. His gaze held hers and he was torn between his head and his urges. If he got out of the water and stepped into her arms, he'd tussle in the sheets with her. If he took the towel from her, there would be no sex that night.

Matt took the towel with a weak smile. Her expression looked shocked for a moment and then she turned away, leaving him in the tub alone.

Damn.

Hannah shouldn't have been disappointed. Matt was exhausted from preparing the barbecue pit and she had no right to expect him to make love. But after the intimate moments they'd shared while he bathed, she'd thought maybe they would.

He had relaxed under her hands and she had completely enjoyed bathing him. But as soon as she'd finished, his gaze became shuttered again, leaving her with nothing but an ache between her legs and hardened nipples.

She washed up for bed and climbed in before she had time to think about being naked. Married people didn't need to make love every night, did they? She fussed around under the covers without really getting comfortable. Matt came to bed within ten minutes and she pretended to be asleep. The truth was she was awake a lot longer than she should have been. As she fell into a fitful sleep, Hannah ached to touch her husband.

Chapter Thirteen

The day of the barbecue Hannah was up before the sun, her heart and body still aching. She dressed quietly, leaving Matt still sleeping. If she had more courage, she might have woken him up, but she couldn't quite make herself do it.

No one else was awake so the house was quiet as she went out to milk the cow. Catherine had shown her how and now Hannah felt confident she could do it herself. The gray light of dawn colored the yard as she made her way to the barn with just a bucket.

She stepped into the barn, and paused at the darkness inside. She hadn't brought a lamp, hadn't thought of it really, so she either needed to go back to the house to get one or go into the gloom of the barn without one. Hannah decided to just get the cow milked and not worry about needing to see. She could leave the door open to shed light into the interior.

The cow lowed at her as she went into the stall. She sat on the stool and placed the bucket strategically to catch the milk. The cow's warm udder felt good in the coolness of the predawn morning. Hannah leaned her forehead against the cow as she milked her, finding the experience relaxing. The soft sounds of the animals, the sound of the milk hitting the pail, they were becoming familiar to her, comfortable. Hannah knew she would be happy here.

It never occurred to her to be afraid or to take precautions to protect herself. She was at home and safe on Graham land. When a pair of strong arms grabbed her, she was so surprised, she didn't make a sound. Her attacker wrapped one arm around her waist, the other around her throat.

Adrenaline surged through her. Her heart had never beat so hard in her life. Who was this and what did he want? The man smelled of sweat, tobacco, and something rancid. She struggled to get free, although her brain told her not to, until his arm tightened so much on her throat she was barely getting any air.

"Let me go." Her shout was only a whisper.

"You listening to me, girlie?"

Hannah managed to make a noise that sounded like a yes.

"That husband of yours needs to stop talking to Armstrong." He tightened his arm again, cutting off her air supply completely. "If'n he don't, I'll come back here and he won't never find your body or that pretty little blonde. You understand me, girlie?"

Hannah tried to nod but his arm was so tight, she couldn't. She scratched at his arm, desperate for air. The only thought in her mind was she didn't want to die before she'd really had a chance to live. He had threatened Catherine, and she had to protect her young sister-in-law.

Black dots swam in front of her eyes, and she mustered up the courage to fight him one last time. She was a Graham now and she would do the name proud. She kicked out hard with her old boot, con-

necting with his shin. He loosened his grip enough for
her to get some air.

"You fucking bitch."

Next she brought her elbow back into his stomach,
but it was padded with so much fat, her blow didn't ac-
complish anything. She tried to kick him again, but he
was ready for it. He replaced his arm with his hand
and really started choking her with fingers like talons.

Hannah was angry enough not to care what he did.
This stranger had dared to hurt and threaten her and
her family. She started fighting him for all she was
worth, scratching and kicking. As the black dots became a roar of blackness in her mind, her last thought
was of Matthew.

She should have woken him up that morning and
told him she loved him.

Matt awoke as the sun crept in through the lace
curtains. He knew he was alone the second he opened
his eyes. To his surprise, he was disappointed Hannah
wasn't there, and not just because his cock was
painfully hard. He wouldn't admit it to anyone, but he
enjoyed spooning with her, feeling the heat from her
body mix with his. Other than riding Winston, it was
about the only time Matt felt at peace.

Today there would be no spooning and no ride.
The neighbors could start arriving at any time and his
shift at the pit started at eight. Judging by the position
of the sun, it was just past six, so he had time to eat
some breakfast.

When the door to his room burst open, he was just
climbing out of bed. He was about to yell at whomever
it was, but Catherine started yelling first.

"Mattie, come quick! Somebody hurt Hannah!"

Matt didn't remember putting his pants or boots on but he was wearing them as he ran across the hard-packed dirt to the barn. Hurt Hannah? Who would hurt her? His gut clenched as he stepped into the barn. She lay on the straw-covered ground, as still as could be.

He dropped to his knees next to her. When he took her hand, he realized his own were shaking. What kind of cruel God would take so much from him? She was warm, and through the haze of confusion and grief, he recognized she was also breathing.

A whoosh of pure relief zinged through him. He slid his arms under her and picked her up. She moaned and her head lolled back. Anger replaced all his emotions when he saw fingerprints on her neck.

Somebody had choked her.

"Is she okay?" Catherine practically danced beside him. "I came to milk the cow but she already done it cause I showed her how, and she was lying there like a doll on the floor."

"You did good, sprite." He didn't want to scare his sister with his fury, so he kept it contained. "Get the door open for me."

Matt brought Hannah into the house, past a surprised Eva, and into their bedroom. As he laid her on the bed, her eyes fluttered open. She gazed at him for a few beats before she smiled.

"Love you, Matt."

Then she was out again. Matt thought he had been shaking before, but now his damn knees were knocking together. First he'd found out that someone had tried to kill her, and now she'd told him she loved him.

Matt wanted to cry.

"*¿Que pasa, hijo?*" Eva was right on his heels, pushing him out of the way. Mrs. Dolan knocked him aside, too.

"Somebody choked the hell out of her." Matt stared at the marks on her neck. He was torn between staying at her side and tearing off after the bastard who had done this to her.

"*¿Porqué?*" Eva unbuttoned Hannah's blouse, exposing the entire length of her neck. Mrs. Dolan gasped and to his surprise, cursed under her breath.

"Damn." Matt couldn't help cussing himself.

Eva pushed Hannah's hair out of the way and examined the back of her neck. "I think whoever the *bandido* was, he only bruised her. I don't think there is permanent damage."

"I don't care if it's permanent or not, I want to rip his arms off." Matt ignored Catherine's gasp behind him. "How dare he hurt my wife?"

Eva turned to him. "Stop complaining and help me. I need water, as cold as you can get it. Martha, I need rags, too."

Mrs. Dolan went to get the rags. Matt didn't want to leave the room, but he did because he knew cold water was for the swelling. If they could keep the swelling down, Hannah would fare better. He grabbed a bucket from the kitchen, then stomped out to the well and pumped it until the water gushed good and cold.

When he returned with the bucket, at least three of his sisters had woken up and were currently crowded in his bedroom doorway.

"Move."

They scattered like feathers in the wind, lucky for them. Matt was in no mood to be patient with anyone. He set down the bucket and Eva immediately dipped a rag in the water. Mrs. Dolan stood at the foot of the bed, watching. As Eva wrung it out, she gestured to Hannah.

Matt looked down, surprised to see his wife's eyes open. "Hannah." He took her hand and squeezed it gently. "You don't get to milk the cow anymore. You spilled half the milk."

She tried to laugh, but winced at the attempt.

"It's okay, honey." His damn knees shook so, he sat down on the edge of the bed, watching Eva press the cold rags against Hannah's neck. "Do you know who did this?"

She shook her head.

"Did you see him?"

She shook her head again. "Message." Her rusty whisper made him want to roar at the heavens.

"A message to me?"

Hannah nodded. "No Armstrong."

Matt's blood ran cold. "Somebody choked you to give me a message to stop talking to Armstrong?"

Her gaze looked scared and angry at the same time, but she nodded.

He pressed her hand between his as he struggled with the rage that poured through him. Not only did the message have the opposite effect from what the son of a bitch wanted, but Matt would personally hunt him down and use his balls for coyote bait.

"Don't do anything stupid, Mateo." Eva changed the cold compress and speared him with one of her *"bruja"* glares. "Today is the barbecue and your wife needs you here."

"Shit." He'd completely forgotten about the barbecue and his shift at the pit. The last thing he needed was to be polite to his neighbors. For all he knew, Stinson was the one who had sent the mongrel to choke Hannah. "We need to cancel the barbecue."

A chorus of nos came from outside the room. It seemed that every one of his siblings was out there.

"It's too late. The meat will go to waste if we don't have it." Olivia spoke up from the doorway.

Matt turned to see them all looking between him and Hannah; their identical expressions of worry almost made him forget how angry he was.

"Besides we need to show whoever it is we're not scared of them," Caleb offered. "Maybe they'll expect us to tell everybody to go home."

"We need to show them what Grahams are made of." Nick stuck out his jaw just like Pa used to do.

"Yeah, we're no cowards." Elizabeth was generally the quiet one, but even she looked fierce.

"We'll find out who hurt Hannah so we can hurt them back." Catherine climbed into the bed and snuggled up against Hannah.

"I like your kin, Matthew." Mrs. Dolan grinned. "I think we need to stand together."

His family had all gathered around his wife as if she had been part of the Graham clan forever. The sight dampened his fury so much that he could see the logic for not canceling the barbecue.

Whoever was behind the attack on Hannah would expect them to cancel. His brothers and sisters were right. They might just flush out the person responsible for not only Hannah's injuries but for his parents' death and Benjy's disappearance. The hunt was on. And he'd make damn sure everyone there knew he'd been talking to Ranger Armstrong.

The Grahams were going to war.

Hannah's throat hurt, especially when she talked, but she was well enough to get out of bed an hour after she woke up in it for the second time that morning. Matt kept hovering, along with Granny and Eva. None of them would let her move.

"I need to help." Her voice was raspy but she managed to be heard without too much pain.

"Pshaw, child. There ain't nothing that important for you to do." Granny sat like a sentry in a chair next to the bed.

"Everyone else is working." Hannah gestured to her throat. "I don't need this to help."

"Wait until folks start arriving, then you can get up. In the meantime, rest." Granny gestured to Eva, who stood in the doorway. "Do you have a scarf she can wear?"

"*Sí*, I have a pretty one *mi mama* made when I got married." Eva disappeared, leaving Granny and Hannah alone.

"That husband of yours was white as a sheet when he brought you in."

Hannah stared at her grandmother. "He was scared?"

"Oh, scared and angrier than I've ever seen anyone. He would have torn apart the man who hurt you, but he was too busy fussing over you." Granny chuckled. "I do believe your husband is falling in love with you, child."

Hannah managed not to let her mouth drop open. Granny was a smart lady and a good judge of people. Hannah had to believe she was right about Matt, but he surely didn't act it around her. The man was still bossy and cold outside the bedroom.

"Good thing, too, because you done told him you loved him."

This time, Hannah's mouth did drop open, "I did no such thing."

"Oh, yes you did. Plain as day. Me, Eva, and him

heard it." This time Granny's cackle made Hannah panic.

"I couldn't have. I mean, I don't remember." She searched her memory and the last thing she could recall was the man choking her in the barn. When she woke up in the bedroom, she could hardly talk much less confess her love. What if Granny was right and she had told Matt she loved him?

Was it such a bad thing?

Yes, if he didn't feel the same. And in such a short time? Two weeks was hardly long enough to fall in love, but she was well on her way.

"He must know I was out of my head." Hannah pushed the thought out of her mind. She had other things to worry about. If Matt had heard her, then he could darn well ask her about it.

Eva appeared with a beautiful scarf in her hand. The colors were so vibrant, it looked like a sunset, with gold, red, green and orange, even pink and purple. They all blended together to form the most beautiful thing she'd ever seen.

"Eva, I can't use this." She knew she'd either rip it or stain it with the food she'd be serving.

"Of course you can." Eva helped her sit up. "Hold up your hair, *hija*."

Hannah wanted to protest some more, but as soon as the scarf touched her bruised neck, she closed her eyes at the sensation. It was magnificent, the most wonderful fabric she'd ever had the privilege of touching. Eva tied the scarf to cover the bruises, then stepped back.

"*¡Que bonita, hija!*" The housekeeper clapped her hands. "The color was made for you."

Hannah wondered how Eva could possibly think she was beautiful, when plain was all she'd ever be.

She got out of the bed, grateful to be on her feet. No one protested, so she walked over to the small mirror on the wall and peered at her reflection.

Her hair was a cloud of curls, forming a halo of brown. The scarf stood out as if someone had painted an explosion of color on her neck. Even her mud brown eyes looked different because of the scarf.

"Wow."

"*Sí, hija, muy bonita.*" Eva picked up the brush and worked on the snarls in Hannah's hair. "Now let's get you ready to meet the neighbors."

Hannah endured ten minutes of discomfort until her hair was neatly contained, as much as possible anyway, in a braid. Eva stepped back to admire her handiwork, then turned to Granny.

"What do you think, Martha?"

"She's a beauty, just like her mother was." To Hannah's surprise, tears appeared in her Granny's eyes. "I can't believe you're all growed up and a married woman."

Hannah took her grandmother's hand. "I'm still the same girl."

Granny held up Hannah's hand, the silver band winking in the sunlight. "No, child, you're not. And it's a good thing."

"A wagon is coming over the rise. We need to get ready." Matt put one foot in the room, barked his orders, then turned and left.

Hannah wanted to kick him.

"Don't worry about him. He's deeper than he thinks he is." Granny winked at her. "Now help me up so we can get cracking."

The three women went outside together, prepared as best they could be for the day. Hannah's throat hurt, but the scarf actually made her skin feel better.

"Wait, what if people ask me about the scarf?" Hannah kept her gaze on the very full wagon headed toward the house. Her stomach did a jig at the sight.

"No one will ask you why you are wearing it. If anything they will be jealous of how beautiful you look in it." Eva smiled and took her arm.

Granny took her other arm. "Eva's got the right of it. Just keep smiling."

Hannah took a deep breath and got ready to face the second half of the hardest day of her life.

Matt was still seething inside. Nothing was going to quench that fire until he found who had hurt Hannah. Some lowdown snake thought a Graham would fold like a deck of cards. That fool was going to have the entire family on his ass, with blood in their eyes.

He managed to act polite for his neighbors, but he scrutinized every one of them for guilt. Throughout the next few hours, he also kept Hannah in his line of sight. Always.

At first he had trouble finding her until he realized she was the striking woman wearing a bright scarf. He'd never thought of her as beautiful, but the colors in the scarf made her shine like a vibrant flower in the sunlight.

He told himself he wasn't staring at her because he was struck dumb by how pretty she looked. Hannah was his wife, so he didn't need to be fussing about her looks. He watched her only out of concern for her safety.

Nick and Caleb, however, thought his fascination with his wife was hilarious. They kept coming up behind him and talking in a falsetto voice.

"Oh, Mattie, don't I look pretty?"

"Mattie, will you kiss me?"

He punched them both at least once; then they got smart and moved out of the way before he could reach them. Of course that made them laugh harder. Matt found himself feeling angrier by the second, and wishing the entire barbecue would just be over.

Wishing it so did not make it happen, of course. Matt had to endure the teasing, be polite to the neighbors, and mind the pit. He kept his eye on Hannah while he searched the crowd for Ranger Armstrong. That man had a lot of questions to answer, starting with why someone would almost kill his wife to stop the two of them from talking.

Lorenzo and Javier pronounced the meat ready around four in the afternoon. With Nick and Caleb, the four of them managed to move the meat to the tables, already groaning with the food the neighbors had brought. Matt supervised, unwilling to leave his position where he could see just about everyone. The only neighbors who had not arrived were the Stinsons. He didn't know if he should read anything into their absence. Guilt, perhaps?

"Looking for me?" Armstrong appeared beside him, much to Matt's consternation. Still dressed in black from head to foot, the ranger was like a living shadow.

"Dammit, man, are you part Indian or something?"

Armstrong turned his cold blue gaze on Matt, but didn't answer. Perhaps he was part Indian and Matt had just insulted him. It didn't matter one way or the other. He wasn't interested in the man's feelings, just what he knew.

"I was looking for you." Matt glanced at Hannah. "You see that scarf my wife is wearing?"

One dark eyebrow went up. "You wanted to show me your wife's scarf?"

"No, I wanted to show you the bruises on her neck where some bastard almost choked the life out of her this morning." The fury he'd felt came rushing back at him like a black cloud. Matt had to clench his fists and teeth to keep from howling.

Armstrong pulled him back toward the side of the barn before he spoke. "Tell me."

"He gave her a message for me. Said to stop talking to you. He used your name, Armstrong." Matt glanced at Hannah and a wave of worry for her hit him. She smiled and chatted with the neighbors as if she hadn't been nearly killed eight hours earlier.

"What exactly did he say?" Armstrong's jaw had a tic.

"I don't know. I wasn't there." He gestured to Hannah. "I can go get her and she can tell you herself."

"Fine then. Go get her." Armstrong was as bossy as he could be, but right about then, Matt didn't care. He just wanted his family to be safe.

He walked over to where Hannah was chatting with young Maggie McRae, the fifteen-year-old daughter of the neighboring rancher. Matt took Hannah's elbow and whispered in her ear.

"I need you." He hadn't meant to say it that way, but that's what came out of his mouth. Of course, what he meant was he needed her to talk to Armstrong. Her reaction told him she read a lot more into his statement than intended. Hell, he didn't know his ass from his head right about then. "The ranger is here."

Her smile faded and she nodded. "Excuse me, Maggie. I'll be right back."

They walked over to where the ranger waited. Hannah didn't take his arm or his hand, and he told himself he was not disappointed. Armstrong stood where Matt had left him. The lawman seemed as tough as leather the way he was so still, so unyielding.

"Ma'am." He tipped his hat to Hannah. "Name's Armstrong."

"Mr. Armstrong. Pleased to meet you. I'm Hannah Fol—I mean Hannah Graham." Her cheeks pinkened as she stumbled over her married name. Matt wasn't bothered by it. Hell, he wasn't used to introducing her as his wife.

"Your husband tells me someone gave you a message." He gestured to the scarf. "One that left marks."

Her gaze narrowed and the shyness disappeared. Hannah looked as angry as he felt. Her rusty voice was a testament to what she'd endured that morning. "Yes, some lowdown snake hid in the barn and choked me until I blacked out." She glanced at Matt. "He told me my husband needed to stop talking to Armstrong or he'd never find my body or Catherine's."

Hannah's words were like a slap. Matt reeled back, unhappy she hadn't shared the entire message with him before now.

"What? Why didn't you tell me that before now?"

"I told you." Hannah frowned. "The important thing was Armstrong's name."

Matt took her arms and yanked her against him until they were nose to nose. "The important thing was that he threatened your life again, and the life of my sister. I don't give a shit about Armstrong if you are in danger because I'm talking to him."

Her gaze searched his. "Matthew." The husky whisper was enough to drive him over the edge.

Before he realized what he was doing, his lips slammed into hers and he kissed her with all the pent-up fury and emotions churning inside him. Her mouth opened beneath his as his body hardened, inch by inch.

"Ahem, Graham, this isn't really the place to do that." Armstrong's voice broke the haze of pure passion Matt had fallen into.

He stepped back from Hannah and took a shaky breath. Her lips were reddened and moist from his kisses. Damned if her nipples weren't hard beneath her blouse, too. What the hell was wrong with him?

"Sorry. I, uh, let's get back to the stranger." His body throbbed with lust for his wife, but Matt managed to tear his gaze away from Hannah to look at Armstrong. "And why he would warn me away from you."

Armstrong frowned. "There aren't many who know I'm here, and if they do, they don't know why I'm here."

"Somebody does. I want to find out who." Matt knew something dark was going on in their little corner of Texas and he wanted to know who was behind it.

"Not any more than I do. I'm supposed to be a ghost around here." Armstrong glanced at Hannah. "Is there someplace private we can talk?"

"I'm going to hear what you have to say, Mr. Armstrong. Don't think for a minute I'll simply walk away." Hannah surprised Matt again with the vehemence in her voice.

"Fine, but I don't care if you're a woman or not. If you repeat anything I tell you, I will take action." Armstrong didn't need to say what he would do, but Matt understood just the same.

"You don't need to threaten my wife."

"I'm not threatening her. I'm warning her and you." Armstrong's jaw clenched so tight, the scar on his face whitened. "I don't share information, ever, but since you two are already involved, I reckon I need to tell you. Otherwise you might just keep being a thorn in my paw."

"Then start talking." Matt couldn't imagine what the ranger was doing in their neck of the woods that was so secret, but he knew it was the key to what had happened to his parents, his brother, and his wife.

Armstrong looked hard at both of them for a few moments before speaking. "Sam Houston himself asked me to investigate what's been happening. I told you about the other ranches. Word of the violence got to Sam's ear and he wanted to find out who was behind killing the citizens of Texas."

Matt was impressed. Sam Houston? Ranger Armstrong was rubbing elbows with some big men.

"What does that have to do with Hannah?"

"Someone saw me here talking to you yesterday. That means that person knows why I'm here." Armstrong glanced at the crowd of people eating and talking. "More than likely one of those folks right there."

Matt turned and realized he didn't know whom to trust. His family, the people he loved, had a murderer in their midst. The thought made his blood run cold.

"How can we help?" Hannah pulled their attention back from the barbecue.

"I can't ask you to do that. Just know that I'll be around looking into things." Armstrong frowned. "I don't need you fiddling with my investigation."

"I refuse to do nothing." Hannah put her hands on her hips. "I was attacked and that vermin threatened my little sister."

"Mrs. Graham, I can't let you—"

"You won't *let* me do anything." Hannah poked one finger into the ranger's chest. "I decide, not you."

Armstrong stared down at her, his scowl deeper than the pit they'd dug for the barbecue.

"You're bossy, if you don't mind my saying so."

"So are you." Hannah looked like a rabbit facing the big, bad wolf.

Matt didn't know whether to spank her or kiss her, but Hannah seemed to change the ranger's mind. He relaxed his stance and nodded.

"Fine, but if I tell you to get out of my way, you do it."

"Agreed." Hannah touched the scarf. "I don't want to ever feel afraid again. I find myself ready to shoot the man who made me feel that way."

Matt swore the ranger nearly cracked a smile.

"You're quite a woman, Mrs. Graham. Too bad you're married." Armstrong pushed his hat back a smidge, staring at Hannah.

Matt found himself fighting a pang of jealousy. He needed to get the ranger's attention back on the problem. "Can you tell us what you know?"

Armstrong's gaze moved back to the crowd. "The attacks come when the ranch hands are out on the range, so it's someone who knows the comings and goings of the ranchers. They kill women, take at least one if not two children, and burn what they can."

"Why?" Hannah frowned so hard her eyebrows touched.

"I don't know. That's what I'm here to find out. If I can figure out what they're after, I can stop them." Armstrong's expression was one of frustration.

"What happened to the other ranches after the attack?" Hannah's voice had dropped.

"Five of the ranchers lit out of Texas completely. Two of them hunkered down and now carry guns." Armstrong hesitated.

Matt knew there were ten total and realized there were other ranches not accounted for. "And the other three?"

Armstrong shook his head. "All dead or missing."

Hannah stepped away, her arms wrapped around her belly. She stared out into the open range, her gaze shining in the mid-afternoon sun. Matt wondered if she was thinking about her brush with death or his own parents' murders. Either way, her thoughts were heavy enough to make her fight for control.

Matt hadn't realized there was a pattern to the attacks, that there were other people who had lost loved ones, had suffered fear and grief. Hannah was right. They had to help stop this mayhem so others didn't have to endure the dark hell left behind by these bastards.

"Do they leave anything behind? Anything that might point to who they are?" Matt hadn't found a thing.

"No, but there is a pattern." Armstrong's gaze flickered to the fancy wagon heading toward them. "Someone has been buying the land either left behind by the dead or sold by the ones who ran."

Matt knew who it was before Armstrong even said his name. And at that moment, the Stinsons' buggy rolled onto his ranch. His hands clenched into fists.

"Stinson has a lot of money and a lot of land. He's got a lot more now, and I hear he's building a big herd of cattle, too." Armstrong stepped back into the shadows. "Be careful, Graham. You, too, Mrs. Graham."

With that, the ranger disappeared from view. The words Matt forced back down his throat threatened to explode when Stinson stopped the buggy. Margaret smiled at him while Jeb waved.

All Matt could think was *murdering bastard*.

CHAPTER FOURTEEN

Hannah could hardly keep a smile on her face. Anger and fear churned in her stomach at all she'd learned from the ranger. How could anyone murder innocent people just to get more land? Was dirt worth more than someone's life? If Stinson was capable of killing their neighbors, there was likely nothing he wouldn't do in the name of greed.

She carefully avoided talking to any of the Stinsons, moving away each time they grew near. Let Eva and Granny be polite to them. Right about then, Hannah might have spit in their faces.

The only good thing about what she'd heard from Armstrong was that he was investigating the crimes. At least the murders wouldn't go unpunished, not if she could help it. Hannah would help the taciturn ranger no matter how much he warned her away. This was her family now and they'd been hurt, not to mention her own brush with death. She would not go down easy.

The barbecue was in full swing when Lorenzo and Javier pulled out a guitar and fiddle. To her surprise, they could both not only play but also had lovely singing voices. Their neighbors, relaxed with food and good cheer, started dancing.

Hannah had never been to a barbecue or a dance, and found her foot tapping along with the beat. The smiles and laughter abounded as the ranchers danced under the waning daylight. She wanted to join in but had no idea what to do, and her husband didn't seem the type to dance.

"Why are you hiding over here, Mrs. Graham?" Frederick Stinson's voice scraped along her skin. She barely stopped herself from flinching.

"I'm not hiding, Mr. Stinson. I'm making sure folks enjoy themselves." She started to walk away but he took her elbow.

"Whoa there, little filly. How about you take a turn around the dance floor with me?" Stinson didn't give her a chance to respond. He simply took her out to the dance floor and started dancing.

Her anger overrode her fear, but she knew if she pulled away from him, there would most definitely be a scene. She gritted her teeth and hoped it looked like she was smiling. To her surprise, Frederick Stinson was a graceful dancer and moved fluidly, regardless of her own clumsiness.

Hannah tried to keep quiet, she truly did, but her mouth started moving and she was hopeless to stop. "Have you met Ranger Armstrong, Mr. Stinson?"

He stumbled but regained his balance almost immediately. "No, I haven't had that pleasure."

"You really should. He is a very nice man." Hannah could hardly stand to touch Stinson. His hands were softer than hers, with no calluses to speak of, and his palms were damp. She needed to get away from him. "Very smart, too."

This time when he stumbled, she broke away from

him. He reached for her again but she sidestepped him.

"Thank you for the dance, Mr. Stinson." She managed to make her way through the dancers, and away from him.

Matt stood at the edge of the dancing with a deep scowl on his face. She turned left and avoided her husband's wrath. Hannah could hardly believe what she was doing, and how alive she felt doing it.

Granny sat in a rocking chair on the front porch and she beckoned Hannah closer. With a quick look behind her, Hannah darted onto the porch and sat beside her grandmother in the empty rocking chair.

"What are you up to, child?"

"Hiding from the men out there."

Granny's eyebrows went up. "Hiding from the men? Has someone hurt you again?"

"No, I'm just, I don't know how to describe it." She rocked back and forth, the cool early evening breeze exactly what she needed. "I'm too full of things right now."

"Too much food?"

"No, I haven't eaten anything yet. There's just so much happening at once, I don't know which end is up." She took a deep breath and blew it out slowly.

"I reckon I know what you mean." Granny nodded. "Sit here a spell and get your wits about you."

Hannah took Granny's advice and stayed put. She saw Stinson walking through the crowd, chatting with people, smiling and acting as if he were the host. She was disgusted that she'd even touched him, much less danced with him.

"You're going to strike sparks with that fiery look," Granny mused. "Who is he?"

"Frederick Stinson."

"The neighbor who snatched that land between the Circle Eight and the new land?" Granny peered through the crowd.

"Among other things."

"He's very handsome."

"Granny! The man is a snake." Hannah saw Jeb Stinson heading toward the porch and told herself not to get up and run again. Jeb likely had no idea what his father was up to.

"You best stay clear of the man then."

Easier said than done, of course, but there were so many things she knew about and could not ignore. That included the Stinsons and the threat to the Graham family.

"Good evening, Mrs. Dolan. Mrs. Graham, may I call you Hannah?" Jeb smiled, his pearly white teeth shining in the setting sunlight.

"No, you may not. It's Mrs. Graham and it's going to stay that way." Matt stepped up beside him. "She's married, Jeb, so quit flirting."

"Hey, I can't help if it I see a pretty lady and I just feel the need to make her smile." Jeb chuckled, earning a surprised smile from Hannah. "You see, it worked!"

Matt's scowl returned. "I need to talk to my wife, if you don't mind."

"Oh, but I do mind. I heard my father danced with the hostess. What kind of man would I be if I didn't dance with her, too?" Jeb ignored Matt's protests, as well as Hannah's, and led her out to the dancing couples.

It was a lively song with a lot of foot stomping and swirling. Hannah couldn't catch her breath as Jeb twirled her around and around. She found herself smiling at his good-natured silliness and enjoyed herself for a few moments.

Then her scarf fell off.

Jeb's eyes widened and he snatched up the scarf, leading her into the shadow of the house quicker than she'd thought possible.

"Hannah, what happened to you?" He reached out toward her neck and she reared back.

"Please don't touch me. I'm fine." She took the scarf and tried to remember how Eva had wrapped it earlier.

"Like hell you're fine. Someone tried to choke you." Jeb's voice grew angry. "I can't believe Graham would do that to you. I'm going to—"

"Matthew did nothing to hurt me, Jeb. I appreciate your concern, but this is none of your business." Hannah touched his rock hard arm. "Please forget you saw my neck and enjoy yourself."

"I can't do that." He moved closer and she suddenly felt very small next to his large body. "You are a good woman and deserve better than a rancher without two nickels to rub together."

Hannah tamped down her panic and told herself to be strong. Jeb wouldn't hurt her. He was just worried about her.

"I love my husband. He is a good man and that's that." She turned to walk away from Jeb, but he took her arm again.

"Please, Hannah, don't run away yet." His fingers twined with hers and she yanked her hand away.

"I did not give you permission to call me by my first name, Mr. Stinson. Don't touch me and don't ever think you can bad-mouth my husband." Her anger returned and with it the courage she needed. "I suggest you get your sister and father and head home."

This time he didn't try to stop her, which was good because she would have kicked him. She ran right into a wall, which turned out to be her husband.

"Matthew." She sounded out of breath even to her own ears. "My scarf fell off and I had to fix it. How does it look?"

The orange glow of the sun gave him a fiery look as he reached out to adjust the scarf. His hand grazed her jaw as his gaze locked with hers. Hannah's body came to life as though he'd cast a spell over her. She nearly fell into the pool of his blue-green eyes.

"Jeb try anything with you?"

"Yes, but I told him you were a good man." She swayed toward him, eager to touch him, to feel him. Her core throbbed with an ache that needed to be satisfied.

"That's not all you told him."

Oh dear Lord, he'd heard her tell Jeb she loved her husband. If he hadn't heard her before when she was out of her head, apparently he'd heard her this time.

Matt moved closer and everything around him fell away. As his lips touched hers, Hannah was able to shake off all the darkness riding her back. She moaned into his mouth as the kiss deepened.

"I guess you weren't kidding, Mrs. Graham." Jeb walked past them in a huff.

Both Hannah and Matt laughed as they moved back a step, taking up where they'd left off.

"Did you mean it?" His softly worded question made her heart hiccup.

Hannah closed her eyes and looked down at her feet. "Yes."

His thumb pressed her chin back up. "Good. You're mine." After a hard kiss, he tucked her arm in his and walked her back to the barbecue.

She didn't quite understand what "you're mine" meant, but it was probably the closest thing to "I love you too" she'd get.

Matt's gut was on fire. At the sight of Jeb dancing with his wife, jealousy had eaten him up like a dragon from a storybook. He'd stomped after them, eager to kick Jeb's ass from one end of the Republic to the other. But when he'd paused to listen, he'd heard Hannah defend him, put Jeb in his place, then confess she loved him.

He'd thought perhaps he'd heard her wrong earlier in the day or maybe she had been out of her mind. This time, however, she was lucid and completely clear when she told Jeb she loved Matt. He had to ask her, he just had to, and she willingly confirmed what she'd said.

His wife loved him.

It had been the strangest, craziest day of his life, but at the end of it, his wife loved him. Matt wasn't about to admit to his own feelings for her, but armed with her love, he felt a little invincible.

Matt walked toward Frederick Stinson with determination in his step and Hannah on his arm. He found the rancher at the bowl of beans, talking to Olivia. In the door of the barn, he spotted Armstrong, who was also watching Stinson with Olivia. What in the hell was going on?

"Stinson." Matt kept his voice even, although inside he wanted to tear the man's arms off for not only touching his wife but obviously sizing up his sister.

"Graham. I was looking for you earlier, but I couldn't find you. I spent the time talking to your lovely sister. How is it this pretty young gal isn't married yet?" Stinson leaned toward her and Matt could swear the other man was looking at his sister's breasts.

He almost lunged for the man, but Hannah caught his arm. Damn, the woman was stronger than she looked.

"Mr. Stinson, we'd like to discuss a business matter with you." Her voice was high and tight.

"Ladies ought not to talk about business. That's a man's job, little missy." Stinson rocked back on his heels. "You let your women run amok, Graham. I saw your wife with no less than three men tonight."

Hannah held his arm tighter. "It is my business because it involves my family." Her smile looked forced.

"We got our land grant, Stinson, but I'm thinking you might know that," Matt began. "We want to offer you a deal to buy that little patch of dirt between this ranch and our new property." There, that sounded reasonable.

Stinson rubbed his chin. "That's a mighty tempting offer, but I don't know that I want to sell any of my land."

The music faded as Lorenzo and Javier turned their attention to what was happening between Matt and Stinson. Conversation around them also seemed to stop.

"I'll have to go near fifty miles out of my way to get from this ranch to the new land." Matt kept his tone as light as he could. "It would be right neighborly if we could either buy that patch of land or work out an arrangement to cross it with our animals."

Stinson shook his head, and then his gaze flicked to a spot over Matt's shoulder. Matt had a feeling Hannah's plan to call the rancher out in front of everyone was working. The last thing Stinson wanted was to be thought badly of. He had a reputation as a smart but tough man; however, most folks respected him. Until his parents' deaths, Matt had been one of them.

Now he knew better.

"I didn't know my owning that strip landed you in such a situation, Graham. I would think the land grant office would be more logical." Stinson shook his head as though he hadn't masterminded the entire thing.

"Seems you had already claimed that skinny piece of land, so there wasn't anything they could do." Matt squeezed Hannah's arm. "I want to build a bigger ranch for my future children and my brothers and sisters. I'm sure you understand that."

Margaret appeared at her father's side. "Daddy, this barbecue is boring. Can we leave now?" She turned a pouty gaze on Matt, and damned if she didn't wink at him.

"Not right yet, pumpkin. Daddy is finishing up some business." Stinson patted her head as though she were a pet, rather than his nineteen-year-old daughter.

"I know the strip of land also borders McRae's ranch." He turned to find red-haired Angus McRae in the crowd. "He probably needs to get across it, too."

Angus nodded his shaggy head. "Aye, that's true."

"What do you say, Stinson?" Matt asked, forcing his own smile.

"For my neighbors, yes, I'll let you use the land. I need to see a map, of course, to make sure I know the patch of land you're referring to." Stinson's smile was as fake as Matt's.

That's when he became certain Stinson was behind

everything. Armstrong was right about all of it. Son of a bitch! Why couldn't he have seen before now just how evil men could be? His father had been such an honorable, strong man, it had never occurred to Matt that others could be so different.

Matt gestured to the house. "I have the map the land grant office gave me. I can show it to you now."

Stinson tutted. "No need to stop the fun because of a business deal. We can talk tomorrow and let folks enjoy the rest of the evening."

"Why don't we meet tomorrow at Angus's ranch at nine? We can make our arrangements then." Matt didn't want Stinson on his land any more than necessary. He figured by putting the meeting on another rancher's property, Stinson might actually agree to it.

"That sounds fine, young Graham. Now why don't you have your Mexican boys start playing again so folks can dance." Stinson's leering gaze landed on Hannah and Matt couldn't stop the growl in his throat.

Javier and Lorenzo must've sensed the tension was about ready to bust wide open because guitar music floated through the air again. Hannah's fingers dug into his arm and he recognized just how close he was to losing control. He was actually vibrating with anger.

"Come dance with me." Her whisper tickled his ear, pulling him from the edge.

"I can't dance."

"Me neither, so we'll make fools of ourselves together." She tugged on his arm. "C'mon, cowboy."

Matt didn't want to dance, but he didn't want to commit murder in front of half the county either. He let Hannah lead him toward the open area folks had been dancing in. Javier starting singing a Mexican ballad.

Hannah managed to wrap her arms around him and took his hand. "Now dance."

They swung back and forth like a bell; neither one of them had a lick of rhythm. Somehow just touching her, breathing in her air as she let it out, calmed him. She had some kind of magic in her and he was glad for at least the dozenth time that day that she was his wife.

Other guests joined them and soon ten couples were swaying to Javier's beautiful ballad. By the time the last notes fell away, Matt felt better. He didn't want Hannah to know how close he'd come to accusing Stinson of murder. It would've jeopardized Armstrong's investigation and any chance of actually catching the bastard.

To his surprise, he spotted Armstrong talking to Olivia on the side of the porch. He assumed the ranger was just pursuing his investigation but Matt would have to keep his eye on the other man just the same.

"Better?" Hannah took his hand and looked at him inquiringly.

"Yeah. I won't shoot anybody. Yet." He blew out a frustrated breath. "Why don't you go check on Eva and I'll go talk to Armstrong?"

Hannah frowned but she squeezed his hand and walked away, leaving him to his own choices. He could kick Stinson's ass but that wouldn't get him anything. Instead he went toward Armstrong, and to his consternation, Olivia walked the other way as soon as he got close.

"What are you doing with my sister, Armstrong?"

"Just talking. Can't investigate without talking to folks." Armstrong nodded. "Nice work getting Stinson out of his house tomorrow. I can be in and out while he's gone. I expect the son to go with the father to McRae's house. He follows his Pa around like a puppy."

Matt hadn't thought of it before, but it was true Whenever he saw Frederick Stinson, Jeb was two steps behind him. It wasn't strange for a son to want to be like his father, but by the time he was sixteen, Matt had been working the ranch and not following his father around. Jeb was nice enough, but the man didn't have any skills beyond smiling and flirting.

"Now we need to make sure the girl is gone, too. I asked your sister to invite her for tea or something." Armstrong frowned at Olivia's retreating back. "She's got quite a mouth on her for a young lady."

Matt didn't really care if Olivia cussed at the ranger, but he felt better somehow knowing she didn't have romantic notions about the man.

"Good idea. Livy and Margaret are friends." Matt didn't want his sister to feel obligated to help, but knowing her, she heard a lot more than she ought to about what was going on. "Then what do we do?"

"*We* don't do anything. I go in and snoop around." Armstrong's gaze dared Matt to contradict him.

"You can't get in there and out without someone noticing you. Stinson has fifty people working for him. You're not a ghost, Armstrong." Matt folded his arms across his chest. "You have someone you trust to be your lookout?"

Armstrong stared off into the distance for a few moments before his cool gaze met Matt's. "No, but I don't need one."

"I don't necessarily believe you, but I'm trusting that you will do what you can to find what you need."

"I'll be leaving now. Make sure you get on over to McRae's by nine. I'm counting on you." Armstrong melted into the deepening darkness behind him, leaving Matt to wonder if he was trusting the right person.

He had to be because if he wasn't, the future of the Graham ranch might never happen.

Hannah washed the dishes with a feeling of relief. She absolutely hated washing dishes, but the normalcy of the chore somehow calmed her frayed nerves. The entire day had been like a dream, perhaps more of a nightmare.

Eva left her in the kitchen, seeming to understand that Hannah needed to be alone. The low hum of conversation outside centered around the bonfire the boys had built just beyond the barn. Peace had settled over the Graham ranch, and the guests were nearly gone.

Matt was nowhere to be found; perhaps he was hiding someplace, too. After all they'd found out today, she wouldn't blame him a bit. His neighbor was probably behind his parents' murders and his brother's disappearance. Missing children were generally thought of as dead, but the ranger's information made it sound as if the children had been taken, not killed.

There were so many reasons why people chose evil, but when the life of a child was involved, she just couldn't understand how anyone could commit such a crime. They were innocent, untouched by the ugliness of the world. Now Benjamin Graham was gone, subjected to who knew what. He would never regain the innocence snatched from him, but she prayed he was still alive.

Her heart hurt for the Graham family. She hoped that by helping Ranger Armstrong, they could put the ugly past behind them and really start living again. Oh, they ate, slept, and breathed each day, but Matt had just proven to her that he wasn't living. He just existed from day to day.

Hannah knew he would never truly fall in love with her until he banished the demons that haunted his every moment. He had nightmares in his sleep, often moaning out loud. She hadn't told him about it, for fear she'd embarrass him, but the unsolved crimes were slowly eating away at him, bite by bite.

She rinsed the last plate in the cool water in the bucket and set it on the pile. The barbecue had been a success, albeit one of the strangest days she could remember. Life at the boardinghouse had been so boring and mundane. Her new life on the Circle Eight was nothing if not unpredictable. She was up for the challenge though. Hannah was so glad she had accepted Matt's proposal even if someone had tried to kill her because of it.

The memory brought jitters to her whole body, and she knew she had to sit down. The chair was blessedly solid beneath her.

"*Hija*, are you okay?" Eva poked her head in the kitchen from the hallway.

"Yes, no, I don't know." Hannah leaned forward and cradled her head with her arms.

Eva rubbed her back. "Ah, *hija*, you need sleep. In the morning, you will feel better." She touched the scarf. "Let me check your throat."

Hannah sat back up and untied the scarf. "Thank you for letting me use this. It's the most beautiful thing I've ever worn."

"It is the person who makes a thing beautiful, not the other way around." Eva smiled as her fingers gently explored Hannah's neck. "There will be bruises so you keep the scarf. *Mi mama* would be happy for you to wear it."

Hannah nodded, her throat tight with the generosity of this woman who barely knew her. "Thank you again."

Eva kissed her forehead. "Anything for *mi hija*." Eva turned to leave.

"Wait, I need to ask you—" Hannah's eyes pricked with unshed tears. "Why?"

Eva frowned in confusion. "Why what?"

"Why did you welcome me into your home? Why do you treat me like one of your *hijas*? I'm not your daughter and you don't even know me." Hannah struggled not to burst into tears. "Why?"

Eva folded her into a hug. "You love with all your heart and soul, Hannah. I knew as soon as I met you that you were someone to trust, someone who will love Mateo with everything she has. Catherine loved you right away, too. She knows, just like me, you are one of us."

Hannah had never realized what she'd been missing in a family. Granny had done her best, but she was old when Hannah came to live with her. Without brothers and sisters, without a mother and a father, Hannah had always been lonely. The Graham family had taken her in immediately, filling the hole in her heart.

"Thank you, Eva."

"How about some tea before bed?" Eva stoked the fire in the stove to heat a pot of water. "I have some herbal tea I make myself."

"Tea would be really nice." Hannah was torn between being sad and being absurdly happy. She had everything she wanted, now she just had to find a way to keep it.

Tomorrow Matt would be at the McRae ranch for a while. Perhaps if she went over to the Stinsons', she might find something to help Armstrong with his case against the rancher. When she'd been at the ranch several days earlier, she had passed by what appeared to be Stinson's office. If she went by for a visit, she might just get lost and end up there for a look around.

Hannah would help her husband whether or not he liked it.

Matt made sure the bonfire was completely out before he headed back to the house. Everything was dark except for a solitary light in the kitchen. Eva always left one burning if one of them wasn't home when she went to bed. It kept everyone from getting bruised shins and it was a welcoming sight after a long day.

He made his way into the house and blew out the lantern. The night before, Hannah had bathed him, shown him how much she loved him without words. He grew hard at the memory, felt the rush of heat he'd experienced several times that day for Hannah.

It was late, nearly midnight, and she'd be long since asleep. She'd started the day by nearly getting killed, then played hostess to the biggest party they'd ever had at the Circle Eight without letting on once she had been attacked. Hannah had surprised him more than once that day, proving to him he'd found the right woman to be his wife. Even if it had been because of some turnips.

When he opened the bedroom door, he was surprised to see her standing at the window. She turned to face him and the moonlight turned her into an ethereal being. His body hardened almost painfully as he closed the door behind him.

"Hannah." His voice was a rusty whisper in the stillness of the room.

"I'm yours."

He shed his clothes quickly, almost falling while taking off his boots. As he approached her barefoot, his cock was like a divining rod pointing straight toward exactly what it wanted.

She opened her arms and he pulled her against him, his mouth slamming onto hers with a ferocity that he had never known before. Her softness cradled his hardness as his blood rushed around his body, pounding past his ears.

"I need to feel your skin."

To his delight, she pulled off her nightdress to reveal nothing but what God had given her. He ran his hands down her shoulders, back to her round buttocks. She moaned low and soft in her throat when his touch moved to the front of her body. He cupped her breasts, loving the weight of them in his hands.

Matt dropped to his knees and took a nipple in his mouth. She trembled as he lapped, nibbled, and sucked at her. He moved his hand between her thighs, gently parting the incredibly soft skin until he found what he wanted. She was wet and welcoming, making his cock thump against his belly.

"I need you, Matt."

He would have responded in kind but he couldn't find his voice. So he scooped her up and brought her to the bed instead. When she lay there looking up at him, her brown eyes like liquid heat in the silver moonlight, he paused to stare at her. His wife was a gift and he wanted to be sure she knew that.

Although he didn't have a lot of experience with women, he knew enough to make Hannah feel good. Together they could learn everything they needed to know about keeping each other happy.

He dropped to his knees again and parted her thighs. Her glistening cleft waited, its pink folds enticing him to taste, touch, pleasure. He kissed her nether lips, earning a surprised gasp from Hannah. When his tongue found her clit, the gasp turned into a full-fledged moan. Her tangy taste coated his tongue, exciting him to the point he found his hand sliding up and down his shaft.

Lick. Tug. Lick. Tug.

As her thighs quivered against his cheeks, he lapped and sucked at her. When he pushed two fingers into her, she clenched around him so tight, he knew he wouldn't last long if he entered her too soon. He needed to make sure she came first.

His fingers thrust into her as he increased his tongue's rhythm. She made a funny, kittenish sound in her throat, which turned into a low keening moan as she grew closer to her peak. When he started sucking on her clit, she grabbed the quilt and dug in her heels.

"Maaaaattttheeeewwww—" She drew out his name as she came, her juices becoming sweeter, her channel tighter.

He couldn't wait a second longer. Matt stood and plunged into her welcoming core. He came almost immediately, filling her with his seed as her own orgasm shuddered around his staff. Stars swam behind his eyes as he experienced the most powerful ecstasy of his life. He held onto her hips, plunging in with each wave of pleasure. When he was wrung dry, he collapsed beside her, shaking with the force of what he'd just experienced.

Whether he would admit it to her or not, Matt knew he was in uncharted territory. Nothing had ever felt like that with any other woman. It was she who made the difference. For the first time in his life, he was afraid he couldn't stop himself. Matt was falling in love with Hannah.

After he caught his breath, he tucked them both under the covers, naked as the day they were born. When they spooned together, their body heat mixed to form a cocoon around them. It felt safe, comfortable. As he listened to his wife breathing softly, Matt promised himself he would find a way to control himself around Hannah. If he didn't, he might never be the same.

CHAPTER FIFTEEN

Matt kissed Hannah before he left for the McRaes', leaving a stupid smile on her face. The girls made silly kissing noises in imitation while the boys make disgusted sounds. To Hannah, the embrace meant the world to her. Perhaps he was starting to feel things for her. The possibility lit a glimmer of hope in her heart that there was a fighting chance for the love she needed from him.

As soon as he was out of sight, she ran into the house and changed into her riding skirt. Olivia appeared wearing one as well and looked at Hannah in surprise.

"Are you going somewhere?"

"I just needed a little time to myself. Yesterday was so busy." Hannah's smile was forced but she hoped her sister-in-law didn't notice.

"Matt would have our hides if we let you ride off by yourself. Take Caleb or Javier with you." Olivia pulled on her gloves with a frown. "I'm going to the Stinson ranch for tea with Margaret."

Inspiration hit Hannah like a knock to the head. "May I come?"

Olivia's brows went up. "You want to have tea with Margaret?"

"No, I mean yes. I just want to get away from the ranch for a little while." This was a perfect opportunity to get into the Stinson ranch without having to sneak.

"She's bound to be catty to you." Olivia looked guilty. "I know she's not the nicest person in the world, but she's my friend."

"It's okay. I won't mind, really. It will be my first real tea." Hannah shrugged. "Not much opportunity for ladylike teas at a boardinghouse."

"Or on a ranch for that matter." Olivia smiled. "You should put on the scarf first. We don't want to give Margaret any more reason to be, ah, difficult."

Hannah was delighted to put on the scarf and go out to the barn with her sister-in-law. She didn't know what she would have done without the escort to the Stinson property. Now she had the perfect excuse to be there.

Javier saddled their horses for them, frowning the whole time. "Matt will not like this."

"He's not my boss so he has no say in what I do, or what Hannah does for that matter." Olivia got up on her horse with more agility than Hannah could ever hope to have.

After using a mounting block to awkwardly mount Buttermilk, Hannah was ready to face the lioness in her den. With a grim smile, she nodded to the worried-looking Javier and the two women started riding toward the Stinson ranch.

She would show Matt just what she could do for him.

*   *   *

Matt rode up to Angus McRae's ranch with a knot in his gut. He wasn't surprised to see Stinson's prize stallion already there, tied to the hitching post in front of the sprawling ranch house.

He dismounted and retrieved the map from his saddlebags. This was the moment he would have to stand firm against Stinson and his greed. He sure as hell hoped his father was somewhere nearby, giving him strength to face the challenge and not lose his temper in the process. Strength and logic would win the day, not anger and passion.

Matt knocked on the door and Maggie opened it. The redheaded younger daughter blushed when she saw Matt. The fifteen-year-old had always followed him around from the time she could toddle. But he was almost ten years older than she and certainly didn't want her pining after him.

"Good morning, Maggie. I'm here to see your father."

She stammered a response and led him into the house. The men were seated in Angus's office in the front corner of the house. He had put in a large picture window so he could watch his five daughters whenever they were outside. With no sons to take over the ranch, McRae knew there would come a time when too many young men would be sniffing around his land and his daughters.

The big red-haired man sat behind his desk while Stinson leaned on the corner of it, as if he owned the room. Matt considered accidently pushing him off his perch, but decided it would be a bad start to the meeting.

"Did you bring the map, Graham?" Stinson didn't seem the least bit concerned he was about to be exposed as a thieving murderer.

Matt laid the map out on the desk and the three of them stared at it. "Right here is my ranch and here is yours, Angus." He traced the outline with his finger. "Here is my new land grant and here is the two-mile gap between them."

There was a moment of silence before Stinson laughed. "That little wiggly line? What is it?"

"It's your property." Matt wanted to punch the laughing jackass.

"No, it's not. Why in the hell would I buy a piece of property like that?" Stinson straightened up. "You got your facts wrong, Graham. Maybe next time a grown-up ought to come with you." His cocky grin made Matt's temper almost bubble over.

Then a sudden thought struck him, snatching the anger as quick as a hawk. "What do you mean it's not yours?"

"Just what I said. There ain't no money to be made on such a small tract of land." Stinson frowned at Matt. "What makes you think it's mine?"

Matt's stomach fell to his knees. "I saw the deed. It's in your name, along with another half dozen pieces of land west of here."

This time it was Frederick's turn to look surprised. "What the hell are you talking about?"

"It's not you, is it?" Matt was suddenly very afraid for his sister. "It's Jeb."

"What's Jeb? Graham, would you start making sense?" Stinson was a jackass, but he was a straight shooter who would tell a man to his face what he thought of him. This whole situation with the land, the murders, the missing children, didn't point to him.

It pointed to his son. The twenty-five-year-old with

nothing but a big smile who waited to inherit his father's ranch. Impatiently.

"I think Jeb has decided to snatch up as much land as possible, perhaps even arrange for you to have a riding accident." Matt ignored the confused anger on Frederick's face. "Armstrong was right. It was a Stinson all along, but not the one he suspected."

"Graham, I think you have gone loco." Stinson folded his arms across his chest but Matt saw a glimmer of uncertainty in his gaze.

"Someone wants as much land as he can get no matter what the cost. My parents, Benjy, and half a dozen other families are all gone, either dead or disappeared. Their properties were purchased by you."

"The hell you say. I didn't kill nobody and I haven't bought any property." Stinson glanced at the map. "You saw the deed with my name on it?"

"Yes, I did, and so did Hannah. I'm guessing if we travel to Houston, we'd find quite a few deeds with your name on them." Matt couldn't believe the affable Jeb was behind it all. "Where is Jeb?"

"At home like always. He said Margaret was having company so he stayed to flirt with 'em." Stinson's gaze didn't leave the map.

"At home? Oh my God, Olivia is the company. She was going to have tea." Matt knew he had to get to Stinson's ranch immediately. "Angus, go to town and get the sheriff. Meet us at the Stinson place." He turned to Frederick. "You ready to find out the truth?"

Stinson's eyes met his and Matt saw confusion and anger swirling in their depths. "I don't believe a word of what you said but if someone is buying land in my name, I want to find out who and why. You're going to have some apologizing to do when we get to my ranch." He slammed his hat on his head. "Let's go."

The two of them left Angus's office in a hurry. As they untied the horses from the hitching post, Matt hoped Winston was ready to fly.

After Olivia knocked on the door, Hannah waited beside her on the ornate front porch of the Stinson ranch. She was trying to figure out how to get into the office without anyone noticing. It was imperative she find some scrap of evidence that Stinson was up to no good.

When the door opened, she knew Olivia was as surprised as she was to see Jeb in the doorway. He smiled and bowed at Olivia.

"Welcome, Miss Graham. I'm so glad to—" He spotted Hannah standing a few feet away. "I didn't expect to see you though, Mrs. Graham. What a lovely surprise." His grin was unsettling and made her warning bells ring loudly.

"Margaret is expecting us for tea." Olivia glanced at Hannah. "Well, just me really, but I convinced Hannah to join me."

"Please come in. Both of you." Jeb opened the door and gestured with his arm for them to enter.

As Hannah walked in, she swore she felt Jeb's breath on her neck, and she hurried to catch up to her sister-in-law. She took Olivia's arm.

"Something's wrong," Hannah whispered.

Olivia frowned at her, then turned back to look at Jeb. "Where is Margaret?"

"She's feeling poorly this morning after the barbecue." Jeb put his arm around their waists and led them through the house. "However, our housekeeper had the tea and sandwiches all ready. Margaret asked me to host in her place."

Hannah stared at the handsome, charming Jeb, wondering just what it was that set her on edge. He seemed so friendly and sincere, but she didn't quite feel comfortable with just the three of them. What if Hannah hadn't accompanied Olivia? Her sister-in-law would have been alone, unchaperoned with Jeb.

That could have been exactly what he wanted. Jeb Stinson was hunting for a wife, if Hannah wasn't mistaken, and could ruin Olivia just by being with her alone. Possibly even take it a step further and rape her.

Hannah was doubly glad she'd come. Now she could stop the snake from defiling her sister-in-law and find evidence his father was swindling, murdering, and kidnapping folks. Her smile was genuine if a little self-satisfied.

"Poor Margaret. Does she need a poultice or some of Eva's special tea?" Olivia turned to go toward what Hannah assumed was Margaret's bedroom, but Jeb stopped her.

"Oh, she wouldn't want you to see her like this. She's been, ah, vomiting all night. Probably some bad beans or something." Jeb ushered them back toward the terrace, toward the garden that had seemed so lovely a week earlier. Now with the clouds hiding the sun, it seemed almost sinister and the bright flowers had lost their vibrancy.

On a small table were a teapot with two cups and a plate of tiny sandwiches. There were also only two chairs and Hannah knew she'd been right about Jeb's nefarious motives. Maybe Margaret wasn't even sick. Perhaps he'd done something to his sister so he could get Olivia alone. The possibilities were endless.

"I think we'll need another cup and chair, Jeb." Olivia frowned at him.

"Of course. I shall be right back. Why don't you two lovely ladies enjoy some refreshments while I go rustle up what we need?" He disappeared back into the house, shutting the glass paned door behind him.

"That snake." Olivia snatched up a sandwich. "He was going to have tea with me alone."

"I thought so, too. Olivia, I don't trust him. I think he's trying to find himself a wife and he's zeroed in on you." Hannah glanced around the beautiful garden. "There isn't a soul around, which means he could do whatever he wanted to you."

"Matt would kill him." Olivia's flat tone said what Hannah was already thinking.

"I believe you're right. I need to get into the house for a few moments but I don't want to leave you here alone." Hannah had to bring her sister-in-law into her confidence. "I want to look in Mr. Stinson's office for evidence."

"What kind of evidence?"

"I can't give you all the details, but Ranger Armstrong is investigating him. I want to help as much as I can, maybe even help solve your parents' murder."

It was what Hannah didn't say that Olivia heard. Her gaze narrowed and her eyes hardened. "That bastard."

"I want to see what I can find. Will you help me?"

"Damn straight I'll help you. I knew that Armstrong was up to something when he convinced me to have tea with Margaret." Olivia huffed out a breath. "Gave me some humbug story about possibly courting Margaret and wanting my help. Ha!"

Hannah hadn't realized Armstrong was such a good liar, but perhaps as a lawman, he sometimes needed to be untruthful to get what he needed. After all, she was a normal woman who had been about to commit a crime by breaking into her neighbor's house. She couldn't cast any stones against the man.

"He's just trying to help find out who's behind the crimes." Hannah took her hand. "Are you ready? If Jeb catches us, we'll be in hot water."

"I hope he does. I want to call him on this attempted seduction anyway." Olivia tightened her grip. "Let's go find out what Stinson is up to."

When they walked into the house, Jeb was coming right toward them.

"Stay here. I'll distract him," Olivia whispered, then turned a full smile on the younger Stinson. "There you are. I was hoping you'd come back soon. Take me to the kitchen, please. I brought some special tea to share with Margaret, but now I can share it with you."

Hannah stayed in the shadows until they disappeared from view. Heart pounding, she tiptoed down the hallway to the room she thought was the office. As she slipped through the door, she held her breath until the snick of the lock sounded.

It was definitely the older Stinson's office. The weak light from the cloudy day filtered through the large picture window. A huge wooden desk dominated the room, covered with papers, a few old cups of coffee, and a dark lantern. She sat down in the chair, which squeaked like a giant mouse. Hannah froze in mid-motion, waiting for someone to discover what she was doing.

Minutes later, which felt more like hours, she sucked in a shaky breath and started searching. There were plenty of papers: feed receipts, bills of sale, and letters from people like Sam Houston. None of it seemed to be illegal, and some of it was even impressive.

Frustrated, Hannah moved to the drawers, and after more fruitless searching, decided Mr. Stinson must not keep his illegal activities mixed with the legal. The bottom drawer was locked so she used a letter opener to pry it open. He would know someone had been there, but if he was in jail, it wouldn't matter a whit.

Expecting to find a pile of evidence, Hannah was disappointed to find a bottle of whiskey and two glasses. Why would he keep the liquor locked up in his desk? Perhaps one of the staff or even Jeb or Margaret had a problem with drinking too much?

It didn't matter why; there was nothing here. *Nothing* to help the case against Frederick Stinson. She put everything back the way she'd found it and crept out of the room.

"Why, there she is!" Jeb's loud voice made Hannah jump a foot in the air. "I think she must've gotten lost in this big house."

She turned to find Olivia with a panicked expression, her arm in Jeb's punishing grip. "Run," she mouthed.

Hannah shook her head, unwilling to let her sister-in-law face whatever consequences she had brought on both of them. "Not lost, just being nosy." Hannah managed a silly laugh. "I admit I wanted to snoop a bit. Sorry, Jeb." Her grin felt brittle but she offered him one anyway.

"Oh, Hannah, now you know that's not the truth," he said in a startlingly cold voice. "It'll be a sad day for the Grahams when you two go missing, or maybe even turn up dead. You shouldn't have taken that shortcut through the ravine. The coyotes can be mighty hungry when they find a wounded animal." Jeb, who had appeared so sweet and vapid, was finally showing his true colors, and they were as black as pitch. He didn't appear to be loco, far from it. His gaze was clear and calculating.

Hannah had assumed Frederick Stinson was behind the attacks, as had everyone else. They'd been dead wrong.

She ran at him, ready to do what she had to to get Olivia free. To her surprise, Jeb was strong as an ox. He grabbed her braid and twisted it so hard, the pain radiated down her head to her feet. Olivia tried to push him and he retaliated by pulling her hair until she fell to her knees with a loud crack. She cried out in agony and there was nothing Hannah could do to help her.

"I can't let you get in my way, ladies. I had hopes one of you could be the next Mrs. Stinson, but now you will simply be the dead Graham girls." Jeb dragged them both down the hallway by their hair.

Hannah met Olivia's gaze, her face wet with tears and covered with stark terror. She had to do something. Hannah would not be the Graham who let her family down, not when they needed her most.

Jeb dragged them to a dark room under the house. He threw Olivia against the wall and she landed in a soundless heap. Horrified, Hannah was too slow to act. Jeb backhanded her so hard, blood filled her mouth. She spat on the floor, and he kicked her in the stomach with a boot that felt more like a boulder.

"Don't mess up the floor, Hannah. You know how hard it is to get bloodstains out?" He pushed her to her back, then pressed his boot into her chest. "I could crush you right now and not have to worry about you anymore. I knew you were the smart one. Somehow Matt found you, hidden treasure that you are."

Blackness crept around Hannah's vision and for the second time in as many days, she faced death.

"Fuck you, Jeb."

His face registered surprise before he threw back his head and laughed. "I knew I liked you for a reason." His foot eased up. "I just may keep you for myself after all."

Dazed and lightheaded, Hannah could only watch as he tied her up and gagged her, forcing blood down her throat from her mouth. She nearly choked on it before she was able to roll to her side and let it slide out of her mouth. After tying the motionless Olivia up, too, Jeb leaned down and cupped Hannah's cheek.

"Be a good girl now." With that, he left them alone in the cold, dark room under the house. There was not a peep of light and the only sound was a scurrying in the corner. Hannah had to find a way to get free, or both she and Olivia could be dead by the time Jeb came back.

Hannah managed to get into a sitting position, and although her head swam for a moment, she stayed that way. Pride and determination coursed through her. She would make her husband proud and be a true Graham, no matter what.

Matt rode like the hounds of hell were chasing him. To his surprise, Stinson kept up with him. The horses were equally matched, although the older rancher bragged about his prize stallion to anyone who would listen. Appeared as though a gelding could give him a run for his money. Matt didn't want to waste time stopping at his ranch, but knew he needed reinforcements if they were to gain victory. He rode into the yard in a cloud of dust.

"To the Graham!" It was an expression his father always used when he wanted all the children to come to him immediately. He explained that back in the day, it was a battlecry for the Graham clan.

It still worked and everyone came running, including Eva. The one Graham missing was Hannah.

"Javier, Lorenzo, Nick, and Caleb. Saddle up and follow us to the Stinson ranch." He speared Eva with a worried gaze. "Is Hannah feeling poorly?"

"No, she felt fine this morning. She went to tea with Olivia at the Stinsons. *¿Que pasa, hijo?*" Eva stepped toward him but before she even started talking, Matt had turned his lathered gelding east and kneed him into a gallop.

Hannah was there, at the Stinsons' ranch. What was she thinking? She didn't even like Margaret, so why would she have tea with her? Granted, it was safer to travel in pairs, but there was no reasonable explanation for Hannah to go with Olivia.

"Matt!" Caleb shouted from behind him, but there was no way in hell he was going to slow down.

His wife and his sister were in danger. Matt couldn't lose the woman he loved or the sister he cherished because of his own lack of forethought. He leaned low and spoke into his horse's ear.

"I can't let her die, Winston. Help me save her so I can tell her I love her." Matt's heart thumped against his ribs, and cold fear crept into his bones with each passing minute.

Armstrong was supposed to be at Stinson's house. Maybe he was there and would help the women stay out of trouble. This was Hannah and Olivia though, both of them stubborn and strong-willed as mules.

Matt hung on as his horse's hooves ate up the miles. He knew his family and Stinson were behind him, but he had to arrive first. There wasn't any other option.

Armstrong had been in the office reviewing every scrap of paper he could find when he heard a female voice in the house. It had to be Olivia, the outspoken woman had tried to get information from him last night. When he'd refused to give it to her, she'd warned him she wasn't done with him.

Yet here she was in the Stinsons' house, as he'd asked. Truth was, she was probably the most beautiful woman he'd ever met. Instead of talking to her like a gentleman, he'd been short and almost rude. But rather than wilting like a flower, she'd snapped to attention like a warrior.

Even though he told himself to focus on business, he found his dreams full of Olivia Graham. In the morning, he'd woken in his bedroll with a hard-on. He'd shaken off the remnants of his erotic thoughts of her and gotten busy.

Now she was in the Stinsons' house and he had to hope she would follow through on what he'd asked. When the door handle rattled, he disappeared out the large window and ducked into the bushes.

After a few minutes, he'd realized what he'd heard was someone else rifling through Stinson's office. Damn Olivia! She was supposed to keep her hosts busy, not take it upon herself to snoop around.

As he rose to give her a talking-to, he heard footsteps leaving the room and the door closing. Jeb Stinson's voice was overly loud, enough so Armstrong heard him quite clearly.

Girls? What girls? Was the man doing something to his own sister and Olivia? A woman's cry of pain was followed by another and then a horrendous cracking sound. Armstrong had climbed back through the window, unwilling to allow Olivia to be hurt helping him. When he'd made it through the narrow window, he'd eased the office door open and peered out.

The hallway was empty. The only sign someone had been there was the bright scarf lying on the floor. He'd seen Hannah Graham wearing it the night before. Armstrong's heart had slammed into his throat. Quickly, he'd searched the house but now he still had found no other sign of them.

Where were they?

Hannah worked at the gag with her teeth and tongue, fighting the pain until she managed to get it to her chin. She swallowed, almost choking on the blood. Jeb's slap had loosened a few teeth and she'd cut her tongue. She spit out as much blood as she could before she scooted over to where she thought Olivia had landed.

"Olivia?" She moved to her right and sighed with relief when she bumped into a warm body. "Can you hear me?" Hannah heard a small groan and blew out a shaky breath of relief. "I'm going to try to get us loose."

Lucky for her, Jeb had tied her hands and feet together in front, so she could lean down and gnaw at the knots. Her lips grew raw from rubbing against the rope but she finally managed to loosen the knots and slip one hand out.

She wiped the blood from her chin on her sleeve, then finished untying herself. Hannah reached for Olivia, who hadn't made another sound. With shaking hands, she untied her sister-in-law, then reached for her face.

"Liv? Please wake up. I don't think I can carry you out of here." Hannah's whisper sounded as desperate as she felt. "I don't know when Jeb is coming back. We need to get out."

"Hannah?" Olivia's voice was slurred but it sounded like an angel's singing to Hannah.

"Yes, come on. We have to get out of here." Somehow she helped Olivia to her feet and the two of them hobbled to the door.

When Hannah tried to turn the knob, she realized the door was locked. She pressed her forehead against the wood, fighting the panic that clawed at her. There had to be another way out, there just had to be.

She guided Olivia back to the wall and helped her sit. "The door is locked."

"Mm." Olivia didn't sound like she would last long. Jeb had thrown her so hard against the wall, her head was probably broken open. Hannah had never been around someone with such a serious injury, but she heard both Eva and Granny in her head, telling her to stay calm. She felt Olivia's head and her hand came away sticky with blood.

Hannah ripped part of her skirt to make a bandage and wrapped Olivia's head as tightly as she dared. It would have to do until they could get her real help.

"Stay here. I'm going to see if I can get us out of here." She felt around the small room, finding vegetables, jars full of what was probably preserves, and a few baskets. Nothing helpful.

Hannah searched around the door and got nothing but a few splinters. There had to be something she could use to get out.

"Call for help." Olivia's weak suggestion surprised Hannah.

"I can't do that." Hannah had found an inner well of strength and she wasn't going to abandon it just yet. She continued her journey to the right of the door and found a metal bar. With a triumphant grin, she went back to the door. Using all her strength, she pried the metal bar against the door until it splintered.

A shaft of light blinded her temporarily. She tucked the metal bar into her waistband and peered out the door. There didn't seem to be anyone about, but that didn't mean Jeb wouldn't come back any second.

Hannah returned for Olivia and together they crept out of the small cellar room and started toward the stairs.

Matt leapt off his horse the moment he neared the Stinson ranch. There were no horses tied up outside, but that didn't mean no one was home. Without waiting for anyone to open the door, he crashed through it, shouting Hannah's name.

He scared the housekeeper and a cat, but he didn't care enough to even apologize. Shouting his wife's name, he stalked through the house until he reached the veranda doors. He slammed through them too and found Jeb sitting at a table.

The surprise on Jeb's face looked genuine. He set a sandwich down and picked up a mug of what looked like tea.

"Matthew Graham, I never thought you were the rude sort. What are you doing here howling like a fool?" Jeb was either a fantastic thespian or a complete lunatic.

"Where are they?" Matt growled.

"Who? I'm here alone. Margaret went to town with your sister. My father was supposed to be with you." Jeb took a sip of the tea. "I'd offer you a drink but I'm certain you'd refuse. Something sure has put a bee in your bonnet."

Matt stalked over to Jeb and grabbed him by the shirt. They were similar in size, but Matt's daily labors and his fury made him twice as strong.

"I will snatch the life right out of you if you've hurt them."

Jeb's eyes widened and Matt saw a dollop of fear in his blue gaze. "I haven't hurt anyone."

"You killed my parents." Matt's voice was raw with pain and rage. The thought of giving this murderer his friendship made him sick. It didn't matter a bit if he'd been as fooled as everyone else.

"Matt, I don't know what you're talking about."

Matt shook him, his arms shaking with the effort of not killing Jeb outright. "I will not give you another piece of my life. I'm going to ask you one more time, where are my wife and sister?"

Jeb's gaze moved past him. "Hannah, tell your husband you're okay."

Matt turned, hope making him blind to the danger Jeb presented. Too late, he realized his mistake. Jeb brought the cast-iron teapot down on Matt's head with a resounding thud. His teeth slammed together and the ground slapped him in the face.

Armstrong couldn't find the women. He knew they were in the house, but damned if Jeb hadn't stashed them someplace good. He'd looked in at every door in the entire house. To his surprise, he'd found nothing. Where were they?

The scarf hadn't appeared out of nowhere and he knew exactly why Hannah was wearing it. She wouldn't willingly give it up. Someone had done something to both women, and it was up to Armstrong to find out just what it was.

A commotion in the back of the house brought him running as quietly as he could. He peered out the window in the office and saw Matt shaking Jeb like a dog. Armstrong didn't know what the hell Graham was up to, but he needed to put a stop to it.

Armstrong checked his pistol before he stepped cautiously outside. When Jeb slammed the teapot against Matt's head, Armstrong realized he'd been investigating the wrong Stinson. Matt had obviously figured it out, and the ranger was embarrassed to be so slow to recognize the truth.

Now he had to save Graham, as well as the man's sister and wife. Armstrong wasn't prepared for Jeb to pull out a gun and point it at him.

"You know, I was wondering when you would make an appearance." Jeb cocked the pistol. "I was watching you last night, making cow eyes at my intended bride."

"I wasn't making cow eyes at anyone. Mr. Graham invited me to the barbecue when we met last week. I was much obliged for the invite." Armstrong held up his hands. "I followed him over here because he was talking crazy."

"Damn right he was talking crazy. He tried to kill me." Jeb set the pot down on the table. "I never saw such a thing."

Armstrong wondered whether Stinson's innocuous

behavior was all an act or whether he was facing one of the smartest killers he'd ever met.

"Why don't you put that pistol away so I can arrest Graham for attacking you?" Armstrong kept his voice even, calm, although his gut was churning like a twister.

"Oh, no, I can't do that. Matt threatened my life. I won't put the gun down in his presence again." Jeb turned the pistol on Matt's inert form. "I have to protect myself."

Two things happened so fast Armstrong had to blink to be sure he wasn't seeing things. First, Hannah appeared behind Jeb, covered in blood, her hair a wild cloud both blood-streaked and dirty. Then Olivia ran past him, also bloody and bruised, screaming like a banshee from a tale his granny used to tell.

"Don't you hurt my brother!" She threw herself at Jeb just as Hannah conked the man on the head with some kind of metal bar.

The younger Stinson fell to the ground beneath a heap of female anger. Armstrong was there in a blink, pulling both women up and out of harm's way. Of course they didn't seem to care for his assistance and scratched and bit at him.

"Olivia! Hannah! Stop. It's me, Brody Armstrong!" He managed to pull them off Jeb, who looked as though he'd been tossed down a ravine.

"Your first name is Brody?" Olivia had dried blood all over her hair and forehead. He'd never been so glad to see a woman alive.

"Don't remind me. My mother was a true Irish woman and thought I should have a strong Irish name." He pulled both women to their feet. "Now what the hell happened here?"

Hannah was breathing hard as she pushed her hair

out of her eyes, then spat a bloody wad on the ground. Armstrong thought he had seen everything, but these two had just proved him wrong.

"Jeb tried to kill us. We stopped him." Her grin was positively feral and liberally sprinkled with blood.

Truthfully the women were making Armstrong nervous. "Your husband was hurt. You might want to tend to him."

"Matt!" Hannah ran to him and knelt down, pulling his head into her lap. She touched the gash on his forehead with such tenderness, he had to look away.

Olivia had found Jeb's gun and was currently pointing it at him. "I should kill him now."

"Let the law handle him, Miss Graham."

She snorted. "You should call me Olivia. I think we're on a first-name basis by now."

Just then Frederick Stinson, Javier, Lorenzo, Nick, Caleb, and Angus McRae all barreled through the door. When they caught sight of the women, Jeb, and Matt, their expressions were almost comical.

"What in the name of God happened here?" The elder Stinson looked as though he might explode.

"I'm placing your son under arrest for murder, fraud, and kidnapping." Armstrong pulled a length of leather from his pocket. "You can visit him in the jail."

Hannah and Olivia threw their heads back and let loose a battle cry that had all of the men taking a step back. Armstrong could just imagine what kind of children Hannah and Matt would have. Too bad he couldn't stick around to find out.

CHAPTER SIXTEEN

Matt woke slowly, his head pounding as though it had been split open by an axe. He cracked one eye open and recognized his bedroom at the ranch. Confusion was replaced by panic when he remembered what had happened.

He sat up so fast, his stomach came right up with him. Matt bent over the side of the bed and a bucket appeared below him. As he vomited, a soft hand touched the back of his neck and he knew without looking it was Hannah.

When he had stopped making a fool of himself, he lay back on the bed and was finally able to look at Hannah. Her face was bruised an ugly shade of purple and green on one side, her lip split and swollen, and one eye was black, as though she'd been in a brawl. His mouth dropped open when she smiled.

"I'm so glad to see you awake. It's been two days, Matt." She took his hand and kissed the back of it. "You scared me."

"*You're* scaring *me*, Hannah. What the hell happened to you?" He didn't dare touch her for fear he'd hurt her healing wounds.

"I'm fine. Just a bit bruised. You were really hurt." She moved closer and touched the side of his head. "The doctor said Jeb might have cracked your skull. I wanted to beat him all over again when I heard that. Are you in pain?"

"My head does pain me something fierce." Matt reached up, surprised to find a bandage wrapped around his head. The left side was particularly sore. He felt plenty of whiskers on his face. Matt hoped there wasn't a mirror nearby because he didn't want to see what he looked like.

He tried to remember what had happened. Images of blood and screaming women ran through his mind. He wondered if he'd dreamed it or if Hannah had really rescued him instead of the other way around. It shouldn't surprise him. After all, his entire life had been turned on its head since they'd married.

"Did you and my sister attack Jeb?"

She blushed. "Kind of. He'd locked us in the root cellar and we got free. Then I saw he'd hurt you and I didn't hesitate to defend you."

Her brown gaze was so guileless, so completely full of love, he had to look away. His throat had tightened up, and he swallowed three times before he could speak.

"Thank you, Hannah. I, uh, ain't so good with words." He took her hand, embarrassed to see his own trembling. "When I asked you to marry me, I didn't know what was in store for us. Now I can't imagine my life without you."

She blinked a few times and then nodded. "Neither can I."

"Is it okay if you kiss me?" He really wanted to make slow, sweet love but that would likely have to wait at least until he could sit up without help.

Hannah smiled. "I think I can arrange it with your caretaker."

She rose and leaned toward him, and her breath puffed against his lips. He closed his eyes and she kissed him so lightly, she could have been a butterfly.

"You need to sleep and get better. Don't worry; we're taking care of everything."

Sleep crept over him like a warm blanket. The last thing he saw was Hannah's eyes. The last thing he heard was her quiet whisper.

The next morning, Hannah was up before the dawn again. Doing chores helped her to focus, to forget all the horrible things that had happened on the Stinson property. The relief she felt when Matt had opened his eyes had sent her outside to cry after he'd gone back to sleep. She wept for the love she'd thought she'd lost before ever really experiencing it. Hannah had sobbed until her throat was raw and she didn't have a tear left to shed.

When she crawled into bed, she slept for the first time since Matt had been injured. He couldn't spoon up behind her yet but his body warmth and even the sound of his breathing were enough for her. Now he was sleeping deeply and no longer unconscious. Hannah woke feeling refreshed and ready to get back to normal.

The sun was just peeking over the horizon when Granny came into the kitchen. Hannah was surprised to see her up so early.

"Mornin'." From experience, Hannah didn't engage in conversation with her grandmother just yet. Instead she poured a cup of hot coffee and set it down on the table.

"These old bones can't get comfortable no more." Granny sat down with a groan and snatched up the cup. She sniffed in the hot brew before taking a noisy slurp. "Your man wake up?"

"Yes, thank God." Hannah started rolling out the biscuit dough. "He doesn't remember much."

"Good thing. He'd probably pitch a fit if he knew what you'd done." Granny shook her head at her. "Not many women could do what you did."

"What did she do?" Matt's voice made Hannah slip and she nearly dropped the glass she was using to cut out the biscuits.

"She saved your life and captured the bastard who tried to kill you." Granny slurped again.

Matt shuffled into the kitchen, his clothes messy but his eyes clear. His hair stuck up every which way on top of his head, pushed up by the bandages. He was pale and a little shaky, but Hannah thought he'd never looked so handsome and *alive*.

He sat down and she gestured to her own cup. "Go ahead and drink it. I just poured it."

With a grateful sigh, he wrapped his hands around the hot mug and sipped the coffee. "Now tell me what exactly you did to save my life."

"She saved me, too." Olivia didn't look much better than her brother, but she had only been knocked out. The doctor said her skull was hard enough to survive the hit against the wall. Her knees were bruised and she winced when she walked. It would be a while before she could run, but she could get around just fine.

Matt frowned at Hannah. "I think I need to hear more, starting with why you were at Stinson's ranch in the first place."

Hannah started putting biscuits in the pan without

answering. Olivia poured herself a cup of coffee and sat down beside her brother.

"She asked me if she could go with me. When we got there, Margaret wasn't home. Jeb invited us in and we realized he was the one who was behind the attacks, not his father." Olivia met Hannah's gaze; the bond between them had deepened now. "Jeb hit us, tied us up, and locked us in a root cellar of some kind. Hannah managed to untie us and get us out."

Matt's eyes widened. "How the hell did you do that?"

Hannah finished putting the biscuits in the oven and started cleaning up the mess she'd left behind. "My teeth, my willpower, my brain." She shrugged. "Anybody could have done it."

"Like hell." Granny smacked the table with her open hand. "About time you stopped apologizing for being strong and smart."

Hannah jumped at her grandmother's loud pronouncement. "I'm not apologizing."

"Damn right, you are. Tell your husband how you lost two teeth because Jeb hit you so hard. Tell him how you lost skin on your lips gnawing on the rope to get yourself free and how you used a metal bar to pry the door open. How you about carried Olivia upstairs." Granny got to her feet. "Or tell him how you used that metal bar to knock some sense into Jeb's stupid head."

Matt's mouth dropped open and Hannah couldn't help squirming under his gaze. This was what she didn't want, to have what she did laid out for everyone to talk about again. Never mind that Matt hadn't heard it the first time; she still could hardly believe it was true and she'd lived it.

"You did all that?" Matt got to his feet and took her

wrists, turning so he could see the chafing from the ropes. He kissed the inside of one wrist and a shiver ran down her arm.

"Yes."

Matt wiped away her tear with his thumb. "I've got to be the luckiest man in Texas."

Hannah's heart thumped hard as she raised her gaze to meet his. "You lost so much."

He shook his head. "I lost my parents and my brother, but that's part of life. What I gained—Hannah, I can't think of a man who would do what you did. You humble me."

Hannah gave him a small smile. "I'm a Graham. I did what I had to."

Matt pulled her into a hug. "My mother would have loved you, too."

It was the closest she'd come to a confession of love from her husband, and she held onto it and tucked it away. Perhaps one day he might find the words. For now she could be content with what he'd given her because she loved him.

Matt sat on the porch with Armstrong in the afternoon. He felt so much better being out of bed that he ignored Eva and Hannah's clucking and remained outside. The ranger had been staying in the tack room at the barn while everyone healed up.

"Where is he?"

Armstrong didn't ask who; he didn't have to. "Sheriff locked him up but I was supposed to take him to Houston yesterday."

"I appreciate your waiting." Matt knew the ranger was accountable to Sam Houston himself. "Will you get in trouble for not bringing him in?"

"Nah. I sent Sam a wire. I plan on leaving in the morning. I get itchy when I'm in one place for too long." Armstrong took a drag off his cigarillo.

"Two weeks is too long?" Matt shook his head. "I can't imagine being anywhere else."

"I love to wander." Armstrong's gaze flicked to the door as it opened. Olivia shuffled out and the ranger sat up straighter.

"Matt, your wife and Eva are about to come out here and haul you back to bed." Her gaze skittered past the ranger and she looked out at the horizon.

Matt watched her as if she'd changed overnight. The one thing he could count on from his sister was her directness. Now she was acting shy with Armstrong. What else had happened while he'd been unconscious?

"I ain't going back to bed." Matt stretched out in the rocking chair, leaning back until his head just touched the back. "Me and the ranger are talking."

"I can see that." Olivia stepped out and shuffled to the other rocking chair beside Matt.

He didn't know what to think of her behavior, so he ignored her. There was obviously something she wanted to know from Armstrong.

"Did you interrogate him?"

"Yes, but he didn't tell me anything. Claimed he was attacked by your wife and sister." Armstrong took another drag and blew it out before he spoke again. "Says he doesn't know shit about your parents or brother, or about the other ranches. I'm still looking for evidence at the ranch."

A slight breeze tickled Matt's skin, cooling the sweat on his forehead. "What happens now?"

"We keep investigating him. His Pa is giving me free rein to search everything." Armstrong glanced at

Olivia. "I found the room where the girls were tied up."

Matt's hands tightened on the arms of the chair. "And?"

"Blood, rope, a couple teeth and a torn-up door handle. Just like your wife said."

"Jesus Christ." Matt had heard what everyone had said, but to hear the ranger tell it so bluntly made his gut twist.

"We've got Jeb for the crimes against them. In the meantime, we keep digging until we find what we're after."

"That's not good enough." Matt choked on the frustration building inside him. "I want him to swing for my parents' murder, and I want to know where Benjy is." His voice rose until he was shouting, making his head throb in tune with his heart.

"I know, but right now you gotta be patient." Armstrong rose to his feet. "I won't be back before I leave."

"No, you're not leaving with him. Not until I talk to him." Matt struggled to stand. "That bastard is going to have to answer to me."

Armstrong put one arm on Matt's shoulder. "Ain't nothing you can do if you fall off a horse and break the other side of your head. Besides, your wife would likely shoot me if I let you."

Matt's fury had started to grow the more he thought about never finding out what he had to know. "I have to talk to him, Armstrong. I have to."

The cool-eyed ranger stared down at him. "I'll come by with him first thing on my way out of town. You get a few minutes but no more. I shouldn't even let you have that. I could get my ass chapped for doing it. I got to follow the law."

Matt wanted to say the hell with the law and kill Jeb

himself. If he did he'd never find out what had happened, but he might not find out anyway. Armstrong was doing him a favor and he did appreciate it, even if he was angry enough to bite through steel.

"I guess I'll see you in the morning then," Matt said through clenched teeth.

"You're welcome." Armstrong's mouth kicked up in some semblance of a grin. "See you in the morning."

"Good-bye, Brody." Olivia's voice made the ranger almost miss a step.

"Damn." It was a soft curse but the breeze carried it to Matt's ears.

Olivia grinned. Matt shook his head. The ranger kept walking.

The predawn light turned the prairie into a gray world of shadows. Matt paced back and forth on the porch, watching the horizon for Armstrong to appear. He knew the ranger would be on his way early, and Matt had to talk to Jeb before he was taken to Houston.

It was Matt's only chance to talk to the man who had been his friend, who had apparently betrayed him completely. Jeb had become a monster. Matt needed to understand why. The question had danced around in his brain all night long and he had to ask it.

More than likely, Jeb wouldn't give him what he needed. He had to try anyway. There were so many questions Matt needed to ask. The most important one would come first; then he would ask where Benjy was. There was a break in their circle of eight, and although his wife was amazing, he wanted his little brother back.

Hannah stepped out on the porch wearing a shawl.

Her braid sat on one shoulder, curls sticking out as if she'd done it up in a hurry. As she walked toward him, he held up his right arm and she tucked herself underneath it. Her warmth seeped into his bones and he felt better almost immediately.

"You took your bandage off."

He kissed the top of her head. "It was making me itch."

"It was keeping your wounds clean so you can heal." She put one arm around his waist and leaned into him. "You need a bath."

Matt barked a laugh. "I need a shave, too. I'm sure I'd scare small children and dogs looking like this."

"Your smell would, too."

When they'd met, he hadn't realized she had a sense of humor or how outspoken she was. Hell, the woman had practically run from him when he'd spotted her across the turnips. She'd proven to be a treasure beyond his imaginings.

Now he understood what his parents had had, why his father would give up everything for his mother. Matt had thought him less of a man for it, but the truth was, Hannah made him feel more of a man. His heart ached with the overflowing feelings his voice couldn't express.

The bald truth of what had happened at the Stinson ranch, how she had saved him, should have shamed him. It didn't. He was proud of her and how much grit she had. Most women would have simply given in, but she'd dug in and fought.

He loved her.

Matt's vision went a little gray around the edges as the realization hit him. *He loved her.* He'd never believed it would happen to him, fought against it from the second he suspected he had feelings for Hannah.

It had taken a brush with death for him to realize what he had was love.

As he was trying to figure out a way to tell her without sounding like a fool, he heard the sound of horses approaching. His romantic notions tucked away, Matt waited, vibrating with a kettle full of dark thoughts. When the men finally appeared, he stepped away from Hannah and waited on the steps to meet them.

Armstrong held the reins of both horses. Jeb had been tied to the saddle horn and his feet tied to the stirrups. It gave Matt an evil pleasure to know if Stinson did try to escape, he couldn't even get off the saddle.

"Here we are, Graham. Say what you gotta say and we'll be on our way." Armstrong tipped his hat to Hannah. "Mornin', ma'am."

"Morning, Ranger Armstrong." Her head was high although her face was a rainbow of bruises. Matt swelled with pride at the way she stood her ground, shoulders back and chin up. Hannah was a hell of a woman.

"Isn't anybody going to say good morning to me?" Jeb's smile bore only a slight resemblance to a real one.

"I've got things to say to you, but they sure as hell ain't good morning." Matt put his hands on his hips and stared at his former friend. There were so many reasons why Jeb could have chosen the right path, now was the time to find out why he'd chosen the wrong one. "Let's start with why. Why the hell did you do it, Jeb?"

"Do what, Matthew?" His pretended innocence made Matt want to rip his arms off.

"You killed my parents." Saying it out loud made

Matt's stomach almost meet up with his throat. "And you took Benjy. Why?"

Hannah reached for his hand and he held onto her, grateful for her strength.

"Matthew. Are you asking me why men do the evil things they do?" Jeb shook his head. "I don't have an answer for you."

"You son of a bitch." Matt's hand tightened on Hannah's as rage coursed through him unabated. If he'd had a gun, he would have ended Jeb right then and there.

"Most assuredly, that I am. Can't you see that greed is what drives most? You and your happy clan have little and aspire to nothing. You're less than a man, Graham, and it's you I pity." Jeb made a tsking sound with his tongue. "Stuck with a cow for a wife, and a tiny little plot of land. No future, no money. Nothing."

Matt's anger gave way to a bitter acceptance. Jeb would never tell him what he needed to know, likely took pleasure in playing games over it. "Armstrong, I appreciate your bringing him by. Hope you have a safe trip to Houston."

Armstrong tipped his hat to Matt and Hannah, then kneed his horse into action. As they started to move away, Jeb squawked.

"Wait, what? I haven't answered your questions." Stinson fought at his bindings. "Don't leave yet. I-I'm not done."

"Oh yeah, you're done." Armstrong's grin was feral and colder than his blue eyes. "Now shut up or I'll gag you."

They rode off into the grayness, leaving Matt with a hollow feeling inside. No matter what happened, he sure as hell would never understand why. Jeb was a greedy piece of shit who simply took what he wanted, no matter what the cost. That was the truth Matt had to accept.

He'd likely never find Benjy. That was a truth that would be excruciating to accept. Somewhere deep inside, he'd always hoped Benjy had been given to some farm couple to raise, as a last act of cruelty to the Grahams. Now he had to face the possibility Benjy was dead or worse.

It was a dark day for everyone.

The day after the ranger took Jeb to Houston, Hannah was teaching the girls how to sew when a knock came at the door. Matt wasn't allowed to ride or work yet so he was sitting in the kitchen with them. He met her gaze with a frown.

Matt walked to the door while the Graham women watched him. He opened it at the second knock and looked surprised to see Frederick Stinson there. Hannah stood to greet the rancher and was as surprised as Matt by the older man's appearance. He'd aged twenty years in only a week, with sunken cheeks, larger patches of gray in his hair, and pain-filled eyes. Even his shoulders slumped in defeat.

"Please come in, Mr. Stinson." Hannah gestured to the girls to go. Rebecca, Catherine, and Elizabeth listened and took the sewing down the hallway. Olivia remained with them, sitting at the table since walking was still difficult for her to do without pain in her knees.

Mr. Stinson walked in and took off his hat. "I wondered if you would slam the door in my face, Graham. I probably would have."

"It's not your crime. I'm not going to make you pay for it." Matt gestured to the table. "Sit down. Coffee?"

"I'd be much obliged. It was a dusty ride." Stinson sat and looked at both Hannah and Olivia. "I needed to come by and apologize to the two of you."

After everything that had happened, Hannah had contemplated going to see Mr. Stinson but Eva had told her not to. "He is a hard man, *hija*. When he is ready, he will come to us." Since the housekeeper seemed to know people well, Hannah took her advice. Judging by Mr. Stinson's appearance, she was glad she had.

Hannah poured him a cup of coffee and returned to the table. As she set it down in front of the man, she was surprised to see his hand shaking.

"I don't know why Jeb turned bad or why he would hurt our neighbors. I taught him nothing but good things." He shook his graying head. "He wouldn't tell me what happened. Wouldn't even talk about what happened to Margaret." His chin wobbled and his normally steely eyes filled with tears.

"What about Margaret?" Olivia finally spoke although her face was as hard as the table.

"Nobody's seen her since the day Jeb did what he done." He ran his hands down his face, the scrape of the whiskers on his hand loud in the quiet room. "I looked for her everywhere, but she's disappeared."

Hannah saw the shock on Matt's face. No one would ever have suspected Jeb would do something to his own sister. She covered Mr. Stinson's hand with her own.

"I'm so sorry. Is there anything we can do to help?"

"No, but I thank you for the offer." He looked at Matt. "I didn't know what you went through. Now I've lost everything I had."

Matt finally sat down and his shoulders relaxed. "No, you haven't lost everything. You've still got neighbors."

Hannah's chest swelled with pride in her husband. Given how much pain Jeb had caused the Grahams, it took a big man to still offer his father friendship.

"I appreciate that. I surely do." Frederick wiped his eyes with the heels of his palms. "You folks don't owe me a thing."

"That's the good part about being a neighbor. You never worry about owing." Matt's gaze reflected his own pain. She knew he'd been pacing at night, unable to sleep.

Stinson pulled a folded paper from his shirt pocket. "I asked Elliot Barnum in town to take a look at the map. He told me it's all legal."

Matt frowned. "I didn't lie to you, Stinson."

"I know that now. I'm gonna sign over that two-mile patch of land to you and Angus."

Hannah gasped along with Olivia.

Matt's frown deepened. "Why would you do that?"

"I don't have any use for it. And after everything Jeb did to your family, I couldn't keep it." Stinson got to his feet. "I've taken up enough of your time."

He shook Matt's hand and nodded to Olivia and Hannah. With a shuffle that appeared to be that of an old man rather than a forty-five-year-old, he left the house.

The three of them stared at each other in silence for a few moments after Stinson left. Hannah noted his untouched coffee on the table. The legacy of what Jeb had done would affect the Grahams, the Stinsons, and all the other families he'd attacked. Frederick Stinson would live with that burden the rest of his life, and more than likely, die a lonely old man. She truly hoped he would find Margaret. If not, the man had lost his entire family in one day.

"Poor man." Olivia shook her head.

"He was a hard man. He gave his children everything they ever wanted and look what that brought him." Matt stared at the closed door. "I hear his wife died giving birth to Margaret and his second wife left him. Now he is completely alone."

"You were kind to him." Hannah had seen a new side of her husband today.

"He didn't do anything beyond being a lousy father. I meant what I said. Jeb will answer for what he did but his father shouldn't have to." Matt got to his feet and kissed Hannah's forehead. "I'm going to the barn to check on Winston."

He left the two women alone and shut the door gently behind him.

"My brother can be stubborn," Olivia offered.

"I've noticed that." If they were going to move past the tragedies the Grahams had suffered, Hannah had to find a way to break through the walls her husband had erected around himself. She loved him, but she needed to help him.

Matt woke before dawn after a fitful night's sleep. He was going to go riding, come hell or high water. There was no reason he shouldn't—he certainly felt well enough. He missed his early morning rides, that time to himself when he could think.

Three weeks married and he hadn't made love to his wife in a week. She'd been nearly killed because he couldn't protect her, same as his parents and his brother. Matt had failed her, as he'd failed his family. For that, he couldn't forgive himself.

He stepped outside and took a deep breath. The warm air felt good as he walked to the barn. The smell of new wood was still strong, another gift from the neighbors after the old barn had been burned. There had been gifts in his life he would never forget. Hannah was the best of all. He didn't deserve her if he couldn't take care of her.

Winston whinnied the moment Matt got near his stall. The gelding had obviously missed him as much as he had missed the horse. The morning rides were special for both of them.

After he'd saddled the horse, he led him out of the barn and stopped in his tracks. Hannah stood on the porch wearing a white nightdress, her hair unbound.

His body tightened up like a bow string at the sight. She was incredible, so sexy and tempting, he almost turned around and brought Winston back into the barn. As she walked toward him, the wind picked up her hair and it fluttered behind her. He'd never seen anything more beautiful, and damned if his eyes didn't prick with tears. She'd turned him into a fool, but it didn't matter.

He loved her.

Matt knew he needed to tell her, too. As she got closer, her nightdress billowed in the warm breeze, making her laugh. Her smile made his heart skip a beat.

"Going for a ride?" She kept her voice low.

"I go in the morning before anyone else is up. Well, I guess you are now." He thought about all those early morning rides alone. Then he realized this time he didn't want to be by himself. "Come with me."

Her eyebrows went up. "You want me to ride with you?"

Matt pulled her close, until he was close enough to touch her, put his hands in her glorious hair, and kiss her until he had to come up for air.

"Yes, ride with me, honey. I need you to ride with

me." He forced himself to step back, to let go of his warm, tempting wife.

She scrutinized his face for a few moments before she smiled again. "I'll be back in five minutes." Hannah reached up and kissed him hard, then ran for the house.

The wind still kicked up, making her hair and her nightdress billow around her. She had to put her arms out for balance when a strong gust came through. Matt was hit between the eyes with the image of Hannah dressed as she was. She looked like an angel, his angel.

He took off his hat and dropped to his knees, disregarding the horse's curious stare. His heart swelled with the idea she had been sent to love him, to watch over him, to heal him. Perhaps his mother had whispered in God's ear to send a woman to do just that.

Matt squeezed his eyes shut and said a prayer of thanks for finding Hannah. He was a simple rancher's son with too much responsibility to bear, the weight of the world on his shoulders. Matt had been floundering until Hannah came into his life.

She'd given everything to him, including her heart, her blood, and her love. He felt humbled by all of it, sure someone had made a mistake and given him exactly what he needed. Now he had so much, and although he'd lost people he loved, he had gained a partner, a soul mate to stand by his side.

He didn't realize five minutes had passed until her boots appeared in front of him. Matt glanced up to find her braiding her hair, with a hat tucked under her left arm and a curious look on her lovely face.

"Are you praying?"

He jumped to his feet and took her face in his

hands. Before he could stop himself, he told her what was in his heart. "Hannah Graham, I love you."

Her eyes widened and then a beautiful smile spread across her face. "Matthew Graham, I love you, too."

Matt whooped, regardless of the sleeping people on the ranch, picked her up, and swirled her around until she begged him to stop. She slid slowly down his body. Their ragged breaths mingled and he kissed her softly. Matt knew a moment of pure joy and his heart was healed.

"Let's ride."

Hannah nodded and they went back in the barn to saddle Buttermilk.

Hannah could hardly keep the smile off her face. Matt had told her that he loved her. *Loved her!* It was enough to keep her happy for the rest of her life. Their marriage hadn't been a traditional one by any-body's standards, but whatever forces had brought them together had done a good job.

She knew he liked early morning rides. Although he probably shouldn't be on a horse yet, his invitation to accompany him was marvelous. Hannah didn't have a great seat yet on a horse, but she was getting better. The sway of gentle Buttermilk was even be-coming familiar to her.

He led her to the edge of the property, to an en-clave of cottonwood trees with a small pond in the center. It was idyllic, a perfect spot to stop and rest.

Matt dismounted and came over to her, holding up his arms. She shook her head. "I'm too heavy for you."

"That's not true. I'll catch you. Trust me, Hannah." He stared up at her, his beautiful blue-green eyes so full of love, she couldn't help falling into his arms.

To her surprise, he helped her down without so much as a grunt. Hannah was not a small girl, but he surely made her feel like one. He laid out a blanket from his saddle and they both sat, side by side, watching the water. Hannah hadn't felt this relaxed for a month. She'd never expected to feel that way with a man, even her dream man. Of course, her dream man was now her husband and only he would fill her nighttime thoughts.

"I come out here by myself a lot. Winston and me, we don't always like everybody's noise." Matt pulled up a blade of grass and twirled it in his fingers. "I kept this spot a secret until now."

Hannah lay back and put her hands under her head. "Thank you for showing me. I like it. A lot."

He tickled her nose with the grass. "I like you a lot, too."

She took his hand and tugged until he lay on his side, looking down at her. "I was worried about us."

His smile disappeared. "Life ain't been easy if you're a Graham. I keep hoping each bad thing will be the last."

"You haven't given up on finding Benjy or who killed your parents, and I don't think you should." She reached up and touched his cheek. "But I think you need to start the rest of your life."

"I am. I got the land grant, didn't I?" He scowled. "And I married you. What else can I do?"

"You think about them every day. You even dream about them."

His face registered surprise. "I do?"

"Yes, you call for them in your sleep. You even cry sometimes." She turned to face him. "I don't think you've said good-bye to your parents yet."

"I don't know what that means." He got to his feet

and walked a few feet off. His expression was wary and she knew he was pulling away from her. This was the moment that decided how close they would be, how successful their marriage would be.

Hannah rose and walked toward him. "They wouldn't want you to put your own life aside to fuss about them each and every day. Your parents are proud of you, and you have to be the one to let them go."

He stared at her, his eyes wide. She didn't think he would respond and her heart began to sink.

"I can't." His voice was barely above a whisper.

She took his hands. "You can and I can help you. Where are they buried?"

His face paled a little. "By that big tree near the corner of the house. Liv thought they'd like to be in the shade but close enough to keep an eye on us."

"Let's go then." She picked up the blanket.

"Go where?"

"To the graves. You need to say good-bye and that's the best place to do it." Hannah remembered very clearly standing at her mother's grave with its crude cross and crying her eyes out. It was a chance for her to say good-bye, one forced on her by Granny. Now it was her turn to do the same for the man she loved.

"I don't want to."

"Too bad. You're going anyway." She took Buttermilk's reins and tried to get back in the saddle, unsuccessfully, until Matt's big hands pushed her rear end up. Looking down at his handsome face, she gave him a sad smile. "Let's ride, cowboy. We need to bring this one home."

"I wanted to make love to you here."

"And you will. But today we need to put the ghosts to rest and get the grieving done." Hannah was taking her Granny's advice and holding on with both hands. Matt was hers; now she needed to keep him.

He didn't say a word but he stood there for a few minutes, staring into the water. She held her breath while her heart did a funny pittypat, until he hopped on Winston and kneed the horse into action. The ride home was somber but Hannah was determined to make this step.

When they got to the tree, she wasn't surprised to see two bunches of wildflowers on the simple graves. The brothers and sisters obviously took care of them, kept them well swept and let their parents know they loved them and missed them.

Hannah dismounted with less grace than Matt, but on her own this time. She knelt down between the graves. "Hello, Mr. and Mrs. Graham. You don't know me but I'm Matt's wife. I'm sorry I didn't know you, but I feel like I do through your children. Thank you for raising such a bunch of amazing folks. I promise to always love Matt and give him my heart and soul. You can tell God I said thank you for bringing him to me."

She rose and glanced up at Matt, who still sat in the saddle. "You're going to have to get down here to make it work."

"I can't." His jaw was tight enough to make his skin twitch.

"You can and you will." She held up her arms. "I'll catch you. Trust me."

The corner of his mouth went up a smidge. "You're a stubborn woman, Hannah Graham."

"I'm trying." She waited, hoping against hope he would do what he needed to.

Matt finally dismounted and took her hand. She didn't comment on the fact it was shaking or that his palm was clammy. She just walked him over to the graves and knelt next to him.

It took another few minutes and quite a few deep breaths before Matt started talking.

"Ma, Pa, I feel kind of silly doing this. I know you didn't want to leave us, but the man responsible is in the law's hands now. I won't give up on finding Benjy though. I promise." He let out another loud breath. "I miss you and I hope you can be proud of what I've done, what I'll do, and I sure hope you like Hannah. We'll name your grandchildren after both of you." Matt's voice cracked and she tightened her grip on his hand.

His breathing became ragged and she just held on, waiting. Out of the corner of her eye, she saw tears sliding down his cheeks, so she turned and pulled him into her arms. The dam within him must have finally burst as Matt buried his face in her neck. Safe in her embrace, Matt wept and finally grieved for those he'd lost.

It was after midnight when Hannah went in search of her husband. Once he had let his feelings out, he'd returned to the graves twice already, telling his parents this and that. It was good for him, but he needed rest. And she needed him.

Hannah spotted a light in the barn and walked over. When she walked through the open door, she found Matt hanging up some tack on the nails on the wall. His expression was full of guilt.

"Is it late?"

"Very." She leaned against the door. "You missed supper."

"I needed to work." He pushed back his hat and

squeezed his nose. "I didn't mean to be so late though."

"It's all right. You must be hungry." She wrapped her arms around his waist and pressed her forehead against his chest. "You certainly smell like you've been working."

He chuckled and pulled her close. "I can always count on you to tell me I smell."

"I'm sorry." Her voice was muffled against his shirt.

"I know somewhere I can get clean and we can, ah, get close."

She looked up at him with a grin, her heart already starting to pick up. "The pond?"

"The pond."

"It's awful dark out. Won't it be dangerous?" The last thing they needed was another injury. Both of them were still recovering from the last ones.

"We'll ride Winston at a nice slow walk. The moon is bright and I know the way like the back of my hand." He kissed her hard. "Trust me."

"I do." She reached out and cupped his cock.

He groaned and hardened within seconds. "I can't ride with that thing in my trousers."

"Then it should ride in my trousers." Hannah couldn't believe she'd said that, but now that she had, she laughed at her own bawdiness.

"I don't know if I can make it to the pond either." Matt took the lantern and turned the wick down until it was just a glimmer of light. "I have a blanket and a clean stall."

"I'd go anywhere with you, Matt." Hannah meant every word. She had started out a lonely woman and was now a woman loved by her husband, with a family she could love in return.

He took her hand and led her to the back of the

barn, to the stall with all the hay bales stacked in it. Hannah watched as he shut the door behind them and hung the lantern on the hook. Matt's eyes glowed in the meager light.

"Now what?"

"Now we get naughty." He reached for her buttons at the same time she reached for his. The rest of their clothes disappeared quickly. Soon they were both naked and their discarded clothing made a nice blanket on the hay.

She sat down on the pile closest to her and found Matt's cock directly in front of her. Without thinking about what she was doing, Hannah took him in her mouth. He was hot, hard, and salty in her mouth.

"Oh God." His breathing became irregular. "What are you doing?"

"Making you feel good." She licked at him as she would a sweet treat, finding her own body warming up quickly by giving him pleasure.

"You've got quite a tongue."

She would have thanked him but her tongue was busy sliding up and down his staff. Hannah had no idea what she was doing but it had felt good when he had licked her so she was just following her instincts. His cock pulsed in her hand, the base of it so thick she couldn't wrap her fingers completely around it.

A rush of power went through her as she made a grown man tremble at her touch. She tasted him with each pass of her mouth. He tasted of man, of love, and of passion. Hannah could definitely get used to pleasuring him with her mouth. The throbbing began low and deep inside her, as she felt his excitement build. His thighs grew taut and he thrust into her mouth.

"You need to stop, Hannah." He tugged gently on her hair. "I don't want to finish before you even start."

She wanted to continue licking him, but she was also anxious to be joined with him. This would be their first time since he'd told her he loved her. Their joining would be a consummation of that love.

With one last suck and a lick at his tip, she let him go. He let out a shaky breath and leaned over her.

"Lie back, woman." Although he didn't usually talk to her like that, Hannah found herself liking it.

She found a comfortable spot and did as he bade, the hay crinkling beneath her. The soft sounds of the horses, the chirping of the night creatures, were the only things around them. They were in their own paradise, their little piece of heaven on earth.

Her heart swelled with love as he nudged her entrance. She held his gaze as he pushed inside her, inch by inch. The love in his eyes made her breath catch. When he was fully sheathed inside her, he stopped and took a breath.

"What's wrong?"

He chuckled painfully. "I didn't want to come the second I was inside you."

She reached for his hand and placed it on one breast. "Then keep yourself occupied."

This time he didn't laugh. He smiled, then bent down to take the other breast into his mouth. His tongue swirled around the turgid peak, lapping at one nipple while his hand tweaked the other. She grabbed his behind and pulled until he got the message and started moving.

His was a slow pace, one meant to savor the joining, prolong the pleasure. She closed her eyes and reveled in it, contracting around his cock, pulling him in deeper with each thrust.

He bit her nipple and she gasped, her muscles tightening, so he did it again. It was a trigger, one that sent them both careening toward their peak. Hannah felt it in her toes, traveling upward, and in her breasts, traveling down. The tingles and zings of pleasure moved through her until they all coalesced between her legs.

His mouth found hers in a bruising kiss, one that mimicked what his body was already doing with hers. Her tongue slid against his, warm and slippery.

She scratched at his back, urging him to go faster, harder. He didn't need encouragement as his pace had quickened along with the pulsing inside her. She held on when the explosion began deep within her. Her silent scream of pleasure was meant for him, for her love.

She clenched around him, becoming one with him. He bit her again, this time as he found his own peak. Hannah was transported to the stars, her husband by her side. Her heart stopped as the perfect moment made the world around them pause. Exquisite ecstasy showered down around them.

Hannah trembled with the power of what they'd shared. She had always enjoyed making love with Matt, but this was different. This transcended all of those experiences, and crossed into a sharing of souls. She had found the other half of herself.

"Love you, Matt."

"Love you, Hannah."

They snuggled together, using his shirt as a cover, and slept. Matt and Hannah had found what they'd been searching for all their lives. Love.

Have you tried Emma Lang's other books?

Ruthless Heart

He led her astray, and she never wanted to go back . . .

Sheltered all her life, Eliza Hunter never imagined herself alone in the vast Utah plains, much less trailing a mysterious, rugged man hired to hunt down her beautiful younger sister. Unable to reveal the truth about her pursuit of him, Eliza plays student to his teacher, transforming herself in the process. And when she finds herself sharing the warmth of Grady's campfire, wrapped in his arms, hypnotized by his power, soon she is a naive spinster no more . . .

Grady Wolfe is more than a loner, he's a man forever on the run. With a body and soul finely honed from living off the land, Grady knows he should leave the irresistible woman alone, but she stirs something in him he hasn't felt before. Now he's lost in the woods for the first time in his life—with a dangerous job to do. And no one—not even the luscious Eliza—is going to stop him.

Grady had never met a woman like Eliza, if that was even really her name. She talked like a professor, rode around with twenty pounds of books, and could build a campfire like nobody's business. Yet she was as innocent as a child, had a sad story about a dead husband he didn't believe for a second, and seemed to be waiting for him to invite her along for his hunt.

He snorted at the thought. Grady worked alone, always and for good. There sure as hell was no room for anyone, much less a woman like Eliza.

He had damn well tried his best to shake the woman, but the blue-eyed raven-haired fool wouldn't budge. Truth be told, he was impressed by her bravado, but disgusted by his inability to shake her off his tail the night before. Rather than risk having her do the same thing again, he decided to ride like hell and leave her behind. He should have felt guilty, but he'd left that emotion behind, along with most every other, a long time ago. Grady had a job to complete and that was all that mattered to him.

The only thing he was concerned about was finding the wayward wife he'd been hired to hunt and making sure she regretted leaving her husband, at least for the five seconds she lived after he found her.

Grady learned as a young man just how much he couldn't trust the fairer sex. His mother had been his teacher, and he'd been a very astute pupil. No doubt if she hadn't drank herself to death, she'd still be out there somewhere taking advantage of and using men as she saw fit.

The cool morning air gave way to warm sunshine within a few hours. He refused to think about what the schoolmarm was doing, or if anything had been done to her. If she could take care of her horse and build a fire, she could take care of herself. Food could be gotten at any small town, but then again maybe she could hunt and fish, too.

Somehow it wouldn't surprise him if she did. The woman seemed to have a library in her head. Against his will, the sight of her unbound hair popped into his head. It had been long, past her waist to brush against the nicely curved backside. Grady preferred his women with some meat on their bones, better to hang on to when he had one beneath him, or riding him. He shifted in the saddle as his dick woke up at the thought of Eliza's dark curtain of hair brushing his bare skin.

Jesus Christ, he sure didn't need to be thinking about fucking the wayward Miss Eliza. If she was a widow, no doubt she'd had experience in bed with a man. It wasn't Grady's business of course, so he needed to stop his brain from getting into her bloomers, or any parts of her anatomy.

As the morning wore on, Grady's mind returned to the contents of her bags. The woman didn't have a lick of common sense and fell asleep, vulnerable and un-protected. Good thing he didn't have any bad thoughts on his mind or she wouldn't have been sleeping. She even snored a little, something he found highly amusing as he'd rifled through her things.

Her smaller bag had contained a hodgepodge of clothes, each uglier and frumpier than the last, a hair-brush, half a dozen biscuits in a tattered napkin, and some hairpins. A measly collection of a woman's life, and quite pitiful if that was all she had. Perhaps she'd been at least partially truthful about taking everything she owned and hitting the trail. Her husband must have been a poor excuse for a provider if this collection of rags was all she had.

The bag of books was just that, a bag stuffed full of scientific texts ranging from medical topics to some titles he couldn't even pronounce. In the bottom of the bag was a battered copy of *Wuthering Heights*. He didn't know what it was, but it was much smaller than the other books, likely a novel. She obviously put the spectacles to good use judging by the two dozen tomes she had in her bag. He wondered how she'd gotten it up on the saddle in the first place.

"Fool." He had to stop thinking about Eliza and what she was doing and why. Grady would never see her again.

As a child, Grady learned very early not to care or ask questions. It only bought him a cuff on the ear or a boot in the ass. A boy could only take so much of that before he kept his mouth shut and simply snuck around to find out what he needed to know.

As a young man, it served him well and garnered the attention of the man who taught him how to hunt and kill people in the quickest, most efficient way. Grady had learned his lesson well, even better than his mentor expected. When the job was put before him to hunt and kill the very man who had taught him those skills, Grady hesitated only a minute before he said yes.

The devil rode on his back, a constant companion he'd come to accept. He didn't need a woman riding there, too.

Restless Heart

He craved her like the earth craved the rain . . .

Sam Carver had the kind of body that turned a woman's head, and the kind of eyes that had seen more than his share of trouble. But he couldn't get enough of the mysterious, ethereal beauty who had showed up in his little Wyoming town, working at the Blue Plate, keeping to herself.

He knew Angeline Hunter was running scared, pursued by a fanatic who threatened her life. But no matter what it took, Sam would convince his angel to put her trust in him, to put the painful past behind her and learn just how pleasurable the present could be. . . .

"Your beau is here."

Angeline stopped in mid-motion. "Excuse me?"

"Your beau is here. Samuel Carver is here for dinner and I would swear he's spiffed up for it." Alice grinned widely. "He's ordered the ham and potatoes, with apple pie. Do you want to serve him?"

"No, I do not." Angeline felt her nervousness returning and silently cursed Alice for her silly enthusiasm.

"Oh, why not? He asked for you." She waggled her eyebrows. "He might not be rich, but he sure is sweet." With a cheeky grin, she took the plate and left the kitchen.

"You might as well talk to him. Don't listen to Alice prattle on about him being a half-breed. He's a good boy, no matter who his mother was." Marta put ham on another plate. This time it was for Samuel Carver. "If you hide in here, it will make it worse."

Angeline knew she was right. The longer she hemmed and hawed about the gift and the man, the worse it would be. She needed to tell him there could be no future between them.

With a firm spine, she put potatoes on the plate to accompany the ham and nodded to Marta. "I'll be right back."

Angeline stepped into the restaurant and looked around. There were a number of people at tables, but she had no idea what the man looked like. Alice's silly description meant nothing except that he was a man. As if she'd conjured the waitress, Alice appeared next to a man sitting in front of the bay window. She pointed and winked at Angeline.

Now she really was uncomfortable, because Alice had no tact or consideration for other people. The man looked up and saw Angeline standing there.

The ground shifted beneath her.

His hair was the color of midnight, so dark it was nearly blue-black. It hung straight to his shoulders, too long to be fashionable. The ends curled up slightly as if a breeze had come through and ruffled it. His shoulders were wide, but not overly so.

He had an intense stare that made goose bumps crawl over her skin. His eyes were also darker than pitch, black pools that seemed to be bottomless. To her surprise, his skin was lightly tanned, with tiny laugh lines around his eyes and mouth. He could be any age, but she knew him to be twenty-nine. He had the demeanor of a man who had seen too much in his short life.

The bright blue of his shirt contrasted so much with the rest of him, she had to blink to absorb it all. He was a striking man, not classically handsome but fascinating.

Angeline did not ever remember seeing him before, which wasn't surprising because she worked in the kitchen most days.

She managed to swallow, somehow, before she

stepped toward his table with her heart firmly lodged in her throat. He watched her with wide eyes, unsmiling and unthreatening. She couldn't have explained it to anyone, but Marta had been right—Samuel Carver was no threat to her.

"Good afternoon, Miss Hunter." His voice had a lilt to it, one she'd never heard before. It was like warm honey on a piece of toast.

Angeline thought perhaps she would be embarrassed by her reaction, but she wasn't. "Good afternoon, Mr. Carver." At least she set the plate down on the table without dropping it.

He smiled. "I hope you're enjoying the book."

She licked her lips and managed a small smile. "I've never had a new book before. I-I wanted to say thank you, but it's much too extravagant for me to accept.

There, that sounded reasonable and intelligent. He, however, shook his head.

"I can't take it back."

"Please, it must have cost you a lot of money." She put her hands in her apron pockets and clenched them into fists, her right hand pressed up against the book. "It's not appropriate for me to accept it."

He hadn't even glanced at the plate. His gaze was locked on hers. "I know it was forward of me, but I saw you reading on the back steps one day. You seemed to be at peace with a book in your hands."

Angeline unwillingly nodded. "Yes, that's exactly it. It's almost as if the books give me peace."

This time when he smiled, she found herself smiling back. The situation had gotten complicated in less than five minutes.

"I feel the same way about books. So please accept the gift from a fellow reader. It's nothing more."

She was torn between what she had to do and what

she wanted to do. Angeline could not become attached or involved with any man, regardless of her silly heart's reaction to him. It didn't make it any easier to conjure up every other reason why she needed to keep her distance from him.

Books by Bestselling Author
Fern Michaels

___The Jury	0-8217-7878-1	$6.99US/$9.99CAN
___Sweet Revenge	0-8217-7879-X	$6.99US/$9.99CAN
___Lethal Justice	0-8217-7880-3	$6.99US/$9.99CAN
___Free Fall	0-8217-7881-1	$6.99US/$9.99CAN
___Fool Me Once	0-8217-8071-9	$7.99US/$10.99CAN
___Vegas Rich	0-8217-8112-X	$7.99US/$10.99CAN
___Hide and Seek	1-4201-0184-6	$6.99US/$9.99CAN
___Hokus Pokus	1-4201-0185-4	$6.99US/$9.99CAN
___Fast Track	1-4201-0186-2	$6.99US/$9.99CAN
___Collateral Damage	1-4201-0187-0	$6.99US/$9.99CAN
___Final Justice	1-4201-0188-9	$6.99US/$9.99CAN
___Up Close and Personal	0-8217-7956-7	$7.99US/$9.99CAN
___Under the Radar	1-4201-0683-X	$6.99US/$9.99CAN
___Razor Sharp	1-4201-0684-8	$7.99US/$10.99CAN
___Yesterday	1-4201-1494-8	$5.99US/$6.99CAN
___Vanishing Act	1-4201-0685-6	$7.99US/$10.99CAN
___Sara's Song	1-4201-1493-X	$5.99US/$6.99CAN
___Deadly Deals	1-4201-0686-4	$7.99US/$10.99CAN
___Game Over	1-4201-0687-2	$7.99US/$10.99CAN
___Sins of Omission	1-4201-1153-1	$7.99US/$10.99CAN
___Sins of the Flesh	1-4201-1154-X	$7.99US/$10.99CAN
___Cross Roads	1-4201-1192-2	$7.99US/$10.99CAN

Available Wherever Books Are Sold!
Check out our website at **www.kensingtonbooks.com**